US   ng author
Ja   om Vanderbilt
University and works as a nurse practitioner in a family
practice. She lives in the southern United States with
her Prince Charming, their children, their Maltese
named Halo; and a lot of unnamed dust bunnies that
have moved in after she started her writing career.
Readers can visit Janice via her website at: www.
janicelynn.net

Joanna Neil had her future planned. She enjoyed her
work as an infant teacher and didn't envisage any
changes to her way of life. But then she discovered
Mills & Boon. She was surprised to find how absorbing
and interesting they were and read them on a regular
basis. The more she read, the more she had the
overwhelming desire to write one. Encouraged by her
family, she persevered until her first book was
accepted, and after several books were published, she
decided to write full time.

Cheris Hodges was bitten by the writing bug early.
The 1999 graduate of Johnson C. Smith University is a
freelance journalist and always looks for love stories in
the most unusual places. She lives in Charlotte, North
Carolina, where she is trying and failing to develop a
green thumb. www.cherishodges.net

Irresistible Bachelors

Irresistible Bachelors:
Second Chance with the Bachelor

JANICE LYNN

JOANNA NEIL

CHERIS HODGES

MILLS & BOON

First Published in Great Britain 2021
by Mills & Boon, an imprint of HarperCollins*Publishers* Ltd,
1 London Bridge Street, London, SE1 9GF

www.harpercollins.co.uk

HarperCollins*Publishers*
1st Floor, Watermarque Building,
Ringsend Road, Dublin 4, Ireland

IRRESISTIBLE BACHELORS: SECOND CHANCE WITH THE
BACHELOR © 2021 Harlequin Books S.A.

New York Doc to Blushing Bride © 2015 Janice Lynn
Second Chance with Lord Branscombe © 2016 Joanna Neil
The Heat Between Us © 2017 Cheris Hodges

ISBN: 978-0-263-30041-3

MIX
Paper from
responsible sources
FSC™ C007454

This book is produced from independently certified FSC™ paper to ensure responsible forest management.

For more information visit: www.harpercollins.co.uk/green

Printed and bound in Spain
by CPI, Barcelona

NEW YORK DOC TO BLUSHING BRIDE

JANICE LYNN

To Abby, my daughter, an amazing young woman whom I hope reaches for the stars without ever forgetting her inner dreamer. Love you, Baby Girl!

CHAPTER ONE

At first glance, the slim redhead sitting on the funeral chapel's front pew epitomized poise and grace. But as she politely accepted the sympathy being expressed her fingers clenched and unclenched around the crumpled tissue in her hand. Dr. Sloan Trenton would like to hold her hand, let her cling to him to help her get through the next few days, to share the pain they both felt.

No matter how much he felt he knew Dr. Cara Conner, she saw him as a stranger.

Only she wasn't a stranger to him.

From the time Sloan had joined the Bloomberg, Alabama family medicine practice the year before, Preston had enthusiastically talked about his amazing daughter who worked in a downtown Manhattan emergency room. That must be why Sloan had thought of her so much since he had officially met her only yesterday.

He'd stopped by Preston's house to offer his sympathies. His heart had raced like crazy when he'd rung her doorbell, knowing he was finally going to meet her. Despite his exhaustion, his grief over Preston's heart attack, he hadn't been able to stay away. He'd had to go to her, to offer his condolences. He felt as if his own heart had been ripped to shreds at the death of a man who'd treated him as a son. Something Sloan had never had anyone do, blood kin or otherwise.

Probably that was why he felt such a connection to Cara.

Regardless of the reason, he'd been shocked at Preston's daughter's reaction.

She hadn't been out-and-out rude, but she hadn't been receptive to his visit, either, had failed to even invite him into the house and had failed to hide her dislike. He'd stood on Preston's front porch, a house the man had given him a key to, and he'd felt like an awkward inconvenience in Cara's world, like an outsider in a place where he'd, up to that point, finally felt at home.

Maybe it was just grief making her so prickly toward him. After all, she'd just lost her father. Still, his gut instinct warned her reaction ran much deeper than grief over Preston's death.

Sloan swallowed the lump that formed in his throat every time the reality that his mentor and best friend was gone hit him. He moved closer to the brushed steel casket he'd stood vigil by all evening.

Dr. Preston J. Conner had been the best man and doctor Sloan had ever known. He'd been the doctor Sloan aspired to be like. No matter how much he tried, he'd never be half the physician Preston had been.

Just fifteen feet away, Cara stood, wobbling slightly in her black stilettos and slim skirt. Sloan moved forward, determined to catch her if she didn't straighten. Without glancing his way, she headed out of the room, unaware that he couldn't drag his gaze away from her more than a few seconds at a time.

He excused himself from the bank president and a local preacher who had been carrying on a conversation around him and he followed Cara.

Leaving the large old Victorian-style house that had served as one of Bloomberg's two funeral parlors for more than a hundred years, she slipped around to the side garden.

If Sloan followed her, was that outright stalkerish or just the action of a man who was worried about a woman who had just experienced great loss?

He had to at least make sure she was all right.

Hadn't Preston's last words been for him to take care of Cara?

Sloan headed around the side of the building. She was sitting on a bench, looking up at the sky. A pale sliver of moonlight illuminated her just well enough that he could tell she was speaking, but he was too far away to make out what she said or even the sound of her whispered words.

His ribs broke loose and lassoed themselves around his heart, clamping down so tightly that he could barely breathe.

Never had he seen anything more beautiful than the ethereal image she made in the moonlight. Never had he felt such a fascination with a woman.

A commotion behind him had him spinning to see the source, but not before he saw Cara's head jerk toward the noise also, catching him watching her. Great. Now she'd add stalker to whatever other crimes he'd possibly committed.

But he didn't have time to dwell on that. The cause of the noise now had his full attention.

Mrs. Goines, a blue-haired little elderly lady, had fallen while going down the three steps leading out of the funeral parlor. Why she hadn't taken the handicap ramp Sloan could only put down to her stubbornness that she wasn't handicapped or disabled. She had lost her footing and down she'd gone.

He got to the frail little woman almost as quickly as the woman who'd been right behind her—her daughter, if Sloan remembered correctly.

"Mom? Are you okay?" she asked, confirming Sloan's memory of who she was. She leaned over her mother, who moaned in pain.

"I can't move." Ignoring her daughter, Mrs. Goines's gaze connected to Sloan's and she groaned in obvious agony. "I can't get up."

Assessing the position in which she'd fallen and how she'd landed, Sloan winced. She'd landed on her right hip, leg and arm. Her hip and her shoulder had taken the brunt of her weight. He'd seen her in clinic several times since he'd come to Bloomberg. He knew her health history. She was on a biphosphanate medication to strengthen her thin bones, having struggled with osteoporosis for more than a decade. Her weakened bones hadn't been able to withstand the impact of her fall.

"Don't try to move, Mrs. Goines," he ordered in a low, confident tone. "I'm going to check you, but I will need to send you to the hospital for X-rays."

"Is everything okay?" Cara asked, joining them and hunching down next to Sloan. At his dash at the noise, she'd apparently come to investigate. Taking the elderly woman's hand, her expression softened with a compassion that caused Sloan's breath to catch in his throat.

"Mrs. Goines," she chided with a click of her tongue and the twinkle in her eyes that had captured his imagination in Preston's office photos, "were you sliding down the railings again? You know my dad warned you about that."

The woman's pain-filled eyes eased just a tiny bit

with Cara's distracting words. "Remember that, do you, girlie?"

"I remember a lot of things about growing up in this town. Like that you used to sneak me extra peaches when I'd go through school lunch line," Cara told her in a gentle voice. "Can you tell me where you are?"

The woman frowned. "If you don't know, then it should be you being checked by a doctor, not me. It's your father's funeral we're at, girlie."

"You're right," Cara agreed, not explaining that she was checking the woman's neurological status with her question. "Did you hit your head when you fell?"

"If only," Mrs. Goines moaned. "I wouldn't be hurting nearly so much."

"Possibly not, but I'm still glad you didn't hit your head." Cara looked into her eyes, studying her pupils in the glow of the porch and lit walkway. "Can you tell me where you hurt most?"

Completely ignoring Sloan now, Mrs. Goines continued to moan in pain while answering Cara's questions.

Despite the seriousness of the situation, Sloan had to fight a smile at the transformation that had taken place. Gone was the lost, grieving daughter from moments before. In her place was a confident doctor who stepped in and took charge. Truly, she was her father's child.

She moved efficiently and thoroughly, quickly coming to the same conclusion Sloan had while watching her examine the older woman. "She needs X-rays. I'm not sure we will be able to move her. You'll need to call for an ambulance."

He nodded his agreement and motioned to what he held next to his ear. He'd already punched in the emergency dispatcher's number. "I need an ambulance sent to Greenwood's Funeral Parlor," he told the woman who answered the call. "I've a ninety-two-year-old white female who's fallen and can't get up. Probable fractured right hip. Possibly her right humerus, as well."

Cara, Sloan and the crowd that had gathered to see what the commotion was all about stayed with the in-pain Mrs. Goines until the ambulance pulled to a screeching halt in front of the funeral home.

Bud Arnold and his partner Tommy Woodall came up to where Mrs. Goines still lay on the concrete steps at an awkward angle. With her level of pain, moving her had risked further injury so they'd just made her as comfortable as possible where she lay.

"Hey, Dr. Trenton," the paramedics greeted him, then turned to the moaning woman.

"Mrs. Goines, please tell me you didn't try sliding down the handrail," Bud said immediately when he realized who the patient was.

Obviously, there was a story behind Mrs. Goines and handrails. Sloan would get her to tell him about it soon. Maybe when he rounded on her in the morning because no doubt she'd be admitted through the emergency room tonight and he'd check on her prior to Preston's funeral service.

"Hey, Bud," Cara greeted him, causing the man's eyes to bug out with recognition.

"Well, I'll be. If it isn't Cara Conner. Good to see you, pretty girl." Then he recalled why she was in town and his happy greeting turned to solemn remorse. "Sorry to hear about your dad. He was a good, good man. Best doctor I ever knew."

"Thanks, Bud. He was a good man and doctor." She took a deep breath. "Now, let's take care of this good woman lying here in pain. She's going to have to be put on the stretcher. Right hip is broken. I can't be certain if her right shoulder is broken or just shoved out of socket from the impact of her fall. Her right clavicle is fractured, too."

Cara pushed aside the loose material of Mrs. Goines's dress neckline. Sure enough, there was a large bump that had fortunately not broken through the skin but which did indicate that the woman's collarbone had snapped from the impact against the concrete steps.

"I do believe you're right, Doc," Bud agreed. "Let's get this feisty little lady to the emergency room."

The two paramedics lowered the stretcher as far as it would go and positioned Mrs. Goines to where they could slide her onto the bedding.

Cara and Sloan both positioned themselves where they wouldn't interfere with Bud and Tommy's work but where they could help stabilize Mrs. Goines's body as much as possible during the transfer.

"On the count of three, we're going to lift you onto the stretcher," Bud told their patient.

Although Mrs. Goines cried out in pain, the transfer went smoothly.

Sloan turned to Cara and smiled. "You should move back to Bloomberg. We make a good team, you and I."

Her gaze narrowed as if he'd said something vulgar. "You and I are not a team," she said, low enough that only he could hear. "And I will never move back to Bloomberg."

She stood, bent and said something to Mrs. Goines, who was now strapped onto the stretcher to prevent her from falling off while they rolled her to where the ambulance waited. Then she nodded toward Bud and Tommy and disappeared inside the funeral home.

Slowly, Sloan rose to his feet, scratched his head and

wondered what he'd ever done to upset Preston's daughter so completely and totally.

And why he'd never wanted a woman to like him more.

People Cara had known her entire life shook her hand, hugged her and pressed sloppy kisses to her cheek. People told her how wonderful her father had been, what a difference he'd made in their lives, stories of how he'd gone above and beyond the call of duty time and again during his thirty-plus years of practicing medicine in Bloomberg—as if Cara didn't know firsthand what he'd sacrificed for his patients.

She knew. Oh, how she knew.

Everyone milled around, talking to each other, saying what a shame it was the town had lost such a prominent and beloved member. All their words, their faces churned in Cara's grieving mind, a whirlwind of emotional daggers that sliced at her very being.

Her gaze went to the one stranger in their midst. A stranger only to her, it seemed as he was the other person receiving condolences from everyone in the funeral parlor.

Acid gurgled in her stomach, threatening to gnaw a hole right through her knotted belly.

Why was *he* getting handshakes, hugs and sloppy kisses from people like little old arthritic Mary Jo Jones and Catherine Lester? Why did everyone treat him as if he'd suffered just as great a loss as she had?

Preston had been her father, her family. Not his.

Sloan Trenton was an outsider. Someone her father had recruited to join his practice about a year ago when he'd apparently given up on her joining any time in the near future. Then again, maybe not an outsider. How many times had her father said Sloan was like the son he'd never had? How impressed he was by the talented doctor he'd added to his practice? Every time they'd talked, he'd been "Sloan this" and "Sloan that."

So perhaps the bitterness she felt didn't really stem from Sloan being treated as if his grief was as great as her own. Perhaps her bitterness had started long ago while listening to her father go on and on about the man, about how Sloan loved Bloomberg and its people almost as much as Preston himself did, about how Sloan tirelessly gave of himself to the town, that watching Sloan was like a flashback to himself thirty years before, except that he'd been married. Of course, her father had joked, Bloomberg's most eligible bachelor wasn't still single because of a lack of trying on many a female's part.

Sloan. Sloan. Sloan. Gag. Gag. Gag.

Dr. Sloan Trenton could do no wrong in her father's eyes and, deep down, Cara resented that. Although he'd loved her, she had never achieved that complete admiration because she'd had too much of her mother's love of the big city in her blood, too much of her mother's resentment of how much Bloomberg stole from their lives, and her father couldn't, or wouldn't, understand.

She'd had enough of her father in her to love medicine, but she hadn't been willing to have her life light snuffed out by the demanding town that had taken its toll on her family. Give her the anonymity of the big-city emergency room any day of the week.

She huffed out an exasperated breath.

The tall, lean object of her animosity couldn't have heard her sigh, not over the chatter in the crowded funeral home and the distance that separated them, but Sloan turned as if she had called out his name. Filled with concern, his coppery brown gaze connected to hers and held, despite the men still talking to him as if he was focused solely on them.

She narrowed her eyes in dislike, not caring what he thought of her, not caring about anything except the gaping crater in her broken heart. She focused all her negative energy toward him, as if he were somehow to blame for her loss, as if he could have prevented her father from dying. Logically, she knew he couldn't have.

Sloan's handsome features drew tight. He looked almost as exhausted as she felt. But she didn't like him, didn't want him there. Everything about him disturbed her.

Had from the moment she'd opened the door to find him standing on her front porch yesterday during the midst of her major boo-hoo fest. She'd have hated anyone to see her that way, but she especially hated that her father's beloved prodigy had witnessed her meltdown.

Currently, one of his coal-dark brows arched in acknowledgement of her enmity, no doubt questioning her dislike. Why not? Obviously, he was well loved within the community. Her father had sure loved him. The townspeople loved him. With his inky black hair, those amazing eyes, handsome face and a body that, despite her doom-and-gloom mental state, she had to admit belonged on a television hunk rather than a small-town doctor, women loved him. Why would he expect anything less than adoration from her?

"Oh, Cara, your dad is going to be so missed at the hospital," Julie Lewis, Cara's closest friend during grade school, sympathized, plopping down next to her on the long wooden front pew and wrapping her in a tight hug.

Cara leaned her head on her longtime friend's shoulder,

grateful for the excuse to break eye contact with Sloan. Julie's light, flowery perfume filled Cara's nostrils with memories of when they'd first started wearing makeup and perfume. Her friend still wore the same honeysuckle scent as she'd worn throughout high school.

"I can't imagine not hearing his booming voice in the hospital hallways," Julie continued, shaking her head in slow denial, her long brunette curls tickling the side of Cara's face.

Cara remembered reading something online about Julie working in the hospital lab as a phlebotomist.

"This town has truly lost one of its greatest."

"Truly," Cara agreed, soaking in the remembered warmth of her childhood friend. She'd grown up with this woman and yet these days Julie was a virtual stranger. Other than the occasional message or post on social media, she'd pretty much lost touch with her Bloomberg friends years ago during medical school. She'd been so crazy busy, making sure she distanced herself from everything Bloomberg, making sure she'd aced everything she'd done so as not to disappoint her father.

Only she'd been the biggest disappointment of all when she'd opted not to return to Bloomberg to practice.

He'd just not understood her love of the big city and the excitement that flowed through her veins at working in emergency medicine in the Big Apple. Then again, he'd never understood her mother's broken heart at leaving the big city, either. Cara only did from having spent many hours reading her mother's diaries. She'd clung to those handwritten pages of her mother pouring her heart out as a link to a woman she mostly remembered from photos.

"Poor Sloan." Her friend's attention turned to the

man standing near her father's casket. He'd been there all evening. "He's taken this so hard."

Cara's lips pursed. Of course he had. Because he was the son her father had never had. Ugh. She really didn't like the bitterness flowing through her. Anyone who knew her would say she was a positive person, a regular little Miss Sunshine most of the time. But her disposition toward Sloan could only be described as thunderous.

"He idolized Preston."

"No doubt," Cara agreed, in as neutral a voice as she could muster. No one need know of her dislike of Sloan. She wouldn't be here but a few days, then she'd leave Bloomberg forever. Let Sloan give himself to the townspeople to the sacrifice of all else in his life. Cara could give all those matchmakers a hundred and one reasons why they should keep looking elsewhere. A man as devoted to this town as her father had been was admirable but didn't bode well for his wife and kids.

"Rex said Sloan wouldn't leave Preston, that he rode in the ambulance to the hospital, worked alongside the paramedics, stayed in the hospital with him long after he'd been pronounced." Her gaze softened as she looked at the handsome but tired-appearing man being hugged by yet another little old lady. "Poor, poor Sloan," Julie sympathized.

Guilt hit Cara. The man had been there for her father, had tried to resuscitate him, had apparently gotten a heartbeat restarted with CPR, but his damaged heart hadn't been able to sustain a rhythm.

No doubt the stress of the past few days was taking its toll and that's why she felt such irritation toward a man who was obviously a paragon of the community and whom her father had loved. Shame on her.

She didn't usually dislike someone so thoroughly and intensely. Actually, she didn't usually dislike someone, period. That was an honor Sloan Trenton held all on his own.

"He coaches Rex Junior's little-league team, you know."

No, Cara hadn't known.

"And is an assistant pack leader with the Tiger Cubs."

Gee, did he also wear a red cape and tights with a big *S* on the chest? Not that he wouldn't look good in tights. She might not like him but she wasn't blind to the man's physical attributes. Which perhaps made her dislike him all the more. Why couldn't he at least have been ordinary rather than having those amazing coppery eyes and a smile that would leave most Hollywood beaus green with envy?

CHAPTER TWO

"THAT'S WONDERFUL," CARA said to her friend, instead of expressing her immediate thought. Just a few days then she'd never have to think of Super Sloan Trenton or this town again. She'd make her mother proud.

"Yes, he is." Julie elbowed her, causing Cara to scoot a little on the pew. "Some lucky, smart woman is going to have herself a treasure when she lands that man."

Cara's eyes widened. Surely her friend wasn't hinting…not at her father's funeral visitation…not when she knew Cara would never get serious with a mini-me of her father? But when she met her friend's gaze, Julie nodded and grinned from ear to ear.

"He's a good man, Cara." Julie eyed him as if he were Mr. Perfection. "A woman could do a lot worse than coming home to Sloan every night. Just look at him. I love my Rex, but men don't come any hotter than that one."

Any moment Cara expected Julie to fan her face.

Then she did.

Cara resisted an eye roll. Barely.

"As hard as it is to believe, his insides are even better than that yummy exterior. The man has a heart of gold."

"I have a boyfriend, you know." Not to mention that Julie had a husband and child and shouldn't be calling another man yummy and looking at him as if he were chocolate-dipped, right?

"That fancy trauma surgeon you've been dating since your residency? I've seen the pictures of you two and your travels online." Julie gave a low whistle. "He's a looker all right, but something is missing there. He's a little plastic, don't you think?"

Plastic? Not hardly.

"John is a wonderful man." Nothing was missing between her and John. She planned to marry him. Their relationship was wonderful. Wasn't that what she'd told her father repeatedly? What she told herself repeatedly?

"Wonderful is okay." Julie wasn't going to be swayed. "But Sloan is the total package. I'm pretty sure your father handpicked him for you to come home to."

Julie thought… Was that why her father…? No, she'd been with John years before her father had recruited Sloan. He'd liked John. He'd told her he did.

Had the words come from someone other than her father, she might have thought they'd been said only for her benefit. Preston hadn't been known for holding back his true thoughts. He'd have told her if he hadn't approved of the brilliant trauma surgeon she'd taken a liking to when she'd been in residency.

Her father hadn't picked Sloan for her because she'd already picked the man she'd be sharing her future with. She'd told Preston as much, that when John asked her to marry him, she planned to say yes.

That had been last month when her father had flown to New York for a medical conference and spent a few days with her. Of course, John hadn't asked her yet and had been acting a little weird lately, but that was probably only due to how busy his hospital schedule had been the past few months.

"Besides, where is this boyfriend? He should be here with you," Julie pointed out in a tone unflattering to John. Her lips pursed with disapproval. "A man should be with his woman at her father's funeral. No excuses."

"He's a trauma surgeon. He can't just walk away from his job at the drop of a hat. Not unless it was an emergency. There was nothing John could do to help." Or so he'd bluntly told her when she'd mentioned him coming with her. Logically, even if his crassness had hurt, he'd been right. She hadn't pushed for him to drop everything to come with her. But she'd wanted him to do just that, even though, goodness knew, the emergency room would be crazy enough with her unexpectedly gone, much less her and one of the trauma surgeons.

But they would have gotten by... No, she wasn't going to let those thoughts in. John would be here if there had been anything he could do. She couldn't blame him for not wanting to spend time in Bloomberg when he didn't absolutely have to. He loved city life even more than she did.

"Yeah," Julie tsked. "Nothing he could do, except hold your hand, comfort you and keep you from being alone during your father's funeral."

Well, there was that.

Cara didn't want to be having this conversation. Not right now. Not ever. Because as much as she told herself she understood, she also acknowledged that she would have gone with John had their roles been reversed. That he hadn't even considered it hurt more than a smidge.

Ready to end their conversation, Cara managed a tight smile toward her friend and was grateful to see another familiar face waiting to give her sympathy. "Um, okay, I'll keep that in mind, Julie. Thanks for your condolences. Good to see you."

"You do that, and, yes, Cara, it's so good to see you home, but I hate that it's under these circumstances." Her friend squeezed her tightly, filling Cara's nostrils yet again with honeysuckle and another wave of memories. "Your dad will be missed by everyone in Bloomberg. For that matter, so are you."

She chose to ignore Julie's mention of her being missed. Yes, her father would be missed by Bloomberg, but even more so by his daughter. She may not live in Bloomberg, but she did talk to her father several times a week. Usually their conversations had consisted of what new restaurant or show she had gone to that week or she'd recount some odd case that had come into the emergency room. On her father's end, he'd talked about Bloomberg and Sloan.

She'd gotten to where she'd dreaded their next Sloan the Wonder Boy session. Now, she'd listen to her father read the phone book just to hear his voice.

A fresh wave of moisture stung Cara's eyes and she squeezed them shut. She would make it through the next couple of days and then truly leave Bloomberg, better known to her as Gloomberg, the name she'd given the town during high school.

Eventually, the funeral-home crowd began to thin.

Thank God. Sloan felt exhausted. As if being at Preston's visitation wasn't trying enough, Mrs. Goines's fall and Cara's words had zapped what little adrenaline he'd still been operating on.

As the last visitor, who'd just finished talking with Cara, gave their condolences to Sloan, the funeral director came to him to clarify the next day's arrangements.

"I'll check with Cara to see what she prefers," he told Irving Greenwood, the pudgy, balding third-generation funeral-home director. The Greenwood's Funeral Parlor had been serving Bloomberg for more than a hundred years. Lots of Bloomberg's businesses could boast such a rich heritage. That deep sense of family and belonging was what had drawn Sloan to Bloomberg.

That and Dr. Preston Conner.

Bracing himself for whatever Cara threw at him, Sloan's heart picked up pace. Every breath he took sounded loud, forced as he crossed the room to where she sat, hands in her lap, eyes cast downward. She looked lost, alone, elegantly fragile.

Her emotions were everywhere. Understandably so. After all, she'd lost her father unexpectedly. No wonder she was upset. Although he seemed to be the only target of her negative emotions.

"Hey." Sloan gently called her attention to where he stood in front of her. He wasn't sure if she'd been lost in her own thoughts or if she'd purposely been ignoring him. "Mr. Greenwood asked how you wanted the flowers and such handled. I told him I would discuss the matter with you and let him know."

Complexion pale, she blinked up at him as if she'd forgotten he existed, as if their encounter with Mrs. Goines had never happened. "I don't understand. What about the flowers?"

He motioned to the room that could currently have doubled as a florist shop. "They're all yours. Do you want everything not left at the graveside delivered to Preston's house tomorrow afternoon?"

She glanced around at the room that overflowed with flowers, ceramic statues, blankets, bibles and other sympathy mementos. Her expression became confused. "Please, no. What would I do with them?"

Good question. What did a person do with flower arrangements and such following a funeral? Sloan had no idea. He'd never known his parents, had grown up in foster-homes and had certainly never experienced a funeral from this perspective. "I could help you go through everything. There might be a few items you want to keep. We could take the live flowers to the nursing home or hospital, distribute them amongst the patients and staff there, and hopefully add a smile to their day." He smiled, hoping Cara would do the same, even if only a small curving of her lips.

She didn't.

Obviously considering what he'd suggested, she toyed with her bottom lip. "There's nothing I want to keep. It could just all be delivered there to begin with and we wouldn't have to go through anything. Give them to Dad's nursing-home patients, the nurses or whomever you think best. All I ask is that a running list of items and who gave them be kept so I can send appropriate thank-you notes."

Her expression pinched and she rubbed her temple. "Or does the funeral home do that? I've no idea." Fatigue etched on her lovely face, she ran her gaze over the abundance of tokens sent in Preston's memory. "I'd asked that everyone make a donation to the local heart association rather than send flowers. That would have been much easier to deal with, really."

Sloan would have liked to have sat down next to her in the pew. He felt ridiculous towering above her. Despite her momentary politeness, she wouldn't welcome him sitting next to her. He didn't need a genius

IQ to figure that one out. Still, he attempted an empathetic smile.

"I'm sure lots of donations have been made, too. The town's people want to show their love and appreciation for all that your father has done for them over the years. No one has given so much of himself for the benefit of others as your father did for Bloomberg."

She nodded absently, glanced around the room, now empty except for them and the coffin. Her face paled to a pasty white and her knuckles threatened to burst through the thin layer of skin covering them. A sob almost broke free from her pale lips. She managed to stop it, but not before Sloan realized what she'd done. His heart squeezed in a painful vise-like grip.

"Are you okay?" That was a stupid question. Of course she wasn't okay. She'd bury her father in less than twenty-four hours.

But rather than blast him for his ridiculous question, as he'd expected and braced himself for, she just shook her head. "No. I need to get out of here. Please. Just get me out of here."

He wasn't sure what she intended him to do, and there wasn't much he wouldn't do to ease the strain on her face. When she didn't move, he reached for her hand. "Let me help you."

Still looking drained and a bit panicky, she put her hand in his.

Several things registered all at once. Her hand sent chills through his entire body, probably from their sheer frigidness, although he couldn't be sure because there was something electric in the feel of her skin against his, too. Second, she shook. Again, this could be from how cold her hands were but he suspected it had more to do with the situation. Another was how fragile she felt in his grasp. Preston's daughter was a strong, independent woman, a bit of a daredevil and a phenomenal athlete. At the moment, she wasn't any of those things. She was a little girl who'd just lost her father and she looked overwhelmed.

Without a word, Sloan led her to his Jeep, helped her into the passenger seat. She had a rental car at the funeral home, but she didn't need to be driving. Not with the way she was shaking, with how utterly exhausted she appeared. He hadn't slept much the past few days either, between covering his and Preston's patients and his own grief. But at the moment he was the stronger of Cara and himself.

"Sorry I don't have the top on." He rarely kept the top on the Jeep because he liked the freedom of the air whipping about him. "It'll be a bit windy."

"Thank you," she murmured, barely loud enough for him to make out her words. "My mind just wanted to get out of there, but my body didn't seem to know how to leave. Or maybe it was my heart that didn't want to go."

"A normal stress reaction."

"I'm not stressed," she automatically argued, her shoulders stiff.

"Okay, you're not stressed," he agreed, not willing to debate with her since they both knew the truth. He started the Jeep and pulled out of the funeral parlor parking lot, heading down the highway toward the quiet neighborhood where Preston's house was located.

About halfway to Maple Street he glanced toward where she sat, staring blankly out the open doorway. The wind tugged at her hair, pulling strands free from where she had it pinned back. Utter fatigue was etched on her face. He reached across the seat, put his hand over hers. That skin-to-skin electricity zapped him again.

Her head jerked toward him. Had she felt it, too?

Regardless, she looked ready to demand he take her back to Greenwood's, that she'd only temporarily lost her mind in asking for his help. But whatever had sparked to life within her deflated just as quickly. Without a word, she went back to staring out the open doorway. Within seconds her body relaxed and her head slumped against the headrest.

Hand still tucked beneath his, she'd gone to sleep.

He parked the car in front of Preston's gray-and-white Victorian-style home, jumped out and went to Cara's side of the car.

Should he wake her or just carry her inside?

No doubt she'd not slept much, if at all, the night before. If he woke her, would she be able to go back to sleep or would she lie grieving through the long night hours?

Memories of her tearstained face from the day before decided it for him.

Digging his key ring out of his pocket, he unlocked the front door, went back to the Jeep and carefully scooped Cara into his arms.

She was as light as a feather.

And smelled of heaven.

Or as close to heaven as Sloan had ever smelled. Like the soft, sweet fragrance of cherry candy mixed with an amazing, almost addictive freshness that made him want to inhale deeply. Then there were those electric zings. His entire body sparked with excitement.

He held a woman who had fascinated him for months, long before he'd met her. As he'd dated and tried to make a life for himself in Bloomberg, he'd found himself comparing every woman to the woman Preston often spoke of, never satisfied, always feeling as if he was waiting for something more.

Waiting for her to come home perhaps?

Which made no sense.

He blamed Preston. Preston compared every woman Sloan dated to Cara so, of course, Sloan had done the same. The man's dying words had been a request for Sloan to promise to take care of Cara.

A promise Sloan had given and meant.

But, much as he didn't understand his interest in Cara, he couldn't blame everything on Preston. Cara herself had captured his imagination with the various photos of her hanging on Preston's office wall.

Sloan did his best to tamp down the awareness of her that his body couldn't seem to prevent because he was positive that his all-too-male response wasn't what his friend had meant regarding taking care of his daughter. Besides, she was exhausted, grieving for her father. He had no right to be thinking of her as a desirable woman, to be aware of her feminine attributes. He should only be seeing her as the grieving daughter of a man he'd loved.

He kept telling himself that as he carried her into her room, managed to get the covers pulled back, and gently placed her in her bed.

The glow from the hallway light illuminated her lovely face, free from anguish for the first time since he'd met her, with the exception of when she'd been caring for Mrs. Goines. Then her natural nurturing instinct had taken over. He ached to see the twinkle in her eyes that shone in Preston's photos, to hear laughter spill from her full lips, to have her look at him with something other than disdain.

Unable to resist, he brushed a strand of hair away

from her face, stroking his finger over the silky smoothness of her skin.

Based upon her reaction to meeting him, he doubted he'd ever experience any of the things he'd like to experience about Cara, which was a real shame because she fascinated him. Probably because of his love of Preston. Probably.

If only he could convince himself of that.

He turned to leave but her hand grabbed his.

"Don't go."

Sloan stood perfectly still. Was she even awake or just reaching out in her sleep? He turned, met her sleepy gaze. "Cara?"

"I don't want to be alone in this lonely house. Not tonight." Her voice was small, almost childlike in its plea. "Please, don't go."

Sloan knew staying shouldn't be an option. Not in Bloomberg. His Jeep was parked outside. Everyone knew his Jeep. Bloomberg was a small town. Nothing would happen. Not when she was so distraught, but, still, the right thing for him to do would be to leave, to not give gossips anything to gnaw upon.

But walking away from her might take a much stronger man than he'd ever claimed to be.

CHAPTER THREE

CARA CLUNG TO Sloan's hand as if letting go would mean falling into an abyss she might never climb back out of.

She just might.

Goose bumps covered her skin. Her insides trembled. Her teeth fought chattering.

Which was crazy. The house wasn't cold. Not really.

But she felt chilled all the way to her bones, had from the moment she'd lost contact with Sloan's body heat when he'd laid her into her childhood bed. She'd suddenly felt more alone than she could recall ever feeling.

In his arms, and in the cocoon of her exhaustion, she'd felt warm, safe, not alone.

She'd not slept the night before, had tried, but the house haunted her, filling her mind with noises and memories of days gone past.

By the time she'd left for the funeral she'd been grateful for a reason to leave the ghostly haven.

She shivered again and grasped Sloan's hand tighter as she felt his inner struggle on whether to go or stay. No wonder. She didn't like him, hadn't been receptive to any of his friendly overtures. Yet now she was begging him to stay as if he was the only thing protecting her from nighttime monsters.

He was.

"Don't go," she pleaded, grateful for the dim lights. She hated begging. She hated the thought of being alone in this house even more. "I need you."

Still he wavered. "Are you sure, Cara? I don't want to take advantage of you."

Please. She rolled her eyes. Typical man. She just wanted him to ward off the ensuing nightmares and he thought she was offering sex.

Perhaps she couldn't fault him for that because maybe her pleas had sounded as if she wanted more than what she'd meant.

"So long as you keep your clothes on, Casanova, and I keep on my clothes, you aren't taking advantage. I just don't want to be alone. Please, don't make me."

The dark shadows of the room didn't hide him digesting her words. His expression confused, he looked down at where she held his hand. "Just so we're clear, what is it you want from me, Cara?"

Her brain felt fuzzy and she almost said, "Everything." But that was all wrong. All she wanted from him was the comfort of knowing another person was near, that she wasn't really alone in this house, in the world. She needed human contact. Not *him* really. Just another human near to offer companionship, to ground her to reality.

"Just hold me and don't let me go."

He still looked torn. She wished she could read his mind to know his thoughts. But then his lips pursed and he gave one slight nod.

"I can do that."

His answer seemed odd, but perhaps that was her fuzzy, fatigue and grief-laden brain talking. "I never thought you couldn't."

A small smile tugged at one corner of his lips. "I suspect you have a sharp tongue, Cara."

If Cara weren't so cold, feeling so emotionally bereft, if her eyelids weren't so heavy, she might have smiled at his comment. Wasn't that what her father had often said of her mother? That she'd had a tongue so sharp she could cut diamonds with a few well-chosen words? Odd. She hadn't thought of that in years. Instead of acknowledging the memories flooding her, she wrapped her arms around herself and shivered again. "I'm so cold."

Sloan sucked in a deep breath and crawled into the bed beside her, pulling her into his arms and cradling her next to his long, lean, warm body. "You won't be for long, Cara. I promise."

She wasn't.

Instead, she closed her eyes and, although being in bed with him should have kept her wide-awake, she slept, peaceful in the knowledge that he was there.

Not only there but stroking her hair, telling her how sorry he was at her loss, at how her father had been a good man and would be sorely missed. His low, gentle voice soothed aches deep inside her. She snuggled closer into him, knowing that if she wakened and needed him, he would still be there for the simple reason that he'd said he would be.

Funny how much that thought comforted her when he was essentially a stranger and she didn't like him.

Still, her father had liked him, trusted him, which was partially the problem. But in a moment of crisis that had to count for something.

In his arms was the only place she'd found any comfort since her entire world had turned upside down with a phone call he'd been the one to make.

* * *

Sloan lay very still, listening to the even sounds of Cara breathing. She'd gone right back to sleep. That was probably a good thing because no matter how many times he reminded his mind that this was a good deed, his body responded to her closeness in an all-male way.

He inhaled a slow whiff of the scent of her hair. Clean with a soft cherry flavor. That's what she smelled like. Cherry blossoms.

Unable to resist, he ran his fingers into her hair, stroking the sweet softness of her tresses between his fingers.

What was he doing?

Sighing, he let go of her hair and wrapped his arm back around her body, holding her close.

She wriggled against him, causing torturous awareness to zing to life.

"I don't like you," she mumbled under her breath, so low he barely could make out what she said.

"I noticed," he whispered back in resigned acknowledgement of her feelings toward him.

"Even if you are scorching hot and wear sex appeal like a second skin."

Sloan's entire body went stiff. Her breathing was still even and her body hadn't moved away from where she spooned with his. Was she awake?

"You think I'm sexy?" he asked, curious as to whether she'd respond and, if so, what she'd say.

"You are so hot you melt my insides just looking at you—but don't think I'll ever tell you that," she answered, her body still relaxed against his. "I won't, because I don't like you."

Asleep. She was talking to him in her sleep. No way

would she have just said that and not gone all tense if she were awake.

Despite his current uncomfortable predicament, Sloan grinned. It no longer mattered that Cara didn't like him, because apparently she was as physically aware of him as he was her. Somehow, at the moment, that seemed a lot more important in the grand scheme of life than merely being liked.

"Good night, Cara," he whispered against her hair, brushing his lips against the silkiness in a soft kiss. "We have a long day ahead of us tomorrow but we'll get through it. Then we're going to have this conversation when you're awake and not mentally and emotionally exhausted, because looking at you melts my insides, too, and I do like you. I like you way too much."

Cara gradually became aware of her surroundings, drifting somewhere between sleep and an awareness of the world around her. The quietness was the first thing that struck her. No New York City noises in the background of her inner world, as she'd expected.

But her sleepy inner world definitely had noises.

Male noises.

Soft male breath sounds.

And warmth. She felt so absolutely warm that she hated to move and risk letting any coldness seep into her snuggly world.

John didn't usually hold her like this. He wasn't a snuggler and said he couldn't breathe if she was in his personal space, that she made him sweat. Cara slept on her side of the bed and John slept on his. They met in the middle from time to time, but lately that had been less and less frequently.

Actually, Cara couldn't recall the last time she and

John had had sex or held each other. Way before her father's last visit.

She couldn't recall the last time he'd smelled so wonderfully manly, either. A light spicy musk that made her want to remember sex, to remember intimacy, that made her want to wiggle her body against his, and to have him want her, not just want her, but have to have her.

Which she must have done, because his arm tightened around her and his lower half woke up. Way up.

Good. Since her father's visit she'd gone from thinking John was going to propose to wondering if he even wanted her anymore. Maybe she hadn't wanted to admit it to herself or to anyone else, but something had definitely changed in their relationship. These days he certainly didn't seem to care one way or the other if they maintained a physical relationship.

Sex wasn't the most important aspect of a relationship to Cara, but the closeness of being intimate with one's mate was important. Very important, and she missed that intimacy.

She missed being held and touched and loved.

Which was silly. Of course John loved her. He told her every morning and every night just like clockwork. Just as she told him.

She was being held and touched and loved right now in an *mmmm, good* kind of way and she craved the feelings rushing through her more than she'd realized or been willing to admit.

His lips brushed against her hair in a caress that could only be described as worshipful. She rolled over, wanting to feel them against her mouth, to have him kiss her, to make love to her with this newfound passion.

He must have been waiting for her, because he immediately covered her mouth with his. His lips toyed masterfully with hers, teasing, tasting, tantalizing.

Mmmm, she thought. So good. She didn't recall John kissing so well, or with so much passion, but she wasn't complaining. All her insides were coming alive at how he was kissing her so enthusiastically, at how his body moved against hers, making her all too aware of the clothes separating their bodies. She arched into him, ran her hands into his hair, held him close, kissed him back with an enthusiasm that matched his own, awed at the butterflies dancing in her belly. Lower. It had been so long since she'd felt this way, since she'd wanted, felt wanted, desirable, needed. Had she ever?

"Cara," he moaned. "You feel so good."

Only "he" hadn't been the he she was expecting. He wasn't John and all the feelings hastening through her came to a quick halt.

No longer sleepy, Cara's eyes sprang open and her body jerked away from the man in her bed.

In horror, everything came rushing back.

The awful phone call she'd gotten, telling her that her father had died.

Making arrangements at work to be off for her father's funeral.

John refusing to go with her.

Flying to Pensacola, renting a car, then driving across the Florida-Alabama state line to Bloomberg.

The bittersweetness of walking into her childhood home and it being empty of the man she associated with everything about the place.

Sitting at the funeral home, longing to be anywhere else but in Gloomberg.

Her fatigue, fear and utter loss.

Her begging a man she didn't like to spend the night in her bed because she hadn't wanted to be alone.

Oh, yeah, everything came rushing back in vivid color. No doubt her cheeks glowed in vivid color, as well.

"Good morning," Sloan greeted her sheepishly, raking his fingers through his dark hair and smiling at her as if waking up in each other's arms was no big deal. As if the kisses they'd just shared had been no big deal.

She didn't do that. John was her one and only and they'd been together years. She was going to marry him, for goodness' sake!

"What are you doing?" She ignored his greeting and how absolutely gorgeous he looked first thing in the morning with his tousled black hair and thickly fringed coppery-brown eyes. She went on the attack. Much better to be on the offensive than to have to defend her weakness, to have to explain those kisses. How could she explain what she didn't understand? "I asked you to hold me, not molest me."

The light in his molten eyes morphed into dark confusion. "Molest you?"

Not giving heed to the guilt that hit her, she pushed against his chest, needing him out of her bed, out of her room, her house, her life. She couldn't breathe. She needed him gone. He epitomized everything wrong in her life. "It's time for you to leave."

"Stay. Leave. You're a bossy woman, Cara Conner. Then again, I'd heard that about you more than once. That you're a leader, not a follower." He was trying to make light of their situation, to defuse what had just happened between them. Under different circumstances, Cara might have appreciated his teasing, but she felt too raw to let go of the panic inside her. She'd been kissing him, a virtual stranger. She'd enjoyed kissing him! That had to be because of her crazy emotional state over losing her only living relative. Had to be.

"Don't act as if you know me. You don't." His words were her father's. She knew that. But these were horrible times. The worst of times. Times of which he'd been the bad-news bearer. She'd made them shoddier by inviting a man she didn't know to spend the night in her childhood bed. Shame on her.

They were both still dressed and nothing physical had happened, not really, because that kiss and body grinding so didn't mean anything. She felt emotionally violated all the same, as if something had passed between them during the long night hours when he'd held her, keeping her body safely tucked next to his and protecting her from whatever demons she'd feared. No one had ever held her that way. Not her father. Certainly not John.

That didn't mean she suddenly liked Sloan.

To prove it to herself, she narrowed her gaze and practically growled at him.

"You are obviously not a morning person." Sloan sat up on the side of the bed, raked his fingers through his hair again and shook his head. "For the record, you were the one doing the molesting just then. I was just an innocent victim of your early-morning assault and rather fervent kisses."

Cara's face flamed.

"Not that I'm complaining, because I'm not. I quite enjoyed what just happened between us. But I won't take blame for something I didn't do," he continued, looking way too handsome to have just woken up. "Not even from someone who looks as beautiful as you."

Flattery would get him nowhere. "Innocent victim, my—"

"Shame. Shame," he interrupted, wagging his finger at her. "Watch your language. Preston still has his curse-word jar on the kitchen counter. Would hate for you to have to make a donation first thing out of bed."

Immediately, all the oxygen left the room.

Or maybe it was just Cara's lungs that had become deprived, because Sloan seemed to be breathing just fine.

How dared he remind her of her father's curse-word jar?

What right did he have to tell her about her father's habits? Did he think she didn't know? That just because she'd chosen to live her life where she wanted rather than where he wanted her to be made her love her father less somehow? That her location made her forget growing up in this house and her father's habits? Hardly. She remembered all too well.

Her anger toward Sloan grew tenfold.

"Get out of here," she ordered, focusing all her hurt and frustrations toward him and wondering at how the cold blast didn't slam him out of her bed and against the wall like a splattered bug against a windshield. "Now, before I call the law and have you forcibly removed."

Looking way too calm for someone under attack, Sloan glanced at the wristwatch he still wore.

"I need to go home and shower," he said calmly, as if she had just made a comment about the weather rather than demand he leave. "I'll round at the hospital, and then will be back in a little over an hour with breakfast and coffee with all the fixings. Hopefully, you'll have a better disposition at that time. Be ready to go."

Hello. Was he daft? Or just deaf? "I don't want breakfast or a better disposition." Which sounded very childish, even to her own ears. But she had a lot to deal with today and that kiss wasn't going to be added to the list. "I don't want you to come back. I want you to leave my house and never come back."

"Your car is at the funeral home. You need to eat." Could he sound any more calm? Any more logical?

"You have a long day ahead of you," he reminded her, not that she needed reminding of what the day held. "I will be back, will feed you and will drive you to the funeral home. I want to help you, Cara."

"No, you've helped enough." Lord, she didn't mean to sound so ungrateful. "Don't come back. I can feed myself." Not that she felt as if she'd ever be able to eat again with the nausea gripping her stomach. "I'll find another ride to the funeral home."

She'd walk if it meant not riding with him, not having to look at him and feel the total mortification that she felt because she'd asked him, no, begged him to stay with her because she'd been afraid to be alone. Her only excuse was that she'd been exhausted and full of grief. This morning, well, she'd thought she was kissing John. Surely. Otherwise she never would have... Oh! Why was she trying to justify her actions in her head where Sloan Trenton was concerned? She didn't owe him anything.

"Just go." She slumped forward, burying her face against her hugged-up knees.

"This is crazy, Cara," he told her gently, obviously a man of great patience. He touched her shoulder, but she couldn't bear his touch and jerked away.

"Today is going to be rough enough on both of us without you treating me like I'm your enemy," he pointed out.

He probably thought her crazy. No wonder. She thought he was a little crazy, too, for remaining so calm when she felt so...so...agitated...and aware that he was in her bed beside her. Hadn't that kiss frazzled him in the slightest?

"What is your problem with me, anyway?" He genuinely sounded confused.

"Who said I had a problem with you?" she countered, hugging her knees even tighter.

"Just a wild guess."

"Then why are you still here?" For that matter, why was she still in bed with him? Was she really so stubborn that she refused to be the one to get out of the bed when she thought he was the one who should leave?

"You asked me to stay."

Again, his calm and logic irritated her further. She glanced over at him. His expression said there was more to it and she didn't like the knowing spark in his eyes, as if he knew something she didn't.

"That was last night," she responded in as matter-of-fact way as she could manage, scooting a bit farther away from him in the bed.

"And this is this morning?"

"Exactly."

"I'll ask again, why don't you like me, Cara?"

"I don't have to have a reason, do I?"

He studied her so intently she found herself wanting to brush her fingers through her sleep-tangled hair and pinch her cheeks to give her face some color. "Most people have a reason when they dislike someone."

"You took advantage of my vulnerability last night."

"No, I didn't, and we both know it. You asked me to stay and I stayed because it seemed like the decent thing to do. You were upset."

"Staying makes me a charity case?"

"You aren't a charity case. Far, far from it." His patience seemed to wear momentarily thin. "Why are you trying to fight with me? I don't want to fight with you."

He was right. She *was* trying to fight with him.

Because she didn't like him. Because she was embarrassed by the weakness she'd shown. Because he was logical and she was totally illogical, which irritated her because really she was a logical person most of the time. Maybe.

Fighting with him was easier than addressing kissing him.

"Then leave so you won't have to fight."

He shook his head, raked his fingers through his hair. "I'd like to be beside you today."

She rose up and frowned at him. "Can you not take a hint? I don't want you beside me. Not now. Not ever. Just go."

He opened his mouth, no doubt to point out that she'd wanted him beside her the night before. She had. She couldn't deny it. The house that had been home for so many years had felt empty and creepy in the darkness when she'd known her father wasn't there.

This time she interrupted him. "I have to bury my father today. I was emotionally weak last night and asked you to stay. I shouldn't have. I admit I made a mistake. I have a boyfriend and am ashamed of my mistake, of what happened just a few minutes ago. Now I want you gone and am asking you to leave. Can you not just leave, please?"

No longer meeting her gaze, he shrugged his broad shoulders and got up from the bed on the opposite side of her. "You've made your point. I'm no longer needed or wanted." He headed for the door, pausing just inside the frame to turn to face her. "Call if you change your mind about needing a ride to the funeral home. For Preston's sake, I'll do whatever I can to make this day as easy as possible for you."

He left.

Cara burst into tears and sobbed until there were no more tears left.

When she finally got herself together enough to think about heading to the funeral home, her neighbor Gladys Jones stopped by with some homemade brownies that Cara had loved as a girl and a sympathy card. Cara requested a ride and Gladys was happy to oblige so she could question Cara on why Dr. Trenton's car had been parked in her driveway all night.

"I was too upset to drive myself home from the funeral parlor. Dr. Trenton kindly brought me home" was all she told the woman, and changed the subject time and again when Gladys kept bringing up the subject of Sloan.

The drive to the funeral home seemed to take hours rather than mere minutes. Giving Gladys a grateful hug, because really, other than the Sloan questions, she truly appreciated the woman coming to her rescue, she made her way into the funeral home, knowing the roughest day of her life awaited.

Chin high, shoulders straight, she walked into the funeral home. She could do this. She had no choice.

Everything blurred.

People greeted her, hugged her, handed her tissues when she cried. She'd not meant to cry, had kept herself together the night before at visitation, but today she cried.

Brother Elrod from her grandfather's church presented a moving message, as did the hospital's current CEO. Several suited men served as pallbearers, Sloan included, lifting the casket and assisting as it was placed inside a hearse. Then Mr. Greenwood escorted Cara to a limousine and helped her inside the impersonal black car.

The graveside service passed in just as big a blur. The local sheriff's office honored Preston's many years of serving as coroner and medical examiner and they presented Cara with a folded flag.

The late-winter wind whipped at her clothes but she felt nothing, saw nothing. Standing from her seat with legs that threatened to wobble, she dropped a single rose and a handful of dirt onto the lowered casket.

"I'm going to miss you," she whispered barely above her breath. She sucked up her grief and greeted those who remained at the graveside.

All except one person.

She just wasn't strong enough to deal with him. Or with the odd emotions that sparked in her chest every time she glanced his way.

She'd caught him watching her a few times. She hadn't been able to register if he stared at her with disgust or confusion. Probably both. No wonder. He had every right to dislike her as much as she disliked him.

Fine. She had been emotionally distraught to the point she hadn't made any rational sense that morning. She knew that. What did it matter? After this was over she never had to see the man again.

"Cara?"

But obviously he didn't intend to let today pass without one more attempt at conversation. Why? They had nothing to say to each other. The only thing they'd had in common was a man who was now being covered with reddish-brown dirt.

She didn't look at him, maybe she couldn't.

"For whatever its worth, I'm very sorry about your loss."

At Sloan's words, she glanced up, met his gaze, and got locked into those molten copper eyes. So much emotion burned there. Confusion, compassion, and something so intent her knees really did wobble.

He reached out to steady her but she straightened before he could, not wanting him to touch her.

"Thank you, Dr. Trenton. My father was a good man." She'd given him a similar response to what she'd said over and over to guests today.

She half expected him to say something more but instead, his gaze still locked with hers, he just nodded. Then, breaking eye contact, he turned and walked away from her.

Knowing it was the last time she'd ever see him, not sure why that even mattered, she watched him walk away, watched the strong lines of his black suit stretch across his shoulders, watched the whip of the wind tug at his hair. He climbed into his Jeep and she even watched him drive away from the cemetery.

Her throat tightened and she fought back a sob. Determined not to break down in front of the few remaining people, she walked over to Mr. Greenwood.

"Can the car take me back to the funeral home now, please?"

Once back at the funeral parlor, Mr. Greenwood informed her of incidentals, had her sign more papers, then agreed to have all the fresh flowers delivered to the nursing home, to have the goods boxed up and delivered to a shelter for battered women, and that he'd have remaining food delivered to a needy family. He'd forward all the cards to her with a description of whatever they'd been attached to written on the back so she could send thank-you notes.

Cara went through the motions on autopilot, taking

care of what needed to be taken care of. On the outside, she figured she looked mostly together.

Good thing no one could see what her insides looked like.

She drove herself to Preston's, confirmed her flight back to New York the following morning and then paced through the big, empty house, soaking up the memories contained within its walls and yet broken-hearted that no new memories would ever be made here, no new photos would ever line the walls.

By the time she'd left for college this house had felt more a prison than a home. With each step she took, each tearful breath she sucked into her body, those same claustrophobic sensations grew.

She walked into her bedroom, glanced at the un-made bed that she'd slept in with Sloan. Would her bed smell of his spicy scent? Would she be able to sleep if she crawled between those covers alone, knowing what it had felt like to be held in his arms? To have awak-ened to his kisses?

Forget waiting until morning to fly back to New York.

She wanted out of Gloomberg. Stat.

She picked up her smartphone, pulled up her air-line's website, and, not caring at the exorbitant fees, she changed her flight to one just a few hours from the current time. No way did she want to spend the night there alone with the memories of her father or with the memories of the man she'd shared her bed with the night before.

She'd have to return soon enough to settle Preston's estate and get the few personal items she wanted to keep, but she didn't have to stay tonight. It broke her heart to think of selling the big old house, to sell his medical practice, but she wouldn't be moving back to Bloomberg. There was no need to keep any connection to the town.

She'd stay in New York, marry John and live a life far, far away from Sloan.

Um, she meant, far, far away from Gloomberg.

Then again, same difference.

She didn't like, either.

CHAPTER FOUR

THREE WEEKS LATER, Cara's Pensacola flight had been delayed over an hour. She'd had to rush the drive to Bloomberg to keep from being late to her appointment at the lawyer's office.

Although she'd known she'd have to return to Bloomberg to settle her father's estate, she'd dreaded the trip with all her being. For, oh, so many reasons that included one sexy doctor to whom she owed an apology for her overreaction to waking up beside him. All she could surmise was that she'd been exhausted and an emotional wreck. Kissing him hadn't helped matters one bit. She planned to meet with Mr. Byrd then write a short note of apology and thanks to Sloan.

But when she walked into the lawyer's office lobby and the first person she saw was Sloan sitting in the only occupied chair and reading something on his phone, all her good intentions flew out the window. She balked. "What are you doing here?"

She'd planned to make the trip without seeing him. Sure, he was the most likely candidate to buy her father's medical practice, and perhaps even his hospital shares. She'd planned to let their lawyers handle all those details. She had not wanted to actually set eyes on him.

Looking way too calm and handsome in his khakis and polo shirt, he ignored her outburst. "Good to see you again, too, Cara."

But he didn't sound as if he meant it any more than if she'd said the words to him. That was different, because before he'd been over-the-top nice. Today he seemed that if all eternity passed before he had to set eyes on her again, it would have been too soon.

"Nice to experience your sunny disposition yet again," he continued, clicking off his phone and sliding it into his khakis' front pocket.

Yep, that was definitely sarcasm.

"Mr. Byrd sent me a certified letter requesting I be here." He shrugged, as if his comment was no big deal. "So here I am."

"For the reading of my father's will?" She eyed him suspiciously. "Why would you need to be here for that?"

Looking as if she bored him, he shrugged. "Your guess is as good as mine."

She really didn't like him and his casual nonchalance. Or the fact that she'd thought of him way too often over the past few weeks. Blasted man! Yes, she'd intended to apologize for her dramatic morning show, but perhaps her antagonism toward him hadn't been so unfounded. "I doubt that."

"Same sweet Cara, I see."

"Same jerk Sloan, I see."

His brows furrowed at her comeback. He went to question her further, but Mr. Byrd stepped out from behind a door and summoned them to his office.

"I'm glad you could both be here today for the reading of Preston's will." He settled his pudgy body back into an oversize leather chair behind an equally oversize desk. "As you may know, Preston owned the house on

Maple Street, his medical practice, a significant number of hospital shares and had various investments he'd made over the years." The man pinned them both under his astute stare. "He died a very wealthy man."

Cara hadn't really thought of her father as wealthy, not when he'd worked 24/7. She was glad to know that he hadn't had to worry about money, that had he chosen to live another life he'd had that option. He'd lived how he'd wanted, taking care of others.

Mr. Byrd scratched his balding head, looked at them both from above the rim of his wire-framed glasses. "Oddly enough, as fate would have it, or maybe some sixth sense was at play, Preston changed his will about a month ago."

A month ago? Cara's eardrums thudded with a jungle beat that warned danger lurked ahead. That would have been at about the time of his trip to New York. And would explain Sloan Trenton's presence in the lawyer's office.

"He came to me with some very specific changes he wanted made to his last will and testament." He scratched his head and avoided looking directly at Cara as he continued. "The terms he set forth are a bit unusual but ironclad as I drew them up."

A sense of foreboding washed over Cara. She didn't care about the money, would give everything away plus everything she'd ever have to have her father back. But to know he'd so recently changed his will, that the man next to her had also been summoned to the lawyer's office... Sloan had been like a son to him...

What had her father done?

And why? Had she really been that much of a disappointment to him? Or had Sloan just been that much more the child he'd longed for?

* * *

The woman sitting in the chair next to him annoyed Sloan. Greatly. Immensely. Horrifically. She'd whipped into town, attended her father's funeral, blown out quicker than expected and left a tornado's worth of aftermath in Sloan's life.

Because he hadn't been able to stop thinking about her.

Which was crazy. She wasn't a nice woman, had been outright rude to him, used him, then cast him aside, unaware of how much havoc she'd caused. Preston's daughter or not, he should dislike her.

He did dislike her.

Greatly. Immensely. Horrifically. That's what the strong emotions that being near her again evoked within him. *Dislike.*

"Those terms are?" Cara asked, sounding more like a businesswoman than a doctor.

"That Mr. Sloan Trenton is to inherit one half of Preston's medical practice and one half of all real property attached to that business."

Cara's throat worked, but she didn't speak. She didn't have to. Sloan knew what she was thinking, saw out of the corner of his eye how her fingers bit into the edge of her chair.

Mr. Byrd looked directly at Sloan. "He'd planned to eventually sell half the practice to you and make you a partner in the fullest sense. He wanted to ensure that still happened, even if something happened to him, so he'd know Bloomberg would be looked after in his absence."

Sloan was floored. And humbled. He'd figured he'd buy Preston's practice from Little Miss Sunshine or that she'd refuse to sell to him and he'd just open his own practice in Bloomberg. Never had he considered that Preston would give him half of what he'd spent a lifetime building. Never would Sloan have agreed to his doing so. That the man he'd loved had wanted him to have half the practice filled him with so many emotions, including awkwardness, that Preston would have done such a generous thing.

How his heart ached that Preston was gone, that he wasn't there for him to tell him how much his actions meant, not the actual gifts but that Preston would do that for him, a poor kid from nowhere street, Cincinnati, who'd never had anyone really care for him... Sloan took a deep breath, thinking how blessed he'd been to have been a part of such a great man's life, to have loved and have been loved by such greatness, and wished he'd had more time to soak in everything he could learn from Preston.

Cara's gasp, then the clamping tight of her lips told him she was a bit floored by Preston's will change as well. But not in quite the same way as Sloan. No doubt she'd see Preston's actions as the ultimate betrayal or something that Sloan himself had fostered into happening. He hadn't. Not ever had he even dreamed of such a thing. Dreamed? Losing his mentor and dearest friend was a nightmare.

Cara quickly composed herself. Hands folded in her lap, she gave a tight smile to the lawyer. "With the way my father loved this town and respected Dr. Trenton, I can certainly understand that he'd want to ensure he stayed in Bloomberg to carry on his practice."

"Very true," the lawyer agreed, as if his revelation hadn't caused such a torrent of mixed emotions to burst free in the room. "Those were almost Preston's exact words when he came to me to change his will."

Still reeling at the enormity of Preston's gift from the grave, Sloan's ears roared. He wouldn't have left Bloomberg. Preston had known that Sloan had found a peace in the town that he'd never known elsewhere. For the first time in his life, Sloan had belonged and felt a part of something larger than himself, a medical family, a community, a town. He belonged here and would die here. Preston had known that.

"And the remainder of my father's assets?" Cara's voice was as smooth as silk, no inflection of emotion one way or the other. Those fingers in her lap worked overtime, though, clenching into her palm and straightening over and over. Whether she was making an angry fist or releasing nervous energy, Sloan couldn't say for sure.

Mr. Byrd leaned back in his leather chair and met Cara's gaze head on with a steely light that Sloan had never seen the man have before. The look was probably his courtroom, questioning-an-opposing-witness look. Certainly, many a lesser person than Cara Conner would have squirmed under that gaze. She didn't. Other than the fingers, she was the picture of calm, cool and collected.

Was she even aware she was making the telltale finger motions?

"You inherit the other half of Preston's practice and all his other possessions so long as you meet certain conditions." The lawyer paused dramatically, the conditions weighing heavily in the air.

Despite the roaring still taking place within his own skull, Sloan could almost hear the wheels turning in Cara's head.

"What conditions?" Annoyance laced her question.

"Like I said, Preston was very specific about the

terms of his will." The lawyer straightened a stack of papers on his desk that hadn't needed straightening, then he fixed that courtroom look on Cara again. "You have to move to Bloomberg, live in Preston's house and work at the clinic with Sloan for a minimum of forty hours a week for a minimum of six months."

"I can't move here," she gasped, her face contorted with horror and all pretense of composure gone. She gripped the edge of the desk and leaned toward the lawyer. "I don't want to live here. I won't live here. I hate this place."

She shook her head, as if trying to clear what the lawyer had said.

"Hate away." Mr. Byrd didn't seem to care one way or the other. "But not living in Bloomberg is not an option if you want to meet the terms of your father's will. You have to reside in the Maple Street residence for six months."

"I don't want any of his possessions, anyway. I'd planned to sell everything," she said, probably thinking out loud more than actually telling them her intentions.

The lawyer shook his head. "Nothing is yours to sell until the will's conditions are met. After they've been met, you can sell or do whatever you want to with his assets."

Sloan felt Cara's animosity bristling next to him, had a horrible inkling as to what more the lawyer was going to say. *Oh, Preston, what have you done?*

"If I refuse to meet the conditions of his will? Then what? Where do my father's assets go? To charity or perhaps another one of his causes?" Each word sounded ripped from between her tight lips.

"Your father set up trusts for his charities many years ago," Mr. Byrd informed her smoothly. "He formed those trusts as separate entities and they are well taken care of."

Sloan knew Preston had sponsored several local scholarships, kids' clubs and who knew what all other things. Preston's involvement in the community and his determination to make a difference with the Bloomberg community had been just one of the many things he'd admired about the man.

"If you fail to meet the terms of your father's will, Dr. Trenton inherits the clinic, the clinic's real property and your father's other assets, including the house on Maple Street and his vast investments."

Cara's jaws ground together with a loud snap, but she only said, "What? He has no conditions to meet? No jumping into burning buildings to save small children or stopping out-of-control speeding locomotives?"

The lawyer's eyes darkened with displeasure at her sarcasm, but he maintained his professionalism. "Dr. Trenton has no conditions to meet, other than that Preston hoped he'd continue to live in Bloomberg and provide medical care for the community. He trusted that he would."

Cara stood from her seat, moved across the room, then faced the lawyer. Her body shook beneath the cool lines of her skirt and blouse. Not that Sloan was looking that closely at her body. At least, he was trying not to. Hard not to at least be aware of where she paced when she aimed so much animosity at him that at any moment she might launch herself at him in anger.

"Those terms are ridiculous," she said. "I can't imagine them holding up in a real court of law. I live in New York. I have a life there. My father knew that." Her gaze settled onto Sloan and pure hatred shone in her blue-green eyes.

Not looking concerned or surprised by her out-burst, Mr. Byrd shrugged. "I can give you several at-torneys' names if you'd like to pursue contesting the will. However, I should advise you that Dr. Conner left no loopholes. The terms will hold up in court and will be carried out as he wished. I gave my friend my word on that and will personally do all I can, including calling in favors at any level necessary, to ensure my friend's last wishes are adhered to." The man gave her a dis-approving look. "I'd have thought you'd want to honor your father's dying request, but perhaps his wishes for your future don't matter so much when you have your own life to live."

Cara winced at the man's wounding words. Sloan suspected they carried a whopping, salty sting to her raw emotions. Sloan didn't doubt that Cara had loved her father. He'd seen and heard Preston talk about her too much to think that. They'd been close in their own way. No doubt, Preston having changed his will had shocked her, irritated her as it was her father manipu-lating her from the grave to do what he'd been unable to convince her to do while he'd been alive.

Sloan understood her frustration. He wouldn't have wanted to be manipulated, either, from the grave or otherwise. He'd never wanted or expected anything to be handed to him. He'd paid his way in life and had no problem with continuing to do so. He'd tell her that, but her gaze had narrowed with something akin to pure hatred as she stared at him.

"You knew this? That my father had changed his will?"

"Preston and I never talked money unless it had to do with the clinic." True. He and Preston had got along fabulously and had never had cross words. He directed his attention to the lawyer sitting across the desk. "Can I refuse the terms of the will? As long as she is willing to sell me the clinic and Preston's hospital shares at a fair market price, Cara can have everything. The clinic and hospital shares are all I'm interested in and I'll gladly pay for those."

"You can refuse the terms of the will, but Preston's estate would sit untouched for the full six months and an additional six months. After a year had passed, all his belongings would then be auctioned off to the highest bidder. The terms he set forth in his will not being honored would be a disgrace, considering everything Preston was in this community. This is what he wanted. His wishes should be honored." The lawyer's gaze cut to Cara in blatant disapproval of her wanting to fight her father's terms. "By both of you. If for no other reason than out of love and respect for a great man who has made his final wishes known."

Still visibly agitated, Cara sank back into the chair next to Sloan's and gave the lawyer a confused look. "Judge me all you want, but I can't just move to lower Alabama. Real life doesn't work that way. I have a job, responsibilities in New York."

"Why not?"

At his question, she spun towards Sloan. "You stay out of this. You...you...home wrecker."

Taken aback, Sloan flinched at her venom. "Huh?"

Mr. Byrd watched them curiously. Sloan was pretty curious himself. Why would anyone ever call him a home wrecker, particularly Cara? She'd not ever lived in Bloomberg during the same time he had. It would be near impossible to wreck a home that she'd already left for greener pastures years before.

Although perhaps that was unfair. Cara had left

Bloomberg for medical school then had stayed to do a job she loved in a place she'd also professed to love. As an adult she'd had that right. Just because Preston had wanted her home, in Bloomberg, didn't mean Cara had been wrong to live her own life and make her own decisions about where she wanted to live.

Sloan even understood her frustration with Preston's will. From the grave, Preston, thinking he knew best, was manipulating his daughter to do what he'd wanted all along. Cara to return home and work at his clinic.

How many times had he heard Preston say his girl was too stubborn for her own good? That she needed to come home and take her rightful place at the clinic?

One way or the other, Preston had been determined to prove his point to Cara by forcing her to be in Bloomberg.

Which meant she'd be working with him.

As if Cara didn't already detest him, Preston had made him the enemy.

Which meant six months of his life would be in constant turmoil.

He didn't want Preston's money. He also didn't want Cara at the clinic. Their last encounter had left a bad taste in his mouth. One he'd not really recovered from yet.

"Fine." Cara's voice had taken on a detached quality. "He can have my father's worldly possessions. They are just things. I'll move my personal items out of the house and Dr. Trenton can do whatever he wishes with the rest."

"I'm sorry, Miss Conner," Mr. Byrd apologized without really looking sorry at all. Actually, there was a steely spark to his gaze that said he enjoyed putting the squeeze on another human being and especially on Cara as she wasn't giving in to her father's maneuvering. "But if you decline the terms of the will, you are giving up your rights to any of Preston's possessions, including all personal items within the Maple Street home."

"What?" Cara's jaw dropped. Her face pale, she shook her head in denial. "This isn't happening."

Sloan didn't budge in his chair, just watched the events unfold between Preston's lawyer and his daughter. Tension gurgled between them to the point that had they come to physical blows he wouldn't have been surprised.

"You've not lived in that house for several years and therefore all items inside the house would be considered part of Preston's estate and not yours to take."

Cara's bravado sailed out of her on a puff of wind that expressed itself as a pained sigh. "I can't get my things? My mother's things? Her photos and diaries?"

The lawyer leaned forward, stared directly into her eyes, and sealed their fate. "If you decline the will's terms, those items would be Dr. Trenton's things, not yours. Anything you removed from the house would be theft and punishable by law as such."

"Theft?" She blinked, her hands visibly shaking in her lap. Sloan doubted there had been many times in Cara's life when someone had caught her so off guard, but, to give her credit, she had dealt with a lot over the past few weeks.

"Oh, yes. If you take a single item out of that house, it is my duty to have you arrested for theft of property from the estate of Dr. Preston Conner."

"You have got to be kidding me." She blinked as if she were caught up in some crazy movie plot. Sloan understood. He felt that way, too. Actually, he felt sorry for Cara, even though he knew he shouldn't. What had Preston done?

"I assure you, this is no joke."

"Can I purchase the items I want from the estate?"

"Perhaps Dr. Trenton would consider selling you any item of particular interest that you would like. But Preston was a wise man and did leave specifics on that, as well. A year would have to pass prior to Dr. Trenton being able to sell any item from the estate and any sale would have to be via a public auction or bid."

Any moment Sloan expected the top of Cara's head to explode. Literally. He wouldn't blame her. Preston had thought of everything.

Her face had gone from pale to puffy and quite pink. Her hands still fisted and unfisted. Sloan wasn't sure if she wanted to deck the lawyer, him or perhaps her late father.

"Is that everything?" Cara asked, shuffling some papers Mr. Byrd handed her and readying herself to leave the lawyer's office.

"Not quite." Oh, yeah, the lawyer was enjoying this way too much, Sloan thought as he smiled ever so slyly and pulled out two manila envelopes. "Preston left notes to you both."

Cara's head shot up and her breath caught. "He left notes?"

"Yes."

She closed her eyes, took a deep breath. "Were they from before he made the changes or at the time?"

"He gave me both notes in sealed envelopes on the day he signed and put into effect his new will."

Sloan eyed the lawyer, wondering at what further craziness was going to unfold. "You don't know what they say?"

"I've an idea, but no, I haven't read the specific messages. The letters are for the eyes of the beholder only, not mine or anyone else's. That's what Preston wanted and I respect him enough to honor his wishes." The man's inferences couldn't be missed. He handed Cara a sealed envelope with her name written in Preston's bold handwriting on the front.

Sloan watched her gaze go to her name, watched her visually trace Preston's handwriting and then her fingertip followed suit. Her hands shook slightly and he could only imagine the emotions flooding through her. His own hands probably shook, too. He took his letter and tried not to let his own sentimentality get to him. No way would he let Cara know how much all this affected him.

Inside the envelope was his final message from the man he'd loved more than any other person his entire life. Why did he suspect he already knew what his message would be? That somehow his message would echo Preston's final verbal plea to him? That Cara would be involved and that if he wasn't careful she would destroy the life he had made for himself in Bloomberg?

Just look at how one night in the woman's arms had torn him to bits a few weeks ago. Still tore him up. If he'd had any doubt, seeing her walk into the lawyer's office had set him straight. She messed with his head big time.

Even now the cherry candy scent of her filled his nostrils and made him want to lean closer and inhale as much of her as his lungs would hold. Quite literally, she drove him crazy.

A man could only stand so much.

Without another word, he got up, envelope in hand,

and walked out of the lawyer's office. Let them devise whatever they wanted.

He wasn't playing their game.

Cara had instantly disliked Sloan. She just hadn't fully understood how deep that dislike was destined to run.

She didn't need her father's money. With her scholarships, she'd graduated debt-free and had a great job in the emergency room. She had a good life.

Had had a good life.

Because when she'd gone back to New York after her father's funeral, she hadn't been the same.

Had found herself more and more annoyed with John and his lack of attention to their relationship. He talked big, but no action. No ring on her finger. Problem was, she wasn't even sure she wanted a ring. She'd thought she had, but when she closed her eyes, it wasn't John's kisses that haunted her dreams. The kisses of a man she couldn't stand had stolen her breath and her sleeping fantasies. The way he'd held her, the way his body had moved against hers, the intensity with which he'd kissed her…

Ugh. She just wanted to forget him. Everything about him.

But, according to Mr. Byrd, she could choose to either work with Sloan for six months or say goodbye to everything from her childhood—her mother's paintings, her mother's wedding dress, her mother's diaries, her mother's china, her mother's hope chest, which had been Cara's grandmother's. All material things, but things with such great sentimental value that Cara felt a bit bereft just at the thought of not having them to pass on to her own children someday so they'd have a physical piece of their grandmother to hold on to and know the vivacious woman she'd been prior to Gloomberg sucking the life out of her. Her mother must be rolling over in her grave that Cara's father was forcing her to return to the town.

Her father had wanted her to just up and leave her life and play at living her daddy's dream for her.

She glanced at the lawyer, who still watched her closely. "I had planned on staying for a couple of days to sort through the items I wanted to take back to New York with me. Is it okay for me to stay in the house or do I need to move into a hotel?"

"No hotel is necessary, but you can't remove any of the items from the house. Not for a year."

"Yes, I think you've made that point clear already." She sounded snappy and knew it, but the man had just destroyed her life. "The terms of my father's will really aren't fair, Mr. Byrd."

"It's not my job to judge my client's final wishes, just to carry them out. He wanted you in Bloomberg and used every means at his disposal to make that happen. Perhaps, before you make any decisions, you need to think long and hard about that."

Her father had made his wishes known, had left no doubt how he wanted her to spend her life, that he felt her own choices were wrong.

"You're right. I do need to think about all the things you've said."

It would be so easy to just say okay, to give in to the terms he'd set forth and live in Bloomberg for six months.

Yet it wouldn't be easy at all.

She'd give up everything if she accepted the terms—the job she loved, her relationship with John, because no way would he agree to her moving to Bloomberg for six months, her Manhattan apartment, which was so fabulously located and quite a find. When her six months were up, she'd have to start over completely with her career and her personal life.

But could she really say no to her father's final request of her?

How could she say yes?

She stood, nodded at the lawyer. "I'll stay at my father's tonight as planned and will be in touch within the next couple of days to let you know my decision."

"You have thirty days to decide."

She shook her head. "I won't need thirty days, because I can't throw away my life to move back to Bloomberg."

But could she really throw away her past?

"Bloomberg isn't so bad."

"That is a matter of opinion." She gave him a tight smile.

"Your father was a brilliant man and he chose Bloomberg. He loved this town and there were reasons for that. Reasons you may not know or understand because you never attempted to. Perhaps, while deciding your future, you should stop and ask yourself why not."

My dearest Cara,

If you are reading this, then I've gone on to a better place. I don't want you to mourn me or to be sad, because I've lived a good life. I've loved in ways most men never love—your mother and you.

Isabelle never adjusted to small-town life as I'd hoped she would, but you already know that. You have fashioned your life around wanting to be like her. It took me a long time to realize that, to understand that.

As you decide your future course, I'm asking—no, begging—you to fashion your life around wanting to be like me, even if for only six months. Six months is not a long time in the grand scheme of life. Yet six months can change the way a person sees the world, the way a young woman sees herself and her place in the world.

I know you, Cara. I know you're contemplating walking away from Bloomberg. Give me six months to show you my world, to show you Bloomberg through my eyes. Afterwards, if you still want to leave, then go, have no regrets and know you have my blessing in doing so.

I love you, my daughter. I have from the moment you entered the world and I always will.

Dad

Tears streamed down Cara's cheeks. Her eyes stung. Her cheeks hurt. She drowned on postnasal drainage from sobbed-back tears.

No. He couldn't do this to her. He just couldn't.

She didn't want to live in Bloomberg.

How could she not?

Not so she could inherit his assets, but because if she didn't his words, his last request of her, would haunt her all the days of her life.

Whether she wanted to move to Bloomberg and step into her father's world or not, for six months she was going to.

She'd lived in Bloomberg eighteen years. Being back six months wasn't going to change the way she looked at this town or at herself.

She'd carry out her father's request, but at the end of six months she'd leave and never look back.

CHAPTER FIVE

"WE GAVE YOU two slots per patient all week to give extra time to learn the patients, the electronic medical record and the way the office runs. I wish you'd been able to arrive earlier so you could have had the opportunity to meet everyone and get your feet wet prior to starting today," Amie Matthews informed Cara four weeks later on a bright and early Monday morning as they walked toward the back of the clinic. "Other than the EMR, it's not that different from when you hung out here as a girl, but there are some changes. Like doing everything on the computer rather than with paper."

There had been a lot of reasons why Cara hadn't arrived earlier. Mainly, she hadn't wanted to get her feet wet until the clock started ticking on her six months. Today was that day. *Tick. Tick. Tick.* Time flew when one was having fun. Did that mean the next six months was going to drag by?

"Your schedule is full but shouldn't be too bad today," Amie assured her, smiling in a familiar way that used to set Cara at ease. Now she suspected everyone at the clinic just wanted her to finish her time, sell Sloan the clinic and her be done with Bloomberg.

"They started booking the moment we added your name to the schedule, you know." Amie reached out, touched Cara's arm with gentle reassurance. "I think almost everyone just wants to come in and tell you how much they miss your father."

"Possibly." She smiled at the woman who had been her father's nurse for a good twenty years. Amie Matthews had probably known Preston Conner better than anyone other than Cara...and maybe Sloan.

Sloan. She'd not seen him since he'd walked out of the lawyer's office. She'd not even talked to him. Mr. Byrd had handled letting Sloan know that she'd decided she could take a six-month hiatus from her real life to fulfill her father's last request.

In the grand scheme of life, what was six months when it gave her the peace of mind and heart that she'd abided by her father's last wish?

She'd spoken with Amie and with Erica, the office manager, several times over the past couple of weeks as they'd made arrangements for her to join the practice and be official with various state health boards and insurance companies.

"What are you planning to do about the hospital?"

She was sure she'd forgotten a dozen things in her whirlwind relocation, but the hospital wasn't one of them. "The board met last week and approved my privileges. Mr. Byrd and Erica handled all the paperwork on this end. She's great, by the way."

"She has done a great job managing the practice," Amie agreed. "Your father can really pick good help." Amie drew in a deep breath that was full of sorrow then pasted her smile back onto her face. "Thank goodness you have your privileges. Dr. Trenton is spread too thin between here and the hospital. Casey, our nurse practitioner, is great, but she hasn't been able to lighten his load nearly enough."

"I met her when I was home last year." That would have been right before Sloan had started at the practice. Her father had hired his wonder boy but Sloan hadn't arrived in Bloomberg yet.

"She's a gem. As is Sloan."

Of course Sloan was a gem. Everyone thought so.

Her astute eyes studying her too closely, Amie smiled at Cara with the same friendliness and motherly affection she'd always shown her. "You'll like working with him, Cara. We all do. He's a good doctor. He's a lot like your father."

Cara closed her eyes. She was tired of hearing how much Sloan was like her father. She was tired of hearing about him, period. All morning she'd dreaded seeing him.

And yet... That achy, nervous feeling in the pit of her stomach was dread, right? Not excitement. Not anticipation. Not curiosity that perhaps she had overbuilt the man's looks, aura and kissing ability in her mind. Not curiosity and anxiety over how he'd walked out of Mr. Byrd's office. None of those things. Just dread.

She glanced down the office hallway, wondering where the dreaded doctor was, why she hadn't yet seen him. She wanted to get that first meeting over with, to know how he was going to react to her being at the office, invading his space, for the next six months.

Sure, from the moment she'd let Mr. Byrd know that she was going to fulfill the terms of her father's will, no doubt Sloan had known she'd be in Bloomberg, would be working at the clinic. Had he been disappointed at her decision? Of course he had. He had everything to gain by her staying right where she'd been.

Her decision wasn't based on money. She just hadn't been able to stomach the thought of disappointing her father that one last time, of possibly losing her mother's things, of losing her few prized family heirlooms.

Too bad if Sloan Trenton didn't like her decision.

Amie followed her gaze and her smile grew a little too pleased for Cara's comfort. "He texted a little while ago to say he'd gotten hung up at the hospital but that he'd be here as quickly as he could. He's killing himself, trying to keep everything going. I'm so glad you're here. Only I wish…" Amie stopped, her smile completely gone. She winced a little. Cara didn't need her to finish to know what her father's nurse had been going to say. Only she wished it had been sooner, had been while Preston had still been alive, that her father was there to show Cara the ropes, so to speak, as she stepped into her new career.

A smidge of guilt hit Cara. She hadn't thought about Sloan carrying two doctors' loads by himself.

She had thought about Sloan, though.

Way too often she'd thought about the dark-haired man with his mesmerizing copper eyes. She'd thought about waking in his arms and the passion of his kisses. She'd thought about the fact that for six months she'd be thrown together with him. She'd thought about the look of disgust on his face when he'd walked out of Mr. Byrd's office and how that look had punched her in the gut. How had he dared to look upset when she was the one who was drastically changing her life?

But not once had she thought about how her father's death had affected him and his workload. She'd been too caught up in her own grief and life changes and how she felt emotionally blackmailed into returning to a town that had robbed her of her family. Was she really that selfish? Since when had she quit caring about others? Quit recognizing their needs?

Still, she couldn't have gotten relocated much quicker. She'd had to work out her notice in the emergency room, had had to pack her New York life, take care of the legalities of practicing medicine in another state and so forth. She'd come as quickly as she could. Mostly so she could get these six months behind her and then figure out what was next for her.

She'd broken things off with John—why hadn't he cared more at the demise of their relationship? For that matter, why hadn't she? She'd been with the man for years, yet walking away hadn't hurt. She'd thought she was going to spend the rest of her life with him. Walking away should have at least stung a little. It hadn't. He'd even helped her pack and driven her to the airport. They'd parted as friends. If there had been passion, shouldn't he have been begging her to stay? Shouldn't she have been running back from her airport gate and flinging herself into his arms for one last kiss?

Leaving him had been all too easy. For both of them.

She took a deep breath. No time to think about John right now. Today she started her six-month penitence. She'd suck up her grief over her lost life and she'd make the best of the next six months, whether Sloan liked it or not.

"He loved your father, you know."

Amie's words cut into Cara's thoughts. Bitterness burned the back of her throat. "So I've been told."

"He did. Just as Preston loved him like the son he never had."

At any moment a hole was going to appear in her throat from the acid gnawing away at her. She ignored the sharp pain that ate at her body, met Amie's eyes, and changed the subject before she said something she'd regret. "Are you working as my nurse today? If so, I imagine we should get started because it may take me a bit to pick up this EMR system."

In fact, Conner Medical Clinic's charting system wasn't too different from what Cara had used during one of her residencies. Although she asked Amie question after question, she muddled her way through her morning patients. All without so much as a glimpse of Sloan.

How lucky was she?

At lunch, when Cara went back into her father's office—her office—she stopped at the fresh bouquet of flowers on the desk. Had Sloan...?

"We wanted you to know how glad we are to have you at the clinic," a petite brunette said from behind her, stopping Cara's train of thought. "I'm Casey Watson, by the way. We met briefly when you were home last and again at the funeral home, but I'm not sure if you remember me."

Cara shook the woman's outstretched hand. "Sure I do. You were all aglow because you'd just gotten back from your vacation and talked to me about Aruba. John and I ended up going there for a long weekend a few months after that."

"That's right." Casey's smile brightened. "Hope you enjoyed it as much as I did. That was the best vacation I've ever had. Wish I was there now."

Actually, John had gotten a bit of food poisoning and they had spent a great deal of the weekend just lounging around the hotel. Cara had been bored, but had caught up on some reading.

"Are you talking about going on vacation again?"

Cara's breath caught and her gaze immediately went to the man who'd spoken and was leaning against the office door frame. Her imagination hadn't built up a thing. The man was beautiful in every sense of the word. "Sloan."

Saying his name out loud couldn't be appropriate but it popped out of Cara's mouth all the same.

Sloan had avoided bumping into Cara all morning. That hadn't given him as much peace as it should have, though, because he'd still known she was in the building, that for the next six months she'd be a constant thorn in his side.

Actually, it wasn't his side that she pricked but a spot deep in his chest. How could you be half-crazy about someone you'd never met in person? How could you meet that person and instantly trigger such dislike? How could you shove that person out of your thoughts when you realized that your infatuation had been silly and that you weren't even sure you actually liked the person?

Almost a month had passed since he'd seen her last and yet Sloan still hadn't figured out the answers to any of the questions that had plagued him since Preston's funeral.

Preston. Lord, how he missed that man. Would a time ever come that he'd wake up and not instantly recall that Preston had gone on to a better place? That he wouldn't relive a moment of grief and loss every single day?

"Yeah, well, it was a really great vacation. You should have been there," Casey said, smiling at Sloan as if he hung the moon. She usually did. He thought of her as his kid sister.

"I have this feeling that if I'd been there you wouldn't have had nearly as much fun as you claim to have had."

Casey's face flushed a pretty pink. She hadn't mentioned meeting anyone while she'd been in Aruba for a medical continuing education seminar, but Sloan felt confident she had spent the week with some lucky guy. Regardless, whatever had happened, Casey never mentioned anything other than to talk about what a great vacation she'd had.

"You might be right," Casey agreed, standing up from where she perched against Cara's desk. "The reality is that you have to butter me up with the promise of upcoming vacations so I'll keep coming in to work day after day. Otherwise I'd likely just stay at home and avoid this craziness we call medicine."

Knowing Casey loved her career as much as he did, Sloan put his hand over his heart and feigned devastation. "A woman who chooses vacations over me. Say it isn't so."

He and Casey both laughed, but Cara just watched their byplay with narrowed eyes. His gaze went beyond her to the photos hanging on Preston's office wall. What had happened to the smiley, adventurous woman from all the pictures? Did she really dislike this town so much that she would wear a constant scowl for the next six months? Or was it just him she disliked so much? Preston's will couldn't have helped the situation.

Turning his attention back to Casey, he grinned and was grateful at least one of his coproviders was all smiles. "For the record, I really appreciate you putting your scheduled vacation on hold. I'd have been lost without you last week." He winked at her but remained aware of Cara watching them.

"Yeah, yeah," Casey agreed, laughing then taking on a somber look. "You know I wouldn't leave you with Preston…" She glanced at Cara. "I'm really sorry about your father."

Cara's face instantly blanched. Nothing impassive about her expression now.

She closed her eyes and took a deep breath.

Before Cara could reply, Casey's cell phone beeped. She excused herself, but not before adding, "So glad you are here as part of our family, Cara. As you can probably already tell, we are one big family. If you need anything, let me know. I'll help if I can."

Then left Cara and Sloan alone.

Except for the other six or seven people in the building of course. But alone in Preston's office—Cara's office.

Which suddenly felt very awkward. After avoiding her all morning, after keeping all contact they'd had through the lawyer's office, why had he come to her office to look for her?

Why did he always feel so flustered around her? Because of what Preston had asked of him?

"I'm headed over to the hospital to check on a patient I admitted last night for gastroenteritis and dehydration." He gave her what he hoped was a peace-offering smile. "Do you want to go with me?"

She blinked her wide eyes as if he'd sprouted a horn from her forehead. "Why would I want to do that?"

Why? He could give her a hundred different reasons, but he didn't utter a single one. Just waited. Whatever Preston's note to his daughter had said, it certainly hadn't tamped down her anger towards him. If anything, she looked at him with even more dislike than she had that day in Mr. Byrd's office.

"Why wouldn't you want to do that? You are going to work in this office for six months. Learning the ropes from me seems a logical decision."

"I could give you a hundred different reasons why going with you wouldn't be a logical decision at all. Plus, I'm not a newbie. I've been working in a busy emergency department for almost a year now. It's not like I'm wet behind the ears."

"You're a prickly thing, aren't you?" Sloan laughed at hearing her say his own thoughts out loud, only in reverse. He had the feeling they were going to be at opposite ends of the spectrum a lot. Which was going to make for a long six months. Preston's stubborn blood ran red through her. No doubt he'd be the one to have to offer the olive branch. For Preston's sake and for the sake of them all, he'd offer her the whole olive tree if it meant she'd relax a little.

Her forehead wrinkled. "What's so funny?"

Taking a deep breath, he shook his head and decided to put the cards on the table. "Look, Cara, whether we like our current situation or not, for the next six months we are going to be working together. Those six months will go much smoother, for us and for those who work here with us, if we can find some level of peace between us. If you want to hate me outside the office, fine. Hate away. But here at the office let's at least call a truce, because I don't think the others will understand if we're constantly at odds."

She walked away from him, went behind the desk, put her hands on the chair back, and took a deep breath. "You're right."

She didn't look happy. He suspected that having to admit he was right had a lot to do with her displeasure. Still, it was more than she'd given him up to this point.

"So," he ventured. "I'll ask again, do you want to go to the hospital with me to see a patient I admitted last night for twenty-three-hour observation and IV fluids? I can walk you through normal protocol at Bloomberg General Hospital, because I imagine Bloomberg is going to be vastly different than working in a busy emergency department in Manhattan."

Her fingers dug into the leather of her father's chair, her knuckles blanching white. "I suppose that would be the logical thing for me to do."

"It would."

She took a deep breath, nodded her head. "Okay. Let's go so you can show me the ropes."

He'd half expected her to refuse, but maybe she was going to meet him halfway so the next six months would pass without either of them being too scathed.

Maybe.

The awkward silence that ensued wasn't promising, though. She was just as lost in her thoughts as he was in his.

"What did you think of your first morning?" he asked as they walked toward the hospital, searching for something to break the tension. Preston had built his office on a piece of property adjacent to the hospital, which simplified the sometimes frequent trips back and forth to check on patients.

"I didn't kill anyone," she said drily.

"Good to know, especially since the most likely victim would have been me."

She stopped in midstep, causing Sloan to do the same. Color infused her face and her lips compressed tightly.

"Hmm, I better behave or you may not be able to say the same about your afternoon, eh? You didn't have any Mafia connections in New York, did you?"

"Just a few," she quipped, still not moving. The light breeze caught a loose strand of her caught-up red hair and whipped it across her porcelain face. "I really don't like you, you know."

He knew. "Exactly my point."

"You're not helping."

A smidge of guilt hit Sloan. "This is me trying to be helpful and break the ice between us, Cara. I don't want the next six months to be miserable for either of us."

"Seriously?" She eyed him suspiciously.

"Seriously. I know we got off to a bad start, which I don't fully understand since you didn't like me from the moment I showed up on your doorstep. But, for whatever it's worth, I am glad you are here. The past few weeks have been hellish."

As her scowl lifted and her expression softened, he admitted that he was very glad. Because, whether he understood it or not, Cara Conner got under his skin and he had six months to pry her out from under there and lose his fascination with her. Plus convince her to stay in Bloomberg forever. No big deal.

"I'm sorry you've had to carry my father's load for the past couple of months, Sloan." Her gaze met his and her eyes flashed with guilt. "I had things I had to resolve in New York before I could get here."

Her sincerity and how it hit him suggested everything about her was a big deal. A very big deal.

"I've managed, but, like I said, I am glad you're here. Truce?"

Her gaze narrowed with obvious displeasure at their situation, but then she stuck out her hand. "Truce, but I still don't like you, much less trust you. You have a lot to gain by my failing."

He laughed. "Well, at least that's a start and in case you weren't paying attention, I didn't ask for this situation to be thrust on us any more than you did. I cared enough for Preston to want his final wishes carried out, which means I don't want you to fail at all."

CHAPTER SIX

SELFISHNESS WASN'T SOMETHING Cara associated with herself, but apparently she should have. With her father and with Sloan. All she'd thought about had been how her father had forced her into six months of hell. Not once had she considered that he'd also forced Sloan into six months of limbo. Or hell, since he was forced to work with her and she was miserable about the whole thing and apparently determined to make him just as much so.

Maybe he really hadn't dropped hints to her father that he was like a son to him and should be treated as such. Preston hadn't been a foolish, gullible man. Obviously, Sloan had impressed him and won his favor.

Still, she didn't trust him. Shouldn't trust him. But for six months she would be working with him in a close-knit environment and would be fulfilling her father's final wishes. She'd quit being such a Negative Nancy about the whole thing.

He chatted while they walked into the hospital, introducing her to people left and right as if she hadn't lived here eighteen years. She just smiled and carried on, accepting more condolences for her loss.

"Miranda, this is Dr. Conner," Sloan introduced Cara

as they entered the hospital patient room. A pale young girl stared back at them.

"I thought Dr. Conner..." the girl's voice trailed off.

"He did," Sloan continued, smiling gently at the young woman. "This is his daughter, Cara. She's going to be in Bloomberg, helping out at her father's clinic for a while."

She nodded and smiled weakly at Cara.

"Nice to meet you," she told the patient, whom she actually didn't know, and joined Sloan at the computer as he pulled up lab results.

"Am I going to get to go home, Dr. Trenton?" the woman asked in a voice still so weak it should have answered her question for her.

"Not today, Miranda. Your electrolytes are still too low, despite the supplements we've infused. Your potassium has only come up a few points from two point nine to three point one. I'm going to have another bag of potassium infused in hopes of getting you up within normal range."

"Is that why I still feel so weak?"

He nodded and, after skimming over her other lab results, moved to the hospital bed. "It is. I suspect your muscles are still cramping, too."

Miranda winced. "I got an awful 'charley horse' during the night. It woke me up and I had to call the nurse to help me."

"Those should stop once we get your potassium back to normal. Now that your stomach symptoms have resolved I'm hopeful this next bag will do the trick."

"I hope so."

"Me, too." Sloan leaned forward and placed his stethoscope diaphragm on her chest. He listened to her

heart, lungs,and abdomen, then palpated her abdomen.
"Any pain?"

"Just that cramping sensation before I have a bowel
movement, but it's better than it was."

Cara clicked on the radiology file and reviewed Miranda's computerized tomography scan of her abdomen
and pelvis. "I see she had ovarian cysts that showed
up."

"They were an incidental finding but, yes, there were
ovarian cysts bi-lat. No gallbladder disease or appendix
issues were seen."

Cara felt silly for having pointed out the positive
findings to him when he'd obviously already looked
over the results.

"Thanks for the heads-up," he told her, meeting her
gaze and smiling.

Her breath caught. Okay, he was determined to be
nice to her when really he could make the next six
months so much worse, when he could make them so
unbearable that she'd just leave, and then he'd inherit all
her father's assets. But that wasn't what he was doing.
He was being nice to her. Even when she hadn't been
nice to him.

Ugh.

The man had her emotions torn every which way.
He was her enemy and yet…he wasn't acting like an
enemy at all.

The following morning, Sloan popped his head into
Cara's office, catching her studying her computer
screen. "Thanks for checking on Miranda this morning."

"You're welcome. I was hoping she'd be well enough
to discharge this morning after you gave her the extra
fluids and electrolytes yesterday, but she was still pretty

weak. Her white blood count had jumped up to fifteen thousand this morning."

Sloan arched a brow. "What do you think is up with that?"

"I'm not sure. I've ordered a round of antibiotics and a repeat blood count to be drawn. If her numbers are still up or if her symptoms worsen, I think we should repeat imaging."

He nodded. "Sounds like a good plan to me."

Her gaze went back to the computer screen and she frowned.

"Everything okay?"

"No."

"No?"

"I can't figure out this blasted program. I need to fax a form over to the hospital and I can't get it to send. It would be quicker to walk it over."

Sloan walked over to her desk, bent down to glance at her computer screen, quickly spotting what she was doing wrong. "May I?"

"Be my guest." She pushed the computer mouse toward him. "Any moment now the system is probably going to crash thanks to my many failed attempts as there's no telling what I'm actually doing with all the clicking I'm doing."

"Just because you've faxed all our patients' records to Channel Four news doesn't mean our system is going to crash."

Her eyes widened. "I didn't."

He grinned. "You're right. You didn't."

"You're not a very nice man, Sloan Trenton. Here I am, trying to work my way through this crazy computer system and not bother anyone unnecessarily, and you give me a heart attack that I've sent confidential files to the local news station."

"You didn't believe me for a single second," he accused, knowing his words to be the truth.

A small smile played on her lips. "Well, maybe a single second."

Trying not to label the way his blood hammered through his vessels at her partial smile, Sloan clicked through the steps that would send Cara's fax. He also tried not to let the fact that he stood so close to where she sat distract him from his task. But she smelled good. And he'd bet that if he reached out and ran his fingers into that silky red hair she'd feel just as good. And her lips… He remembered all too well how those had felt. He hit the last button, watched the screen confirm that her fax had been sent properly then he straightened before her nearness cost him his mind.

"Thank you," Cara said immediately, glancing up at him from her chair. Her big blue-green eyes met his, locked for a few brief seconds and flickered with something he couldn't read. Her lips parted and then she shook her head very slightly and glanced back at the computer screen. "I'd have eventually figured the fax out, but having watched you send this will definitely make it easier next time."

Next time. Because she was going to be here for six months. Six months and then she'd leave, never to return to Bloomberg because she hated the town he loved. Preston's note flashed in front of his eyes and weighed heavily on his heart. Leave it to Preston to ask for the impossible, knowing Sloan would give it his all to make the man's dying request happen.

Never had he had anyone in his life ask so much of him; never had he had anyone put so much faith in him as Preston had. His last foster parents during high school had been kind to him, and the man, being a family physician, had lived the life Sloan had quickly realized he wanted—to serve others, to be a part of a tight-knit community and family, to make a difference in people's lives, to matter. That foster father had set Sloan on the course to becoming a doctor, but his relationship with him hadn't compared to the bond he'd formed with Preston. Even if he didn't one hundred percent agree with what Preston had requested, he had to do his best.

"For the record, we're all here to help you, Cara." They were. Everyone in the office was excited she was there. Not only because she was Preston's daughter but because he and Casey were in patient overload. So much so they'd already started looking for another nurse practitioner or physician's assistant. He supposed he should start putting out feelers for another physician as well for when Cara left. A pang shot through his chest, but he ignored it.

"We want to help you so, anything you can't figure out, ask. That way we know you're human, just like the rest of us."

She stared at the computer monitor as if it held the code to all life. "I'm all too human."

"Not everyone has climbed Everest or jumped out of a perfectly good airplane."

Both their gazes went to the smiling photos on the office wall.

"I should take those down, but I can't bring myself to change the way he has anything."

Sloan shrugged. "I don't think you should change them. I like the pictures."

"But they're all of me."

Yeah, there was that. He didn't know how to respond because what could he say? That one of the things he'd enjoyed most about Preston's office was the photos of his daughter? How could he possibly explain that to her? Or to himself, for that matter?

"Like I said, not everyone has done the things you've done or been to the places you have."

"Not in this town. In Bloomberg, everyone seems to think the world ends just outside the county lines."

Knowing he'd stayed in her office longer than he already should have, Sloan moved toward the door, pausing to lean against the frame. Surprised that she'd followed him to the doorway, he met her vivid blue gaze. "For them, perhaps it does."

Her gaze narrowed, but for once she didn't look away. "What do you mean?" she practically growled at him.

Apparently, he'd pushed a sensitive button or two. He'd need to tread cautiously or their truce would likely be a thing of the past. "For many of the people who live here there's no reason to go beyond the county lines because everything they love is right here in Bloomberg. Why go anywhere else?"

"Ugh, you sound like my father."

"I take that as a compliment."

Her lower lip disappeared between perfect white teeth and her shoulders lost their stiff edge. When her gaze met his, her eyes were clouded with inner turmoil. "It wasn't really meant to be a compliment."

Sloan battled some inner turmoil of his own, all of which was triggered by the way he reacted to everything about her. He shouldn't like her, but he did. He shouldn't want her, but he did.

The crazy thing was, as much as she'd tenaciously

deny it, he knew Cara fought the same inner battles. Not just because of her sleepy admission about finding him hot but because he saw it in her eyes.

Six months. Then she'd leave. Except he was supposed to convince her that Bloomberg was the place she wanted to spend the rest of her life.

Preston should not have put them in this situation, but he had.

Sloan reached out, brushed a hair away from her face and smiled despite his doubts. Surprisingly, she didn't pull away from his touch. "I know, Cara. I know."

Cara might not want to like Sloan, but the blasted man was growing on her. How could he not, with his constant smiles and teasing? Not just to her, but with everyone he came in contact with. Their coworkers, their patients, the hospital employees. Sloan was the most positive person she'd ever met. Just like her father, he gave his all to his patients.

After working with him for just a week, she understood why everyone said he was like Preston. The man woke up thinking about medicine, worked medicine wholeheartedly all day and, no doubt, went to bed thinking about medicine.

Case in point: his current text. She stared at her phone and read his message again, then typed a note back.

No problem. I will round on her in the morning and make sure another chest X-ray gets done.

Thanks. I'll be at the nursing home until about nine.

She'd noticed his schedule for the following day had been blocked for nursing-home rounds. Not that she'd been looking at his schedule, just glancing at her own to see how her morning appointments looked, to see how many of the names she recognized.

You want to go with me to the nursing home? I can introduce you to the staff and to our patients there so you can take over rounding on Preston's patients. If that's what you want to do.

Truly, Sloan had been gracious to her, had gone above and beyond to make sure her transition into Conner Medical Clinic went smoothly. Because of him, because of their truce, the transition had been smooth.

She wasn't nearly as miserable as she'd anticipated.

Then again, she wasn't a young girl vying for her father's attention while he was too busy caring for the town's ailments. This time she stood in her father's shoes and was the one caring for the townspeople.

Lord, how she missed him. In his house. In his clinic. In his office. Everywhere, he remained. Everywhere was his domain and she was just a secondary player.

Even with Sloan because she was positive that his kindness to her was due to his respect for her father.

I could round earlier than usual and meet you at the nursing home when I finish.

That works. See you in the morning, sunshine.

She wrinkled her nose at the nickname he'd given her that first day when they'd been rounding at the hospital and that seemed to have stuck. She didn't like it, was pretty sure he was mocking her sour disposition about being in Gloomberg, but whatever.

She didn't answer his text, just slid her phone into her pocket and paced across the living-room floor, wondering at the unease that tugged at her very soul.

She'd been in the house for a week.

Her childhood home. Yet she didn't feel at home here. Not really, because something was missing.

Someone was missing.

Although she knew it had been wrong of her father to have manipulated her so, she also knew that if she hadn't done as he wished, she'd regret not having done so for the rest of her life. Six months wasn't such a long time.

So why did the prospect of six months in Gloomberg feel like a nightmarish eternity looming before her?

She walked to her father's closed bedroom door, ran her fingers over the smooth wooden door. She'd not been able to go into his room yet. Silly of her, but she just couldn't. She'd asked Mrs. Johnson, who'd cleaned her father's house for years, not to go into the room, either.

Cara would go when she was ready, but that wasn't tonight.

"You're bright and early, sunshine."

Cara bristled at the nickname. She so wasn't a nickname kind of girl. "The name is Cara."

"Ah, well, that's an improvement, too, as I was beginning to think you just wanted me to call you Dr. Conner, but, then, that makes me feel as if I'm talking about Preston."

Cara flinched at the mention of her father. She couldn't help herself. She'd cried a big portion of the night as she'd replayed her father's visit to New York, as she tried to look for clues as to why he'd made the decisions he had. Then again, why question what she knew?

She'd been a disappointment to her father. He'd always wanted a son. She'd even overheard an argument between her parents once where Preston had even said as much to her mother.

As if he'd realized his gaff, Sloan grabbed her elbow and guided her toward the nursing home.

"I'm not a little old lady who needs help to cross the street."

"Seriously?" He made a pretense of visually perusing her spine. "I kind of thought you were."

She narrowed her gaze.

"Because I'm pretty sure you're so old that you've forgotten the truce we agreed to."

"I haven't forgotten."

"Just decided not to honor it today, because you feel particularly prickly?"

Grr. She hated it when he was right. "This is me during a truce."

"Then may we never be at odds."

She stopped walking just outside the nursing-home entrance and stared at him. "Make no mistake, Sloan. We are at odds. We've just called a temporary truce."

"A six-month one?"

She pushed the closest double glass door open and walked into the building, calling over her shoulder, "If you're lucky."

"And I behave?"

"Something like that."

"This one never behaves," a petite blonde nurse interrupted as they entered the nursing home. As casually as if touching him was no big deal, the woman wrapped her arms around Sloan and gave him a quick hug. "Thanks for the other night when I called you."

Sloan shrugged as if it were no big deal. "No problem."

Why had the woman called him? Personal or professional? What did it matter? What Sloan did outside work wasn't any of her business.

Even if she had spent the night in his arms a month ago and thought about him pretty much nonstop since. She squeezed her eyes shut and forced that memory from her mind. No way did she want that bogging her down today when so much of the night had been spent reminiscing about her father. When she had slept, she'd woken from dreams of the morning she'd woken in Sloan's arms. She'd been grumpy ever since.

"I'm glad you're here," the blonde nurse continued, walking down the hallway with them toward the east wing. "Ms. Campbell is coughing up some nasty green stuff this morning. I want you to listen to her lungs. I heard a few rhonchi in the left lower lobe, but would like your opinion."

"Sure thing. Lilly, do you know Dr. Conner?" He paused, then began again. "Dr. Cara Conner? She's working at the clinic and will be taking over her father's patients."

"You're Dr. Conner's daughter? Wow. I heard you were here, but I didn't realize you were so gorgeous."

"She is, isn't she?" Sloan agreed, grinning as Cara's cheeks flamed.

Cara thanked the woman, then turned all business without any further acknowledgement of her compliment. "Is Ms. Campbell one of my father's patients?"

Sloan answered for the nurse. "She is. Her daughter had her transferred from Mobile about a year ago when she became unhappy with the care she was receiving at a facility there. She's done well overall, but suffers from congestive heart failure and chronic obstructive pulmonary disease thanks to a lifelong smoking habit. Apparently, she didn't quit until she had the stroke that put her in the Mobile nursing home."

"Actually, we've caught her smoking in her bathroom a couple of times when she's convinced people to sneak her one or bummed one off of visitors who smoke," Lilly added, shaking her head in wry amusement. She met Cara's gaze and gave a friendly smile. "She's a handful, but we all adore her because she's so full of spunk."

"Yeah, yeah," Sloan said, rolling his eyes. "Tell her the real reason y'all adore her."

Eyes sparkling, Lilly laughed. "Ms. Campbell has decided that she's going to marry Sloan and is quite persistent in her pursuit of him. She believes he's into older women. Wouldn't surprise me in the slightest if she's faking the cough just so I'd have to call Sloan, except I hear the rhonchi."

Not surprised one bit that women of all ages found Sloan appealing, Cara arched her brow. "Interesting. How old is this Ms. Campbell?"

"Eighty," Lilly answered. "She was always happy seeing your father, but since Sloan checked her the first time, she's come up with a dozen ailments so I have to call him over."

"Is she who we are here to round on today?" she asked the pleasant nurse, who she just might like if not for that hug. Then again, she had no right not to like a woman just because she hugged Sloan and thanked him "for the other night."

She winced. Whether she should care or not, she did.

Whether that should influence how she felt about the nurse or not, it did.

"No," the woman answered, oblivious to the war Cara waged inside herself. "We have a list of patients to see today to update their chart orders, etcetera, but we will go in to check her, too."

"Awesome. I can't wait to meet her."

"And so you shall," Sloan said, eyeing her oddly, as if he could read her mind.

Thank God he couldn't really because the way he affected her confused her enough for both of them. No need to drag him into the chaos.

Sloan was wonderful with the older woman who suffered from mild dementia. He took everything the woman threw at him in his stride. From her suggestive comments to her marriage proposal. He remained all smiles and although he teased the woman back, he never lost his professional edge.

"Now, Ms. Campbell, you know I can't marry you. I'm a confirmed bachelor."

"Marry me and you will be confirmed my husband," the older woman countered, then sputtered with a coughing spell.

"You know it is a violation of doctor-patient relationship for me to marry you. We'll just have to settle with being friends," he told her between listening to her chest with his stethoscope.

"I can find a new doctor." She tapped Sloan's shoulder then pointed an arthritic finger at Cara. "She can be my doctor."

"Actually," he said, straightening to meet Cara's gaze, "she's my partner and is going to help take care of you, too."

His words didn't faze Cara. Really they didn't. That was only a flutter of gas causing her chest to feel funny. She wanted to correct him and say she wasn't his partner, just a temporary stand-in until the required time had passed, but Lilly and the patient shouldn't be privy to that conversation.

"If I had a husband I wouldn't need some woman to take care of me," the woman intoned with a loud sigh that started another coughing fit.

"Perhaps not, but Dr. Conner is an excellent physician and will be taking over her father's patients."

The woman frowned. "Who was her father?"

"Your former doctor. Dr. Conner."

"I don't know a Dr. Conner."

"He was your doctor for the past year," Sloan reminded.

The woman shook her head. "No, you are my doctor. I don't know a Dr. Conner."

Sloan gave Cara an apologetic glance. "Actually, this is Dr. Cara Conner. Her father was Dr. Preston Conner."

The woman didn't look convinced. "Where is he?"

"He died last month."

"That's sad," the woman said in a voice that truly conveyed the emotion. She turned earnest blue eyes toward Sloan. "We better hurry up and elope before you die. You're not getting any younger, you know."

"Now, you know, you're only as old as you feel, so I think I've got that one covered."

"Elope with me and I'll die a happy young woman."

"You're a mess," he advised, laughing, then pressed on her abdomen, checking all four quadrants.

The woman's gaze settled on Cara again. "Is she your girlfriend?"

Cara's cheeks burned but Sloan just smiled and continued to check the older woman.

"She's my partner," he repeated. "Dr. Cara Conner."

"That's a pretty name."

"Yes, it is. A pretty name for a pretty woman."

"I don't like her if she's your girlfriend."

"She's not my girlfriend. You've not been paying attention," Sloan tutted while checking pulses in her feet. "I don't have a girlfriend. I'm a confirmed bachelor."

"Much to all Bloomberg's females' broken hearts," Lilly added from behind them. "My theory is that there's already someone special in his life that he's just not told us about."

Laughing, Sloan shook his head. "Don't go starting rumors. The last thing I need is a bunch of matchmaking mommas trying to mend my broken heart."

Lilly's brow lifted and she showed genuine interest. "So you admit there is a broken heart?"

"Not really, but it sounded a good excuse for why I choose to be alone. Now, let me give you some verbal orders on our girl here."

Later, when they were walking out to the parking lot, Cara turned to him. "Why do you choose to be alone?"

Obviously caught off guard by her question, Sloan stopped walking. "Who says I choose to be alone?"

"You did in the patient room when Lilly said—"

"Lilly and nursing-home patients aren't privy to my personal life. I date, Cara. Not recently, because I've been so busy, but I'm not a monk and neither do I want to spend the rest of my life alone. I want a wife and kids, but not until it's with the right woman."

"Oh." Heat infused Cara's face as she realized that she was attempting to invade his personal space herself. "I shouldn't have pried."

"Why did you?"

Good question and one she wasn't sure of the answer to.

"I was just curious."

"You know what they say about being curious?"

She gave him a blank look.

"Curiosity killed the cat."

"Good thing I'm not a cat, then," she countered, then left him to stare after her while she hightailed it to her car and away from their conversation.

CHAPTER SEVEN

"HEY, BATTER—BATTER, SWING!" a teammate called out, as Sloan eyed the next batter stepping up to the plate.

His catcher stuck two fingers down, indicating the pitch she wanted him to throw. He shook his head.

Her gaze narrowed and she made another hand signal. He shook his head again. The catcher's mask failed to hide the displeasure twisting her lovely mouth. Anger flashed in her blue-green eyes then she gave another signal.

He nodded. Not because of the passionate spark in her eyes but because it was the pitch he'd intended to throw all along. Sloan had pitched against Robert Jenson before. The emergency-room doctor would tear up the fastball Cara had originally suggested, but the man couldn't hit Sloan's curve ball.

The man looked back at Cara, winked at her, then assumed the batter's stance.

Sloan didn't have to be a genius to know the emotion rocking through him was pure green jealousy at that wink and the smile Cara gave back to Robert. It was. The kind that made him want to scream and yell and beat on his chest and tell the man to leave her alone. She was his.

Only Cara wasn't his.

Sure, four months had gone by since she'd moved back to Bloomberg and stepped into her father's shoes. She'd maintained their truce. But that's as far as it went. On the surface she was polite and professional to him, but that's where she kept things. On the surface. She wouldn't let her guard down for one minute to actually get to know him or to let him in.

Was that what he still wanted? After months of them walking on eggshells? For Preston's snippy, snappy daughter to let him in?

Hell. It was.

For four months he'd been telling himself he was being cordial to her for Preston's sake, for the sake of the clinic and their patients, for his own sake because life was simpler if they got along for the time she was in Bloomberg.

Truth was, he was as fascinated by her as he'd ever been. More so.

Sloan twisted his arm around and flung the ball toward Cara's waiting glove.

Not as a curve, but a fastball. Not what he'd intended. Not what she'd been expecting.

Luckily, Robert must have been as distracted by that smiled response to his wink as Sloan had been because he swung half a second too late and the ball sailed by and went straight into Cara's waiting glove.

"Strike one," the umpire called out.

Cara's brow lifted in surprise as she stood and tossed the ball back to him for the next pitch.

Yeah, he'd said he wasn't going to throw a fast pitch. He knew. He needed to get his head in the game and off his pretty redheaded catcher.

Only she said something to the batter and the man's

face lit up like a Roman candle, his smile as wide as any Sloan had ever seen.

Was Cara flirting? For that matter, she could be dating Jenson. Sloan didn't know what she did, where she went, on her off-call weekends. Was she spending them with Jenson or some other man?

Sloan threw the ball. He couldn't say it was the worst pitch he'd ever thrown, but it sailed over to the right of the plate.

"Ball," the umpire called.

Cara gave him a "what's up" look and tossed the ball back his way.

"Hey, batter, batter," teammates and those sitting in the stands at the hospital charity softball game chanted.

Sloan threw another two pitches and the umpire repeated his calls. Ball. Ball. Not good.

He finally managed a decent curve ball with his next pitch. Robert swung and missed.

"Strike two!" the umpire shouted as he jerked his elbow back, indicating the call. "Full count."

Yeah, Sloan knew. He really didn't want the doctor to get onto base. It was the fourth inning and his team was up by two runs. But Becky Wisdom from Accounting had gotten a decent single and was just waiting to take off toward second if Robert nailed one.

Robert turned, said something to Cara that made her laugh. The sound was both magical and irritating. Magical in that he rarely heard her laugh, although it did seem to be happening more and more frequently as she became closer to the women who worked in the office. Irritating because another man had triggered the sound.

Sloan hiked his leg, reared back and threw the ball for all he had.

Robert got a piece of the ball, but it fouled out to the right. The first baseman caught it for an easy out.

Robert gave a disgusted shake of his head, but whatever Cara said to him made him grin and nod his head. Urgh. She was flirting. With the opposing team.

Who were really only their coworkers.

As Robert left the field and the next batter settled in by the plate, Sloan racked his brain, trying to recall just how much time Cara spent with Robert. Who was he kidding? He had no idea what she did in her spare time because although she might smile and flirt with Robert, she still only spoke with *him* when it was absolutely necessary. She was polite, friendly enough at the clinic, and that was it. No such smiles for him.

And definitely no flirting.

He gripped the softball so tightly he was surprised the ball wasn't crushed. He took a couple of deep breaths, reminded himself that what Cara did, who she talked to or flirted with didn't matter, and he gave a nice normal slow pitch of the ball to one of the phlebotomists.

The guy hit the ball midfield, made it to second and brought Becky all the way around to third base.

Cara motioned that she wanted to meet with him and made her way to the pitcher's mound.

"What's up?"

"You tell me."

"Huh?" She looked as confused as he felt.

"You're flirting with the players," he accused, daring her to deny his claim.

"What?"

"I saw the way you and Robert were carrying on." Did his disgust ooze from his words?

"Um, what does that have to do with your pitching?"

Good question. This woman tore him into bits. He sure couldn't tell her the truth.

But the truth must have been all over his face because her eyes widened. "You're jealous."

He was tired of being treated like the enemy. He hadn't had a thing to do with the decisions Preston had made. All he'd done was love the man and been fascinated by his daughter. How dared she hold that against him? How dared she treat him like he had the bubonic plague while she made googly eyes at other men?

He shrugged and held her gaze. "What if I am?"

What, indeed? Cara thought, staring at Sloan in surprise. Sure, he'd been nice to her, more so than she deserved, from the moment she'd arrived in Bloomsberg. But what she was seeing on his face wasn't friendliness or kindness. It was possessiveness.

Which was ridiculous. Why would he be possessive of her? Jealous about her?

Only she knew.

Hadn't she known from the beginning that there was something different about him? Something that sparked between them every time he was near? Only she had so much animosity toward him that she'd pushed aside the chemistry and labeled the emotions brewing inside her as disgust or anger.

Or tried to. For four months she'd been trying to convince herself, trying to stay away from him except when absolutely necessary. Longer than that, really. From that first night.

Only in this heated moment there was no labeling the way Sloan was looking at her and the way her body was reacting as anger.

He was jealous that he thought she was flirting with another man.

Most surprising of all, she liked that flare of passion, that possessiveness in his eyes.

That terrified her, made her want to lash out, made her want to protect herself from possible heartache.

"Get your act together, Sloan," she growled, eyes narrowed, hands on her hips. "We have a game to finish and I don't intend to lose because your head is elsewhere."

Only it was her head that wasn't in the rest of the game.

Cara had always excelled in sports, had always loved the physical demands put on her body. But for the next three innings she couldn't keep her focus on anything other than her pitcher.

With every pitch her eyes met his and when he released the ball and it sailed into her waiting glove it was as if he reached out and touched her. Crazy. An opposing team batter stood between them. Twenty feet lay between them. A crowd of people was around them. Yet they were the only two players. His release and her catch became more and more sensual with each throw.

She felt it. The darkness in his eyes said he felt it.

"Strike three. You're out," the umpire told the batter.

Cara straightened and stretched her legs. She'd worked out and run regularly in New York and had kept up the habit while in Bloomberg, but it had been quite a few years since she'd spent any time in a catcher's squat. Her knees and calves were protesting the seven innings she'd spent in the position.

They had one at bat left.

The game was tied six to six.

Robert Jenson had taken over the pitcher's mound for his team and was throwing some warm-up pitches.

First up to bat for their team was a guy from Finance, a nurse from the medical floor, and then they'd be at the top of their batting line-up again. Sloan and then Cara.

Finance guy struck out in three pitches. Cara held her breath while the nurse stood straight up over the plate, closed her eyes and swung half a mile too late for the ball. There was a reason Gail was their last batter. Sweet, an amazing nurse, but claimed to have never held a bat prior to today's game.

"Bend your body. Swing a little quicker. Keep your eyes open. You've got this," she said, offering encouragement.

Cara had always loved sports. During her long, lonely hours growing up, she'd lost herself as part of whichever team she'd played for. Softball, soccer, basketball, track, golf, tennis, swimming—the sport hadn't mattered. Just that she'd pushed her body to the max and that she'd done her team—and her father—proud. Some kids acted out to try to get their parents' attention. She'd tried to excel at everything instead. Still, it hadn't been good enough to keep her father's attention for more than a few seconds. There had always been another patient, someone who had needed him more than his daughter.

She huffed out a deep sigh, realized she'd totally missed the pitch and Gail's failed attempt to make contact.

"Strike two," the umpire called.

Cara let her gaze leave Gail and go to the man standing in the warm-up spot. A man who had held her father's attention and had been good enough in his eyes.

He was good enough in her eyes.

Um, no! she corrected her brain, which was obviously suffering from heat stroke—and it wasn't even that hot out here.

Just because Sloan's biceps bulged beneath his neon-green and blue T-shirt did not mean he was good enough in her eyes. Just because his baseball pants clung to his narrow hips and muscular thighs did not mean he was good enough in her eyes. Just because there had been some kind of wild sparks passing between them in that last inning when he'd been tossing the ball into her glove time and again did not mean a thing.

Because she was not a superficial kind of girl. Yes, he was gorgeous. No matter how much she wanted to deny that, she couldn't. His coppery eyes, dark hair, and quick grin should be gracing the pages of a magazine. But she so wasn't interested in a man who had achieved what she'd never been able to attain.

Not that she was interested in Sloan. She wasn't. What would be the point? She was big city. He was country.

As if he sensed she was checking him out, he turned, his gaze connecting with hers. That zap burned straight through her. It wasn't his looks or his brain or even his body that got to her. It was exactly what was happening this second. This annoying total-body meltdown that happened when he looked into her eyes and she could see that he wanted her.

Sloan wanted her.

Maybe he had from the beginning.

Maybe that was why he'd automatically assumed she'd been asking him to stay the night with her for sex the night he'd driven her home from the funeral parlor.

Maybe that was why she should ask him to stay the night for sex.

Um, no!

She was not asking Sloan over for sex. What would she say? *Hey, Sloan. I resent that my father thought you hung the moon. It irks me that he forced me to have to work side by side with you to get to keep my mother's things. But, hey, I think you are hot, I haven't had sex in eons and I'd like you to rock my world tonight.*

He would rock her world. She was sure of it. Sure he would rock her world in ways that her world had never been rocked because although she had enjoyed her sex life with John well enough she couldn't say there had been any world rocking going on. But with Sloan...with Sloan, no doubt he'd be as perfect at evoking every drop of passion from her as he was at every other blasted thing.

She *so-o-o-o* didn't like him. Detested him.

Wanted him.

Cara gulped. Sloan's brow rose. She shook her head.

To what exactly she wasn't sure, but maybe Sloan knew because his brow arched even higher. Then he grinned. Not an amused grin but an I-have-you-now grin. Surely the man didn't also list mind-reading skills on his already impressive résumé? Urgh. He was way too perfect.

"Two down. Only one to go," one of their opposing teammates called out, calling Cara's attention back to the game.

Gail had struck out.

Next up to bat was Sloan. No doubt he'd hit a home run and win the game and be the hero of the day. He was that kind of guy. A hero in everyone's eyes but hers. Or at the minimum he'd get on base and then it would be her turn to either keep things going or end the inning. Once upon a time she'd have not even questioned which.

But until today she hadn't held a bat in quite a few years herself. Funny, she'd pretty much given up team sports at some point during medical school. She took a deep breath and replaced Sloan in the next batter-up spot. She'd missed this.

Not Bloomberg, but this being a part of a team, a part of something where people depended on each other and interacted with each other. She'd been part of the emergency room team at the hospital where she'd worked and yet there was a difference. An indifference to each other as coworkers and individuals.

Not here. Not in Bloomberg.

Sloan held the bat high, poised for the pitch, and then the ball sailed towards him. He gave it a good, solid hit into the outfield and made it to third base just as the ball came sailing into the catcher's glove at home plate.

Cara stepped into the batter box. She'd either be the belle of the ball or the disappointment.

Robert smiled at her as he prepped to pitch. Maybe she should accept his invitation of a date. He was a good-looking man, fun, wasn't her father's golden boy, and wasn't looking for a committed relationship any more than she was.

But she wasn't looking for a noncommitted relationship, either. Only Sloan had her thinking about physical needs and that had her body all stirred up. She didn't want to date. She wanted…

Sloan.

She swung the bat as hard as she could and made contact with the ball. Hard contact that ripped through her body. It felt good.

She took off toward first as fast as she could. She'd just rounded first and was headed toward second when cheers went up from the stands. Sloan had made it home.

Whether she ran or walked the rest of the way didn't matter. They'd won the game.

Everyone was gathered around Sloan and high-fiving him when Cara tapped her foot on home.

"Great job, Cara!" Julie praised her, as another teammate slapped Cara on the back and said similar words. High fives and back slaps abounded. Another chest bumped her and, laughing, Cara turned toward the player who'd just stepped up to her, ready to accept more congratulations. Wow. She'd forgotten just how much fun being a part of a team was.

The person waiting wrapped his arms around her and spun her around, increasing her laughter and stirring a whole new type of excitement. Sloan. He came to a stop and slowly released her. She just as slowly slid down his body to stand close to him. So close their bodies still touched.

Her gaze met his and her laughter faded.

"Nice hit," he said, his coppery eyes not leaving her face.

"Thank you," she managed, despite the lump in her throat. Why, oh, why was she thinking about how much she'd like to lick him? He was hot and sweaty and she didn't like him. Licking wasn't an option.

Yet she wanted her mouth on his throat. Wanted her tongue tracing over the pulse that beat wildly at his nape. Wanted her arms back around his neck and her body pressed up against the hard planes of his chest. She might as well just face the truth. Whether she liked him or not, she wanted Sloan.

"Um," she gulped, knowing she had to do something, to say something. "You run good."

You run good? Really? Could she have found more stupid-sounding words to say?

His eyes sparkled like molten copper and his mouth curved into the sexiest smile she'd ever seen. "Thanks for noticing."

Not that she had. She'd had her focus on her own run and he knew that. Which was why he was smiling.

She stepped back from him, turned to the person next to her and started talking enthusiastically about the game. With words that weren't quite so ridiculous as *you run good.*

Anything to break the connection between her and Sloan.

The following night, Sloan parked his car in the doctors' parking lot and jogged into the hospital. There had been a multicar crash that had resulted in multiple injuries, some serious. One had been a car full of local teenagers on their way back from a weekend in Pensacola. Jenson was in the emergency room, but when the call about the crash had come in to get the emergency room ready for multiple victims, Sloan had been called in to assist as the rural hospital emergency room wasn't equipped for the number of victims on their way.

He'd expected utter chaos when he entered the emergency department. What he hadn't expected was to see Jenson and Cara laughing as they set up a patient area.

Jenson said something. Cara laughed and nudged his shoulder with her own. Sloan's lungs quit working and his head spun from lack of oxygen.

The vision of them, the camaraderie, the lack of

tension irritated him. Why could she look at Jenson and smile freely but keep up all her walls with *him*?

Why was he thinking about that when there were lives to be saved? He needed to get scrubbed and help get the emergency room ready for the pending onslaught.

Working multicar crashes was nothing new for Cara. Having worked in the emergency room in Manhattan, she was used to seeing all different types of trauma. So why taking care of a car full of teenagers, an elderly couple and a family of four had her reeling, she wasn't sure.

This was her specialty. What she did best. She loved ER work. It's what she planned to return to when her six-month Gloomberg stint finished.

She sent a kid with suspected internal injuries to get a computerized tomography test of his chest and abdomen, while another got an MRI of his head. The elderly couple were being x-rayed.

As the actual physician working the emergency room, Dr. Jenson was overseeing the driver of the teenagers' car. The kid's consciousness was coming and going. He had multiple internal injuries, including a crushed pelvis. Robert had called to have him airlifted to a trauma hospital in Pensacola and was trying to keep him alive and stable until the helicopter arrived.

Sloan worked on the father of the family of four. The man had multiple facial lacerations and a fractured humerus. The youngest of the family was a one-year-old who had thankfully been in her car seat and had avoided any serious injuries. The little girl sobbed loudly as she clung to her mother. The mother had several lacerations that were going to require suturing, but currently Cara was working on a three-year-old little girl who had a cut that ran down her forehead and into her eyebrow and other bits of embedded glass on her forehead.

Cara had mildly sedated the child, had her restrained in a bed sheet, and worked tediously to remove the bits of broken glass from her forehead in the area of the main cut, which still bled quite profusely.

She rinsed the open area with saline then closed the skin with a special skin glue. By the time she'd finished cleaning up the three-year-old's forehead and turned her over to the nurse who had assisted with the procedure, the girl's one-year-old sister had given up sobbing and slept in her mother's arms.

"Is Adelaine going to be okay? She was bleeding so much. I was so scared," the woman said, lifting her own bandage away from her forehead and looking at the blood-saturated gauze.

"The best we can tell. She doesn't have any major internal injuries. She has a few nasty cuts on her face that I've done my best to remove the glass from and close, but oftentimes bits of glass will work their way out for months after an accident." Cara washed her hands and put on a fresh pair of latex-free gloves. "Now, let's take a look at getting you closed up."

Cara quickly cleaned the wound and stitched the area closed with the tiniest thread the emergency room offered.

"That's a really nice job."

"Thank you." Cara tied off the last suture and tried to pretend she wasn't startled to see Sloan standing next to her or that his praise didn't please her.

"I've admitted your husband for overnight observation," he explained to the woman. "Mostly so we can keep an eye on him."

A fresh wave of panic crossed the woman's face. "Is he okay?"

"I believe he's going to be fine. His right humerus is broken, probably from when the airbag went off. It saved his life but broke his arm in the process. He's bruised, but I don't find any evidence of internal bleeding or organ damage. I just want a close eye kept on him tonight."

"Thank God." The woman breathed a sigh of relief.

Code blue. Code blue. Radiology.

Sloan and Cara both looked at each other. Not good.

Dr. Jenson was still tied up with the teen driver so Sloan and Cara took off for the radiology department.

A nurse joined them, pushing the crash cart.

One of the teens getting imaging had stopped breathing. A nurse who'd been with the teen was performing CPR, but to no avail.

"Multiple internal injuries with head trauma," Sloan said, as they set up the defibrillator and Cara prepped the patient for the electrical shock, checking telemetry. He gave the nurse an order to inject epinephrine and then told everyone to stand clear.

"Now," he said, and Cara pushed the button that would deliver the surge of electrical stimulation to the patient's heart. Nothing.

The ventilator breathed for the patient, providing a steady flow of oxygen, but there was still no heartbeat. Cara gave a set of compressions while the defibrillator reset. Still nothing. They delivered another jolt of electricity. Nothing.

They repeated the process but couldn't get a heartbeat started on the teen. The nurse with them let out a soft cry. "I hate this."

Cara nodded. So did she. That had been the one part

of the emergency department she'd never liked. Death. In Manhattan it had been unfamiliar faces, unfamiliar names she'd dealt with. Here, in Bloomberg, she knew this teen's family, knew the girl's father worked at a bank as a loan officer, knew the girl's mother had played on the high school basketball team a decade or so before Cara had.

She wouldn't be delivering bad news to strangers. She'd be delivering bad news to people she knew. That was the difference between big-city medicine and Bloomberg.

Letting out a pained sigh of his own, Sloan put his arm around the nurse's shoulder. "None of us do, but we did all we could." He hugged her, took a deep breath. "Is her family here?"

Cara felt relief start coursing through her. Sloan planned to talk to the family. She wouldn't have to be the bearer of such horrible news to the girl's parents.

The nurse nodded. "I was told they arrived not long after the ambulance showed up."

Sloan nodded, gave the woman another squeeze around the shoulders then met Cara's gaze. Such empathy and compassion showed there that Cara took a step back. Not that she didn't see Sloan's compassion for his patients on a daily basis at the clinic, but there was such deep sadness there that she ached for him.

"I'll go talk to them," she volunteered, her gaze not wavering from his.

To her surprise, he shook his head. "Jeff is my friend. He was one of the first people I met when I came to Bloomberg. I should be the one to tell him."

Cara wasn't sure she agreed with Sloan but he didn't give her a chance to argue, just turned and left the room.

Cara glanced around at the somber faces still present,

at the young, lifeless body. For all the good they'd done the other crash victims, they'd not been able to do enough for this young girl. Her heart ached at the lost dreams and hopes, at the sadness so many would feel at the loss.

She wasn't a cold doctor in New York, but she wasn't sure she'd ever considered the ripple effect of a loss of life quite so harshly as at this moment. Bloomberg had lost one of its own and the entire town would mourn.

Just as they'd all mourned the loss of her father.

Perhaps there was something to be said about small-town life but, regardless, more than ever Cara just wished she were far, far away.

CHAPTER EIGHT

IT WAS SEVERAL hours later before the emergency room calmed down enough that Sloan felt okay about leaving the hospital. He'd stayed until all transfers, admissions, and discharges had been made and the emergency room was back to doable for Dr. Jenson.

The medical evacuation helicopter had arrived for the teenage boy while Sloan had been talking to Jeff and his wife, Cindy. That had been a hellish conversation. The entire night had been hellish.

"Sloan?"

Surprised at the voice, he turned toward Cara. Her eyes were big, her face pale. She looked as tired as he felt.

"I thought you'd already left."

Because he had looked for her. Hopefully not too obviously, but he had looked and hadn't been able to find her.

She glanced toward where her car was parked a few spaces down from his Jeep. "I…I was waiting on you."

Perhaps he was so tired he was hallucinating, because surely she hadn't been sitting in her car, waiting for him to come out of the hospital. "Why?"

She bit her lower lip, shrugged, and looked as uncertain as he'd ever seen her look.

"I was worried about you," she said finally.

Yep, he was definitely hallucinating. "I'm okay."

"I could tell how upset you were about the Davis kid."

He nodded. What else could he do? The death of someone so young was such a waste, something he'd never understand. Jeff and Cindy's lives would never be the same. So many lives would never be the same after this tragedy of a car wreck that had involved so many from their community. And he prayed the airlifted boy would survive and the town wouldn't be facing an even worse tragedy.

"For whatever it's worth…" She looked pensive, as if she searched for the right words. She looked up at him with her big, clear blue-green eyes that, upon looking closer, weren't so clear but red-rimmed. "I'm sorry."

He studied her expression. She looked genuinely upset, genuinely concerned about him, and she'd been crying.

"You have nothing to be sorry for, Cara." He reached out and lifted her chin, stared into her sad eyes, thinking that a more beautiful woman had never existed than the one shooting awareness through his fingertips. "You were great in there." Lord, her skin was so soft, so delicate beneath his fingers, so very electrifying. "If I ever have to be intubated, I request you do it, by the way. You make that procedure look easy."

"I had lots of practice in New York." Closing her eyes, she shuddered and rubbed her hands over her arms. "I pray you never have to be intubated, Sloan. Never."

He really must be hallucinating because she seemed so lost, so different than who she normally was. The only other time he'd seen her look this fraught had been the night he'd carried her home from the funeral parlor.

A night that hadn't ended well when she'd woken the next morning and treated him as if he had the plague. The memory had left a bitter taste in his mouth and in his mind.

"Odd," he mused out loud, in protective defense mode. "I'd have guessed you'd like to see me gone."

Stepping back from him, she frowned. "That's a horrible thing to say."

Knowing she was right and that memory of the past had influenced his comment, guilt slammed him. "You're right. I shouldn't have said that."

Especially since she'd waited for him, sought him out to have a conversation. How often did that happen outside the office regarding a patient's care? Never.

"I'm the one who's sorry," he continued. Very sorry. "Guess I'm just tired. We'll just say that if I ever have to be sutured, you can do it. Those were some neat stitches you did tonight."

"Okay, deal. I hope you never need to be sutured, but if you do, I'm your girl." Her lower lip disappeared between her teeth then she sighed. "I'm tired, too. Exhausted." Rubbing her hands over her arms again, she glanced around the dimly lit private doctors' parking area. "I'm too wound up to go home to sleep, though."

He waited, not sure where she was going with her statement but determined not to jump to any conclusions. That tended to get him into trouble where she was concerned.

Her gaze cut back to him. "Do you think we could go somewhere?"

Sloan's breath caught. What exactly was she asking him? Because he was having a really hard time fighting those jumped-to conclusions when she looked at him the way she was looking at him. Eyes wide, lips parted, and her expression needy.

"It doesn't matter where. Anywhere is fine," she added, when he didn't respond immediately. Did she think he'd say no? That he could say no to her? He'd like to think he could, but she got to him. She'd always gotten to him. Could you fall for someone based on how another person talked about them? Based on the sparkle in their eyes in a photo? Lord, he was exhausted. Must be with as crazy as his thoughts were.

"It's after eleven on a Sunday night in Bloomberg. There's not a lot of options. There's only one place even open at this time of night."

"Then let's go there," she suggested quickly, sliding her hands into her scrub pockets and waiting for his answer almost anxiously.

"It's a drive-up fast-food place." What was he trying to do? Talk her out of spending time with him?

He should be talking her out of spending time with him.

Or should he? He didn't know anymore. She confused him.

Then there was Preston's will and last request...

That was a kicker of a dilemma that he still hadn't quite figured out how to deal with, how he even wanted to deal with it.

"I know. I used to live here, remember?" She gave him a tentative smile that shoved all thoughts of Preston's will and last request right out of his head.

"How could I forget?"

"We can take my car, if that's okay. Hop in."

Whatever she wanted was okay with Sloan. He was exhausted, but adrenaline that she wanted to spend time with him was taking over, erasing the fatigue from his body. Or maybe it was her half smile directed at him that had his blood hammering through his veins?

While they were driving toward the fast-food place, he studied her profile. She stared intently at the road as if she expected something terrible to happen to their car. That's when he realized just how much the wreck they'd worked had affected her.

"Don't watch me," she ordered, sounding as bossy as ever, but her shoulders sagged.

"Don't watch you drive or don't look at you in general?"

Her fingers gripped the steering wheel tightly. "Both."

Sloan's heart squeezed at the sight she made. So determined to be brave, so determined not to like him, and yet she'd waited. Why? Because she felt the connection between them that they'd been fighting for months?

Sloan was tired of fighting. Fighting her. Fighting the way he felt about her. Fighting his conflicting feelings over Preston's will and last request. He was tired of all of it.

"Hate to break it to you, sunshine, but there's not another thing in sight worth looking at except you."

"I don't like it when you call me that," she reminded him, not glancing his way and not addressing his compliment at all.

"Add it to my list of crimes."

"You don't have a list of crimes," she countered immediately.

"Sure I do." At her questioning glance his way he added, "Maybe not a written one, but you definitely have a mental list of all the reasons you don't like me."

Her grip tightened even more on the steering wheel, blanching her knuckles. "That's the problem."

"What?"

"I don't want to like you, Sloan."

"But?"

"But I can't seem to help myself," she said, so softly he had to mentally repeat her words to absorb them.

"Why is that a problem? I'm not your enemy, Cara."

"I think you are."

"Why would you think that? Because of your father's will? I had nothing to do with the changes he put into effect. I don't like them any more than you do."

"You have everything to gain by those changes." She hesitated just long enough that he wondered if he was wrong, if it wasn't really the will that was the problem.

"I lost more when your father died than any will can ever replace."

"He loved you." A rough sound escaped her lips that Sloan wasn't sure was a gasp or a sob.

"Yes," Sloan agreed, knowing Preston truly had cared for him. Then what Cara had said, how she'd said it, soaked in. "Your father loved you, too, Cara. More than life itself that man loved you."

She slowed the car then pulled into a vacant building parking lot and put the ignition into park. The street-light across the street and the dashboard lights lit the car just enough to illuminate her features.

"I know he loved me." She was definitely crying now, crying and trying to keep him from realizing that's what was happening. "In his own way."

"In every way." How could she doubt Preston's feel-ings for her? The man had thought she walked on water and shined brighter than any star in the sky.

"I was too much like my mother for him to un-derstand me." She sucked in a little air and lifted her shoulders, her hands gripping the steering wheel, then sliding down them to rest in her lap.

Sloan ached to wrap his arms around her and comfort her. "Doesn't mean the man didn't love you with all his heart."

She gave a low laugh. "He wanted a boy."

What? He had never heard Preston say anything to that effect. But he hadn't known the man nearly as long as his daughter had. Perhaps Preston had said something at some point that made her believe that.

"Most men think they want a son, but it's their daughter who wraps them around her finger." He reached across the console and took her hand into his, stroked his fingers across hers, and was quite positive Cara could easily wrap him around her finger.

She stared down at their hands but didn't pull away from him. "My father wasn't the kind of man to be wrapped around anyone's finger."

"Perhaps not," he agreed, thinking of the powerful man Preston Conner had been, "but he adored you, Cara. You were what he was most proud of."

She shook her head. "I failed him." Her voice broke just a little and Sloan's heart squeezed a lot.

"You didn't," he said, knowing it was true. As much as Preston had wanted his daughter in Bloomberg, he'd been proud of her and her accomplishments. Sloan didn't doubt that for a second.

"You don't understand. He wanted me to move home and I refused."

"That was your right and definitely doesn't make you a failure," he assured her, wishing he had the right to lift her hand to his lips and press a kiss to her skin. Wishing he had the right to pull her to him and hold her close. He hadn't really thought about how the teen's death might trigger Cara's own grief over her father, but it had. Obviously, she was struggling and dealing with an emotional onslaught.

"If I'd known…"

"Hindsight is always twenty-twenty. Most all of us would do things differently if we knew what the future held."

She turned toward him, giving him a truly confused stare. "Why are you being so nice to me?"

If she weren't so serious, he could have laughed at her question. But she genuinely didn't understand. "Because, despite what you think, I'm not your enemy."

She sighed, leaning forward and putting her forehead against the steering wheel. "So you keep saying."

"Sunshine?"

"I ought not answer when you call me that," she admonished, a little of her usual spark coming through as she straightened back up in her seat.

"If you'd let me, I'd like to hold you."

She turned toward him, her forehead wrinkled. "Here? Now? In the car in a vacant parking lot?"

"Yes. Here. Now. In the car in a vacant parking lot. I feel as if I'm giving an answer through the words of a childhood story." He laughed, hoping her expression would also lighten. He couldn't bear the sadness in her eyes.

"Why would you want to hold me, Sloan?"

Why? He could tell her how seeing her tears touched places inside him he wasn't sure had ever been touched. He could tell her how he wanted to share her grief over a man they'd both loved. He could tell her how he craved to feel her body against his again, because holding her for that brief celebratory spin the day before had left him longing for much more. He could tell her how the night he had spent holding her haunted his dreams. He could. But he wouldn't, because what would be the point?

"Quit asking questions," he ordered instead, "and just say yes or no."

"Yes or no."

His lips twitched. "Smart-mouthed woman."

With that, Sloan didn't wait for permission, just leaned toward her, ran his fingers into her hair and gently tilted her face toward him. Her eyes caught the reflection of the streetlight, making them sparkle in the dimly lit car.

Her gaze held his, almost daring him to say more, to do more, to take what he wanted from her. Her lips parted, teasing him with the promise of entrance into that gorgeous mouth of hers. He wanted to taste her, longed to taste her. The morning he'd woken up with her in his arms seemed so long ago. Surely he'd dreamed the passion, the sweetness of her kisses?

He really needed to know.

He leaned toward her, his gaze zeroing in on his destination. "Such a beautiful, tempting mouth to hold such a sharp, sharp tongue."

Sloan was about to kiss her. Cara should stop him. Their emotions were just high from the emergency-room drama. At least, hers were. She knew that.

She also knew that she had been thinking about Sloan kissing her for the past four months. Longer.

From the morning she'd woken up to his body moving against hers, to his lips covering hers, she'd wanted more kisses, wanted his body against hers.

Yesterday, when he'd spun her around and let her glide down his body, every nerve ending in her body had been aware of him. She'd wanted to wrap her arms around his neck, mash her body against his and kiss him.

Kiss him and kiss him and kiss him until they'd both been breathless and clinging to each other the way they had that morning. More. Way beyond that. She wanted everything.

She wanted everything now.

Cara leaned forward and closed the gap between their mouths, pressing her lips to his.

Instant pleasure rewarded her action. Oh, how sweet Sloan's mouth was against hers. Hungry and passionate and demanding. Flutters shimmied in her belly. Warmth spread through her being. She scooted toward him, wishing the car didn't have bucket seats, wishing she could be as close to him as she wanted to be. Her fingers wound into his hair, almost painfully, she was sure, daring him to move away from her mouth. She needed his kisses. Needed what he was eliciting in her body. She needed to feel alive and Sloan made her feel more alive than she'd ever felt.

"Woman, you're killing me," he breathed against her lips.

"Me? How?" she asked, kissing him again, loving the taste of him, loving the strength she felt in his every touch.

"Because I want you, Cara, and five minutes from now you're going to realize who it is you're kissing and you're going to hate yourself for kissing me. Then I'm going to be the bad guy again."

He was right. "You're the bad guy right now."

Drawing a shaky breath, he pulled back from her, but she refused to loosen her grasp on his hair so he didn't go far. "I don't want you to stop kissing me. I want you to kiss me, Sloan. I desperately want you kissing me. Just don't stop and then I won't have regrets."

Then he was kissing her again. Over and over, demanding and yet tender. He kissed her with the passion she craved. He kissed her with reverence and yet masterfully. He kissed her even better than her memory had recalled.

Sloan kissed her and her crazy, unbalanced world slid into perfect harmony.

"I'd like to go to your place, but I'm not going to," Sloan told her much later, when they sat in her car back in the hospital parking lot. After their make-out session, she'd driven them back to the hospital parking lot rather than the now-closed drive-up restaurant.

"I didn't invite you to my place," she immediately reminded him.

He sighed. "You're right. You didn't. I shouldn't make assumptions where you are concerned. I know that."

"You shouldn't, but, to be fair, if I thought you'd say yes, I'd invite you, Sloan." Her gaze held his. "Because I'd be lying if I said that wasn't what I wanted."

Heaven help him. How was he supposed to do the right thing and not beg her to invite him when she'd admitted that she wanted him there?

"Don't say that."

"Why not? It's the truth."

"Because you don't understand how much willpower it requires for me to do the right thing where you're concerned."

"Not going to my place is the right thing?"

Earlier tonight he'd been her enemy in her eyes. She still claimed to see him that way. A relationship between them based on lust went against everything his head told him. "Yes, I believe it is."

She took a few moments to consider his comment. "Because of my father?"

An affair sure wouldn't win him any brownie points toward giving Preston what he wanted. "Because of a lot of reasons, but mainly because you see me as your enemy."

She didn't deny it, but offered, "You could show me all the reasons why I shouldn't see you that way."

He wanted to show her a lot of things, like how good it could be between them. Unfortunately, they wanted very different things in the long term and he was already so wrapped up in her that he wasn't sure he'd recover from an affair with Cara.

"Don't get me wrong," he admitted. "I'd like to do exactly that, but sex would only complicate things between us."

She leaned back in the driver's seat, put her hands on the steering wheel, stared straight ahead, then shocked him with what she said next. "Things are already complicated between us. We can both deny it, but we both know it's true. Besides, what's a little sex between enemies?"

Which was exactly why they shouldn't have sex.

"You aren't my enemy. Just as I'm not yours." He reached out, ran his finger across her cheek. "And, for the record, there wouldn't be a 'little sex' between you and I. If, and when, we take that step, it'll be big. Gigantic even."

"Sheesh. Men." She rolled her eyes. "I wasn't referring to your size."

"Neither was I, but in all regards sex between you and I would be huge." He let the last word roll off his tongue slowly, liking the way her eyes closed, her throat worked, and her fingers gripped the steering wheel tighter.

"But you aren't willing to go home with me tonight, are you?"

Blast Preston for the position he'd put them in with his crazy requests. Blast himself for caring about Cara and not wanting to take advantage of her current emotional state. Blast having scruples and not wanting to have sex with someone who regarded him as her enemy.

Sloan shook his head. "Not tonight. Too much has happened today. Our emotions are too raw. If you still want me in the light of day, we'll talk."

"Perhaps you misunderstand." She tapped her fingers against the steering wheel. "Talking isn't what I want."

He groaned. If his words had affected her body, hers had done so tenfold to his. Did she have any idea how difficult this was on him? How difficult pulling away from their heated kisses had been?

But the next time Cara spent the night in his arms he wouldn't have her telling him to get out when she woke up. The next time she'd spend the night with him willingly, with no regrets when morning came. The next time wouldn't be triggered by her not wanting to be alone in her house because she was grieving for her father.

There would be a next time. He believed that with all his being, which was what gave him the strength to lean forward, press a kiss to her cheek, and then open the car door. "Good night, Cara. I'll follow you home and make sure you get inside safely. Sweet dreams."

"Can you look over June Lucada's labs? She's on the phone, wanting her results," Amie informed Cara, poking her head into her office.

Rubbing her temple, hoping the throb there would ease, Cara fought a yawn. "Sure thing. Is it in my inbox?"

"Yep. It's there. You want me to have her hold or tell her we'll call her back in a few?"

"Have her hold, and I'll take a look now." Fighting another yawn, Cara opened her electronic inbox and reviewed the patient's labs. She picked up the phone and gave the woman the results and advised her to schedule a follow-up appointment to address her elevated cholesterol.

"How's your husband doing?" she asked, referring to the man she'd seen the previous week. "Is his big toe any better?"

While she listened to the woman explain how the man's gout had improved with the medication Cara had given him, Cara glanced up to see she was being watched by a tall, lean specimen of perfection leaning against her door frame.

Almost perfection, because, thanks to him, she was as exhausted this morning as she'd been when she'd crawled into bed. How had she been supposed to sleep after those heated kisses? Obviously she hadn't because all she'd done had been to lie in bed and think about him. That was, until she'd finally crawled out of bed, gone down the hallway and opened a closed wooden door. Her father's room. As much as it had ached to enter the room, it had been time. Past time. She supposed the girl's death had pushed her into the room. Or maybe entering the room, dealing with painful emotions, had been the only way to clear her mind of Sloan.

Either way, she hadn't slept and she hadn't been able to quit thinking about Sloan.

She'd kissed him last night. Kissed him over and

over. She'd run her fingers through those coal-black locks, molded her hands into his neck and shoulders, tasted his masculine goodness.

She'd practically thrown herself at him!

He'd turned her down.

Heat filled her cheeks. Had he come to gloat? Fine. Let him gloat. Perhaps he even deserved gloating rights. The man kissed like a dream.

She finished the call, hung up the phone, then met Sloan's gaze. "Can I help you?"

He didn't speak, just nodded, shut the door behind him, clicked the lock and crossed over to her desk. "Tell me I'm an idiot for leaving you last night."

That was an easy request to comply with. "You're an idiot for leaving me last night."

He laughed, took her hands and pulled her to her feet. "You enjoyed that too much."

"You are an idiot for leaving me last night," she repeated, enjoying saying the words again as she stared up into his eyes. Her heart raced and her head spun a little at his unexpected entrance into her office, at his unexpected words.

"I want to kiss you, Cara. Right now. Despite the fact that it's first thing in the morning and we've an office full of patients to see. I want to kiss you, because I didn't sleep for lying in bed, wishing I was kissing you."

Elation spread through her and she smiled up at him. "You are an idiot for leaving me last night," she said for a third time.

He laughed again and took her into his arms. She thought he would take her mouth, but he didn't. He just held her in his arms and brushed his lips across the top of her head.

"You're right," he whispered into her pulled-up hair. "I am an idiot for leaving you last night."

"Just so we're clear," she said matter-of-factly. "You are an idiot for leaving me last night."

He laughed yet again then became serious, leaned back to stare down at her. "I didn't want you to have regrets this morning and instead I'm the one with regrets."

She pulled away, walked across her office to collect her thoughts. "Actually, you were probably right to leave."

He frowned.

"But I can't say I was happy you did."

"How can I make it up to you?"

Giddiness percolated in her stomach, swelling to mammoth proportions in her chest and threatening to spill over as happy giggles. "We'll figure something out."

He nodded. "Soon."

"Sloan?"

"Hmm?"

"I don't want anyone to know."

"I wasn't planning on walking out of your office and making an announcement over the intercom system that we kissed."

She couldn't quite read his expression to know if he was annoyed or amused.

"I just thought we should be clear on that. I think this, whatever this is, should just be between you and me."

"As crystal."

"Are you upset?"

"No, I agree. This is something that should just be between you and me. No need to make people wonder what's going on when you'll be leaving in a couple of months."

Leaving in a couple of months. Two months and her time in Bloomberg would be over. She'd be able to leave and know she'd done as her father had wished. She'd leave and Sloan would stay. She'd never see him again. It was how life would be.

But she wouldn't think about that now.

"Then again, a lot can happen in two months," he surprised her by adding.

"True, but don't think I'll stay just because we get involved, Sloan. Living in Bloomberg would be a nightmare to me. Whatever happens between you and I has a two-month shelf life."

"Shelf life? You are so romantic," he accused, a grin spreading across his face.

"I'm being honest."

"Which I appreciate, but no worries. Two months works for me. I'm a confirmed bachelor, remember?"

She remembered, but someday some lucky Bloomberg woman would win his heart and they'd settle down into boring Bloomberg life and have a boring Bloomberg wedding and have boring Bloomberg babies. The thought made her ache a little inside, but she didn't fool herself that it could be any other way. Bloomberg life wasn't for her.

No matter what happened between her and Sloan, staying in Bloomberg was not an option.

Just look at what staying had done to her mother.

CHAPTER NINE

THE DAY DRAGGED. Each time Cara glanced at her watch mere minutes had passed when she felt as if hours should have come and gone. Surely Mother Nature had slowed down the passing of time?

Throughout the day, Cara saw routine medication refills, common colds, a few rashes and nothing out of the ordinary until Amie flagged her down.

"You might want to go into room two next. Abdominal pain. Nausea. Vomiting. Diarrhea. Says she feels as if she's dying. She's a walk-in and requested Sloan, but it's going to be a while before he's available to check her. He's in the middle of an ingrown toenail removal. She looks pretty miserable."

Cara's toes curled into the soles of her shoes. She'd done a few toenail removals during residency but none since. Thankfully, there weren't many opportunities for toenail removals in the emergency room. Just the thought of sticking a needle into someone's foot to do the nerve block gave her the heebie-jeebies. She'd gladly see the walk-in abdominal pain so long as he kept doing the toenail removals. "Gastroenteritis?"

"Maybe." But Amie didn't look convinced. Cara trusted the long-time nurse's instincts. Amie was good at what she did, which was why she'd been her father's nurse for so many years. "She's hurting in the left lower quadrant."

Left lower quadrant pain was oftentimes from constipation, but the woman had diarrhea. Perhaps a blockage or diverticulitis.

"Hmm. Possibly not just gastroenteritis, then, although it's still something to be ruled out," Cara mused, heading toward the room. "I'll check her now."

The young woman in her early twenties practically writhed on the examination table. Just looking at her made Cara's insides cramp in sympathy.

"I was hoping to see Dr. Trenton," the woman said immediately when she saw Cara.

Every single female from five to ninety hoped to see Dr. Trenton, Cara included.

"He's in with another patient at the moment. The nurse felt you should be seen as quickly as possible, rather than waiting, as he'll be in that room for a while."

The woman grimaced and nodded. "She's right. I'm pretty sure my insides are ripping apart. You'll do for now."

Cara didn't know whether to say thanks or not. The poor woman did look as if she felt as if her insides were being shredded. "When did your symptoms start?"

"This morning." The woman's arms crossed over her belly and she pulled inward. "I woke up in pain and the hurt just keeps getting worse."

"Have you taken anything?"

"Everything I could find." The woman mentioned several over-the-counter pain relievers and antacids. "Nothing helps."

Cara ran through a myriad of questions while looking over the girl's history. She hadn't had any surgeries so anything was a possibility.

Cara did a quick ENT and neck examination, then listened to her heart and lung sounds. All normal.

"Lie back on the table."

Amongst a lot of grunting and groaning, the woman lay back on the examination table. Her hands immediately covered her stomach. Eyes wide, she pleaded, "Be easy."

"I will be as easy as possible," Cara promised. "But I need to make sure I do a good assessment so we can figure out what's causing your symptoms. While I'm checking you, tell me what you've eaten the past twenty-four hours."

The only significant food intake was popcorn.

Cara finished examining the woman's abdomen, noting the extreme tenderness over her descending colon. "I think you have something called diverticulitis, which is an inflammation caused by bits of food that get trapped in pockets in the colon. Certain foods like seeds and popcorn kernels can get trapped. As the body tries to break them down, it causes cramping and a lot of the symptoms you're having."

Cara sat down at the small desk area and pulled out a form from the top desk drawer. "I'm going to send you over to the hospital to be admitted and to get some imaging of your abdomen and pelvis. I know your chart says no known drug allergies, but I like to confirm that. Are you allergic to anything, specifically any contrast dyes?"

The woman shook her head. "I don't have any allergies."

"Knock-knock," Sloan called through the closed examination room door, while actually knocking his knuckles against the door, as well.

"Come in," both Cara and the patient called.

"Hey, Stacey," he greeted the woman while he washed his hands. "What's going on?"

While he examined her, she ran through everything she'd told Cara, adding a few details about how much she hurt and how much she preferred seeing him to the new lady doctor. "I just prefer a man to check me. No offense meant," the girl added, with a quick look toward Cara.

"None taken," Cara assured her, signing her name to the hospital admission form she'd completed while Sloan was reexamining the woman.

"You getting a CT?"

Cara nodded. "I'm doing a direct admission with an urgent with-and-without-contrast CT order."

"Perfect." He turned back to the patient. "Looks like the new lady doctor has you on the right track. Do what she tells you to do and one of us will be by the hospital later today to check on you."

"I hope it's you." The woman nodded at him as if he hung the moon and dotted the sky with stars, as well.

Puh-leeze. Cara wanted to stick her finger in her mouth to make a gagging sound. Then again, she had kissed him and perhaps he had hung the moon and dotted the sky with stars. He'd been that good. But Stacey didn't know that.

Did she?

A streak of green a mile wide flashed hotly through Cara. A streak of green she'd never felt before. A streak of green she didn't like. She wasn't the jealous type. Sure, she and Sloan had kissed, but that didn't mean she had any right to feel possessive about him. To wonder about his relationships with other women. Now she wished she'd paid more attention when her father had been going on about all the women chasing after Sloan.

No, it didn't matter who was chasing him. They had no future together. Just a small wrinkle in time together.

"I'll get Amie to give you something for pain so long as you have someone to assist you next door," Cara offered, thinking that having Sloan in the room seemed to be working fairly well to distract the patient from her pain and distract *her* from everything but him, as well.

"My sister is in the waiting room. She can help me."

"Great," Cara said, determined to get back to professional because she didn't like the green monster inside her. "Amie will be in soon with something to ease your discomfort. I'm going to call the medical floor and let them know you are on your way over."

Cara paused outside Sloan's open office door. He sat at his desk, skimming over a paper, and then signed his name at the bottom.

Lord, he was a beautiful man. No wonder female patients preferred him and threw themselves at his feet. She couldn't blame them. Not that she planned to throw herself at his feet ever, but just looking at him could definitely make a person feel better.

Could justify a woman feeling possessive about him, could justify a woman feeling a little green that other women might have experienced those spectacular kisses.

She'd kissed him less than twenty-four hours before. And thrown herself at his feet. At all of him.

Heat flooded her body. How embarrassing. She'd never done anything of the sort before, but, at the time, having Sloan go home with her had seemed imperative.

Because she hadn't wanted to be alone because the teen's death had shaken her? Or because she'd wanted to be with Sloan?

If she was honest, she'd have to admit the truth had been a combination of both.

Sloan glanced up from his desk, catching her watching him. Good grief. He was probably going to start lumping her in the same category as all the other Sloan-starved women in Bloomberg. No wonder. She *was* Sloan-starved. Pathetic.

"What did Stacey's CT show?"

"Definitely diverticulitis, with a possible perforated colon."

"Ouch." He set his ink pen down on the desk and motioned for her to come into his office. "She really was in pain."

Cara's heartbeat took on a wild jungle tempo. Any moment she expected her mouth to open and a Tarzan call to echo around the building. That's how wild her heart beat in her chest. The image of Sloan in a leopard-skin loincloth popped into her head. She imagined the planes of the body she'd been pressed up against at the ball field. Strong, hard, chiseled. Would he have chest hair or have a smooth chest? In her vision, she imagined he'd have at least a smattering of chest hair that tapered down a southward path.

"I've requested a surgical consult," she said to ground herself in reality, walking into the room and sitting down in a chair across from him. She crossed her legs then immediately uncrossed them and tucked her hands under her thighs to keep from fidgeting. "Anything else you want ordered since she is technically your patient?"

He studied her for a few moments then offered, "I can take over her admission, if you prefer."

Flustered that her awkwardness was coming across

all wrong, Cara shook her head. "No. I've got her taken care of."

"Are you okay?"

She didn't need to ask why he'd think she might not be. She was acting like a nervous schoolgirl. What was wrong with her? This so wasn't her. "I'm fine. It's just been a long day."

"Can I buy you dinner to make up for it?"

"For my having a long day?"

"Just imagine how long my day would have been if you'd not been here."

"True, but you don't owe me anything, Sloan. I'm doing this for my father. No other reason."

"I know that. But I do appreciate you being here. I know Bloomberg is not where you want to be."

She shook her head. "You're right. It's not."

But was there anywhere she'd rather be at this moment than with him? No. No. No. She wasn't going to think that way.

He leaned back in his chair. "Tell me, Cara, what is it about Bloomberg that you dislike so much?"

"Everything," she answered immediately.

"I don't believe you."

She arched her brow at him.

"Come on, there must be something about the place you like."

"I like being so close to the gulf."

He looked surprised. "Have you been to the beach since coming home?"

"Every chance I get. I've driven down every weekend I've not been on call."

"Let's go." He shocked her by saying it.

What? "We can't go to the beach."

"Why not?"

"Well, for starters, we've admitted Stacey Jones and already have two patients on the medical floor. Plus, I'm on call tonight."

"That's right." He shrugged, then grinned. "We'll go this weekend."

She opened her mouth to say no. She didn't need to go to the gulf with him.

"Casey is on call this weekend," he reminded her before she got a word out. "There's no reason we couldn't drive down on Friday night after we finish here. We could come back on Sunday afternoon."

"Spend the entire weekend with you?"

He searched her face, no doubt trying to read her thoughts. "Yes. Spend the weekend at the beach with me, Cara."

She knew what he was saying, what would happen if they went away together. There could be no regrets of having been caught up in the moment. If she said yes, it was because she wanted him. Wanted them.

She didn't want them, but she couldn't deny that she wanted him. Which made no sense. She didn't have flings. But if she agreed to go with him, wasn't that exactly what she'd be agreeing to? They had no future, no possibility of a future. A fling was all there was to be had between them.

She hesitated. "I thought we agreed this morning that we didn't want anyone to know. We can't both disappear for the weekend. Everyone will know we're together."

"You'll be leaving before long and you'll never have to see these people again. What anyone in Bloomberg thinks won't matter in the slightest."

"Good point, but what about you? You plan to stay in Bloomberg forever. Surely you don't want a fling with me ruining your reputation?"

"I wouldn't call our going to the beach together a 'fling'."

She knew what their going away together for a weekend would entail. How they labeled the weekend didn't change what would happen. "How would you describe our going to the beach together?"

Sloan thought a minute, then met her gaze and took her breath away with the intensity in his coppery eyes. "A fantasy come true."

She bit into her lower lip, barely registering the metallic twang that filled her mouth. "You make it impossible to say no."

He grinned. "Good, because you saying no isn't the idea. I want you to say yes."

A slow smile spread across her face. "I hope I don't live to regret this but okay, Sloan. I will go to the beach with you this weekend."

Sloan couldn't believe she'd said yes so quickly. He felt like jumping into the air and pumping his fist. Instead, he just smiled. "You know what will happen if we go away together?"

"We'll get sunburned?" she asked, blinking innocently.

"We may not even see the sun."

"I know," she admitted on a sigh, looking a little pensive. "It's inevitable. It has been from the morning I woke up kissing you."

"You've thought about that morning?" He wished they weren't at the office, weren't where anyone could come interrupt them. Okay, Amie was the only one who hadn't gone home for the day. No doubt she would approve. She'd said more than one thing to that effect since Cara had started at the clinic. Then again, Amie and Preston had been close. She probably knew what Preston wanted, what he'd asked of Sloan.

Cara's thoughts obviously going where his had, she glanced over her shoulder down the empty office hallway. "I've got to go to the hospital to check on Stacey."

Sloan laughed. "Chicken."

"A wise girl knows when to speak and when to hold her tongue."

"Silence can be an answer in and of itself."

"Silence is what I expect from you regarding this weekend. Like I said, regardless of whether or not I'm leaving in two months, I don't want my private business discussed all over town. If for no other reason than out of respect for my father."

"I respect that."

"I'm sure you do," she said, stared at him a moment with something akin to dislike, then took off to disappear down the hallway, turning at the last moment to meet his gaze. "I'm off to pack my bikini. Have a good evening."

Imagining her in a bikini, Sloan groaned.

Lust was a crazy thing. No doubt Cara wasn't the first woman to fall into lust with the wrong man. Not that Sloan was a bad man. He wasn't. She wasn't so obstinate that she couldn't see all his good qualities and what a blessing he was to Bloomberg. On that matter, she understood her father. But she wasn't into affairs and that was all she and Sloan could ever have.

Whether she was into affairs or not, she'd essentially agreed to have one. With Sloan. Crazy.

Would they only have this weekend or did he intend them to continue until she left Bloomberg?

To continue beyond this weekend would just be ask-

ing for trouble, would be asking for feelings to develop
between them that she didn't need.

She'd go this weekend, get her fill of Sloan and then
they'd go back to being coworkers, only the sexual
tension between them would be abated because they
wouldn't be wondering about each other. A perfect plan.
Or so she kept telling herself.

Friday evening seemed to take forever to come and
yet it got there before Cara was ready. She'd spent longer in the bathroom the night before than she had in
years. She'd shaved, waxed, plucked, buffed, lotioned,
perfumed and conditioned herself until she knew she'd
done all she could to look good in Sloan's eyes.

She wanted to look good in his eyes.

Crazy, because she knew he wanted her. He'd told her
as much and she saw it in how he looked at her. Each
day the tension between them had continued to build,
to the point that just seeing him or hearing his voice
revved her engines.

A man as beautiful as Sloan had probably had a lot
of women, but she refused to think about that, about
her lack of experience. All that mattered was that this
weekend the two of them would assuage the heat that
burned between them, and then they'd be done.

"Hi," she said, trying not to sound nervous when she
let him into her father's house.

"You ready?"

"As ready as I'm ever going to be."

He laughed. "That sounds more as if you're going for
a colonoscopy than away to the beach for the weekend."

"Sorry. I'm a little nervous."

"That's okay, Cara." He moved close to her, cupped
her face. "I understand. I couldn't sleep last night for
thinking about us."

She took a deep breath and knew she needed to clarify one more time the boundaries of their weekend. "There is no us. What happens between us physically this weekend is all that there can ever be."

"You can deny it all you want, but we both know there is an us."

Cara's stomach churned. "Not beyond this weekend, there's not."

"Do you really believe that?"

"For us to go beyond this weekend would be foolish. There's absolutely no chance of anything further happening between us. I won't risk it."

"Risk it?"

"Being entangled in a relationship in Bloomberg."

"You don't think this weekend will make you feel entangled in a relationship with me?"

"I won't let it," she admitted. "I won't stay in Bloomberg and one, or possibly both, of us will end up hurt if we pretend otherwise."

His grip on her face tightened just the slightest, then he stroked his fingers down the side of her cheek. "You're right. Only this weekend it is, then."

Relief flooded her that he'd agreed. Some other twinge of something also flooded her but she wasn't sure what that emotion was so she smiled and focused on the man in front of her. "Come on. The beach is calling my name."

While she locked up the house, he grabbed her suitcase and stowed it in the back of his Jeep.

"Are we staying in a hotel?"

He shook his head. "I've rented a one-bedroom house on Santa Rosa Island."

A house. More privacy. Good.

"I love Santa Rosa." She fastened her hair back so the

wind wouldn't whip it around so crazily when they took off. "My parents used to go there when I was a baby."

It was the one place where her mother had been happy. She'd looked so carefree and content in the photos taken there. Just as her father had.

"I know. I've seen photos."

Pausing with her hands still in her hair, her brows shot up. "How have you seen photos of that?"

There weren't any large framed shots of their family outings on her father's office wall or even anywhere in the house. Just some four-by-six shots taken on her mother's camera that were stuck into an old album and some photos of her mother laughing on the beach that he'd kept in his bedroom.

Sloan shrugged and started the ignition. "Your father showed me your photos one night when we were at his place. Your mother was a beautiful woman. You look a lot like her."

Elation filled her at his statement that she looked like her mother. But shock also hit her.

"Dad pulled out old photo albums?" That so didn't sound like Dr. Preston Conner. He hadn't been a man given to sentimental gestures.

"He was very proud of you."

She laughed a little nervously, not sure what she thought of her father and Sloan having pored over old family albums. What else had her father shared with Sloan? A twinge of jealousy hit her that her father had sat and looked at the old albums with Sloan, something she couldn't recall him ever having done with her. Then again, Sloan had been like a son to him and he'd always wanted a son. Doubt hit her.

All the old feelings about her father and Sloan were still there, but new feelings were there, too. Feelings that kept her from demanding he take her home. Feelings that had her simply saying, "I'm sorry you had to suffer through baby photos of me."

"I'm not. I enjoyed them." He actually sounded as if he really had.

"Why?"

"Why wouldn't I? I cared deeply for Preston and he cared deeply for you."

She sank her teeth into her lower lip, wincing when she caught an already sore spot.

They rode in silence until they were a few miles outside Bloomberg.

"How did you end up in Bloomberg?" she asked, curious as to how he'd come to such a tiny town to practice. He was good enough to work anywhere he wanted. Why Bloomberg?

"I was working in Columbia, Ohio, and met Preston at a medical conference in Nashville. He convinced me that I'd enjoy small-town practice a lot more than living in the city. It didn't take much. I'd always planned to move to a small town to practice someday."

"And settle down?"

"I do want to marry and have kids but, obviously, I'm not in a rush."

She nodded. Women would line up to audition for the role.

"What about you?" he asked, glancing toward her. "What's next on your life agenda after your Bloomberg stint?"

She shrugged. "Back to New York."

"Back to pick up where you left off?"

"I let John…" Her voice trailed off.

"That's your ex?"

She nodded. "Sorry. Anyway, I let him have the lease

on my apartment. I quit my job when I came here. I love the city, so I'll go back there, but I'll probably work at a different facility."

"To avoid seeing your ex?"

"Not really. We're still friends and have talked a few times since I've been here."

That seemed to shock him and he asked, "Do you think you'll get back together when you return to New York?"

She shook her head. Of that she was positive. Whatever had been between John and herself wasn't what she wanted for the rest of her life. Yes, they'd had fun together on their adventures and both had felt passionate about their trips. Too bad they'd not felt as passionately about each other. Too bad neither of them had realized that.

"I may take a few months off before going back to work, maybe travel a bit, do some mission work, while I figure out what I want to do the rest of my life." She was thinking out loud, testing the idea as she said it.

"Maybe you could do a travel medicine stint. Sign on for a year or something," he suggested.

"Maybe." Why did his offering suggestions on places for her to go sting? It wasn't as if either of them expected her to stay in Bloomberg so to be hurt was just ridiculous.

He pulled onto the main highway and the increased speed made further chitchat seem silly as they'd practically have to yell at each other to be heard over the wind noise.

Cara flipped the radio station on then, curious about what type of music he chose to listen to, she hit the CD button.

"Johnny Cash? Really?" she called toward him, her

hair whipping about her face despite her earlier efforts
to contain it.

He glanced her way then grinned.

No wonder her father had been so crazy about Sloan.
Johnny Cash had been her father's all-time favorite.
Medicine, Bloomberg and Johnny. Sloan really was her
dad's mini-me.

Which was yet another reason why she shouldn't be
with him this weekend, but she wasn't going to worry
about that. Instead, she planned to not worry about anything beyond the weekend. Time enough for that later.

Sloan paid the toll going onto the Santa Rosa Island
Bridge and stole a peek at Cara. She had been antsy the
entire drive. They'd started the trip talking, but once on
the highway they had settled into singing along with the
radio. Now she refused to even look his way.

She was such a contradiction. Strong, fiercely independent, yet vulnerable and unsure of herself. She was
nervous about this weekend.

So was he.

She'd lived with a man in New York, so he didn't
kid himself that she was inexperienced. But, other than
John, he'd never heard her father mention other boy-
friends or men in her life. Sure, he'd seen photographic
evidence of high-school dance dates and the like, but
no guy had ever managed to be in more than one photo.
Interesting, that.

Had she never let herself get close enough to anyone
in Bloomberg because she hadn't wanted to risk falling
for someone there?

Once onto the island, Sloan turned left at the main
intersection and headed east past hotels and a few restaurants and shops. Soon they were in a more residential

section of the island. He made a right turn and within minutes he was pulling the car up to the beachfront bungalow-style house he'd rented.

"This looks nice," Cara said, hopping out of the Jeep and reaching for her bag out of the backseat.

"I hope the inside looks as great as it did online." He grabbed his bag and tried to take hers from her, but she refused to let him. He unlocked the door with the pass code the rental agency had given him.

"You haven't been here before?" Cara asked once they were inside. The decor was very typical beach house. Lots of blues, whites, shells, sailboats and a framed print of a lighthouse that dominated the airy room.

"No." He walked into the bedroom, set his suitcase down, then turned back to her. "I have visited the beach with a few friends who came down from Ohio to visit and have made a few day trips, but that's the extent of my beach trips."

She put her suitcase on the bed and began unpacking. "Some friends had beach houses in Atlantic City that we'd stay in from time to time, but the beaches up north just aren't the same as the white beaches here."

She continued to unpack and talk, almost as if she was afraid for there to be a second's silence between them.

"Come on," he said, when she had almost finished unpacking her bag and was still prattling on about New Jersey beaches. "Let's go for a walk."

"But I thought…" Her gaze went to the bed, then jerked back to him. Tension poured off her body. The same tension that had continued to increase on their drive.

"That I brought you up here to immediately ravage

you and that I didn't plan to let you have a moment's peace?"

Her face flushed.

He walked over, took her hands. "We have all weekend, Cara. Let's walk, then we can grab something to eat. I paid the rental agency extra to stock a few items in the fridge for breakfast and snacks, but I've been looking forward to some fresh seafood all day."

He'd been looking forward to kissing her, too, but this weekend wasn't just about sex for him. He wanted to spend time with Cara, to get to know her away from Bloomberg. He wanted her relaxed.

She smiled. "Sounds good. I love the beach."

He took her hand and they took off toward the water, being careful not to disturb the dune as they crossed over to the beach.

Cara let go of his hand and, laughing and kicking off her sandals, raced to the water, pausing as waves lapped at her bare feet.

Turning, she smiled at him. "Sugar-sand beaches, gorgeous blue water, very few people, and just smell the breeze." She inhaled deeply. "Don't you just love Santa Rosa?"

"I do now."

She laughed and ran her hands through the water, sending a spray his way. "Come on and get wet. Unless you're chicken."

He laughed. There went that competitive spirit.

He got into the water then surprised her by sending a large splash her way. She didn't squeal or squirm away, just went on the attack and soaked him.

Laughing, they splashed each other, then he caught her by the waist and spun her around. A wave shifted the sand beneath his feet, sucking it outward and he lost his footing.

"Oh!" she yelped, as they plopped down into the water.

"Come on." He grabbed her hand and helped her onto her feet. "Let's get that walk in before the next wave pummels us."

She glanced down at her soaked clothes. "Not like it would matter much at this point."

Her clothes were plastered to her body, outlining her lean shape. Sloan gulped and tried to sound normal. "Do you want to go inside and change into dry clothes?"

Oblivious that his mind had gone from playful to wanting to throw her over his shoulder and carry her to their bedroom and do exactly as she'd been expecting on their arrival, she shook her head. "Nope. We're supposed to be wet. We're at the beach."

Struggling to get his body under control, because his clothes were wet, too, Sloan watched her pluck the material away from her skin and fan it outward. He wasn't sure how much that was going to help dry the material, but it wasn't doing a thing for his imagination. Maybe she'd been right and they should have just gotten sex over with to break the tension between them.

At the moment the anticipation of peeling her clothes off her was about to kill him. But he'd always been a patient man, and now wasn't the time to waver from that lifelong course.

This weekend was monumental and Sloan knew it. What happened between them would be a turning point in their relationship. Either in a good way or a bad way.

It was up to him to steer them in a good direction.

Hand in hand, they walked, stopping to pick up a shell here and there. By the time they'd walked, turned and got back to the house he'd rented, Sloan was a mess, but Cara was a relaxed beach bum. She hummed as he sprayed the sand off her feet with a water hose. Water trickled over her rosy-pink toenails. He brushed off a stubborn bit of sand and couldn't resist running his fingertip up the side of her foot.

"Hey, no fair," she protested, wiggling out of his grasp.

"Ticklish?"

"Obviously." She moved away from the water spicket. "I'm going to change while you wash the sand off, then let's go find some of that fresh seafood you were talking about. I'm starved."

Sloan was, too, but crab legs weren't what were foremost in his mind.

"So you never knew your parents?" Cara asked, cracking open another crab leg and sucking out the delicious meat inside.

His gaze zeroed in on her mouth, Sloan shook his head.

Cara bit back a smile at his expression. Okay, so perhaps it was wrong of her, but since she'd relaxed, she'd been enjoying herself. A great deal. Sex appeal and her father aside, Sloan really was a great guy.

Okay, so the sex appeal definitely played into her current merriment. Sloan wanted her. And she was enjoying every second of their foreplay.

There could be no more accurate name for what passed between them. Sure, some might call it dinner and conversation, but she knew what it really was.

Every word, every expression, every touch, whether intentional or accidental, were all preludes to what the night would hold.

She'd never considered herself a tease or a seductress but, with Sloan watching her, she felt like a sultry combination of both. Because every move she made turned him on and she liked it. A lot.

Just as she liked him. A lot.

Beneath the table, she slid one foot out of her sandal and slid her toes along the hairy plane of his shin. "There wasn't anyone else who could take you in?"

Eyebrow lifting at her under-the-table play, he shook his head. "I have a few aunts and uncles, but they had their hands full with their own kids. I went into the foster-care system at six and stayed there until I graduated high school. It wasn't so bad. My last foster family was good to me, encouraged me to apply for scholarships and go to college. I still talk to them every so often, but haven't seen them in years."

"I can't imagine." She really couldn't. Her admiration for him, for what he'd accomplished in life, rose even higher, as did the foot that toyed along his leg. She stretched, grazing her toes behind to his calf.

He took a long haul of his drink. "This is perhaps the strangest conversation I've ever had."

"Why's that?" she asked, truly curious and liking the hard calf muscles her toes toyed with.

He leaned toward her, his eyes locked with hers. "Because this topic isn't one I like talking about. It's usually a total turn-off."

"But?"

He took her hand into his. "I'm not turned off."

Excitement fluttered through her body. "You find the conversation stimulating?"

"Something like that." He gestured to her plate. "You about done?"

She didn't even glance down, just held his gaze. "Not nearly."

His lips twitched. "Want dessert?"

"Something like that." She tossed his words back at him but made no move to eat another bite. She didn't want food and they both knew it.

He glanced at the ticket, pulled out his wallet and threw down a few twenties. "Let's go."

Not hesitating, she slipped her sandal back on and took his hand.

He helped her into the Jeep, then drove the few miles down the road to their house. The moment he parked the car under the covered porch Cara hopped out of the vehicle and took off up the stairs. Why, she couldn't exactly say, just that she didn't want to linger in the car with him. When he made it to the top of the stairs he found her leaning over the balcony, staring out at the moonlit waves.

"It's so beautiful and peaceful here. It's like all the cares of the world just vanish. Like nothing else matters or exists."

"It doesn't," he agreed, causing her to turn to look at him.

The breeze caught at his hair, toying with the dark tufts. His eyes were dark molten copper pools that beckoned her to take a plunge.

She planned to. She planned to dive in and not look back.

"I want you," she told him with all honesty.

"The feeling is mutual," he assured her, unlocking the house door, pushing it open, then moving to stand beside her, his hands at her waist. "So very mutual."

She didn't wait for him to kiss her. Instead, she took what she wanted. Him. She couldn't say she exactly launched herself at him but she probably couldn't deny it if accused, either.

Either way, within seconds her body was wrapped around his, melting against him, kissing him as she clung to him. The sound of the waves behind them played the perfect melody. His hands moved over her body, cupped her bottom, molding her tighter against his hard frame.

Her inner thighs squeezed, hugging his hips, eliciting a husky growl from deep within his throat.

"I want you here."

Did he think she was going to argue with him? She wasn't. She was burning up for him, yearning to feel him inside her.

"But I want to see you. All of you."

She'd just as soon he didn't, but was too far gone to argue. Especially when him seeing her meant she'd get to see him, too.

He carried her inside the house and into the bedroom. She slid down him, went to reach for his shirt, but he moved away, opened the sliding glass door that opened onto the balcony. Sounds of the waves crashing against the beach filled the room, but he left the curtains drawn, blocking the view and protecting their privacy should anyone be walking along the beach.

"Nice," she said as he flicked on a bedside lamp.

"Very," he agreed, pulling his T-shirt over his head.

"Oh, my," she breathed. Sure, she'd known he was buff beneath his clothes, but the man was gorgeous. How many hours did he spend working out a week, anyway? She knew he ran most mornings before the crack of dawn, played and coached sports, but he got in some gym time at some point, too.

"Your turn."

Cara gave a slightly nervous laugh then complied, lifting her shirt over her head to reveal her silky bra. His intake of breath was all she needed to boost her confidence another notch, and without questioning herself she hooked her fingers into her shorts and slid them down her hips. She stood before him in her cream-colored silk bra and panties and let him look.

She wasn't in as good a shape as she'd been a few years back and should have felt self-conscious, but under his gaze she just felt beautiful. How could she not when his eyes ate her up and his voice broke when he said her name?

"Your turn," she said, using his words because she wanted to look at him, too. She wanted to see him, to touch him, to caress and taste him.

He outdid her, of course, removing both his shorts and his boxers together. Naked, he stood before her.

Cara swallowed. He'd been right. Whatever happened between them would be huge.

But she didn't have time to think anything else because he closed the distance between them and began touching and kissing her. All rational thought disappeared and wouldn't be found until long after the sun came up.

Cara's soft moans and undulations against him were driving Sloan wild. He'd been fighting the urge to strip her panties off her and take what he wanted for what had seemed like eons but which had probably only been minutes.

He made haste with her bra, tossed back the bedspread and pushed her down onto their bed. She lay there looking up at him with eager eyes and he almost lost it.

But he got a grip on himself and slowed himself down. He wanted this to be good for her. He wanted her as starved for him as he was for her. He moved atop her and kissed her. He kissed her mouth, her throat and her breasts.

"Sloan," she cried against the top of his head, clasping her fingers into his hair. He smiled. She was getting close. So very close.

He teased her with his tongue, over and over, back and forth, until she cried out his name again. Then he moved lower and pulled off her panties. Within seconds she was whimpering, moving against him, tugging him toward her.

"Please. I need you."

Sloan had enough sense to get out a condom he'd put in the end table drawer earlier and slipped it on.

"Hurry," she pleaded, pulling him to her. "Sloan. Please."

He moved between her legs, kept himself raised off her and positioned himself at her entrance. Rather than push inside, he met her gaze and waited, watching her face, looking into her passion-filled eyes and knowing he'd done that. He'd put that expression on her face.

Never had she looked more beautiful to him.

Her fingers found his shoulders and dug in. Her pelvis lifted and he slid inside and knew what he'd been denying to himself for months.

His gaze met hers and he wondered if she could see the depth of his emotions. Either way, it didn't matter because he couldn't hide what suddenly felt so obvious.

"I've been waiting for this moment for a lifetime."

CHAPTER TEN

CARA COULDN'T GET enough of Sloan. Not at the beach. Not after they returned to Bloomberg. So what if Gladys Jones had baked several batches of brownies that had been delivered with questions about Sloan's Jeep spending the night at her place?

So what if everyone at the clinic looked at them with knowing smiles?

They hadn't told a soul, but so what if they all knew, anyway?

Cara didn't care. She'd thought she would, but the reality of being with Sloan was so much more than she could have ever imagined.

For the past two months she'd walked around in a daze. A happy, euphoric daze of working side by side with Sloan and burning up the nights with him.

Like tonight, for instance. She stretched out in his bed, happy, content, her body achy, but in an, oh, so good way.

They usually went to her house, but tonight they'd called by his place to pick up a change of clothes for the morning and they'd ended up in his bed.

They had not talked about what would happen in two days when her time in Bloomberg was up.

Honestly, she wasn't sure herself what was going to

happen. John had called her, told her he missed her and that she was welcome to move back into their apartment.

That one had been easy.

Several of her friends who worked at the hospital had called, asked her about returning to her old job. That had been more difficult.

She'd liked her life before her return to Bloomberg, had liked her job and her coworkers, but the idea of going back didn't appeal as much as it should.

But she would go back.

Not to John.

Or even to her previous job most likely. She'd find a new challenge, something where she gave more back within the community she chose to live in, and she'd make a new life for herself. A better one than she'd had before.

A better one than she had now. Which currently seemed pretty impossible.

If only Sloan wasn't meant to stay in Bloomberg.

"What are you thinking about?"

She rolled over, tucking the sheet under her arm, and smiled at him. "Nothing."

"Your expression went from happy to sour."

Should she tell him?

"You were thinking about New York?"

Could he read her mind?

She shrugged. "I guess that's normal as my time here is almost up."

"Just because your six months is up it doesn't mean you have to leave immediately, Cara. Unless you've lined up something you haven't mentioned, there isn't a reason to rush back to your old life."

"I haven't lined up another job yet."

"Then what would staying a few more weeks hurt?

You can take your time and figure out what it is you want from life."

What indeed?

Part of her feared she'd never be ready to leave so long as Sloan was there, but eventually this heat between them would burn out and the glittery shine would fade and then leaving would be easy, right? She really didn't have to rush away.

"I want you to stay, Cara." He traced his fingers over her bare arm, causing her flesh to goose-bump. "Stay with me."

She closed her eyes and tried to picture being back in New York, being away from Sloan. All she saw was the misery and loneliness of missing him.

All she saw if she stayed was ending up like her mother. Her mother had wanted more for her than Bloomberg. Cara wanted more than Bloomberg.

Not answering him, she ran her fingers along the muscles in his shoulders, liking the way his flesh responded similarly to how hers had.

Searching her eyes so intently her breath caught, he took her hand in his. "In case you haven't noticed, I'm in love with you, Cara. Tell me you'll stay with me."

Forever. The word wasn't said, but Cara heard it all the same. The air between them tensed and she felt as if they were talking about a lot more than just a few weeks. An invisible fist tightened around her throat and she struggled to breathe as claustrophobia set in.

Sloan had just said he was in love with her. Could it be true? Did she want it to be true?

She must because her heart was making ecstatic leaps in her chest. But fear gripped her, too. Fear that if she said the wrong thing, she'd end up a shriveled ghost of a woman, the way her mother had. Some said pancreatic cancer had killed her mother, but Cara had always believed she'd died of a broken heart.

"I will leave Bloomberg, Sloan. Maybe not when I originally planned, but I will leave this place. To stay would suffocate me."

He nodded as if he understood, but she was pretty sure he didn't. She leaned forward to kiss him, to reassure him that she didn't plan to leave any time soon, but to her surprise he got out of bed.

"I'm going to grab a shower," he said, without turning around.

Cara watched him walk into the bathroom and replayed their conversation. He'd told her he loved her and she'd focused on the leaving part. No wonder he was upset.

But did he really think she was just going to let him walk away from her in mid-conversation like that? To tell her he loved her and then take a shower alone? Wrong.

Knowing where her going into the bathroom with him was likely to lead, she opened his nightstand drawer to get a condom out of the box she knew he kept there.

She pulled the condom out and was shutting the drawer when an envelope caught her eye.

An envelope very similar to one she had. Same handwriting. Different name.

She shouldn't touch it. Had no right to touch. But her fingers couldn't not touch it.

She traced Sloan's name, fighting an onslaught of conflicting emotions.

Her father had written his name. Just as he'd written the letter inside.

She pulled her hand away and closed the drawer. She had no right to read Sloan's letter. No matter how curious she was about what her father had told him. She had no right.

So why wasn't she on her way to join him in the shower, as she'd intended? Why was she reopening a drawer she had no right to open? Opening an envelope she had no right to look inside?

God, that woman frustrated him to no end. How could she be so blind to what they shared? To how special and amazing what was happening between them was?

She was so intent on making sure she left Bloomberg that she'd blinded herself to the truth. Or maybe he was the one blinded?

Blinded with love.

He'd known better. Known that an emotional entanglement with Cara was a bad idea, but he'd been emotionally entangled with her long before he'd met her in person.

He'd fallen in love with her through her father. He'd gotten to know her through Preston's eyes and heart and he'd fallen hard. No wonder every woman he'd tried to date had fallen so short when he'd compared them to Cara. Because she'd already had him.

The stubborn woman would leave him just to leave Bloomberg, even if it wasn't what she wanted. Not that she knew what she wanted. She didn't. Not other than him. He wasn't so blind that he didn't know exactly how much she wanted him. She enjoyed their time together as much as he did. She craved their time together as much as he did. Not just for sex, but for their runs, their trips to the beach, when she'd taken on helping him coach his T-ball team, when they rounded together at the hospital, consulted each other regarding patients. They were perfect together. Only they weren't together.

Because if he asked her if they were a couple, she'd say no, they weren't. In her eyes they were having a short-term fling.

He tossed his head back, letting the hot water run over his hair, down his shoulders.

He should be in his bed, reminding her of all the reasons why she shouldn't leave Bloomberg, the number-one reason being him.

When he kissed her, she didn't talk about leaving. When he kissed her, she begged for more, gave more, gave everything.

He rinsed, towel-dried himself, then wrapped the towel around his waist. She may plan to leave, but she wasn't gone yet and he planned to show her all the reasons why she should stay.

"Look, Cara, I'm sorry if you feel like I'm pushing you to stay, but the reality is I don't want you to leave and I'm not going to pretend otherwise."

Her back was to him and he couldn't see what she was doing. If he'd thought about it, he'd have realized something was up, but he was already upset over the prospect of her leaving.

"I am never going to want you to leave, because I meant what I said. I'm in love with you and I think you love me, too."

That's when she turned and he saw what she held.

His gaze lifted to hers, saw her tears, and a sinking feeling took hold of his insides and plummeted.

"How could you?" she accused.

"How could I what?" Preston's letter didn't say anything that Sloan had done, just requested things Preston wanted him to do, such as convince Cara to stay.

"It must be great to have my father's blessing regarding all this." She stretched her hand out over their love-tangled sheets.

"He suggested I marry you, not take you to my bed."

"Guess that one stretched the limits of your friendship too far, eh?"

Sloan closed his eyes, took a deep breath and recalled exactly what Preston's letter had said. He'd read the thing so many times he could quote it word for word. "I wouldn't marry you or anyone just because Preston wanted me to."

"No, you didn't think you'd have to. You'd just make me want you so much that I couldn't bear the thought of leaving you."

"Do you, Cara? Do you want me that much?"

"No," she burst out immediately. "Whatever I felt, this killed it all." She waved the letter between them. "How dare he use you to coerce me to stay? How dare he?"

Sloan didn't answer. He didn't agree with Preston's methods, but he knew why. Preston had figured out that Sloan had feelings for Cara. No wonder. He'd probably been as obvious as a brick through a windshield. How many times had he asked Preston about her, if he'd talked to her recently? How many nights had he and Preston sat around, talking about Cara? Too many.

Thank God he'd declined Preston's attempt to bring him to New York for that last conference he'd attended. No doubt he'd have played matchmaker right then and there, despite the fact Cara had been living with another man.

What a tangled mess they'd weaved.

Sloan,

My last wish and desire is that my daughter move home to Bloomberg. It's where she belongs even if she doesn't realize it. It's where she's always belonged. You probably think I'm crazy for the wheels I've set into motion, but I know my daughter and I know you, son.

My death will have brought her home. Please see to it that she rediscovers Bloomberg and its people. Bloomberg is her heritage and a part of who she is, even if she doesn't want to admit it. If I'd ever had a son, I would have wanted him to have been like you.

Nothing would have made me happier than for you to have married my daughter and truly been my son. You're exactly the kind of man Cara needs in her life. Exactly the kind of man I want for her. Please take care of her.

My biggest regret is that in my grief over losing my wife and throwing myself into work to help me cope day by day, I failed Cara. In my death, I don't want to do the same.

You are a man of integrity. I know I can trust you to help her heal old wounds she doesn't even realize she has. Take care of my daughter, Sloan. If I ever meant anything to you, take care of my daughter and raise my grandchildren in Bloomberg.

Preston

Hands shaking, Cara dropped the letter that had scalded her insides. She shouldn't have read Sloan's letter. To have done so was wrong.

But for her father to have asked Sloan to take care of her, to marry her, was just as wrong.

More wrong.

Anger coursed through her. Anger at her father. Anger at Sloan. What kind of game was he playing with her? And why?

"Cara?" Sloan walked around to where she sat on the bed. A towel hugged his narrow hips. She wanted to scream that her body responded to his nearness, to his beautiful nakedness.

She didn't want to want him.

Not now.

Not when she suddenly questioned every kindness he'd ever shown her. Not when she suddenly questioned every look, every touch, every word.

"Why?"

Sloan stared down at where she sat, but he didn't answer her question.

She stood, wrapping the sheet around her as she did so. She stretched on her tiptoes, not wanting to be at any disadvantage to him. "Tell me why, damn it!"

"I can't explain his letter."

"I'm not talking about his letter. I'm asking why you did it."

"Did what?"

"Went along with his stupid request. How could you do that? Why would you do that?"

"I didn't."

"Yes, you did."

"No, Cara, I didn't."

"That—" she motioned to where the letter had landed on the floor beside them "—isn't what the past six months has been about?"

"No. Not really." He raked his fingers through his hair, the motion stretching his arm, flexing his chest muscles.

She closed her eyes, let her anger consume all other emotions. "You told me once there wasn't anything you wouldn't have done for my father."

His voice took on an angry quality of its own. "Don't say it, Cara, because you know it's not true."

"Do I?" She opened her eyes, glared at him. "Do I really know that you haven't just been buttering me up for the past six months so you could convince me to stay?"

"You told me earlier tonight you aren't staying so that would have been a pointless endeavor, now, wouldn't it?"

"And you told me you loved me," she accused, anger and hurt overwhelming her, making her legs wobble and her heart shatter. She hit his chest with her fist, the sheet still tightly gripped in her fingers. "How could you say something like that when you didn't mean it?"

"What do you care? It's not as if the words meant anything to you or as if you said the words back to me."

Had that stung? That she'd failed to return his words? With all the Bloomberg women falling at his feet, that she'd resisted his claim of love must have stung.

"Oh, you'd really have liked that, wouldn't you?" she blasted. "If I fell in love with you and then you could manipulate me into doing whatever you wanted?"

He took a deep breath, put his hands over her fist, and held it still against his chest. "I could see how you would equate love with manipulation, Cara, but what I told you had nothing to do with Preston's letter. I wanted you to stay for me."

Even in her anger, she couldn't deny her body's response to his touch, to his bare chest with the trail of hair that ran down his flat abs and disappeared beneath the towel. Good Lord, even the man's bare feet got to her. But for once her body's reaction to him just fueled her anger. Never had she felt so betrayed.

By her body. Her father. Sloan.

Sloan was with her because her father had asked him to be with her.

"You can stop pretending."

His grip remained tight on her hands. "What do you mean? Pretending?"

"You told me in the same breath as you said you loved me that you wanted me to stay," she reminded him. "I know you were just trying to convince me to stay so you could give my father what he wanted."

"I do want you to stay." His forehead creased. "Or I did."

Or he had. Implying he no longer did. Because she knew everything now?

"Fine. It doesn't matter, anyway, because I'm not staying." She jerked her hand free, dropped the sheet and picked her clothes up off the floor. "There's nothing in Bloomberg I want and nothing that could convince me to stay in this horrible town."

CHAPTER ELEVEN

A BLAST OF frigid air hit Cara in the face as she stepped outside her apartment building. She pulled her coat and scarf tighter around her body and reminded herself that she loved this city.

She did. She just…

Oh, no, she wasn't going there. Not this morning. Today was a new day and today she wasn't going to think about Bloomberg or Sloan or anything from the South. She wasn't.

Six weeks had gone by since she'd flown home to New York. Six weeks in which she'd cried her silly heart out to her ex and he'd offered to let her stay in his spare bedroom. She'd taken him up on the offer for a couple of nights, but had quickly found a more permanent place to stay, subletting a room from one of the emergency-room nurses.

The place wasn't nearly as great as the apartment she'd shared with John, but at least it was close enough to work that she could walk.

She'd done what she'd planned not to do. Returned to her old job at the emergency room.

She was right back in her old life.

Except more alone than she'd ever felt.

Which was crazy because she was surrounded by millions—literally—of people.

Cara worked her shift, grateful for the heavy workload because it kept her mind busy so she really didn't have time to dwell on anything other than the next patient.

"Um, Cara, the next guy requested you specifically," her nurse, and roommate, told her as she stepped out of the bay in which she'd just finished seeing a patient.

"What's wrong?"

"Hand laceration. Says he sliced it when getting out of his taxi."

"That's crazy. How'd he do that?"

The nurse shrugged. "Who knows? But he's a looker. Single, too. Apparently, he's just moved here and says he's hoping to find work soon."

"Probably an actor or an artist."

"I didn't ask. I was too busy staring into his eyes. I've never seen eyes that shade of brown before."

Cara's heart gave a jerk. How ridiculous that her nurse's description made her think of Sloan.

She left the nurses' station and crossed the room to the bay where the next patient waited. She pulled back the curtain and looked into eyes that were a particular coppery shade of brown she'd only ever seen on one person.

"Sloan."

God, she looked good. Too good. Maybe he had been wrong to come here. Wrong to think that Cara had felt the same about him as he had about her. Wrong to think she'd have missed him a fraction as much as he'd missed her.

He had missed her. Without Cara, life had lost its

luster. It had been as if he'd been living in a color-filled world and had suddenly been shot into black and white. Nothing glittered. Nothing shined. Nothing captured his interest.

His coworkers had known it. His patients had known it. His friends had known it.

Losing Preston had devastated him. Losing Cara had destroyed what was left.

Even more so when he'd realized, really realized, why he'd lost her. He'd been so wrapped up in what he wanted, a life in Bloomberg, that he hadn't let what Cara wanted ever register. Not really. He'd been no better than Preston, trying to emotionally manipulate her into doing what he wanted of her.

"What have you done to yourself?"

Her question had his gaze dropping to his hand. The nurse had given him a stack of gauze to keep pressed to his cut to slow the bleeding.

All professional, she squirted sanitizer into her hands, rubbed them together vigorously, then gloved up.

Without actually touching him, she lifted the stack of bloodstained gauze from his hand. She flinched at the jagged cut that ran along the frenulum of his thumb and pointer finger.

Her gaze lifted to his, full of confusion and something more. For all her professionalism, she couldn't hide that seeing him affected her.

"Why are you here?" Her voice was low, husky, accusing.

"I'd think that was obvious." He nodded toward his hand. "You promised to sew me up if I ever needed sutures."

Her gaze dropped back to the cut, then lifted to his.

"A trip to New York for simple sutures is a little pricey, don't you think?"

"There's nothing simple about what I need from you."

"Please tell me you didn't cut your hand intentionally."

"You know me better than that."

"No, I don't."

"Yes, you do."

She closed her eyes. "Okay, I know you well enough to know you wouldn't cut your hand on purpose, but no way are you going to convince me that it's a coincidence that you cut your hand and just happen to be in my emergency room."

"You're right. That isn't a coincidence. I came here with the sole intent of finding you."

"So I could suture you?"

"No, that happened when I got out of the taxi." He glanced at the cut again. "I'm not even a hundred percent sure how it happened. I was getting out of the taxi and brushed my hand across a plastic name plate on my suitcase that apparently had a very sharp edge."

Cara just stared at him. "Why are you in New York?"

"Because you are in New York." He glanced around the emergency-room bay. She'd pulled the curtain behind her, but there was no real privacy in the area. "Your shift should be about over. Sew me up, then let me take you to dinner and I'll tell you about the past six weeks."

"No."

"No, you won't sew me up?"

Without another word, she began prepping the wound for suturing. When she was ready to anesthetize him, she asked, "Are you allergic to anything?"

"Just penicillin."

"Noted." She injected the numbing agent into the area of the wound. The medication stung, but within seconds he could no longer feel anything she did.

She opened the suture kit, pulled out a needle with attached Ethilon and a pair of needle holders. As she pushed the needle through his skin and pulled the gaping flesh together, she sighed. "Sloan, this isn't fair."

"I'm the one at your mercy. What isn't fair?"

"I don't want you here."

Hearing her words hurt more than any physical wound that could be inflicted. If he'd believed her, her words would have created wounds no physician could heal.

"I'm banking on that not being true."

She wrapped the Ethilon around the tip of the needle holder repeatedly, tying knots then wrapping in the opposite direction to strengthen the overall effect of the suture's hold. She snipped the thread and quickly set about putting the next suture in.

"I don't understand why you're here. You've got everything you wanted from me already."

"You're wrong."

Her hands trembled ever so slightly, but she kept going, put in another perfect stitch and started a third one. "Before I left Bloomberg, I signed over my father's practice to you, his things. What more did you want?"

"His most prized possession."

"What's that?"

"You."

She tied off, snipped the thread on the third stitch and started a fourth. "You can't have me."

He watched her put in the fourth stitch, knew he was running out of time because five would close the wound completely. "Go to dinner with me."

"I've still got another—" she glanced up at the clock on the wall "—thirty to forty-five minutes before I get off work."

"I'll wait."

"What would be the point?"

"I flew to New York to see you."

"I didn't ask you here."

"You left without telling me you were leaving."

"There was nothing left to say."

"You sold me your father's practice for a dollar."

"It wasn't worth even that."

"You don't mean that."

"Quit telling me what I don't mean."

"You're right. I shouldn't do that."

"You shouldn't," she agreed.

"You left your father's things in the house."

"I didn't want them. I took the only things I wanted."

"Your mother's things?"

"Yes." She tied off the fifth suture, dropped the needle holder, needle and thread onto the sterile tray.

"You need to forgive him, Cara."

"I already have."

Cara had. It had taken her a while to work through her feelings toward her father. The reality was he was gone and she'd never be able to ask him why he'd chosen to do the things he had. But she had a good idea.

Preston had wanted her in Bloomberg. Wanted Sloan to be his son. Wanted his future grandchildren raised in Bloomberg. To him, manipulating their lives to where they would be thrown together had made perfect sense. He had been a man used to taking action, used to making things happen. No doubt her unwillingness to give him what he'd wanted had driven him crazy.

His manipulations had driven her there.

Or maybe it was that she'd actually fallen for Sloan that had driven her crazy.

She should have known better.

"This wasn't how I planned this, you know."

"That you had a plan at all is wrong."

"I should have flown to New York without a plan?"

"You shouldn't be in New York at all."

"Sure I should. I've moved here."

She stopped everything and stared at him. "What?"

"Go to dinner with me and I'll tell you everything."

She didn't want to go to dinner with Sloan. She'd actually told John she'd go to dinner with him and a couple of their friends at a nearby Irish pub. "I just can't, Sloan."

"Can't or won't?"

She hesitated. "I have other plans."

Something in the way she'd said it must have made him think she was seeing someone else, because his expression hardened. "You're seeing someone else already?"

"That's really none of your business."

"The hell it isn't."

She took a deep breath and waited. One. Two. Three.

"Dr. Conner, is everything okay here?" her nurse asked, popping her head behind the curtain.

"Everything is fine, Haley. I'm just finishing with Dr. Trenton."

"Doctor?" the nurse asked, looking impressed as she raked her gaze over Sloan. "What kind?"

"Family medicine. I've just moved here from out of state and actually have an interview here tomorrow with…" He gave the name of the human-resource director and the emergency-room director and gave the nurse a smile that was so amazing the heavens might have opened up and angels sung a tune. "You two are the only people I've met, but I'm really hoping to make friends here soon."

"Oh, wow. Nice to meet you." The woman smiled at him, took his bait, and did exactly what Cara didn't want her to do. "A bunch of us, Cara and I included, are going to O'Grady's, a couple of blocks from here. You want to join us?"

Sloan smiled at the woman, then at Cara. "That would be great."

"Seriously, you invited a total stranger to dinner with us?" Cara rounded on her nurse and roommate.

"Hello, are you blind? The man is gorgeous, intelligent, a doctor." Haley emphasized the words. "And will likely be our coworker very soon. Why wouldn't I invite him to dinner? If he's lucky, I'll invite him to more than that."

"No."

"No?" Her roommate's brows rose. "You calling dibs?"

"No." Cara put her fingers to her throbbing temple. "Yes." She rubbed the pounding. "No. Oh, I don't know. The man drives me crazy."

The woman's eyes rounded and her jaw dropped. "That's him, isn't it?"

"Him who?"

"The Southern doctor you dumped John for."

"I didn't dump John for another man. I left to go home to settle my father's estate. Sloan just worked at my father's practice. That's all."

Haley gave her a "duh" look. "Apparently not if the

man packed up his belongings and moved to New York to be near you."

"He didn't move to New York to be near me."

"Right." Haley looked convinced—not. "Keep telling yourself that."

"There's nothing between Sloan and me."

"Sure, because men quit their jobs and move to another state to follow a woman there when there's nothing between him and that woman." Haley leaned against the nurses' station and pinned Cara with her gaze. "Besides, it's not as if every one of us can't tell that something changed while you were down South, because you came back a different person."

"What do you mean?" she asked, knowing she sounded defensive.

"Because you rarely smile, never want to go out with us any more and look like you lost your best friend."

"My father died," Cara reminded her.

"True, and maybe that's all it is, but now that I've met Dr. Sexy from the South in there, I'd put my money on him being involved."

"You'd lose your money."

Her friend smiled and shook her head. "I don't think so."

Cara wanted to scream. How dare Sloan show up in her emergency room and cause all kinds of chaos? All kinds of speculation about what she'd been doing for the six months she'd been in Bloomberg?

Oh, how she despised him.

Only she didn't and no matter how many times she let the thought run through her mind, it wouldn't take hold.

Why was Sloan in New York? Had he really left the practice in Bloomberg and was moving here permanently? She didn't believe it. He loved Bloomberg. He'd never betray her father that way.

Did she really want to spend the rest of the evening under the watchful eyes of her friends, of John, with Sloan there?

She marched out to his examination bay, practically stomped over to where he sat, his suitcase on the floor beside the bed. "I will go with you, but just because I don't want my friends privy to the explanations you're going to give me as to why you're here."

"Okay," he agreed, as if he'd expected her to go along with what he wanted all along. "When can we go?"

"Dr. Koger is already here. Let me make sure everything is okay, grab my coat and then we'll head out. For a walk. Not dinner," she said, just to feel as if she had some control over the situation.

"Whatever you want."

"We've already established that this isn't about what I want, because I don't want you here."

For the first time he looked pensive. "Do you mean that? Do you really not want me here, Cara? Knowing that I've left Bloomberg and come to New York to find you and do my best to make things right between us, do you really want me to not be here?" He sighed, fatigue washing over his handsome features. "Because if that's the case, I'll go and I won't bother you again."

Cara's heart flip-flopped in her chest like a fish out of water. She wanted to tell him to leave. It's what she needed to do because he could only bring her pain.

But he was here.

He had left Bloomberg and was in New York.

Because he'd come to find her and make things right between them.

"I don't want you to go."

Relief washed over his features. "Thank you."

"For?"

"Being honest."

She narrowed her eyes at him. "I expect the same from you."

"That's easy. I miss you and want to be wherever you are. If that's New York, then I'll live in New York. Wherever you are, Cara, that's where I want to be."

"I've missed you, too." Darn it. Those were tears streaming down her face. She didn't want to cry. Not at all, but especially not in front of Sloan.

"Don't cry, Cara. I never want to hurt you. I'm so sorry that I did." He moved to her, stroked his good hand along her face. "Forgive me."

Cara squeezed her eyes shut. Forgive him. For what exactly? Her father had been the one to do the manipulating. Like herself, Sloan had been a pawn. A willing pawn but a pawn all the same.

"I can't bear to see you hurt." With that he bent and kissed her cheek, kissing her tears away.

Cara turned her head, causing her lips to meet his. She kissed him. She kissed him with all the angst swelling in her chest, with all the ache of not having seen him for six weeks. She kissed him with the passion that had rocked her whole world when she'd walked into the emergency bay and seen him sitting on the examining table.

"So good," he whispered against her mouth, kissing her deeper.

He was right. They were so good.

"Ahem." Haley cleared her throat. "I guess this means you're calling dibs after all?"

CHAPTER TWELVE

SLOAN PUT HIS suitcase down next to Cara's sofa and glanced around the tiny apartment she shared with her nurse. Tiny apartments. Busy streets. Tall buildings. No big open fields or clean air to breathe.

He'd just left Bloomberg and already he missed the town. He'd left a piece of himself when he'd packed his bag the night before and driven himself to the airport.

Six weeks he'd waited for Cara to come to her senses. Six weeks when he'd kept telling himself she would. Six weeks before it had sunk in that she was too much her father's daughter to admit she'd been wrong to leave him. She wouldn't be coming back and for him to try to manipulate her to was just as wrong as all that Preston had done. If he wanted Cara, he'd have to go to her. Would have to give up the life he wanted because being with her was more important than Bloomberg, his practice, the life he'd envisioned there.

Cara was that important.

He'd rather be with her anywhere than without her at the grandest place.

Now all he had to do was convince her of that because, despite their kiss, he knew she was nowhere close to letting him behind her walls.

"Maybe we should have gone with my friends after

all. There's not a lot to eat here," Cara said, turning from having hung their coats in the tiny closet just inside the front door.

"I didn't fly to New York because I wanted to eat, Cara."

"We're not doing that, either," she told him, obviously thinking he meant sex.

"I'd actually rather talk."

She walked across the room and sank onto the sofa. "Because you have a pattern of preferring talking to sex."

He grinned. "You're right, but this time I do."

She stared at him from where she sat. "So, talk."

He ran his finger over the bandage on his hand. "I had exactly what I wanted to say all figured out on the flight here."

"Then this should be easy."

"Nothing about you is easy, Cara."

"Probably not. I'm sorry."

"Don't be. It's one of the things I love about you."

She sucked in a deep breath. "Please, don't say that."

"That I love you?"

She nodded.

"Whether or not I say it doesn't change the truth. I'm in love with you. I have been for longer than you'd believe." He took a deep breath. "Actually, I fell in love with you before we'd even met."

"That doesn't make any sense."

"Probably not, but it's true. Your photos on Preston's office wall fascinated me. Your smile, the sparkle to your eyes, your daring spirit."

"Looking at my photo and wanting me is called lust, Sloan. Not love."

"True, but the way I felt about you went way beyond

lust." He met her gaze. "And Preston knew it. I'm not sure when he figured out that I was in love with you, but he knew."

"What makes you think that?"

"The way he talked about you, teased me about you, shared things about you that I don't believe he shared with anyone else. He let me see you through his eyes and, Cara, that's a beautiful and amazing view."

"I don't know what to say." She was floored by what he was saying. Was it even possible?

"You don't have to say anything. Just listen." He stood and paced across her apartment. "Cara, I'm not single because I want to be alone. I'm a man in love with you and no other woman would do. Will do."

Hope grew in Cara's chest. Could he be telling her the truth? Please, let him be telling her the truth.

"When Preston died I was devastated. Truly, the man was like a father to me, loved me like a son, but I believe that was because of you."

"What do you mean?"

"He knew how I felt, Cara. He knew and he encouraged my feelings, fed them, never let me forget you were out there, waiting for me. Only you weren't waiting for me, because you didn't know I existed outside the fact that your father had a new partner."

"I knew you existed. I detested you."

"I knew that, but I never could figure out why."

"Because you had my father's love and admiration without even trying to. I worked so hard to try to earn his love and respect and he just freely gave it to you. I was jealous. I…I think I still am."

"He loved you, Cara. He really did. He had a hell of a way of showing it, but he did love you."

"The will…" Her voice tapered off.

"Was a ridiculous attempt at playing matchmaker. It wasn't meant to hurt either of us. He just wanted to ensure we had the opportunity to work together, to get to know each other."

"How do you know that?"

He shrugged. "I just know."

"But Bloomberg…"

"Your father loved that town and its people, but he loved you more, Cara. In his mind, you were like him, not your mother. I can't tell you how many times I heard him say that you were just like him. He can't have been talking about looks because you're the mirror image of your mother. He thought if you saw Bloomberg through adult eyes, through eyes not clouded by the past, you'd love the town the way he did."

"I…" She almost said that she did, but did she? Or was she just getting choked up?

"I struggled with your father's requests of me from the beginning. Not because I didn't want you, not because I didn't want you to stay in Bloomberg, because I did. I do. I struggled because I was looking at everything through Preston's eyes and not yours."

"I don't understand."

"Preston believed you really loved Bloomberg and so deep down I believed that, too. Like him, I believed that if you just gave the town, the people, the clinic, a chance, you'd be like me and never want to leave."

"But you did leave."

He nodded. "I don't want to be somewhere you hate, Cara."

"I don't hate Bloomberg. I—"

"It doesn't matter. I've already found two doctors to work at the practice. Casey and another nurse practitioner I've hired are breaking them in. I'm not going back."

"Why not? You can't really be serious about moving to New York."

"I'm moving to wherever you are if you'll have me."

"Sloan…" She couldn't take any more. Not another moment. She stood and walked over to where he sat across from her. Dropping to her knees, she stared up at him. "I didn't want to like you."

"I know."

"Instead, I fell in love with you."

He dropped to the floor beside her, on his knees, cupping her face with his hands. "Tell me we have a chance."

Tears streaming down her cheeks, she nodded.

"I won't give up on us, Cara. I'll do whatever it takes to make this work."

She nodded again because words failed her.

"I want you to be just mine."

"I already am."

"I want us to do this right, to date each other without Preston between us. I want you to spend time with me because it's what you want, and when the time is right I want you to walk down the aisle to me and let me show the world how much I love you."

Her eyes widened. "You want to marry me?"

"This isn't a fling, Cara. I told you that long ago."

"But… Because of my father?"

"Because of you. Because of me. Because I love you more than life itself and I want to wake up beside you, go to sleep beside you every day for the rest of my life."

"I think I'd like that." Then she kissed him.

Neither of them heard the front door open, not until Cara's roommate cleared her throat.

"Fine," Haley intoned. "You get dibs on him, but I'm calling dibs on the bathroom first."

Why did you tell me I really a sense went from with her... - said - and I was - am - her... I was - you - can - not - can - where - you - you was - I... - do... - no... - I... - to her... - she was - up at her... I - her...

I - and I - was you.

He wore you - me - down - hi - to her - with you...

EPILOGUE

CARA ROLLED OVER in the bed and reached for her husband, only to find his spot empty. A slow smile stretched across her face. She knew exactly where he was.

Stretching first, she climbed out of bed, reached for her dressing gown and tiptoed out of her room. He wasn't where she first looked, but she soon found him sitting on the front porch, wearing only his pajama pants, rocking back and forth in the double rocker that had sat on the porch for as long as she could recall.

He smiled when he saw her. "We were trying to keep from waking you."

Her gaze traveled over the precious two-week-old snuggled against his chest, peaceful in the comforting reassurance of his father's heartbeat.

"I'd say you should have, but I must have needed the rest because I didn't hear you get up." She climbed into the chair next to him and reached out to touch their son because she couldn't resist the feel of his soft skin. "Hello, there, little guy. What have you and Daddy been up to out here?"

The baby looked at her from eyes that still partially crossed, yawned, then closed his eyes again.

"I've been telling him about how much I love his mom and how she grew up in this house and used to climb those trees over there and that someday he and I would build a tree house up there where those branches bow out."

"I always wanted a tree house in that tree," she mused, knowing the exact place he spoke of.

He took her hand. "I know. Your dad told me one night when we were sitting out here, talking. He told me if I ever had a kid to be sure to build them a tree house, because he'd never built yours."

"He told me he would," she recalled softly, trying not to let sadness seep in. She'd long ago forgiven her father for his unorthodox methods.

"That's what he said. That you two had bought the supplies and were going to build it together, but then he got called to the hospital and the tree house never got built."

"I remember."

Sloan squeezed her hand. "There will be times I get called to the hospital, Cara."

"There will be times I get called to the hospital, Sloan," she countered.

"But I promise you that Conner will have that tree house."

She knew what he was saying, that it wasn't the tree house he was really promising but that he would be there for their son in ways that she'd felt her father hadn't been for her.

"I know he will." She squeezed his hand back and laid her head against his shoulder, staring at their precious son. "He wasn't a bad father, Sloan."

"He was a good man, a great doctor and the best father he knew how to be at the time," Sloan agreed.

They'd discussed her father many times in the year

since Sloan had come to New York to be with her. Not that they'd stayed.

Her father had been right about many things. Sloan. Bloomberg. Her being a lot like him.

"I owe him everything," Sloan surprised her by saying.

"Why do you say that?"

"Because he brought you into the world and into my life."

Never had she felt so loved as she had the past year. Never had she felt she truly came first with another person until Sloan. He'd taught her so much about herself, about her father, her mother, who she was and who she wanted to be. The wife of a loving man. The mother of their son. A small-town doctor. A member of the community.

"I love you, Sloan."

"Love me forever and that'll be almost long enough."

* * * * *

SECOND CHANCE WITH LORD BRANSCOMBE

JOANNA NEIL

For my family, with thanks for their unfailing
love and support through the years.

CHAPTER ONE

'IT'S BEAUTIFUL OUT HERE, isn't it?' Jake smiled as he looked out over the sea and watched the waves rolling on to the shore. 'I never get tired of looking at that glorious view. I'm just glad I get the chance to come and sit here after work sometimes.'

'Me too.' Sophie returned the smile and then concentrated on carefully spooning golden sugar crystals into her coffee. It gave her a bit of time to think. She *ought* to be content, no doubt about it, but she couldn't get rid of this nagging feeling that before too long everything in her world was going to be turned upside down.

On the surface everything was running smoothly. What could be better than to be here on a late Friday afternoon, taking in the fresh sea air with Jake, on the terrace of this restaurant in the delightful little fishing village they called home? On the North Devon coast, a small inlet in a wide bay, it was an idyllic place to live.

A faint warm breeze was blowing in off the blue water, riffling gently through her long honey-blonde curls and lightly fanning her cheeks. From here she could see the rocky crags that enclosed the peaceful cove and she could hear the happy shouts of children playing on the beach below, dipping their nets into rock pools that had been left behind by the outgoing tide. She had every reason to be happy.

The truth was, though, that she'd been on edge this last couple of weeks…and there could be only one reason for that. Ever since Nate Branscombe had returned to the Manor House her emotions had been on a roller-coaster ride. Maybe she should have expected him to come back once he'd heard about his father's health taking a downward turn. Deep down, she'd known all along he would have to visit his father, Lord Branscombe, sooner or later, but when she'd heard he'd actually turned up she'd been swamped by a feeling akin to panic. She'd gone out of her way since then to avoid running into him.

'This is the perfect place to relax,' Jake said, oblivious to her subdued mood. He sipped his coffee and then glanced at his watch. 'I can't stay for too much longer, though…much as I'd like to—I have a meeting to go to.'

'Ah—the joys of working in hospital management!' She glanced at him, her mouth crinkling at the corners. It was what he was born to do, streamlining what went on in various departments of the local hospital.

Jake Holdsworth was a clever, likeable young man, good-looking, with neat dark hair and compassionate brown eyes. He was a couple of years older than her at twenty-eight, but they'd known each other for several years since he used to regularly come to the village to visit a favourite aunt. They'd become firm friends. Eventually, though, they'd gone their separate ways when they each left home to take up places at university— she went to Medical School and Jake went off to study Hospital and Health Services Management. It was one of her proudest moments when she was at last able to call herself Dr Trent.

'Oh, yes! Budget meetings, purchasing committees, dealing with the complaints of clinicians! It's all go!'

'But you love it.' Their lives had been busy, as each of them worked towards building their careers, and it was only lately they'd met up again. Jake had a keen sense of humour and she liked spending time with him. He always managed to put her at ease, to help her set aside her troubled family situation for a while, to make her forget that life could be a struggle sometimes. He was a restful kind of man and she enjoyed talking to him.

He was nothing at all like Nate Branscombe—the very opposite, in fact. She frowned. Somehow, Nate had the knack of stirring up strong passions in her—for good or bad—but, either way, they were feelings she would far sooner forget. More often than not, he left her in turmoil.

Nate had the kind of bone-melting good looks that sent her heart into overdrive the moment she saw him. Women couldn't get enough of him but, as far as he was concerned, it was all easy come, easy go. His girlfriends each thought they would be the one to change him, but she could have told them they were wasting their time. He would never make that final commitment.

Maybe that was why Sophie had always held back from him. He wanted her, there had been no doubt about it, and she'd been so…so…tempted, but she wasn't going to fall for him, like all the others, and end up being hurt. Nate liked women, enjoyed being with them, having fun, getting the most out of life, but she wondered if he'd ever meet the woman who was right for him. Or maybe Nate was aware that the women he'd dated simply didn't make the grade to be the wife of a future lord.

'Are you okay? You're a bit quiet today.' Jake studied her thoughtfully. 'Have you had a tough day at the hospital?'

'Oh—I'm sorry. I was miles away.' Jerked out of her reverie, Sophie made an effort to pull herself together. 'No, it was fine.'

'Is it some problem closer to home, then? Are you worried about your family?' Jake gave her a wry, coaxing smile before finishing off his coffee and resting his hands on the table, his fingers loosely clasped.

She shrugged her shoulders. 'The usual, I suppose. According to my brother, Rob, my mother's acting weird again, and Jessica's a bit upset because Ryan has to go away to work.'

He gave a sympathetic nod. 'It's not the best timing, is it? How far advanced is her pregnancy?' He hazarded a guess. 'Third trimester?'

She nodded, smiling. 'Thirty-seven weeks or thereabouts. The baby could decide to put in an appearance any time now.'

His mouth made a flat line. 'Not a great time for her to be on her own, then?'

'No.' Sophie frowned. 'Mum and my stepdad are fairly close by for her, though.'

She glanced around as she heard the sound of footsteps approaching. 'Your table's over here, sir,' the waitress was saying, showing Lord Branscombe to a table set in a quiet corner by the wrought-iron balustrade. As he followed her, Lord Branscombe was walking slowly, each step measured and cautious. He straightened, looking towards the table. A bright spray of scarlet surfinia spilled over from a tall cream-coloured planter nearby and beyond the rail there was a mass of green shrubbery, providing a modicum of privacy from some of the other diners.

James Branscombe acknowledged the waitress briefly, but came to a halt halfway across the terrace. He seemed to be struggling for breath, a hand clutched to his chest, and the waitress watched him worriedly.

'Are you all right?' she asked. 'I didn't think— The steps up to the terrace are quite steep… Perhaps I should have taken it more slowly…'

'Please, don't fuss,' he said in a gruff voice. 'Just bring me a whisky, will you?'

'Of course. Right away.' His command had been peremptory but, even so, the girl escorted Lord Branscombe to his table and made sure he was seated before she hurried away to get his drink.

Around them, Sophie noticed the hubbub of conversation had died down. People cast surreptitious glances towards the occupant of the table in the corner and then began to speak in hushed voices. Lord Branscombe, for his part, ignored them all, lost in a world of his own. In his early sixties, he looked older, his hair greying, his face taut and a deep furrow etched into his brow.

'Perhaps he shouldn't be out and about,' Jake murmured, echoing what everyone must surely be thinking. 'He doesn't look well.'

'No, he doesn't,' Sophie said, a touch of bitterness threading her words. 'But when did that ever stop him?'

'True.' He sent her a quick worried look. 'I'm sorry. Of course, you know that to your cost.'

'It's probably the reason Nate's back at the Manor House,' she said, ignoring his last statement. She wished she'd never said anything. After all, what was the point in raking up past history? 'He'll be worried about his father.'

'Hmm…about the estate too, I imagine.' Jake frowned. 'You must have heard the rumours going around?'

'About Lord Branscombe's business venture overseas?'

He nodded.

'Yes, I've heard them.' She winced. 'According to what I've read in the national papers, he's lost an awful lot of money.'

'Nate won't like that—the fact that the press have got hold of the story, I mean.'

'No, he won't.' Nate already hated the press after the coverage his father had received a couple of years ago when he was taken ill at the controls of a light aircraft. This new story would have stirred his dislike of them all over again. 'What makes it worse is that he didn't want his father to have anything to do with the so-called development out there in the first place, but Lord Branscombe wouldn't listen.'

'Oh?' Jake raised a brow. 'How do you know that?'

'I heard Nate and his father having a heated discussion one day when I was out walking the dog. Lord Branscombe wouldn't listen to reason…but then, he never has.' And it was James Branscombe's refusal to take heed of what people said that had left her father in the state he was now. Her lower lip began to quiver slightly and she caught it between her teeth to still the movement.

Jake laid his hand over hers, clasping her fingers in a comforting gesture. 'This must be really difficult for you, after what happened to your father.'

'It is.' She closed her eyes fleetingly. Her father had been a passenger in the single-engine plane that crashed nearly two years ago. James Branscombe had taken the controls against all advice and that decision had left her father with life-changing injuries. He'd suffered a broken back, shoulder and ankle, whereas Lord Branscombe had come out of it relatively unscathed.

Even now she had trouble coming to terms with what had happened.

Jake was concerned. 'You must be upset at the thought of Nate coming back. You and he had something going for a while, didn't you? Until the accident put an end to it.'

'Maybe I had feelings for him, years ago, when I was a teenager, and then later it all came to the fore again just before my father's accident…but we wouldn't have made it work. I realise that, now. We were both studying in different parts of the country for a long while, so I didn't see him very often…and, anyway, Nate could never commit to a relationship. Things went badly wrong for us after what happened to my father. I think Nate only stayed around long enough to make sure his father was okay. He's been back a few times since then, but I've kept out of his way.' She braced her shoulders. 'Do you mind if we don't talk about it?'

Right now she couldn't cope with having it all dredged up again. She steeled herself to put on an appearance of calm and she and Jake talked quietly for a while.

A few minutes later, though, her outward composure was all but shattered once more. She looked up and saw a man striding confidently across the terrace, heading towards the corner table.

'Nate?' The word crossed her lips in a whisper of disbelief and Jake gently squeezed her hand in support. It was a shock, seeing Nate standing just a short distance away from her. When she'd seen him, soon after the crash, she'd been upset, out of her mind with worry, and they'd argued furiously over his father's actions. But when he went away, in her mind, in her soul, she'd still yearned for him.

Nate hadn't seen her yet as he stopped briefly to speak to one or two people along the way. Her mind skittered this way and that, trying to find some means of escape, but of course it was hopeless from the start.

He saw her and his eyes widened in recognition. For a moment or two he seemed stunned. Then he started towards her, a long, lean figure of a man, his stride rangy and confident, the muscles in his arms hinting at a body that was perfectly honed beneath the designer T-shirt and casual trousers he was wearing.

The breath caught in her throat. She couldn't think straight any more. All she could do was drink in his image—the broad shoulders, the sculpted cheekbones and the black, slightly overlong, unruly hair that kinked in a roguish kind of way.

'Sophie.' His voice was deep and warm, a hint of satisfaction there, as though he was more than pleased to see her. He stopped by her table and looked at her, his brooding green gaze all-encompassing, tracing the slope of her cheekbones and the soft curve of her mouth and lingering on the golden corkscrew curls that tumbled over her shoulders. 'It's good to see you again. You look wonderful.'

Unsettled by that penetrating scrutiny, she lowered her gaze. She didn't know how to react to him after all this time. She was distracted by a whole host of unfamiliar feelings that were coursing through her.

His glance trailed downwards, taking in the way Jake's hand covered hers. Then he lifted his head, making a faint, almost imperceptible nod. 'Jake.' He gave him a narrowed look and Jake must have begun to feel uncomfortable because he straightened, slowly releasing Sophie's hand.

'Hi there, Nate. We haven't seen you in a while,' he said.

'I've been busy, working away for the last few months.' Nate's gaze swept over Sophie once more, meshing with hers in a simmering, wordless exchange.

Images flashed through her mind, visions of times past when they'd walked together through the woods on the estate, when her feelings for him were growing with each day that passed. Nate had held her hand, that last day before she went away to Medical School, and led her into a sunlit copse. She'd been eighteen then, troubled about going away and perhaps not seeing him again. She recalled how the silver birch trees had lifted their branches to the clear blue sky and he'd gently eased her back against the smooth white bark. He'd lowered his head towards her and his kiss had been warm and tender, as soft as the breeze on a hot summer's day.

Even now, thinking about it, she could feel his body next to hers, remember how it had been to be wrapped in his arms, to have her flesh turn to flame as his lips nuzzled the curve of her neck.

Jake's voice broke the spell. 'I'd heard something about you being in the States for a while,' he said. 'You've been doing well for yourself, or so they say.'

'I guess so.' Nate turned his attention to Sophie once more. 'I was hoping we might run into one another.'

'I suppose it was inevitable.' Sophie pulled in a deep breath to steady herself. 'You're back here for your father, I imagine?' She looked up at Nate, amazed to find that her voice worked, with barely a trace of nervousness showing through.

'I am. He's not been doing so well these last few weeks, though he would never admit it.' He frowned, glancing to where his father was sitting alone at the table. 'I should go and join him.' There was a hint of reluctance about his mouth as he spoke. 'But I'd like to see you again, find out how you've been doing. I've tried to keep up with how things were going for you and your father, through Charlotte, mostly.' He looked at her intently. 'Perhaps we could talk later?'

She gave a non-committal movement of her head. Charlotte was the housekeeper at the Manor House and she might have expected her to let Nate know what was happening in the village. As to talking with him, surely it would be best, from her viewpoint, to steer very clear of both Branscombes, but especially Nate? Already she was conscious of a knot forming in her stomach and a fluttery feeling growing in her chest. In every way he was dangerous to her peace of mind. Her alarm system was on full alert.

Nate must have taken her gesture for agreement. He nodded once more to both of them and then left, walking over to the table at the corner of the terrace. As Nate went to sit opposite his father, Sophie saw that another man had come to join them—a man she recognised as Lord Branscombe's Estate Manager...his most recent

Estate Manager. Her father had done the job for a good many years before him. She sucked in a sharp breath.

Jake's gaze followed them. 'I wonder what will happen to the estate if Lord Branscombe really has lost most of his money overseas. That's what the newspaper articles are saying…that he's gambled his son and heir's inheritance on a doomed investment and lost.'

'I think there's a lot more to worry about than Nate's inheritance. There are more than two dozen houses on the estate with tenants who will be worried about what's going to happen to their homes.'

Jake's expression was sombre. 'And your father's one of them. It's understandable if you, of all people, feel angry about the way Lord Branscombe's behaved.'

'Maybe.' She frowned. 'But, like I said, I think I'd prefer not to talk about that right now.'

'Of course. But at least it sounds as though Lord Branscombe's finally getting his comeuppance.'

She didn't answer. The waitress came and refilled Sophie's coffee cup, glancing surreptitiously over to where Nate was sitting. Absently, she went to pour a refill for Jake.

'None for me, thanks,' he said, covering his cup with his hand.

'Oh, okay.' Still casting quick looks in Nate's direction, the girl slowly walked away.

Jake made a wry smile. 'He's lost none of his charm, has he?' he murmured, glancing at Sophie. 'He still has that charisma that had all the girls hankering after him.' There was a hint of envy in his voice.

'Mm hmm.' She was hardly immune to it herself—no matter how much she'd told herself in the intervening years that Nate didn't have any power over her feelings, it had taken only a few seconds in his company for him to prove her profoundly wrong. 'I suppose so.'

They chatted for a while, about Jake's work and her job as a children's doctor, until, reluctantly, he glanced once more at his watch. 'I should go,' he said. 'Do you want me to see you back to your car?'

She shook her head. 'No, that's all right. I still have to finish off this coffee. You go ahead. I'll leave in a minute or so.'

'Okay.' He stood up, leaning over to give her a quick, affectionate kiss on the cheek. 'I'll see to the bill on my way out.'

'Thanks.' Sophie watched him leave and then slowly sipped her coffee. It was hot, a new brew fresh from the pot, so she had to take her time. Lord Branscombe, she noticed, glancing idly towards his table, was picking at a plate of food with hardly any appetite, while his Estate Manager was tucking in to a steak and all the trimmings. Nate wasn't eating. The three men seemed to be having an avid discussion about something—the way forward, she supposed.

A short time later she pushed her cup away and picked up her handbag, getting ready to leave.

'You're going already?' Nate must have been watching her because he suddenly appeared at her side, his hand coming to support her elbow as she stood up. 'I didn't want you to leave without my having the chance to talk to you again. Perhaps I could walk with you?'

'I… Yes…I mean…' She was flustered, startled by the way he'd homed in on her, and she stayed silent as he accompanied her down the stairs. By the time they reached the lounge area of the restaurant, though, she had managed to recover her equilibrium enough to say, 'Won't your father be expecting you to keep him company?'

'I'm sure he'll be fine without me for a while. Besides, I've said all I need to say to him for now. He knows my opinion. I've no doubt he and Maurice will be battling things out for another hour or so yet.'

They walked out of the white-painted building and stood by the railings on the cliff path, looking out over the rugged crags to the beach below. 'I suppose I shouldn't have been surprised to see you with Jake,' Nate said. 'You were always good friends…but I saw that he kissed you. Are you and he a couple now?' He was studying her intently. 'Are things serious between you?'

She blinked at the suddenness of the question. She'd forgotten how direct he could be. 'Oh, we met up again fairly recently,' she answered cautiously. 'I think he's fond of me but, really, we're just friends.' She suspected Jake would like to take things further, but after a couple of ill-fated relationships over the last few years, she wasn't about to step into another one in a hurry. Perhaps *she* was the problem. She'd seen what had happened with her parents' marriage and she wasn't ready to put her trust in anyone any time soon.

'I see.' He studied her closely as though gauging her response. He didn't seem to believe the 'just friends' scenario. 'I've always cared for you, Sophie. You know that, don't you? It was hard for me to see you hurting so much after what happened to your father. I felt perhaps you blamed me in some way—perhaps you thought I should have tried to stop my father from flying—'

'You must have known he had angina.' She stared at him, and the pain must have been clear in her eyes. 'Surely there was something you could have done?'

His gaze travelled over her, searing her with its intensity. 'You know what he's like. He never admits to weakness. And I was working at a hospital in Cornwall at the time.' His mouth flattened. 'Sophie, I never wanted there to be this rift between us. You didn't seem to want me around but I always hoped—'

She stopped him before he could say any more. 'No— let's not go there,' she said quickly, anxious to ward off complications. He'd gone away to work abroad, leaving her to pick up the pieces. Perhaps, like he'd said, it was hard for him to see her pain, to witness the heartache his father had caused. 'A lot's happened in the last few years. I'm sure we're very different people now—leastways, I know I am. These past two years have changed me.' She braced her shoulders. 'So what's happening with you? Is there someone in your life these days?'

He pulled a face and shrugged. 'You know me,' he said. 'Can't settle—too much going on all the while.'

'Hmm. And it's going to take time, isn't it, to find the right woman…the one with the class and breeding to take her place at Branscombe Manor?' She said it with a smile, with the wry knowledge that he would most likely exhaust all possibilities before making his pick.

'Oh, you know me so well, don't you?' he said with a short laugh, reading her mind. 'Or at least you always thought you did.' He sobered, studying her thoughtfully.

'Oh, cryptic now, are we?' She let that one pass and asked seriously, 'So…have you come back to sort out the estate?'

He raised a dark brow. 'Can you imagine my father letting me do that? He's never listened to any ideas that don't go along with his way of thinking, from me or anyone. That's why we argued and it's another reason why

I left. He's always been a stubborn man, determined to do things his own way.'

'Yes, but you can be a bit like that sometimes,' she said, challenging him. 'Isn't there a bit of *like father, like son*? After all, you decided on medicine as a career and went your own way, even though you knew your father was set against it.'

'True,' he conceded, 'but I felt very strongly about becoming a doctor. I'm lucky, far more fortunate than a lot of people—I was able to dip into my trust-fund money to get me through university because he wouldn't support me in my choice. He wanted me to go in a completely different direction and learn everything there was about Estate Management so that I could take over one day, but I couldn't do what he asked. We settled the argument eventually, but it was always a sore point with him.'

'Some people around here think you don't care about the estate, or the village.'

'Is that what you believe?' He shot her a lancing green stare.

'I think I know you better than that…but I'd like to hear your side of things.'

He made a grimace. 'It's not true that I don't care. Of course I care. It's my heritage. The Manor has been in our family for generations and I want to keep it that way. I would have been fine with taking on the estate when the time came. I would have done whatever was needed, with the help of managers and estate workers, but my father wouldn't tolerate any of my ideas. Whenever I suggested changes that I felt would be for the better, he said things were all right as they were. He made things impossible for me. I wasn't prepared to be just a figurehead, keeping things ticking along in the same old way.'

She nodded, acknowledging the truth of that. Her father had often hinted at how difficult it was to work with Lord Branscombe. 'How are you getting along with him now that you're back?'

He shrugged. 'We still don't see eye to eye, but we get on fine. When I heard that his angina was worsening I had to come back, to make sure he's all right. I didn't see that I had any choice. My father can be difficult, but he's all I have and I'm his only son, so, despite our differences, we have a strong bond. We've come through a lot together over the years and we've learned to understand one another.'

'And how is he, really? He hasn't been looking too good lately.'

'Do you care?' His gaze narrowed on her, a muscle in his jaw flexing. 'After what happened to your father, do you actually care what happens to him?'

She winced as his shot struck home. 'If I'm honest, I'd like to be able to say...no, I don't care...but I'm a human being and I'm a doctor, so it's probably inbuilt in me to show concern for anyone who's suffering. I still blame him for what happened to my father, but I can't do anything to change the past, can I? Somehow, I have to try to accept it and move on.'

He sighed. 'I'm sorry, Sophie. I'd give anything for it not to have happened.' He reached for her, his hand lightly smoothing over the bare skin of her arm. His touch disarmed her, sending a trail of fire to course through her body and undermine all her carefully shored-up defences. Against all common sense she found herself desperately wanting more.

She couldn't think clearly while he was touching her, holding her this way. She looked at him, absorbing his strong features, the proud way he tilted his head, and wished more than ever that things could be different between them. But it could never be. Not when his father was responsible for the accident that caused her father's terrible injuries.

'I know you're sorry…but it's too late for regrets now, isn't it? If you'd known about his angina earlier, you might have stopped him from taking off that day. But you didn't.' The words came out on a breathless whisper as she gently eased herself away from him. A look of anguish briefly crossed his face and she said quietly, 'I suppose Charlotte has been making sure you knew how your father was getting along?'

'Yes—if it had been left to him I would never have known how serious his condition had turned out to be. He's far too stubborn for that. But Charlotte has been keeping me up to date, especially after the newspaper stories came out about the investments failing and he took a turn for the worse. We all thought his angina was under control, but his condition has deteriorated and it's become unstable of late.'

She nodded. 'Charlotte's always been more than just a housekeeper to you, hasn't she—from when you were little?'

He smiled. 'That's right. She's looked out for me ever since I was nine years old—from when my mother died. She was always there for me when I needed her. She always seemed to know what was going on in my head, the things that frustrated me or made me happy. Truthfully, she's been like a second mother to me. I'll always want to keep her close.'

She smiled. 'I know. I've always liked Charlotte.' She gazed up at him. From a very young age he'd had a number of pseudo-stepmothers foisted on him as his father brought home a succession of girlfriends, but Charlotte had stayed through it all, his salvation, the one fixed point in his young life that never wavered.

It had been hard for him back then. Going round and about the village with him and their friends as they grew up, Sophie had seen the effect the loss of his mother had on him. Perhaps seeing his vulnerability was what had drawn her to him in the first place. His father hadn't known how to deal with such a young, bewildered and frustrated boy and simply lost himself in keeping up with his contacts in the business world, in the City. Gradually, Nate had built a shell around himself. No one was going to penetrate his armour…no one except Sophie. Her parents had been going through a difficult time in their marriage and she and Nate had been like kindred souls.

Nate shot her a quick glance. 'She told me she hasn't seen your father in a while. Usually she sees him around the village, at the post office or the grocery store at least once a week, but lately she's missed him.' His voice deepened with concern. 'How is he? Is he still able to get about in the wheelchair?'

'Yes—he's not been out and about lately because he's getting over a nasty chest infection but he manages very well, all things considered.'

'I heard he was having specialist treatment?'

'Yes, that's right. He was in hospital for a long time, as you know, and we were afraid he might never walk again—but thankfully he's making progress. His spinal cord wasn't cut right through, but it has taken a long time to heal, along with the broken bones—he still has physiotherapy several times a week. It's a struggle for him, but he's not one to give up. He generally tries to take things one day at a time. We're hoping that he'll be able to walk with a frame before too long.'

'I'm so sorry, Sophie. If there's anything I can do—' He tried to reach for her but she took a step backwards. It was far too unsettling to have him touch her. Frowning, he let his arms fall to his sides.

'It's all right; I know you would do anything you can to help.'

'My father said he tried to make amends but your father won't talk to him—all their communication is being carried out through lawyers.'

'That's right.' She shot him a quick glance. 'Do you blame him?'

'I suppose not…but nothing's ever going to be achieved by not talking to one another.'

Her back stiffened. 'The accident changed everything. He should never have gone up in that plane with your father—Lord Branscombe seemed unwell from the first but he insisted he was perfectly fit and able to fly. We'd no idea he was suffering from a heart condition. He should have been stopped. It wasn't even as though the journey was important. He just wanted to check out the site of a new golf course he was planning.' She wrapped her arms around herself in a protective gesture. 'It was totally Lord Branscombe's fault, but afterwards he replaced my father as Estate Manager and didn't even offer him a desk job overseeing things.'

Nate frowned. 'My father said he and the lawyers were talking about compensation.'

She gave a short humourless laugh. 'Compensation? What compensation? Your father had been having angina attacks for some time without telling the authorities. He knew it would affect his pilot licence if he said anything—and when the insurance company found out about that they wouldn't pay out. My father lost everything—his job, his house. He had to sell up and go into rented property.'

'I know—he's in one of the houses on the estate.' Nate's eyes darkened. 'It was me who made sure he had somewhere to go... As for the rest, my father said everything was being dealt with. I'm sorry if that wasn't the case...I've been working away quite a bit in the States, so I couldn't oversee things for myself. I wanted to, but... you didn't seem to want me around and then this job came up...I thought, perhaps, you would find it easier if I wasn't around...'

She turned her back to the sea and leaned against the railing, facing him. She wouldn't be drawn into that conversation again, not now. It was too difficult. 'Will you be going back there?'

'No, this last stint was just a six-months contract in the paediatric intensive care unit in Boston. I have a job lined up here in Devon, so I'll be able to keep an eye on things from now on. It's what I've been working towards. This business with my father just moved things forward a bit.' His gaze moved over her, gliding over her slender curves, outlined by the simple sheath dress she was wearing. 'Better still,' he said in a roughened voice, 'it means I'll be able to see more of you. Perhaps you and I could start over...?'

Her heartbeat quickened and her cheeks flushed with heat. 'Oh, I wouldn't be too sure about that,' she countered in a low voice, her throat suddenly constricted. If Nate thought he could erase the last two years and swoop back into her life, he had another think coming.

'Are you sure about that?' He was looking at her in

that devilish way that had her nervous system on red alert and he was moving closer, the glint in his green eyes full of promise…

It was a promise that never came to fruition. Shouts came from above them, shocking her system and acting like a dash of cold water to propel them away from one another.

'Help, someone…come quickly—we need help here! Is Nate Branscombe still around? Is that his car in the car park?'

Startled, Sophie looked up to where the sound came from, up on the restaurant's terrace. She saw people getting to their feet, rushing towards the corner table, barely visible from this angle.

A man came to lean over the balustrade, looking down at them, waving his arms urgently. 'Nate, will you come up? It's your father. He's collapsed.'

'Call for an ambulance,' Nate shouted back. He was already taking the steps, racing to get to his father, but instead of following him Sophie hurried towards the car park. Her medical bag was in the boot of her car. Her instincts told her they might need it.

When she reached the corner table a few minutes later, she could see that James Branscombe was sitting propped up against the balustrade. His skin looked clammy, ashen as he groaned in pain. Sophie guessed he was having a bad angina attack, which meant his heart wasn't receiving enough oxygen and had to work harder to get what it needed.

Nate had loosened his father's shirt collar and was kneeling by him, talking to him quietly and trying to reassure him. 'Is your nitro spray in your pocket?' he asked, but James Branscombe was barely able to speak.

Nate searched through his pockets until he found what he was looking for and then quickly sprayed the liquid under his father's tongue. The medication would dilate the blood vessels, allowing blood to flow more easily and thereby lessening the heart's workload.

Nate glanced at Sophie as she came to kneel down beside him. His expression was grim; his fear for his father was etched on his face. He seemed relieved to see that Sophie was by his side, though. 'You have your medical bag?' he said. 'That's good. Do you have aspirin in there?'

'I do—they're chewable ones, or he can dissolve them on his tongue.' She opened the case and handed him the tablets. They would thin the blood and hopefully would prevent blood clots from closing up the arteries.

After a few minutes, though, it was clear that Lord Branscombe was still in a lot of pain. His features were grey, his lips taking on a bluish colour, and beads of cold sweat had broken out on his brow. Sophie guessed this was more than a bad angina attack. She was worried for Nate; this must be something he'd dreaded, the real reason he'd come home.

'Morphine?' Nate asked, and she nodded.

'Yes, I have it. I'll prepare a syringe.'

'Thanks.' He administered the pain medication and soon afterwards wrapped a blood pressure cuff around his father's arm. 'He's becoming hypotensive,' he said, frowning. 'I'll put in an intravenous line—as soon as the paramedics get here we can put him on a saline drip to stabilise his blood pressure.'

They didn't have to wait too long. The ambulance arrived shortly, siren blaring, and the two paramedics hurried on to the terrace. They nodded to Sophie, rec-ognising her from her work at the hospital.

Nate swiftly introduced himself and said, 'I think my father's having a heart attack. We need to get an ECG reading and send it to the Emergency department.'

'Okay. We'll make sure they're kept informed.'

'Thank you.'

One of the paramedics set up the portable ECG ma-chine, whilst the other man began to give the patient oxygen through a mask. Nate helped them to lift his fa-ther on to a stretcher, and then together they carried him down to the waiting ambulance.

'His blood pressure's dropping.' The paramedic sounded the alarm and Nate reacted swiftly, setting up a saline drip and giving his father drugs to support his heart's action. Sophie stood by as the three men worked on Lord Branscombe.

'He's gone into V-fib. Stand clear.' Nate called out a warning as his father's heart rhythm went awry and the defibrillator readied itself to give a shock to the heart. He checked his father's vital signs. 'And again, stand clear.'

Her heart went out to him as he exhausted every ef-fort to save his father's life. She saw the worry etched on his face and suddenly wanted to put her arms around him and comfort him, but of course she couldn't do any-thing of the sort.

'All right,' he said eventually. 'He's stable for now. I'll go with him to the hospital.'

The paramedic nodded. 'Okay, we're ready to go. The emergency team's alerted and waiting for him.'

'That's good.' Nate turned to Sophie, who was wait-ing by the ambulance doors. 'I want to thank you for all your help,' he said softly. He reached out and gently cupped her arms with his long fingers. 'I owe you. I'll make it up to you, Sophie, I promise.'

She shook her head, making her soft curls quiver and dance. 'There's no need for you to do that. I was glad to help.' No matter what bad feelings she might harbour about James Branscombe, she couldn't have stood by and done nothing to save him. Working alongside Nate, though, had been another matter entirely. She hadn't been prepared for that and the effect it had on her at all.

The paramedic closed the doors of the ambulance and climbed into the driver's seat. Sophie stood by the roadside and watched the vehicle pull away and it was as though the world was sliding from under her feet. She reached out to rest a hand on a nearby drystone wall.

Nate had been back for only five minutes and already she felt as though she'd been hit by an electric storm. How on earth was she going to cope, knowing he meant to stay around and once more make his home at Branscombe Manor?

CHAPTER TWO

'COME ON IN, then, Charlie.' Sophie let herself into her father's kitchen and then stood to one side to let the excited yellow Labrador follow her. He was carrying his lead in his mouth as usual—she always let him walk home the last few yards untethered. She went over to the sink and filled the dog bowl with fresh cold water. 'Okay, I'll swap you—you give me the lead and I'll let you have the water.' It was a ritual they followed every time they went out.

Charlie obligingly dropped the loop handle and she unclipped the lead from his collar and put it away. He drank thirstily and then dropped to the floor, panting heavily and watching her as she washed her hands and then filled the kettle and switched it on.

She gazed out of the window at the neat lawn and the garden with its bright flower borders. There were scarlet surfinias in tubs that reminded her of that day at the restaurant when she'd met up with Nate. It had been almost two weeks ago and she hadn't seen anything more of him since then but she guessed he was probably spending a lot of his time visiting his father in the Coronary Care Unit.

'He looks suitably worn out.' Her father wheeled himself into the kitchen, breaking into her thoughts and smiling as he looked over at the dog. 'Just as well, if the physio's coming here later on. Charlie can be a bit too exuberant at times.'

Sophie smiled with him and pushed a cup of tea across the table towards him. 'He's not slowing down at all, is he? You'd have thought at eight years old there would have been a few signs of maturity by now, wouldn't you?'

'You would.'

Her father had bought Charlie as a pup, a couple of years after his marriage to her mother had broken down. He'd taken him with him everywhere, even to his work on the estate, and they'd roamed the woods and fields together, man and dog.

'How's the work going with the physio?' she asked now, as she slid bread into the toaster. Every morning before work, she came over to the house to have breakfast with her father.

'We're getting there, I reckon.' He paused, thinking about it. 'When she came yesterday I stood for a while with the frame, and I even managed to take a couple of steps.'

'You did?' He looked deservedly pleased with himself and Sophie stopped what she was doing and rushed over to him. 'Oh, that's wonderful.' She hugged him fiercely. 'I'm thrilled to bits for you. That's amazing.'

'Yes, it's definitely a step forward…' He chuckled at his own joke and she laughed with him. 'Seriously, with all the treatment I've been having at the hospital, and now these sessions at home with the physio, I feel as though I'm making progress. It's been a long job, but I'm getting there at last.'

They ate cereals and toast and chatted for a while, but Sophie soon realised her father had something else on his mind. 'I've been hearing rumours,' he said, 'about Branscombe losing all his money and the estate houses being put on the market. Do you know anything about that?'

'Not really.' She frowned. 'I don't suppose we'll know anything more until Lord Branscombe is out of hospital. Nate's looking after things in the meantime, but—'

'You've seen him again?' Martin Trent's voice was sharp, his whole manner on the alert all at once.

'No…no, not since I saw him that day at the Seafarer when his father was taken ill.' Sophie hastily tried to calm him. It was true. She hadn't *seen* him. She wasn't going to tell him that she'd phoned the Manor House the next day to find out how Lord Branscombe was faring. After all, it had been an innocent enquiry—she'd expected to talk to Charlotte, and it had been a shock to have Nate answer the phone.

'I haven't seen him,' she said again, calmly, concerned that her father was still looking tense, his fingers gripping tightly on the arms of his wheelchair, 'so I assume he's busy visiting his father and talking to the Estate Manager to see how they can keep things jogging along.'

'Hmmph.' He slumped back in his seat. 'I don't want either of us to have anything more to do with that family. James is an arrogant, self-centred womaniser and his son is likely no better.'

'We don't know that Nate is like that,' she said in a reasonable tone. 'He hasn't been around here for any length of time these past few years, has he, so how can we judge him?'

'He can't escape heredity,' her father said flatly. 'It'll be in the genes. That's all you need to know. Besides, he upset you...I know you and he argued but you were broken-hearted when he went away.'

'It was a bad time. You were injured and struggling to come to terms with being disabled and I was confused and lashed out.' Sophie sighed inwardly. She understood her father's dislike of the Branscombes and his hostility towards them. After all, he'd worked for Lord Branscombe for years and had suffered in the end because of it, but it was hard for her to share his animosity towards the son. Her mind drifted back to that last conversation she'd had with Nate.

He'd been more than pleased to talk to her that day when she'd telephoned the Manor House. Despite his troubles, his voice was warm and welcoming, sending little thrills to run along her spine. Just hearing him had made her feel that he was close by, almost as though he was in the room with her. She'd been concerned for him, though, wondering how he was bearing up, and tried to keep her mind on the business in hand.

'They're assessing my father in the Coronary Care Unit,' he'd said when she asked about Lord Branscombe. 'I think they're planning on removing the blood clot and putting a stent in one of his arteries. It's looking as though he'll be in hospital for some time.'

They'd talked for a while and he said, 'I'm sorry things turned out the way they did—both for my father and for selfish reasons... It was good seeing you again, Sophie. I'm sorry our get-together came to such an abrupt end.'

'Yes...though I wasn't expecting you to turn up that day or I—' She broke off.

'Or you'd have gone out of your way to avoid me.' She could hear the wry inflection in his voice and she flinched, knowing what he said was the truth.

Seeing him again had stirred up all sorts of feelings inside her that she'd thought were long since forgotten… or at least pushed to one side. But she didn't want to go there again—to start up something that would only end in distress.

Suddenly uncomfortable, she sought for a way to bring the conversation to an end. 'I'm sure your father's in good hands, Nate. He'll be glad to have you by his side as he recovers.'

'Yes, he seems calmer, knowing I'm here for him.'

'That's good.' She hesitated, cautious about getting more deeply involved with him, and then said, 'I should go. Maybe I'll see you around.'

'Sophie, couldn't we—?' Nate started to speak but she quickly cut the call before she could change her mind.

'Bye.' She had no idea what he must have made of her rush to get away, but he already knew she was trying to keep her distance from him.

'Anyway,' her father was saying, 'it looks as though the tenancies could be at risk if what the papers say is true.' His brow was furrowed with anxiety. 'I've grown used to living here since the crash—I have wheelchair access, handrails…I don't want to have to move…to have to go through the upheaval all over again…'

'It probably won't come to that,' she said, trying to soothe him. 'I suppose we're all in much the same boat—my place is rented too. But, as far as I know, the press stories are just speculation. It's too soon yet for anything to have been decided.'

'Yes, I suppose you're right.' He glanced at Charlie,

snoozing in the corner of the kitchen. 'Thanks for taking him out for me every day. It's good of you and I do appreciate what you do for me—I know how hard you work.'

She smiled at him and stood up to clear away the breakfast dishes. 'I like to keep an eye on you. I was worried when you had that chest infection, but you look so much better now.' She finished tidying up and then glanced at her watch. 'I must go,' she said. 'I have a date first thing with those gorgeous little babies in the Neonatal Unit.'

'Ah…that's the bit you like best of all about your job, isn't it? Looking after the tiny infants.'

'It is.' She gave him a quick kiss and a hug, patted a sleepy Charlie on the head and headed out of the door.

She drove to work, following the coast road for a while, uplifted as always by the sight of the wide, sweeping bay and the rugged landscape of cliffs and inlets. After a mile or two she turned inland, driving along a country road until gradually it gave way to suburbia and eventually the local town came into view. She parked the car at the hospital and made her way inside the building.

There was one baby in particular she was eager to see this morning. Alfie had been born prematurely at twenty-seven weeks and had been looked after in Intensive Care for the last couple of months. She'd followed his progress day by day. Now that he was a little stronger and in a better stage of development, Sophie had been able to withdraw his nasogastric feeding tube and she was keen to see how he and his mum were coping with him taking milk from a bottle. They'd had a few attempts at feeding him over the last couple of days, but so far it hadn't been going too well.

'Hi there, Mandy,' Sophie greeted the young woman who was sitting by the baby's cot, holding the infant in her arms. She looked down at the tiny baby, his little fingers clenched, his pink mouth pouting, seeking nourishment. 'Isn't he gorgeous?'

Mandy smiled agreement, though at the moment the baby was squirming, crying intermittently and obviously hungry. The nurse on duty brought a bottle of milk and handed it to Mandy, who gently placed the teat in her baby's mouth.

Alfie sucked greedily, gulped, swallowed and forgot to breathe, causing him to choke on the milk, and Mandy looked anxious. 'He keeps doing that,' she said worriedly.

'It's all right, Mandy,' Sophie said softly. 'It's something they have to learn, to remember to breathe while they're feeding. Sometimes they stop breathing for a few seconds because the heart rate is a little slow—as in Alfie's case—but we've added a shot of caffeine to his milk to give him a little boost. There's supplemental iron in there too, because being born prematurely means his iron stores are a bit low.'

'Will he always have this low heart rate?' The young mother was full of concern for her baby.

'No, no. Things will get better as he matures. In the meantime, the caffeine will help. You can relax. He's doing really well.' Sophie lightly stroked the baby's hand. 'Look, he's sucking better already.'

She left the unit a few minutes later, after checking up on a couple of other babies, and then went along to the Children's Unit. An eleven-year-old girl had been admitted a couple of days ago, suffering from septicaemia, and she wanted to see how she was doing.

'Sophie—I was hoping I might catch up with you at some point today.' A familiar deep male voice greeted her and stopped her in her tracks. An odd tingling sensation ran through her.

She'd been lost in thought, but now she looked up to see Nate standing by the nurses' station, tall and incredibly good-looking, dressed in dark trousers that moulded his long legs and a pristine shirt with the sleeves folded back to the elbows.

She stared at him, her blue eyes wide with shock, her heart beginning to thump heavily. 'Nate—what are you doing here?' She was startled to see him standing there, and more than a little alarmed to have her sanctuary invaded. This was one place where she'd always thought she was safe.

'I've started a new job here as a locum consultant,' he explained. 'It's a temporary post for the next few months until they appoint a new person for the job. They tell me I'll be in the running for that too.'

She pulled in a steadying breath. 'I'd no idea you were looking for work over here. I suppose you must be pleased that you found something so soon…and so close to home.' Why did it have to be here, in her department? How on earth was she going to cope, having him around?

'I am; I'm very pleased. The opportunity came up and I decided to go for it. This will give me time to decide what I want to do—and of course it means I'll be on hand to visit my father in the Coronary Care Unit here, which is an advantage.'

'Yes, of course.' She looked at him in concern. 'I hope he's doing all right.'

He nodded. 'They went ahead and put a stent in the

artery to prevent another blockage there. He's a lot better than he was.'

'That's good.' Her mind was reeling. It was difficult enough, knowing that Nate was back in the village… but to have him here, working alongside her…that was something she'd not contemplated. How was her father going to react to that news? But she didn't confide any of that to Nate. Instead she did her best to keep things on an even keel. 'I hope you enjoy your time here—I think you'll find it's a very friendly, supportive place to work.'

'I'm sure I will.' His green eyes glinted as he looked at her. 'Knowing that you're here too makes it even better.' His glance moved over her, flicking appreciatively over her curves, outlined by the close-fitting lavender-coloured top and dove-grey pencil-line skirt she was wearing. 'I'm more than glad to know that I'll be working alongside you.'

'I—uh…' She cleared her throat. 'Yes…well…I think I should make a start on seeing my patients. I was just about to do a ward round.'

He inclined his head briefly. 'I'll come with you and try to get acquainted with everyone. I've already met some of the doctors and the nursing staff…like Tracey and Hannah over there…' His mouth made a crooked shape and he gestured towards a couple of the nurses who had been watching him from a distance but who now felt dismayed at being discovered and quickly seemed to find a reason to be going about their work.

She acknowledged their reaction with a faint grimace. Nothing had changed, had it? No doubt the nurses and female doctors had been falling over themselves to get to know him. He seemed to have that effect on women.

They simply couldn't get enough of him. And he probably liked things that way.

'Okay. I thought I'd start by looking in on Emma.' She began to walk towards one of the wards, a four-bed bay close to the nursing station.

He seemed to be searching his memory. 'That would be the child with sepsis?'

She looked at him in surprise. 'You've looked through the notes already?'

He nodded. 'I like to know who and what I'm going to be dealing with, if at all possible. There isn't always time but I was in early today, so I was able to take a quick glance at the notes on computer. They only give the bare essentials, of course.'

She had to admire his thoroughness. 'Well, she and her friend apparently gave each other body piercings—they wanted to wear belly bars but Emma's mother wouldn't allow it, so they did it in secret. Emma's wound became infected and the little girl was too worried about what her parents would say to tell them what was happening. It was only when she started to feel ill that she finally admitted what she'd done. Her parents brought her to A&E but by then the infection was in her bloodstream.'

He winced. 'You have her on strong antibiotics?'

'We do. We had the results of tests back from the lab—it's an aggressive infection, so we've put her on a specific treatment now. Of course she needs support to compensate for failing internal organs while her body's under attack.'

That was the reason the little girl was on a ventilator to help with her breathing and was receiving vital fluids through an intravenous line. Her parents were sitting by her bedside, taking turns to hold her hand. They were pale and distraught, and Sophie did her best to reassure them.

'Her temperature's down,' she said, glancing at the monitor, 'and her blood oxygen levels are improving, so it looks as though the antibiotics are beginning to have an effect. It will take time, but there's a definite improvement.'

'Thank you.' Emma's mother was still sick with worry. 'I just blame myself. I should have known.'

'I doubt anyone would know if a child made up her mind to keep something to herself,' Nate said, his voice sympathetic. 'It's all the rage to get these piercings, but I expect she'll be wanting to give them a miss for the time being, at least.' He smiled and the woman's mouth curved a fraction.

'Let's hope you're right about that.'

Sophie went on with the ward rounds, conscious all the time of Nate by her side. He talked to the young patients, getting a smile from those who were able and bringing comfort to those who needed it. He was a dream of a children's doctor. It was a role that could have been made especially for him.

'Shall we go and get some lunch in the hospital restaurant?' he suggested a couple of hours later, when she had seen all her patients and finished writing up her notes.

'Yes, I'd like that. I'm starving.'

He grinned. 'I thought you might be. You always burned up energy like a racing engine. From what I've heard, the food's pretty good here.'

'It's not bad at all,' she agreed. 'That's mostly down to Jake's intervention, I think. Soon after he was appointed as a manager, he brought in new caterers and the whole place was reorganised. It's only been up and running for a few weeks. They do hot and cold food and there are sections where you can help yourself and get served quickly.'

He pushed open the door and slipped an arm around her waist as he guided her into the large open-plan area. She felt the warmth of his palm on the curve of her back through the thin material of her top and a sensation of heat spread out along her spine. Try as she might to ignore it, she couldn't get away from the fact that she liked the feel of his hand on her body...so much so that she was almost disappointed when he let go of her and led the way to the service counters.

There were several of them, each offering a variety of food—salads, sandwiches, cold meats, and then there were the hot food counters, serving things like jacket potatoes, chilli con carne and tomato-and-basil quiche.

Nate studied the menu board. 'Looks like today's specials are lasagne or shepherd's pie,' he said.

She pulled herself together and tried to concentrate. 'I think I'll have the lasagne,' she said, and added a rhubarb crumble to her tray. Nate opted for shepherd's pie and runner beans but didn't bother with a dessert. He added a pot of tea and two cups to his tray.

'No pudding... Now I see how you keep that lean and hungry look,' she commented.

'Oh, I prefer savoury food above all else.' His gaze travelled over her. 'But the puddings don't seem to have done you any harm at all. You're as slim as ever—with curves in all the right places.' He smiled as a swift tide of heat swept over her cheeks. 'It must be all the exercise you get, working here and helping your father. Charlotte mentioned to me that you walk the dog and do your father's grocery shopping and so on.'

'I do what I can.' They chose a table by the window and sat down to eat.

'I imagine your father and Jake get on pretty well,' Nate said after a while. 'Jake's easy to get along with, isn't he?'

'I guess so. I mean, he and I get on all right. We always have done.' She frowned. They'd always been friends, a bit like a brother and sister, really. She looked at Nate. 'Actually, he hasn't had all that much to do with my father, up to now. They know one another, of course, from when we were younger, but I haven't had occasion to take him home as yet.'

'Hmm.' His green gaze was thoughtful.

'What's that supposed to mean?'

'I expect Jake wants to move things on… He'll want to be more than just friends.' He studied her intently as though memorising every one of her features. 'Any man would.'

She moistened her lower lip with her tongue. 'I don't know about that. I've been down that road before and I've discovered to my cost that things don't always work out too well.'

He raised a brow. 'Perhaps you've known the wrong people.'

'Perhaps.' The truth was, the only man she'd ever really wanted was Nate, but there had always been so many obstacles in their way that it just felt that maybe it was never meant to be. 'You must know from your father's experience that it isn't easy to find the right partner in life,' she said. 'My own mother and father couldn't make a go of it.'

'I think the truth is my father never really got over losing my mother,' he admitted. 'He was something of a lost soul after that. But, as to your situation, it always struck me—as a child growing up—that your father did his best. He wanted the relationship to work.'

'I'm sure he did.' She pulled a face. 'But, well, you know my mother... She could be...flaky, I suppose you'd call it. She was unreliable and her behaviour was odd sometimes. It made her difficult to live with, but of course we didn't know then that she was suffering from bipolar disorder.'

He slid his fork into his shepherd's pie. 'It must have been difficult for you when the marriage broke up and she took you and your brother and sister away to live in Somerset.'

'Yes, it was. It was hard leaving my father, and everything we'd ever known back here.' She frowned, thinking about it. 'Though it wasn't so bad for me because I was getting ready to go to Medical School. I was more worried about leaving Rob and Jessica behind at that time. They were still very young—nine and eleven by the time Mum remarried. It broke my heart to leave them.' Her mouth flattened. 'I still worry about them after all this time—eight years later.'

'But they come to stay with you quite often, don't they? Charlotte told me a long while ago that they're back here whenever they have the chance.'

'That's true. Jessica's married now, though, so I don't know if she'll be over here quite as much.'

His eyes lit up with interest. 'I heard about that—and that she's pregnant. Is she okay? Is it all going well?'

She paused for a moment to savour her lasagne. 'Yes, she's fine. Money's a bit tight—but she and Ryan managed to buy a small terraced house in an old part of town. They're young and they were impulsive, I suppose, in a hurry to be together. Only now Ryan's taken a job which means he has to work away for several days at a time. I'm just hoping they won't have too much of a struggle financially, with a baby on the way.'

He shrugged lightly. 'Young people are resilient. If the love's there I'm sure nothing much else matters.'

She smiled. 'I think that's what I've always liked about you—your optimism. Yes, I'm sure things will turn out fine, eventually.'

He poured tea for both of them. 'And Rob—how's he getting along? He must be sixteen or seventeen by now…'

'He's just turned seventeen. Rob's a typical teenager—full to bursting with teenage hormones right now.' She made a start on her dessert, enjoying the brief moment of sweetness as she tasted the creamy custard on her tongue. 'I think he worries about Dad.'

'I'm sure he does. The relationship between a father and his son is an important one.' He studied her closely. 'It applies to fathers and daughters too. Your father always looked out for you, didn't he? I had the feeling he didn't want you getting too close to me.'

'He was just trying to protect me. I guess he knew you weren't one to settle. And your family heritage is something you can't get away from—you lead a vastly different life to most ordinary people and I suppose he felt in your eyes and your father's eyes I would always be the Estate Manager's daughter.'

He shook his head. 'That's not true. I always thought you were special. I was miserable when you left to go to Medical School—I was glad for you that you were doing something you'd always wanted to do, but sad for myself. We were bound to be separated for a great amount of time, studying in different parts of the country.'

She smiled, unconvinced. As a teenager she'd longed for Nate to look at her the way he'd looked at other women, but it was only when her family was uprooted and she was desperately vulnerable that things had changed between the two of them. He'd reached out to her and offered her comfort, a shoulder to cry on.

But it had been too late. She'd made the decision to leave home to go and study medicine. Those last few times they had been together, he had held her in his arms and there had been the occasional stolen kiss, enough to make her long for more. How could she have allowed herself to get more deeply involved with him back then? He was often away, studying to be a doctor, and when he was home she was too conscious of the great divide between them to let it happen.

Perhaps it was true he had missed her for a while. But he must have known that they were miles apart in other ways. Nate's family, unlike hers, was completely orderly, old school, following age-old traditions, their ways of going on passed down from generation to generation. She sighed inwardly. She would never fit in.

Now, he reached for the milk jug and frowned as he caught sight of a newspaper lying abandoned and open on a nearby table. Sophie followed his gaze and scanned the headlines. There was a picture of Branscombe Manor with a larger image of Lord Branscombe in the foreground.

Lord Branscombe puts Village up for Sale! the headline screamed. *Villagers mount protest!*

'Wretched rumour-mongers,' Nate said under his breath. 'Why do they have to go talking to the press?'

Sophie studied the headlines in consternation. 'Is it true? Is the estate up for sale?'

'Nothing's been decided yet,' he answered shortly, his jaw tense. 'But that doesn't stop the rabble-rousers from going tattling to the papers, raking up trouble, does it?'

'People are worried about the future of the village,' she told him with a frown. 'They know what's happened with your father—how he lost a great deal of money—and they want to know what he's planning on doing about it. Surely you can understand that?'

'Of course I do. But my father is too frail to cope with estate matters right now, and stories like this aren't going to help. He made a mistake—he knows that now. He thought he was buying land with a huge potential for development but it failed spectacularly. He's lost millions of pounds. It's a tragedy for everyone concerned and I know how worried people must feel. Right now, though, he's too ill to deal with any of it and he's passed the reins over to me. Somehow or other I have to negotiate a way out of the mess.'

'I'm sorry.' She laid a hand on his arm, sympathising with his predicament and wanting to offer comfort. 'That's a huge burden for you to take on.'

'It's a headache, I grant you.' He squeezed her hand lightly, sending a warm tide of sensation to ripple through her.

As their lunch break drew to a close, they finished their meal and headed back to the Children's Unit. When they reached it, they found everyone on high alert.

'A little boy's being transferred here from Emergency,' Tracey told them. 'I was just about to page you.

He'll be here in a few minutes. His name's Josh. He's five years old—apparently, he ran out from behind an ice-cream van yesterday and was hit by a car. He was tossed in the air and hit his head on the ground.'

Sophie sucked in a breath. It was one of the worst things a doctor could hear…and as to the child's parents, they must be in torment. 'How bad is it?'

'His skull's fractured in four places and the CT scan shows there's a blood clot forming under the bone. The A&E team decided it would be best to keep an eye on things rather than operate. At the moment he's under sedation and on a ventilator.'

'Okay, we'll keep him that way for now. Let's make sure everything's ready for him.' Sophie quickly stifled her emotional response and switched to being professional. 'I'll take a look at him and then go and talk to the parents. Are they being looked after?'

'Hannah's with them at the moment.'

'Good.' Sophie started towards the side ward, getting ready to receive the little boy. She was very much aware of Nate walking along with her, silent and concerned, his expression taut. He'd been rigidly attentive, on the alert the whole time.

'Does this bring back memories for you?' she asked. 'I know you suffered a head injury as a child.'

'Ah…yes, that's very true. I was nine years old and fell from the roof of an old outbuilding near to the Manor House. One of the gardeners found me unconscious on the ground.' He frowned. 'Apparently, my mother was beside herself with worry back then… She stayed with me through two nights, thinking that I might not make it.'

Sophie was concerned for Nate. 'That must have

made a lasting impression on you.' It must be one of the last major memories he had of his mother. She'd been killed in a car accident a few months later.

'My accident was the reason I wanted to study medicine. I was so impressed, even at that young age, by the way the doctors and nurses looked after me. I was convinced I had to be able to save lives the same way they saved mine. But my mother's death coming so soon afterwards—the car accident that killed her—was horrendous. It was such a shock. It had a tremendous impact on me and it's something I've struggled to come to terms with over the years…in order to carry on.'

She nodded, understanding. Sophie was almost four years younger than Nate, but even back then, as a little girl, she'd been aware of Nate's unhappiness, the way he'd withdrawn into himself. Now, as an adult, she could still feel terrible sadness for that vulnerable little boy.

'I can't imagine how any child could handle something like that.'

He made a brief faint smile. 'As I recall, you were very gentle and caring with me over the next few years. You talked to me and tried to bring me out of myself. I appreciate that, even now.'

'I'm glad if I was some help.'

She prepared herself as the injured child was wheeled into the side ward. He was deathly pale, breathing oxygen through a tube that had been inserted in his windpipe, and there were tubes and wires connecting him to equipment and monitors used in the transfer.

Immediately, she did a quick but thorough examination. 'Tracey, will you do fifteen-minute observations, please?—limb movement, pupils, blood pressure, temperature and verbal response and so on. We'll need to monitor intracranial pressure. A small blood clot might resolve on its own, but if the swelling gets worse he'll have to go up to Theatre to have it removed, so everyone needs to be looking out for that.'

'I'll see to it.' Tracey started on the first round of observations, noting the results in the patient's chart.

Sophie and Nate went to talk to the parents. They were sitting in the waiting room with Hannah, still very upset, but they were calm enough to recount the incident.

'I carried him to the ambulance,' his father said. 'He was bleeding from his ear and he was so quiet and limp in my arms. I was scared. I didn't know what was going to happen to him.'

Stressed, Josh's mother clasped her fingers together. 'We're still in shock,' she said.

'It's a difficult time for you,' Sophie agreed. 'But I promise you we're doing everything we can to make sure he's comfortable.'

'Is he…is he going to be brain damaged?' The father voiced what both parents must be thinking.

'I wish I could give you definitive answers,' Sophie said, 'but it isn't possible just now. The healing process takes time but he's young, and young people have remarkable powers of recovery. We have to be patient and wait and let nature do its work.'

'Dr Trent is very experienced in looking after children with these types of injuries,' Nate said, and Sophie absorbed his comment in surprise. Had he checked up on her qualifications? As the new locum consultant, he would probably have access to staff records. Or maybe the head of the unit had told him all about her. 'We'll let you know about his progress every step of the way,' Nate added. 'You'll be able to sit with him as soon as we have him settled, and we can arrange overnight accommodation in a room close by if one or both of you want to stay with him.'

'Thank you…thank you so much.' Josh's mother wiped away a tear. 'He's so tiny. I can't believe this is happening.'

They talked for a little while longer, and then Sophie and Nate left them in Hannah's care. The nurse would take them along to see their son in a few minutes.

Sophie spent the rest of the afternoon making sure that Josh's condition remained stable and that her other small charges were being looked after. She scanned lab reports and dictated her notes and then handed over to the doctor who was coming on duty to take her place.

'Are you off home now?' Nate asked, coming after her and watching her retrieve her bag from her locker. 'I expect you have plans for the evening?' He didn't ask her about Jake, but somehow she guessed that was on his mind. He just wouldn't believe that Jake was only a friend…

'Yes, I do, but I have to go and walk Charlie and pick up a few bits from the shops first of all,' she said. 'Aren't you about due to finish your shift too?'

He nodded. 'I'm just going to stay and tidy up a few loose ends before I go. I'll walk with you to your car, though, if that's all right. I could do with a breath of fresh air.'

'That's fine.' They left the hospital together, walking out through the landscaped gardens to the car park beyond. All around them, stretching far into the distance, they could see the beautiful Devon moorland.

Nate took a moment to take it in as they came to stand by her car. 'I love this county,' he said, looking around.

'Whenever I've been away, no matter where I am in the world, I always want to come back here.'

'It's a wonderful place to live,' she agreed. 'I'm certainly glad I came back to the village.' She glanced at Nate, a small line creasing her brow. 'Your ancestral home is here, though, isn't it? How's that going to work out for you? Will the Manor House be safe, with everything that's been happening? You haven't really said anything about how you're going to be affected by all this.'

'I think the house at least should be secure,' he said. 'My father hasn't mentioned any problem with it.'

'But the estate *is* at risk, isn't it?' she persisted. 'I know you don't like to think about it, but the stories in the papers aren't unfounded, are they? Is there any chance that your father will sell up?'

His shoulders moved stiffly. 'He was approached by a would-be buyer—Peninsula Holdings—some time ago. He was considering their offer, but then he had his heart attack and everything's been put on hold. He's handed all the business dealings over to me, and I have to make a decision soon, but I still need to make up my mind on the best course of action.'

Sophie frowned. 'I've heard of that company,' she said, suddenly uneasy. 'They're a business conglomerate, aren't they—a company that likes to pull down properties and build hotels in their place?'

'It's true—they're a company generally interested in development, but that doesn't automatically mean they'll want to knock down the cottages on the estate. They might prefer to keep up the tenancies.'

'Really?' She raised a brow at that. 'From what I've heard of their other operations, if they do that they're quite likely to put up the rents—to a level that people can't afford.' Perhaps her father had been right to be worried all along.

'The rents are quite low, and have been for some time,' Nate said calmly. 'There was some talk of offering people the opportunity to buy their properties rather than rent.'

'My father wouldn't be able to do that.' Sophie shook her head, making her honey-gold curls dance. 'And I'm not sure *I'm* in a position to do that right now either. I'd need to come up with a substantial deposit, and that won't be easy at the moment. I've been doing what I can to help out Jessica—she needed funds when they bought the house—and now I'm helping my father. He's having private physio treatment at the moment, and that doesn't come cheap.'

She frowned. 'Is this development company going to put me out of a home, along with all the rest? Can't you do something to put this right, Nate?' Her blue eyes pleaded with him. 'There are too many people who stand to have their lives turned upside down the way things are at the moment.'

'You don't have any need to worry, Sophie. I won't let anything bad happen to you.'

'No?' She looked at him uncertainly. 'What could you do to make this go away?'

He smiled, a compelling, enticing smile that made her insides quiver with excitement and longing. He slipped his hands around her waist and drew her to him. 'You could always come and live with me at the Manor House. You could have anything you want there. You know I've always wanted to keep you close.'

He lightly caressed the curve of her hips and wrapped

his arms around her, drawing her into the shelter of his long, hard body.

Her mind fragmented, her willpower crumbling as she felt the heat emanating from him, felt the powerful muscles of his thighs against her legs. 'I've always wanted you, Sophie,' he whispered.

A pulse throbbed in her temple, and a wave of heat ran through her from head to toe. Her wilful body was saying *yes, yes, please* to the temptation of being with him, locked in his seductive embrace, but the sensible part of her mind was telling her this was madness. What was she thinking of, letting him coax her this way?

'I can't,' she said huskily. 'There's just too much water under the bridge with us, Nate—you know that.' She closed her eyes briefly at the thought. 'Plus, my father would have a stroke.'

'Ah…I wouldn't want that to happen,' Nate murmured. 'But maybe you could bear my offer in mind… for some time in the future, perhaps? There is still something between us; I can feel it…'

She pushed against his chest with the flat of her hand. 'I think that's highly unlikely,' she said.

'Maybe.' A smile played around his mouth. 'But, like you said, I've always been an optimist.'

CHAPTER THREE

'OH, THAT'S GOOD to see. He's feeding much better now, Mandy.' Sophie watched in awe as the tiny infant lay in his mother's arms, suckling hungrily at the bottle of milk formula she was holding. He was wrapped tenderly in a beautiful super-soft Merino wool shawl. Alfie's eyes were wide open, the deepest blue, and he looked up at his mother with perfect trust.

A lump formed in Sophie's throat. She worked with babies and children all the time, but would she ever experience that profound joy of holding her own baby close to her heart? It was a difficult question to answer. The father of her baby would have to be the one and only man for her, the love of her life, because after the disasters that had occurred in her family she didn't want to make the same mistakes they'd made. She wanted a relationship that would stand the test of time…but was that going to be possible?

She closed her eyes briefly. Nate would make a wonderful father… She could see him holding their child in his arms…holding the baby against his bare chest. Unbidden, the image came through in startling clarity, along with a rush of heat that suffused her whole body. Nate was everything she was looking for in a man. He could turn her blood to flame with a single glance and just thinking about him in that way caused a wave of dizziness to engulf her. It could never be…he would never settle, and he wouldn't choose to spend his life with her, the daughter of a man who had worked for his father, would he? How could she contemplate such a thing? She must be out of her mind, even thinking along those lines!

She'd do far better to concentrate on the job in hand, wouldn't she? Chiding herself inwardly, she straightened, finished checking up on her tiny charges and with a new, brisk determination left the Neonatal Unit and went to look in on the rest of her young patients on the Children's Ward. Thankfully, Nate was nowhere to be seen. She didn't think she could cope with having him around just now.

'He's gone up to the Coronary Care Unit to see his father,' Hannah said when Sophie came across her a little later on. The young nurse frowned, pushing back a stray lock of chestnut-coloured hair. 'They were aiming to get Lord Branscombe out into the rehabilitation garden this morning but he wasn't well enough, apparently. He's been very breathless lately.'

'I'm sorry to hear it.' Sophie frowned. 'Nate must be very worried.'

Hannah nodded. 'He is.' She'd obviously been talking to Nate quite a bit lately. That was the way with him—he got on well with everyone, and the nurses especially had taken to him. Did he return their interest? Sophie wasn't at all happy with the way her thoughts were going—it was quite possible that he would start dating any pretty girl who caught his eye… Wasn't that warning enough that she should steer clear of accepting Nate as anything other than a colleague? Her stomach churned uneasily.

She left Hannah after a minute or so and went to look through the patients' files in the wire trolley by the desk, searching for five-year-old Josh's notes. She and the rest of the team were worried about the little boy's head injury and she wanted to check up on his medication and observation chart. A further CT scan this morning showed there was a very slow bleed beneath the skull bones and the pressure inside his head was rising.

Looking at the little boy this morning had left her feeling worried. Pale and unmoving, his fair hair tousled against the pillow, he'd seemed incredibly vulnerable and her heart turned over at the sight of him. If the medication didn't resolve the problem, she would have to do something fairly soon to prevent a dangerous downturn in his condition.

'Hi there, Sophie.' Jake walked towards her and greeted her, smiling. 'I've been looking for you.'

Surprised to see him, she gave him a quick answering smile. As a hospital manager, he spent most of his time in his office, so she hadn't expected him to venture down here. He wasn't an impulsive man. 'Hello, Jake. Is everything okay?'

'Yes, absolutely fine.' He nodded. 'On the face of it, I'm down here looking for Tracey. I need to ask her to try out a new batch of disposable syringes—but I was hoping to see you. I wanted to tell you that I won't be able to come with you to the village fête on Saturday, after all.'

'Oh, that's a shame.'

'It is.' He looked genuinely downcast. 'I'm sorry—I was really looking forward to spending the day with you, but I have to go and talk to a couple of people I used to work with in Cornwall. They've been trying out a new supplier for things like cannulas and rubber gloves—

equipment we use all the time—and they've supposedly made a huge saving in their hospital budget. I'm thinking of using the same supplier here, but I want to know how their trial went before I do that. Saturday's the only day we can all meet up.'

'That's all right. Don't worry about it.' She made an impish grin. 'I'll have Charlie for company. I dare say he'll drag me through all the mud in the playing field before we get to the enclosure where the dog show's taking place.'

'Playing field?' He lifted a brow. 'Oh, you don't know about the change of venue, then?'

'It's not going to be at the school?' She shook her head. 'No, I haven't heard anything…but then, I've been very busy lately, with one thing and another.'

'The school had to cry off—the mobile classroom unit is being delivered ahead of time, so the headmaster asked around to see if any other organisation could offer a field. Nate Branscombe stepped in and told the committee they could use the grounds of the Manor if they wanted. There'll be marquees if the weather turns bad, or the old stable block—it was a better alternative than the village common, by all accounts. Anyway, they're busy putting up notices all over the village.'

'Oh, I see.' That had come as a bit of a shock. She wasn't sure how she felt about spending the day in the grounds of the Manor. She studied Jake thoughtfully. 'How do you know all this—you're not on the committee, are you?'

He shook his head. 'Nate told Hannah and she told Tracey… You know how the grapevine works.'

'Hmm.' Apparently it didn't extend as far as Sophie, but in this instance that might be because they were worried about how she'd feel about going to an event at the home of her father's arch-enemy. They were probably right to have their doubts...but most likely they were waiting to tell her at the last minute.

'Is it going to be difficult for you?' Jake had picked up on her thoughts. Certainly, her father would be annoyed if she went there—he was already in a grumpy mood after she'd told him she was working with Nate, but she didn't see how she could get out of going to the event when she'd been roped in to open the proceedings on behalf of this year's charity—the Children's Unit.

'I think my biggest problem will be telling Dad,' she told him. 'He's already upset because Peninsula Holdings have sent out men to conduct land surveys on the estate—the tenancies could all be at risk—so any dealings I have with the Branscombes are likely to set him off.'

'Oh, dear.' Jake put an arm around her and gave her a hug. 'It's going to take a while for him to get over this latest blow, isn't it?'

'I think so, yes.' She nodded, comforted by the brief hug, until she looked up and saw with a faint shock that Nate had come into the room and was watching them, his green eyes assessing their clinch with obvious suspicion.

'Something wrong?' he asked.

Sophie eased herself away from Jake and braced her shoulders. 'Nothing I can't handle,' she said.

'That's always good to hear.' He studied Jake, his expression taut. 'Is there something we can do for you, Jake?'

Jake took a step backwards as if he was getting ready to move away. 'No, no... I'm looking for Tracey—I need her to road-test some equipment I've ordered from a new supplier. Trying to save money wherever, you know...'

'She's taken a child down to X-ray,' Nate said curtly. 'I expect she'll be on her way back from there by now.'

'Oh, okay, thanks... I...I'll go and find her.' Jake raised a hand in a goodbye gesture to Sophie and headed for the exit doors.

'He's doing his best for this hospital, you know,' Sophie said, her blue eyes narrowing on Nate. He wasn't being uncivil towards Jake, but there was a definite friction in the atmosphere.

'Yeah, I know.' His green gaze lingered on her, dark and unfathomable.

She frowned. 'But you seem to have a problem with him...?'

'Mmm...you could be right...' His glance shimmered over her. 'It's what he's doing for you that bothers me.'

Her mouth made a faint wry quirk. Her relationship with Jake was none of Nate's business...but it kind of made her feel warm inside to know that he might be just a bit jealous. Perhaps he did actually care for her, deep down. Would there ever be a chance his feelings went further, and that she and Nate might get together? A strange tingling sensation started to run up and down her spine at the thought.

She gave herself a mental shake. She really couldn't afford to explore that notion, could she?

'Perhaps we'd do better to concentrate on the job in hand?' She gave Nate the file she'd been reading. He studied her, his eyes dark and brooding, but she ignored that and commented instead on the patient's folder. 'I'm concerned about Josh Edwards. I don't think the medication alone is going to be enough to resolve the situation,' she said. 'I think we should get him up to Theatre so he can be fitted with a drainage tube to relieve the pressure inside his head. The steroids and diuretics on their own aren't going to keep things under control.'

He glanced through the file and came to a swift decision. 'Okay. Notify the surgeon and ask Hannah to prep the boy.'

'Do you want me to talk to the parents?'

He shook his head. 'No, I'll do it. You might want to go and talk to the little girl with the belly piercing—she was asking for you.'

'Was she?' She smiled. 'From what she was saying yesterday, I expect she wants me to reassure her that there won't be a scar and that she can eventually go back to wearing crop tops. I looked in on her earlier this morning, but she was sleeping peacefully. The antibiotics seem to be dealing with the infection at last.'

'That's good. It's always nice to know when the treatment's working.'

'It is.' She glanced at him. 'Is there any news about your father? Is he making any progress?'

His mouth flattened. 'It's going to take time, I think. The heart attack caused damage to the heart muscle and he's finding rehab a strain. I'm booking him into a convalescent home so that he can rest and get the help he needs. We'll be transferring him there on Friday, so I should be able to check on him on Saturday morning and still do the honours at the fête in the afternoon. I've said I'll call out the winning raffle numbers.'

She nodded. 'I only heard about the change a little while ago. Jake was telling me that you're letting the organisers use the Manor. Aren't you worried about the damage that might be done to the grounds—your father's always been very particular about the way they look?'

'Not really. He's left everything up to me, and as far

as I'm concerned, the old saying is true—what the eye doesn't see, the heart won't grieve over... Anyway, we have skilled groundsmen who know how to put things right afterwards. I'm more worried that villagers might boycott the event because of everything that's been in the newspapers about my father and the estate. There's been a lot of bad feeling, and word soon gets around. It would be a shame if that happened—it would be good to raise money for the Children's Unit. I certainly wouldn't want to jeopardise that in any way.'

'I don't think you need have any worries on that score. Everyone wants to contribute—I know a lot of people have been working very hard to try to make sure it's a success.'

'Well, let's hope it all turns out okay.' His gaze moved over her. 'I'll see you there, I hope?'

She hesitated, thinking about the implications of that, and his gaze darkened. 'Yes,' she said. 'I'll be there to represent the Children's Unit.'

'I suppose Jake will be with you?'

She shook her head. 'He has to go to a meeting with some ex-colleagues in Cornwall, so he cancelled on me. But I'll have Charlie with me. I've entered him in the dog show, and I'm just hoping he'll walk properly on the lead and not show me up! He gets excitable if there's a lot going on. He might try to head for the flower borders if I don't keep a tight hold on him.'

He grinned. 'Oh, I can imagine... Charlie's quite a character, isn't he? I remember when he was a pup I was back home for a couple of weeks in the summer, and he dug up the lawn at the back of the Manor. My father was apoplectic when he saw a dozen or so holes appear in his pristine turf, but I couldn't help seeing the funny side. Your father was chasing Charlie, trying to stop his antics, but Charlie thought it was all a good game and kept stopping to dig a bit more. As soon as your father caught up with him, he ran off. The more he was chased, the more fun it was.'

Sophie rolled her eyes. 'He's always been a handful. But hopefully he'll behave himself on Saturday. At least he's grown out of digging holes.'

He smiled. 'I'm glad you're going to the fête.' A gleam of anticipation sparked in his eyes. 'I'll look forward to seeing you there.'

A quiver of nervousness started in the pit of her stomach. 'Yes, you too.' She set her mind on her work and went off to sort out the arrangements for Josh's operation.

To her relief, everything went smoothly. The neurosurgeon treated the request as an emergency and the little boy was whisked up to Theatre. Once there, the surgeon implanted a small silicone tube into the subdural space in Josh's head to draw off blood that was forming there, and the pressure on the little boy's brain was instantly lessened.

Sophie went home that day feeling much happier about his progress. Josh was still sedated for the moment, but she knew he stood a much better chance of recovery.

The day of the fête arrived—a gloriously sunny afternoon—and Sophie set off early with Charlie to walk to the Manor. Their route took them along the cliff top, with moorland stretching away into the distance. Soon, Branscombe Manor came into view, situated high up on a hill, looking out over the landscape, a beautiful yellow stone mansion formed in an elongated U-shape with two gable-ended wings making the U. Over the years there had been side extensions added towards the back of the house, again with magnificent gable ends.

The house was architecturally superb, with stone mullioned windows fitted with leaded panes. The glass sparkled in the sunlight and she paused to gaze at the house in wonder as she approached it from the long curving driveway. But then her attention was distracted by the arrival of a large white catering van turning in off the lane.

There would be burgers and hog roasts and all manner of refreshments laid on for the hungry visitors. Stalls had been set up on the sweeping lawn at the front of the building, with striped marquees to one side where people could sit at tables and enjoy a cup of tea or coffee. Further along she saw another marquee where alcoholic drinks were being served.

Sophie looked around. As a teenager, she'd come here often with her father, helping him as he carried out various tasks around the Manor. All those memories came flooding back now, as she gazed once more at the imposing house and well-tended gardens. At the side of the house there was a walkway through a stone arch that led to a rose garden and beyond that there was a landscape of trees and shrubs.

'Hi, Sophie. Things are looking good, aren't they? We've a great crowd here already.' Tracey greeted her cheerfully, her fair hair tied up in a ponytail, her grey eyes lighting up as she saw Charlie. She bent down to stroke him. 'Shall I take him for you while you go and do the honours?'

'Oh, bless you. Thanks, Tracey.' Sophie handed over the dog, who went willingly, pleased to be fussed and patted and generally crooned over. His tail wagged energetically.

Sophie stepped up on to the dais and set about formally opening the proceedings. 'We want you to have a great time here today,' she told everyone. 'We've all kinds of fun things for you to see and do this afternoon—there's face painting for the children, a karate demonstration taking place in the South arena at two o'clock, and music from our favourite band all afternoon. Don't forget to look in on the flower and plant marquees while you're here, and there are all sorts of cakes, jams, pickles and chutneys for sale in the home produce section. Above all, remember that any money you spend here will go towards buying much-needed equipment for the Children's Unit at the hospital. Please—enjoy yourselves.'

'Well said. That's the aim of the day.'

Sophie glanced around, her stomach tightening in recognition as she saw that Nate was waiting to take his turn on the stand. He looked good, wearing casual chinos and a crisp open-necked shirt that revealed a glimpse of his tanned throat.

Gesturing to him to come and take the microphone from her, she introduced him to the crowd and then stepped down. The atmosphere changed almost immediately as he took to the stage. People weren't sure how to react to him—it was clear in the silence that fell over them and in the way their expressions changed from smiling to sombre. His father's poor investments and lack of judgement had come down to haunt the son.

'Thank you, Sophie,' Nate said. He looked briefly at Charlie, who was busy trying to wind his lead around Tracey's legs in his efforts to get back to his mistress, and then he looked out at the sea of faces. 'Ah...I should mention there's a dog show too, for any of you who haven't yet had time to glance through your programme. It'll be held in the East Meadow at two-thirty.' He looked bemused as Tracey swiftly tried to untangle herself and Charlie began to pull her exuberantly towards Sophie and a child who was licking an ice cream.

'Among other things, there will be an obedience training exercise. I'm not sure if Charlie here will be a good candidate for that—he might be considered a bit of a disruptive element.' There was a ripple of laughter among the crowd as Charlie's ears pricked up at the mention of his name. The dog quickly turned tack, heading up on to the dais, pulling Tracey along with him. Worried, Sophie followed.

Nate grabbed hold of the leash from a relieved Tracey and then wound it firmly around his palm. 'Of course, he might do well in the sledge-pulling event.' Another murmur of amusement. He looked at the overexcited dog and said briskly, 'Charlie—sit!' To Sophie's amazement, Charlie sat, looking up at Nate with an expectant, adoring expression.

'Okay...' Nate turned his attention back to the audience. 'I'll call the raffle results at the end of the afternoon—we've a television as first prize, a hamper to be won, bottles of wine, and a whole array of wonderful things which you'll see on display when you buy your raffle tickets. Go and have a great time.'

Nate stepped down from the stage, bringing Charlie with him. 'Are you okay, Tracey?' he asked.

The nurse nodded. 'I just feel a little silly, that's all. I didn't expect him to go racing off like that.'

'I'm sorry,' Sophie said. 'Perhaps obedience classes

would be a good idea, after all—except he's probably a little too old for them by now.'

'That's up for debate,' Nate said, laughing.

Tracey walked with them for a while as they wandered around the stalls and checked out the games on offer. Sophie tried spin-the-wheel and won a cuddly toy. 'That's one for the Children's Unit,' she said happily, holding on to the golden teddy bear. At the first opportunity she would pass it on to one of the organisers.

Nate had a go on the rifle range and hit the prime target, sending a spray of water to fall on Charlie's head. The dog promptly shook himself and showered everyone in the vicinity. 'Aargh, I'm sorry,' Sophie said, pulling the Labrador away.

'My fault,' Nate commented with a smile. 'I might have known he would try to get his own back.'

Tracey met up with a friend and went off with her to buy candy-floss, leaving Sophie and Nate to walk round the rest of the stalls together. They bought burgers from a van and walked along, eating them as they went. It was fun, until they began to be interrupted by villagers who stopped Nate and asked him about the tenancies on the estate and about the activities of Peninsula Holdings.

'What's going to happen to my home?' one man wanted to know. 'This company—Peninsula Holdings— has been sending men to measure up and ask a lot of questions. My tenancy's up for renewal in a few weeks. It always used to go through automatically, but what's going to happen now? Am I going to be put out of my home? Where am I going to go with my family?' He was understandably angry, disgruntled by the way things were going, not knowing how to plan for the future.

'Like I've told everyone else who's asked,' Nate said,

'nothing's been decided yet. Peninsula Holdings are looking into things to see if they want to do a deal. I may decide it isn't going to work. In any case, no one's going to be turned out at a moment's notice. It could be that you can go on renting, or any new buyer might want to offer the properties up for sale, but you would be given first option to buy. In any event, we'll make sure you're offered alternative accommodation.'

'And what if I don't want it? What if I don't want to move away? We've lived here in the village, in this house, all our lives.'

'I know…and I'm really sorry. I understand this is a difficult time for you.' Nate tried to soothe him, to calm all the people who came to complain or ask about what was going to happen, but nothing he said could appease them. Sophie could understand how they felt. It was all so unsatisfactory, with everything left up in the air, but she sympathised with Nate. She didn't see how he could tell them anything different if he was still awaiting the outcome of negotiations.

They headed over to the East Meadow for the dog show and watched the dog trials taking place. Sophie sighed. 'They're all so clever, aren't they, listening to what their owners say and going where they tell them to go?' She glanced at Charlie, who was panting, eager to get involved. 'Not so with this one, though,' she said with a smile.

Nate chuckled. 'He's one of a kind,' he said, tickling Charlie's silky ears. 'I think dogs need to listen if they're to learn, but he's never seemed to have that connection between ears and brain.'

She laughed. 'Oh, well, here goes… It's the competition for the best-looking dog—that's one thing he *is* good at. He's always been beautiful to look at.'

He watched her get ready to walk the dog over to the line-up. 'You make a perfect team,' he said. His glance shifted over her slender figure, neatly clad in blue jeans and a sleeveless top. She was wearing her hair loose, the curls tumbling down over her shoulders.

Unexpectedly, he took his phone from his pocket and swiftly took a photo. 'Two beautiful blondes.' He looked at the image on the screen and a glint of satisfaction came into his eyes. Sophie was oddly still for a moment, the breath catching in her throat at the casual compliment. Then she collected her thoughts and set off with Charlie, conscious all the time of a warm glow starting up inside her.

She came back to Nate a few minutes later, but there was no rosette to show for their efforts. 'I can't believe you were outshone by an Afghan hound,' she told Charlie. 'Don't let it bother you—you're way better-looking than any dog here.'

Nate smiled. 'Better luck next time, maybe.' He glanced at Sophie, his expression sobering. 'I'm still being pounced on from all sides. Shall we try and get away from here for a bit, before anyone else comes up and tries to waylay me? Have you seen everything you want to see for the time being?'

'Yes, okay. Where do you want to go?'

'I thought we might take Charlie for a walk by the river—that might wear him out for a bit.'

She smiled. 'Okay. I think he'll definitely be up for that.'

They left the meadow and walked along a footpath until they came to the riverbank. The water was fairly deep at this point, flowing freely on its downward tilt towards the sea. It was fed by the lake in the grounds of the Manor, a favourite beauty spot when she had been a teenager. The lake was on private land belonging to the Branscombes and was supposed to be out of bounds, but she and her friends had often gone for walks there on hot summer days. Further along, she recalled, there was a weir, where they'd stood and watched the water tumble over stone and form white froth.

'You must love this place,' she said now, watching the ducks glide on the water, dipping their beaks every now and again among the reeds as they searched for morsels of food. 'It's so peaceful and unspoilt.' They were following a well-worn path by the river, where clumps of yellow fleabane grew along the banks and here and there were shiny deep pink blooms of musk mallow and star-shaped ragged robin. Charlie was sniffing among the blades of grass, seeking out the flower petals and sneezing when they tickled his nose.

'I do.' He sent her a sideways glance. 'It's even better having you here to share it with me.'

'Is it?' She was pleased but looked at him curiously. 'I wasn't expecting to see you at all outside of work, but I suppose when you opted to have the fête on the Manor grounds you felt you had to put in an appearance.'

'That's true…but I'd have turned up anyway, just so that I could spend some time with you.'

'Really?' Flattered though she was by his persistence, she wasn't about to fall for his charm the way countless other girls had in the past. 'That might have been awkward if Jake had been around.'

'Ah, but he isn't here, is he?' His eyes glittered. 'What

was he thinking, choosing to go to a meeting and missing out on the chance of being with you?'

Impishly, she decided to play him along. She'd never said there was anything going on between her and Jake, but Nate seemed concerned about their relationship. 'He's very passionate about his work.'

'More than he is about you?' His dark brows rose in disbelief. 'Doesn't he know he's leaving you open to being chatted up by the likes of me?'

She smiled. 'We're just friends.' She sent him a fleeting blue glance. 'Besides, there's so much history between our families...'

'Yes, there is,' he said, trying to ignore the elephant between them. He checked his watch, a stylish gold timepiece that looked good on his strong tanned wrist. 'We've an hour or so left before I have to call the raffle results—we could go back to the house and get Charlie some water and I could show you round, if you like? You've never seen the inside of the Manor, have you?'

'Only the lodge, where my father had his office.' She smiled. 'I think I'd like that. I've always wondered what such a grand house was like inside.'

'Come on, then. We can take a shortcut from here across the field to the back of the house.'

He showed her the way along a narrow path that led to a hedgerow and a wooden stile. He held Charlie's lead while she swung her jeans-clad legs over the railing and stepped down into the field beyond. From here she caught a glimpse of the Manor House through the thicket of ancient trees that surrounded it.

'Are we going in through the servants' entrance?' she asked with a mischievous smile as they approached the back of the house. There were no stalls set up out here, and there was no sign of people coming away from the main event and wandering about. She guessed he'd had it temporarily fenced off.

'There's no servants' entrance nowadays,' he said, 'but it's not quite as grand as the archway at the front of the house.'

'Oh, I don't know about that...' She gazed at the covered portal. 'It's quite impressive.' The lawn and gardens here were beautiful, with wide flower borders and tall trees and a verdant shrubbery. Sophie went with Nate into the house through a pair of wide, solid oak doors and then stopped to look around in wonder.

She was standing in the kitchen, a huge room with gleaming pale oak floorboards and golden oak units all around. There was a large central island bar with a white marble top, and to one side there was a dining table with half a dozen chairs set around it. Above the range cooker there was a deep, wide cooker hood with a tastefully designed tiled splashback. All along one wall were feature windows with square panes and two of the windows were decoratively arched. The room was light and inviting—it was the most wonderful kitchen she had ever seen.

'Oh, I'm almost speechless,' she said, gazing around. 'I wasn't expecting anything like this. It's so traditional, yet completely modern.'

Nate smiled. 'I persuaded my father a couple of years back that it needed updating. I'm pleased that for once he took note of what I said.' He went to the sink and poured cold water into a large stainless-steel bowl and set it down on the floor for Charlie. The dog drank thirstily and then flopped down on the tiles, watching them, his head on his paws. 'What would you like to drink?'

Nate asked Sophie. 'Something cold, or tea, coffee…? Something stronger, if you like?'

'A cold drink would be lovely, thanks. It's so warm today—it's left me with a real thirst.'

'Watermelon?'

She nodded and he took two glass tumblers from a display cabinet and filled them from a dispenser in the front of the tall double-door fridge. 'This is a mix of watermelon, a dash of lime and a hint of cucumber,' he said. 'I think you'll like it.'

She took the glass and swallowed deeply. 'Mmm… that's lovely. Thank you.'

'You're welcome.' He finished off his drink, tipping his head back. Sophie watched, fascinated as his throat moved, but she lowered her gaze as he put the glass down on the table. 'I'll show you the rest of the house,' he told her, 'the main part, at least. It would probably take too long to go through the East and West Wings.'

'Okay.'

There were several reception rooms, one used as a library and another as an office, all tastefully furnished with the same pale oak used in carved, decorative panelling on the walls and in the bookcases and desks. The drawing room, though, facing out on to a paved terrace, was very different.

'We went for a much lighter touch in here,' Nate said. 'There's no panelling, as you can see, but we chose a very pale silk covering for the walls.'

'It's lovely,' she murmured. 'It's all so restful.' She looked around. 'You've kept the original inglenook fireplace, but everything blends in perfectly.' The fireplace was a pale stone arch with a wood-burning stove set into the recess. There were two cream sofas in here, with splashes of soft colour in the cushions and in the luxurious oriental design rug and floor-length curtains. Again, the windows were tall, with square panes, and there were glazed doors opening out on to the terrace.

'I'm glad you like it.' He smiled. 'Let me show you upstairs.' They went out into the large hall, almost a room in itself, and Sophie looked up to see gleaming pale oak rafters and a mezzanine floor set off by a beautifully carved oak balustrade. 'I have my own office up there,' Nate said, following the line of her gaze. 'I like to sit up there in the room and look out over the moors. You can see the lake from there, and a good deal of the estate. Come on, I'll show you.'

He reached for her hand and led her up the wide staircase to the open balcony that looked down on to the hall. His fingers engulfed hers and instantly she felt a thrill of heat pass through her at his firm touch.

The room opened out on to the internal balcony. There were a couple of easy chairs up here, with bookcases to hand along with a small glass coffee table. She imagined him sitting here, reading and being able to look down into the hall when anyone arrived downstairs.

Further back in the room, through a wide, square archway, there was a bespoke furnished study, with a built-in desk and units and glazed square-paned display cabinets above them. The main features, though, were the two wide arched windows that took up a good part of the back wall.

'Come and see.' Nate took her with him to stand by one of the windows. 'See what I mean?' He slipped his arm around her waist, holding her close. She knew she ought to move away but it felt good to have him hold her, to have him so close that she could feel his long body by her side, and she couldn't bring herself to break that contact. Instead, she wanted him to wrap his arms around her. His nearness was intoxicating.

'Oh…it's incredible!' She gasped softly in delight. 'You're so lucky to have such a wonderful view.' From here, with the house situated at the top of the hill, she could see all around for miles. She saw the lake and the copse, and beyond that she glimpsed some of the houses beyond, white-painted and nestled into the hillside. She looked at him, her lips softening with enchantment. 'It's all so lovely. I've never seen it set out like this before.'

'*You're* lovely,' he said huskily, his gaze lingering on the pink fullness of her mouth. 'It means so much to have you here with me like this. I've missed you, all those years we've been away from each other. I kept thinking about you all the time we've been apart.'

'Did you? Me too…' It was true. She'd never been able to stop thinking about him. And now she was lost in his spell, enticed by the compelling lure of his dark eyes and mesmerised by the gentle sweep of his hands as they moved over the curve of her hips, drawing her ever closer to him. He bent his head to her and gently claimed her lips, brushing her mouth softly with his kisses. Her whole body seemed to turn to flame and she melted into his embrace, loving the way his arms went around her. Her limbs were weak with longing. She wanted his kisses, yearned to know the feel of his hands moving over her.

'I've been desperate to kiss you ever since I saw you that day at the Seafarer,' he said, his voice roughened with desire. 'I wanted to hold you, to feel your body next to mine.'

She felt the same way about him, but his words made her stop and think about what she was doing. Her father had been upset when he'd heard about that meeting. He'd warned her about falling for Nate all over again. They'd never made any commitment to one another but, whenever he was around, she was drawn to him like a moth to a flame and, even though they'd argued, she'd been upset when he went to work in the States after her father's accident. How would she feel when his job here came to an end and there was the possibility of him leaving once more? It was better, surely, not to let things get out of hand?

'I wanted it too, Nate, but...I can't let this happen. I'm sorry if I led you on in any way. I'm very confused right now. I need time to think...'

'Why, Sophie? Tell me why.'

She looked up at him. 'I know you're not right for me,' she said quietly. 'It would be madness if I were to fall for you...again. We're worlds apart.'

'You don't know that.' His hands circled her waist. 'You seem absolutely perfect to me. I'd do everything I could to make you happy.'

She shook her head. 'But you can't. And what you're going to do will hurt my family and friends. Think about what you're doing—you're planning to sign away the homes of everyone who lives in property belonging to the Branscombe estate. It's no use saying you haven't made a decision yet. It's what you'll do to make sure that you can keep this house, isn't it? I understand that—the Manor has been in your family for generations; you said so. But do you really know the pain you will cause?'

He ran his hands lightly over her bare arms. 'If it came to that, if I have to sell the properties, I could negotiate a deal for you so that you could buy your house for a rock-bottom price.'

'And my father's home? What will happen to that? Can you tell me it won't be demolished to make way for a hotel or shopping mall? Isn't that what that company does? Will anything be left of our lovely tranquil village when they've finished?'

He winced. 'I'll make sure that your father gets a better place. He won't suffer.'

'He's already suffering. He's only just getting used to going around in a wheelchair and negotiating ramps. The last thing he needs is to be uprooted all over again.' She sighed heavily. 'It's as though you're moving chessmen on a board, deciding their fate.' She gazed searchingly at his face, studying the taut line of his jaw and the bleak sea green of his eyes. 'Nate, isn't there anything you can do to stop this?' She lifted her hand to his chest and ran her palm lightly over the warmth of his ribcage. 'Can't you find another way? Please?'

For a moment, his expression was agonised. 'I wish I could, Sophie, but a place like this, with all the land and outbuildings associated with it, costs a fortune in upkeep. I'll do what I can. You know I'd do anything not to hurt you.'

'I know you will. But things don't always work out the way we want them to, do they?' She eased herself away from him and took a couple of steps backwards. 'It's getting late. There's the raffle to draw and I should go and see what Charlie's getting up to. It's time we set off for home. He should be rested well enough by now. Thanks for showing me around.'

He walked with her to the kitchen. 'I could take you home in the Range Rover. Charlie could go in the back.'

'No, it's all right. We'll walk.' She needed to be alone right now, away from him, so that she could clear her head. With him around, it was impossible.

CHAPTER FOUR

'HI, JAKE. How did your weekend down in Cornwall go? Did things work out all right for you?' Sophie walked into Jake's office at lunchtime on Monday, greeting him with a bright smile. She was glad to see him. He was a calming influence—everything Nate was not.

She should never have gone back to the Manor House with Nate. That had been a big mistake, and she might have known he wouldn't be one to miss an opportunity. After all, he had nothing to lose.

Even now, she remembered how it had felt to be in his arms, to know the touch of his lips on hers. Her whole body tingled with nervous excitement at the memory.

'Oh, hi, Sophie.' Jake looked up from the mound of paperwork on his desk. 'Yeah, it went okay, thanks. We managed to get quite a lot sorted.' He frowned. 'The hotel was a bit crowded, though. There was some sort of event going on in town—a music festival—so it was quite noisy.'

'But it must have been good to meet up with your friends?'

He nodded. 'Yes…yes, it was.'

She hesitated momentarily. He seemed harassed and out of sync with things, not at all his usual self. 'I came up here to see if we might have lunch together?' she suggested. 'Maybe you can tell me all about it over a plate of spaghetti?'

He frowned again, glancing at his watch, and then started shuffling through papers. 'I'm sorry, Sophie. I've a stack of work to wade through and I have to get a report ready for a meeting with my boss this afternoon. Do you mind if we give it a miss and meet up later?'

'No...no, of course not... That's all right.' She tried to hide her disappointment. 'It was just a spur-of-the-moment thing...I hadn't heard from you, so I thought I'd come and see you on the off chance. It doesn't matter.'

'Ah, yes...I should have phoned you. Everything's been a bit hectic.' He grimaced. 'How about I give you a call when I'm free?'

'Yes, okay. That's fine. No worries.'

She had plenty of other things to occupy her mind when she went back to the Children's Unit after grabbing a quick bite to eat in the hospital restaurant. She checked up on her patients, taking time to look in on Josh, the five-year-old boy with the head injury, and she was thankful that his condition was at least stable now. He was still under sedation while they waited for the fractures to begin the healing process and while the swelling inside his head subsided. His parents were obviously worried about his prognosis and whether he would be brain damaged in any way, but Sophie reassured them as best she could before going in search of her next patient.

As she was walking by a side ward, though, she heard a series of monitor alarms going off. Instantly concerned, she looked into the room to see what was happening.

Nate was in there looking after a young girl who appeared to be around ten years old. When Sophie walked further into the room, she could see that the child was thrashing around on the bed, her limbs moving uncontrollably, her head tipped back and her body arching. She was having a full-blown seizure and Sophie hurried over to Nate and said quietly, 'Can I help?'

He nodded, giving her a quick smile. 'Thanks, I'd appreciate that. The nurses are all very busy just now... Would you try to hold her still while I give her a shot of anti-convulsion medication? She only just seemed to come out of one seizure and now this...'

'Of course.' Sophie gently restrained the child while Nate drew up a syringe and inserted it into the intravenous cannula that was taped to the girl's arm. 'Are her parents around?'

'Her father had to leave to go to work. I sent her mother to take a break and get some coffee. These last few weeks have been a worrying time for her and she's stressed out. Luckily, she missed seeing these latest seizures.'

'Do we know what's causing them?'

He nodded. 'I think so. Lucy has been suffering from really bad headaches, nosebleeds and vomiting for some time now. Her blood pressure's frighteningly high—it's been getting steadily worse over a couple of years despite treatment. It isn't responding very well to antihypertensive drugs.' He withdrew the syringe and put it aside. Glancing briefly at Sophie once more, he said, 'It might be a good idea if you were to stay with us while I explain things to her mother. She's quite upset by what's happening to her daughter, and it might help her to have another woman present. I'll need to get her consent for angiography.'

'All right, I can do that.'

Slowly, as the drug took effect and as Lucy recovered consciousness, Nate began to speak to the child in a low voice, soothing her and trying to keep her calm. Even Sophie began to feel more relaxed under the comforting influence of his gentle tones.

'How do you feel?' he asked the girl after a while. 'Is your headache still as bad as before?'

'No, it's a bit better.' Lucy was silent for a moment and then her face suddenly paled, small beads of perspiration breaking out on her brow, and she said urgently, 'But I'm going to be sick again.'

Sophie quickly found a kidney dish and held it for the little girl while she vomited, and then gave her a tissue so that she could wipe her mouth when she was finished. 'I'll just get rid of this,' Sophie said, removing the dish and replacing it with a clean one. 'I'll be back in a minute or two.'

When she came back into the room, Lucy was resting, leaning back against her pillows and looking completely washed out. Her dark hair was damp with perspiration. Her mother had come back from the cafeteria and Nate was sitting on the end of Lucy's bed, gently explaining the results of tests that had been carried out earlier. 'As you know, we've done lots of tests, along with ultrasound scans and a CT scan, and from those results we can be fairly certain about what's causing the high blood pressure.'

Lucy's mother frowned. 'You said it might be something to do with her kidneys.'

'Yes, that's right. From what we can see on the radiology films, the blood vessels to her kidneys are narrowed and that's what's causing the problems she's been having.'

'But you can fix it with tablets, can't you?'

Nate shook his head. 'I'm afraid not.'

The woman stiffened and Sophie pulled up a chair and went to sit with her at the side of the bed.

'There's some sort of blockage in the arteries,' Nate explained, 'and that is what's making her have high blood pressure and causing the severe headaches and so on. It also means that the blood flow to her kidneys is not what it should be. We have to do something that's more invasive, I'm afraid. If we don't do anything, things could get much worse and there might be damage to the kidneys.'

The woman's hands started to shake and Sophie covered them with her own, wanting to comfort her and at the same time not wanting Lucy to see her mother upset. 'We need to do a procedure called angiography,' she explained. 'This will clear the blockage and open up the arteries, but Lucy will be anaesthetised so she won't feel anything or need to worry about what's going on.' The little girl was watching and listening through all this, wide-eyed, and Sophie glanced at her. 'How do you feel about that, Lucy?'

Lucy paused briefly to think about it. 'Will it make me better?'

'It should do. That's what we're aiming for.'

Lucy was quiet for a moment or two, thinking about it. 'If it's going to help, I think it's okay.' Seemingly older than her years, she glanced at her mother and said, 'I'd like to stop feeling this way, being ill all the time.'

Slowly, her mother nodded. She exhaled heavily. 'All

right. I'll phone your dad and explain things to him.' She looked up at Nate. 'When will you do it?'

'Tomorrow morning, most likely. I'll speak to the radiology consultant who'll be carrying out the procedure. He'll want to see Lucy, and he'll explain things to you...but basically he'll thread a catheter from the groin through the blood vessels to look at the kidneys. Then he'll place a small balloon inside the artery and inflate it to open up the blood vessel and restore the circulation. When that's been done satisfactorily, he'll withdraw the balloon and catheter. He'll need to do the process for both arteries.'

Lucy's eyes grew even wider. 'Are you sure I won't feel any of it?'

He nodded and smiled. 'I'm quite sure. You might feel a little bit sore at the injection site afterwards, but you'll be given painkillers, so it shouldn't be a problem.' He studied her expression. 'Are you still all right with it?'

She nodded.

'Good.' Nate stood up and smiled. 'We'll leave you to talk to your mum and dad about it, and I'll let the nurse know what's happening so she can answer any of your questions.'

'Thanks.' Lucy's mother smiled at both of them as they went to leave the room. 'I'm really grateful to you for the way you're looking after her.'

They went over to the computer room so that Nate could type up his case notes and confirm things with the radiology consultant.

Sophie wrote up her own notes on Josh, and when they had both finished, Nate swivelled round in his chair to look at her. He said, 'I'm glad we've finally managed to catch up with one another. It's been so busy here we haven't had a chance to talk…but it was good being with you on Saturday. I wanted to tell you I enjoyed the whole afternoon, walking with you, spending time at the house…especially spending time at the house…' He smiled, but she couldn't be persuaded to do the same. She was still struggling with anxiety at her lack of self-control after the way she'd responded to him that day.

'It's certainly a beautiful house,' she said, dodging around the issue.

His mouth tilted at the corners. 'You won't admit you liked being with me, will you?'

'How can I?' She sighed. 'I feel I shouldn't have let things get that far.'

'I don't see why.' His shoulders moved in a nonchalant fashion. 'Anyway, it was just a kiss.'

She sucked in a silent breath at that. Just a kiss? Had it meant nothing to him? She was shocked.

'It was exquisite…sensational…wonderful…' he added. 'But it was just a kiss, after all. I don't see that you've any reason to regret it. It was instinctive. We didn't plan it. It just happened.' His glance flicked over her, moving from her burnished shoulder-length curls to glide down over the simple sheath dress she was wearing and trace the long line of her shapely legs. 'Though I wouldn't have been sorry if it had gone further.' His green eyes darkened. 'I always wanted you, Sophie… from back when we were teenagers. And I would definitely have staked a claim there and then if you hadn't decided to skip off to Medical School and disappear from my life for endless years.'

'Oh, really?' She pretended to be surprised. 'But you didn't try to find me, did you, and am I to believe you didn't go out and console yourself with any other girls in all those years?'

'If I didn't come after you it was because life got in the way. And as for any other women, trust me, no one could ever hold a candle to you.' All at once his expression was sincere, his gaze steady, and she almost faltered under the influence of that persuasive, utterly convincing guise until she managed to collect herself just in time. Was she a naive teenager?

'Well, that's good to hear.' She sent him a flashing blue glance. 'Although…you know I don't believe a word of it, don't you?' She frowned. 'There's no Irish in you, is there? I'm wondering because somewhere along the line you seem to have kissed the Blarney Stone.'

He tried to look offended but failed due to the faintly amused quirk of his mouth. His dark brows shot up. 'Not a drop. How could you say that to me? My ancestry is founded in the deepest combes—in the hills and valleys of ancient Devonshire—as you well know. I would never resort to such tactics.'

'Hmm. That's yet to be proved.' She pulled a wry face and might have said more but her phone rang and she unclipped it from the purpose-made jewelled clasp on the narrow belt around her waist. Then she glanced at the small screen and frowned. 'I'm sorry; I ought to take this,' she told him. 'It's my sister, Jessica. She almost never rings when I'm at work.'

'That's okay. Go ahead.' He was immediately serious but turned back to the computer while Sophie walked a short distance away to take the call.

'Oh, Sophie—' Her sister's voice came over the airwaves. 'I wasn't sure what to do—I didn't know whether to ring you or not. I don't know what to do.'

'It's all right—try to calm yourself.' Sophie used a soothing tone. 'I'm sure we can sort it out, whatever the problem is.' Intuitively, she asked, 'Is everything okay between you and Ryan?'

'Yes, except that he's had to go off to Canada on an engineering job—right now when my due date is so close.' Her sister pulled in a quick breath. 'I've been feeling so tired lately. I'm nearly full term, my back hurts, I'm getting these odd contractions—the midwife says they're Braxton Hicks—and he's away, working. It came up out of the blue and he said he had no choice but to go.'

Sophie tried to soothe her. 'I expect he's gone because he wants to boost your funds. Everything's been a struggle for you up to now, hasn't it, financially? He'd have known that Mum and Tom were close by if you needed them.' They hadn't counted on a baby coming along quite so soon.

'Yes, that's true. He's doing everything he can to make sure we're okay. It was all right till I had to stop working. I didn't realise how much we relied on my salary. We were doing all right, but then the boiler broke down and it's too old to be repaired, and now there's a problem with the plumbing that needs to be sorted but the plumber says he can't fix it for at least three weeks.' She sighed. 'I can't stay here but I don't know what to do. Can I come and stay with you for a while?'

'Oh, Jess…of course you can. Pack a case and catch the earliest train down here and I'll get the spare room ready for you. We'll book you in with a local midwife and arrange for you to have the baby in the local hospital. I'm sure everyone will be accommodating once we explain the situation.'

'Could I? Would you?' Jessica's words were tumbling

over themselves in her relief. 'Oh, thank you, Sophie. Thank you. Oh—' She broke off suddenly and Sophie could feel there was something more to come.

'What's wrong?'

'Well, it's nothing wrong, exactly, but I think Rob wants to come and stay with Dad for a while. You know what he's like once he makes up his mind about something. He's very impulsive. He keeps saying he wants to help look after him. Mum's okay with it, and I know Dad will be happy, but I don't know where he'll stay— Dad's spare room is being used for storage at the moment, isn't it?'

'I'm sure we'll sort something out.' Sophie tried to stay focused on the situation in hand. 'See if you can get the evening train over here. I think there's one that gets into town at about nine o'clock. I'll come and meet you at the station. We'll work out what we can do about Rob, but the priority is to get you settled first. You have to think about your health and about the baby.'

'Okay, I'll do that... Thanks, Sophie. You're the best.' Jessica cut the call a minute or so later and Sophie frowned as she turned back to Nate, trying to work out what she needed to do. She would have to go home after her shift and make sure everything was ready for her sister.

'Trouble?' Nate was sympathetic, ready to listen.

'Not really. It's just that I need to get organised.' She explained what was happening with Jessica and how Rob wanted to come over.

'I don't see how she can stay on her own in those circumstances...but I'm sure she'll be glad to have her big sister's support.' He gave her a brief smile before asking seriously, 'Is there any way I can help out with Rob?'

It warmed her through and through to know that he would do what he could for her. 'I'm not sure, to be honest,' she said. 'But thanks for offering.' It was good of him—there had been no hesitation; he was ready to help in an instant.

She paused for a moment, thinking about what she was going to do. 'I won't be at all surprised if my mother turns up at my place some time soon. This is just the kind of thing that would set her off. With all the changes going on, she'll probably forget to take her medication.'

He nodded. 'That could happen. She used to take off for days at a time, didn't she? I often wondered, back then, how you coped. You were only about sixteen when your parents' marriage broke up, as I recall, and your mother was in a bad way for a long time. I caught up with everything that was happening whenever I came home from Med School and Charlotte would phone me every week and let me know all the village news.' Nate's expression was pensive. 'Yet you seemed to take it all in your stride—you took on the role of mother to Rob and Jessica. They must have been…' he worked it out in his head '…seven and nine at the time?'

She nodded. 'That's right. They were very young, so I tried to be strong for them. It was hard because I was upset and hurting too. Dad was unhappy and not coping very well. It was still hard when Mum married Tom and we moved to Somerset. It was a new life, a new place, but we felt as though our roots had been torn.'

'I can imagine.' His gaze narrowed thoughtfully. 'I don't suppose there's room for Jessica at your mother's place?'

She shook her head. 'When Jess married they turned her room into an office. Anyway, she craves peace and quiet—mentally, if not physically.' She shot him a quick, amused look. 'A bit like you, really. You'd never be able to put up with some of the organised chaos we live in.'

His mouth curved. 'Probably not. I'm used to things running smoothly, like a well-oiled machine. I suppose Charlotte had a lot to do with that.' He glanced briefly at his watch. 'Your shift's about due to finish—why don't you go home and make a start on getting things ready? It's going to be a bit of a squeeze for you in your small cottage, I imagine—and you'll need to make room for a cot in case the baby arrives in the next couple of weeks, won't you?'

'Oh, heavens! I hadn't thought of that! What am I going to do for a cot?'

He was thoughtful for a moment or two. 'There might be one stashed away in the attic back at the Manor. In fact, now I think about it, I'm sure there is. My father has things up there going back generations. He never throws stuff out.'

'Oh, bless you! That would be marvellous.' She studied him cautiously. 'Is there any news on your father?'

He pulled a face. 'There's been no change, really. He's being well looked after at the convalescent home, but his recovery's going to be a long haul, I think. He's very breathless and needs a lot of rest.'

'I'm sorry. It must be difficult for you.'

'Yes. Thanks for asking.' He sent her a quick glance. 'Is your father making any headway?'

She nodded, smiling. 'He managed to stand and bear his own weight for a short time. It's a start. He took a couple of steps with support. I'm keeping my fingers crossed that he'll keep on making progress.'

'I'm glad.'

She left the hospital a few minutes later, her mind racing, full of things she had to do. It occurred to her that Jake had mentioned seeing her later, so she tried calling him. When he didn't answer, she sent him a text message telling him what was happening. He was probably in a meeting.

As soon as she arrived back at the village, she checked up on her father and heated up a beef casserole she'd made earlier.

'Rob told me he wants to come over,' he said as they ate together. 'I told him I'd love to have him stay with me but there's only the box room and that's filled with physio equipment and so on. It would take a bit of work to sort it out.'

'Don't worry about it, Dad,' she said. 'We can deal with that later.'

'And what about Jessica? Are you going to have room for her and perhaps for a baby as well at your place?'

'I'm sure we'll manage.' She looked at him thoughtfully. 'Anyway, how did you get on with the physio today—it was your day for the hospital workout, wasn't it?'

He grimaced. 'It was okay. I managed a couple of steps again, with a lot of help. Some days I don't seem to have the strength…'

'You're getting there—that's the main thing. A year ago we wouldn't have thought you'd come this far.' She clasped his hand warmly and smiled at him and he brightened, seeming to absorb some of her optimism. 'Now—I'll take Charlie for his walk and then I'll have to love you and leave you. I've a dozen things I need to do before Jessica gets here.'

Charlie's ears perked up at the mention of a walk and

they set off along the moorland path, heading for the local village shop. Sophie stocked up on extra provisions and then dropped Charlie back home.

She went back to her own white-painted cottage and put away the groceries. With any luck, Jessica would be arriving in the next couple of hours and by then she would have everything more or less in order. She put fresh linen on the bed in the guest room and made sure there were plenty of clean towels in the bathroom. When she had finished it was still light, so she went out into the garden to breathe in the fresh air and gather some flowers from the border. She loved her garden with its curving lawn and pretty display of colourful blooms. There were trellis panels covered in sweet peas in warm pastel shades, with deeper lavender, mauve and blue colours interspersed.

The sun was setting on the horizon when she turned back towards the house, carrying a wicker trug filled with bright pompon dahlias and a posy of delicate sweet peas.

'I thought I might find you out here.' Nate's deep voice startled her. He walked around the side of the house and came across the small terrace towards her, smiling. 'I rang the doorbell and knocked, but I saw your car outside, so I guessed you were still at home. I brought the cot and came to see if you needed any help.'

'Oh…I didn't expect you to look for it right away.' She was a bit breathless all at once, seeing him standing there. He looked wonderful, dressed in casual chinos and an open-necked shirt with the sleeves rolled up. All the nervous excitement of the last few hours seemed to flow out of her as she looked at him, to be replaced by a warm feeling inside. It was so good to have him here.

'That's really thoughtful of you,' she said. 'It's good to see you, Nate.' She started towards the house once more, heading towards the open square-paned French windows. 'I was just going to put these flowers in water. Jessica likes sweet peas, so I thought I would put some in her room—and the dahlias will look good in the living room.' She was babbling, startled by his arrival, but thrilled to see him.

'Have you heard anything from your brother?' He followed her into the kitchen.

'No, nothing. I tried calling him but I couldn't get through. I expect his battery's low.' She set the trug down on the white table, then switched on the kettle and set out a couple of porcelain mugs for coffee. 'I'll just put these flowers in water. Sit down—I can get you some scones to eat if you're hungry.'

'No, thanks, I'm fine. Besides, you have enough to do without bothering about me.' He watched her as she arranged the sweet peas in a glass vase. 'Look—why don't I go and meet Jessica at the station? She'll remember me from before your family left the village—and we met up briefly in the village last time I was home.'

'Are you sure you don't mind doing that?'

'Of course not. I told you, I want to help.'

'Thanks. That would be such a relief. I'm really grateful.' She made the coffee and slid a mug towards him. 'I've been thinking about her, wondering if it will all go smoothly.'

He looked at her curiously. 'You don't show your feelings to the world, do you? You look very calm and composed on the outside, but I know you're a little anxious inside. That's probably what makes you such a good doctor. You get on with the job in hand—no panic, no fuss, just sheer concentration and doing the best you can.'

She gave a small broken laugh. 'You make me sound like a robot!'

'No! Never.' He stood up and laid his arm around her shoulders. 'It's all right to admit that you worry sometimes. I'm here for you, Sophie. I need you to know that.'

She reached up and touched his hand, and his fingers closed around hers. The warmth and gentle strength of that grasp encouraged her and somehow gave her a renewed burst of energy. With him around she could cope with anything. 'Thanks. I'm glad you're here.'

'Me too.' He released her and seemed to brace himself as though he was cautious about holding her for too long. Reading her thoughts, he said, 'Just being near you drives me wild. You can't imagine how difficult it is for me.'

'It isn't easy for me either...but, no matter what you say, I can't help feeling I need to keep my guard up. I don't want to fall for you, Nate. It's way too risky for my peace of mind.'

He looked at her, his dark eyes brooding. 'We need to work on that.' He started to walk away. 'I'd better go and get the cot—it's in the back of the Range Rover. There's a nursing chair as well—it rocks gently, so Jessica will be comfy when she feeds the baby.'

She went with him, following him out along the path to where he was parked at the front of the cottage. She didn't know quite what she was expecting—perhaps a very old, serviceable child's cot—but what she saw made her gasp with delight.

'Oh, it's lovely! I didn't realise it would be a crib that

swings from side to side.' The white cradle had beautifully carved spindle sides and was supported on a sturdy white wooden frame. The rocking chair was a perfect match, white-painted with spindle legs.

Nate carried them into the house and put them down in the guest room she had prepared. 'There, the cot looks good next to the bed, doesn't it?' He studied it, looking pleased.

'Oh, it's just perfect. I never imagined you'd bring anything as lovely as this.'

'It was mine, apparently. I remember my mother talking about rocking me in a cradle at the side of the bed. She said it sent me off to sleep every time.'

'Thank you. I'm so grateful to you.' Forgetting everything, without thinking, she turned towards him and hugged him tightly. He was there for her when she needed him without her even having to ask. That meant a lot to her.

His arms closed around her, folding her to him in a warm embrace. 'You're very welcome. Any time.'

She looked up at him, his handsome face just inches away from her own. She felt safe in his arms. He only had to bend his head a fraction more towards her and their lips would be touching. A surge of longing swept over her, filling her body with aching desire.

His green eyes shimmered with answering passion and he slowly lowered his head. He breathed in raggedly. 'Sophie,' he said softly, 'you need to think about what you're doing, about what you want…because I'm just a man and I'm finding it really hard to resist you. I don't want you to blame me afterwards for anything that might happen between us.'

His gentle words brought her back swiftly to reality. What was she doing? She pulled in a shaky breath. 'Ah… I wasn't thinking. You're right. I'm sorry.' Her hands were trembling as she dragged herself away from him. 'I don't know what's wrong with me. I haven't been able to think straight ever since you came back. It's like I'm eighteen again, as though the intervening years count for nothing.'

His hand lifted, his fingers tangling in the soft mass of her silky curls. 'I wish we could go back too…I want to turn the clock back and start again, and this time no bad things would happen to tear us apart. If I could write my own story, I'd make it one where you and I could be together and nothing would come between us.'

She gave him a tremulous smile. 'That would be good, wouldn't it? But this is real life, Nate. It never seems to go smoothly for either of us, does it?'

He shook his head and slowly took a step back from her. 'No, it doesn't.' He straightened and said quietly, 'I should go and pick up your sister.'

'Yes…thanks.' She nodded, taking a moment to get herself together. 'I'll send her a message to let her know you'll meet her instead of me.'

After he'd gone, Sophie looked once more at the room she'd prepared for her sister and the baby. She would have to buy bedding for the cradle, and maybe a mobile to hang above it, and she would find some soft cushions for the chair. They could be her gift for the baby.

It grew darker outside but there was no sign of Rob turning up and she busied herself with a few chores. At last the doorbell sounded and she opened the door to Jessica and Nate.

She greeted them with relief. 'Jessica, I'm so glad

you're here.' She reached for her sister and put her arm around her. 'Come and sit down in the living room and put your feet up for a bit. You look exhausted.' Jessica's complexion was pale against the soft gold of her fair hair. Sophie glanced at Nate, who was following them along the hallway, and mouthed silently, 'Thank you.'

He smiled. 'I'll put the kettle on, shall I? I expect Jessica could do with a cup of tea…and maybe one of those scones you mentioned. From what she tells me, she hasn't been eating too well—too much heartburn lately.'

'Oh, it happens, doesn't it, when the baby gets bigger and presses on everything? It must be horrible.' Sophie helped her sister into a cosy armchair and pulled up a footstool for her. 'Perhaps you need to snack little and often. I have some of your favourite strawberry jam to go with those scones.'

Jessica smiled, her pretty face lighting up. 'Oh, it's good to be here with you, Sophie. I'm feeling better already.'

'I'm glad to hear it. We'll get you sorted out with a midwife and so on tomorrow. For now, you just need to rest.'

Nate pulled up a small side table and set down a cup of tea beside her chair. 'Why don't you girls try to relax for a bit and enjoy being with one another? I'll leave you to it. I'm sure you have a lot of catching up to do.'

Sophie followed him along the hallway to the front door. 'Thank you for everything.'

'You're welcome.' He leaned forward and dropped a light kiss on her forehead before opening the door and walking swiftly down the path to his car. She watched him go, hoping that nothing would cause their new closeness to fall apart. It meant a lot to her that he was around.

But how was she going to square that with her father's feelings towards the Branscombes? He, of all people, had reason to be hostile towards them and he would worry in case she was hurt again.

CHAPTER FIVE

A SHARP RAPPING sound startled Sophie just a few minutes later. She finished stacking plates in the dishwasher and went to see who was knocking at the door.

She hurried along the hallway. Jessica had gone to her room, exhausted, and she didn't want her to be disturbed by the noise. She opened the front door.

'Hey, Sophie.' Seventeen-year-old Rob stood on the doorstep looking tired, sheepish and dishevelled, his fair hair spiky. 'Can I stay with you for a bit—just till I clear out the box room at Dad's house? I didn't want to tell him I was coming over. I wanted to surprise him.'

'Of course you can. Oh, come here—let me hug you.' She wrapped her arms around him and held him close for a minute or two. 'How did you get here?'

'I thumbed a lift with a couple of lorry drivers. But the last one dropped me off a few miles from here and I had to walk the rest of the way. Then Nate Branscombe saw me and offered me a lift.'

'Nate saw you?' she echoed. 'But he— Where is he?' He wasn't here with Rob and she couldn't see beyond the tall hedge that obscured the road.

Rob carefully extricated himself from her arms and tilted his head towards the front gate. 'He's cleaning the headlamps on the car—we went through a bit of muddy water.'

'Oh, I see.' Gathering her thoughts, she ushered her brother into the house. 'Go and make yourself a hot drink, Rob. There's food in the kitchen. I'll just go out and talk to Nate for a minute.' She frowned, a sudden thought occurring to her. 'Did you and he get on all right?'

'Yeah, I guess. I wasn't sure how to react to him but he told me you knew I wanted to be with Dad.' He winced. 'I know Mum doesn't want us to have anything to do with him—she still cares about Dad even though they're not together any more. She's always saying how Nate's father caused Dad to break his back, but I don't think Nate had anything to do with that. He always seemed okay to me—a bit of an 'us and them' divide, sort of, but okay. But I suppose you never know. He comes from a different world to us and things are passed down in families, aren't they? It's all in the genes—character traits, some kinds of illnesses and so on?'

'Sometimes. Go in and get warm. I'll be back in a minute.' She suspected Nate was cleaning the headlamps to give her and Rob some time to themselves but she wanted to thank him for finding her brother.

She went out to greet him. 'Hi there.'

'Hi.' Nate smiled in the darkness. A streetlamp lit up his features and she had to resist the impulse to put her arms around him and hold him close. She was so glad to see him, and so grateful that he'd taken the trouble to bring Rob home.

'Thanks for bringing my brother back to me,' she said. 'I'm overwhelmed, the way things are turning out. You must be tired by now. It's very late and we had a busy day at the hospital.'

'Yes, it is, but I'm okay.' He studied her, seeing that she was still dressed in jeans and a sweater. 'You're still up.'

'Yes, I wanted to make sure that Jess was comfortable. Do you want to come in for a coffee or tea or something?'

'Hmm…' He seemed to be thinking about that and his mouth curved. 'The "or something" sounds very tempting.'

Her cheeks flushed with warm colour. 'You know what I mean.'

'Yes…' He gave a soft, amused sigh. 'Unfortunately, I do.' He studied her, his eyes glinting, his gaze running over the tousled mass of her honey-blonde hair and the hot flare of her cheeks. 'I think, in order to avoid temptation, I'd better pass on the offer of a drink tonight. And, as you say, it's late.' He braced himself and came back to the matter in hand. 'Are you going to find space for Rob to bed down here?'

'He'll have to use the sofa.'

'I thought so. I offered to find him a room at the Manor House but he very politely refused. He said he didn't think it would be a good idea, given the way your parents feel about the Branscombes.'

'I'm sorry about that.' She pulled a face. 'He's probably right, though. If my dad found out, he would be very annoyed. I'd sooner not upset him right now or it could set his progress right back.'

He nodded. 'It's okay. I see your point. Actually, I think Rob will do better staying with you—he seems a bit down at the moment and I get the feeling he needs family around him. Too much going on in his life, perhaps…worries about college.'

She frowned. 'I know he wasn't enjoying the course he was on. I think he feels he chose the wrong subject. Or it may be something else altogether.'

'I'm sure you and Jessica will manage to help him get through it.' Nate smiled. 'I'll say goodnight, then, and leave you to go and look after your brother. I take it Jessica's okay? I told Rob she was here with you.'

'She's fine, thank you…and she absolutely loves the cot and the chair. She was amazed when she walked into the guest room and saw them there. She wants to thank you personally for giving them to her but she asked me to tell you if I saw you in the meantime. I think she's probably fast asleep right now.'

'I'm glad she's all right.' He slid behind the wheel of the Range Rover and started the engine. 'Shall I see you back at the hospital in the morning?'

'Yes, I'll be there. See you.'

She watched him drive away and turned to go back into the house. She was pleased Rob was home, and even more glad to know that Nate had been the one to find him.

What she had to do now was send her parents messages to say that Rob and Jessica were both safe and sound with her. With any luck, they would read them first thing in the morning so she wouldn't have woken them.

She went back into the house and found pillows and a duvet for Rob. Like Sophie, he was exhausted, and after he'd had a meal of a hot Cornish pasty and soup, along with a hot drink, she helped him to settle in the living room.

'You can bed down on the sofa for now,' she said. 'It's quite comfortable, so all being well, you should be able to get some rest. We'll talk in the morning before I leave for work, and then maybe we'll be able to have a proper chat later on. Nate said you were feeling a bit low.'

Rob sat down on the sofa and pulled a face. 'I'm always up and down lately. Sometimes life seems black and empty and yet other times I'm on top of the world. I don't understand it.' He sent her an anxious look. 'Sometimes I worry that I might be bipolar, like Mum.'

She knelt down beside him. 'I don't think you need worry about that, Rob. We would have noticed signs before this if you suffered from the illness she has. I think what you're feeling is just part and parcel of being a teenager. Maybe we need to find a better way of supporting you.'

He nodded absently, absorbing that. 'I hope that's all it is.'

'Well, Jessica's here, so you'll be company for each other—and it will make me feel better knowing you're here to keep an eye on her. You can let me know if she shows any sign of going into labour.'

His brows shot up and he said in a faintly alarmed tone, 'Is that likely to happen? She's not due yet, is she?'

'No…she still has a few days, possibly, but the baby seems quite big and there's not a lot of room for him in the womb, according to her last session with the midwife. Things could start happening any time.'

Rob looked worried and she laughed. 'It'll be fine, Rob. A first baby always takes a few hours, so there'll be no need to panic. Just ring me if anything seems to be starting.'

He nodded vigorously. 'I will—definitely.'

'Okay.' She smiled. 'Try to get some sleep.'

* * *

Despite having a disturbed night, Sophie was up early in the morning, preparing breakfast and getting ready for work. Rob appeared in the kitchen, bleary-eyed, as she was scrambling eggs at the hob, and he pulled out a chair by the table and sat down. 'Dad rang, didn't he?' He yawned and stretched his limbs. 'I heard him on the phone to you. You seemed to be trying to calm him down.'

'He wasn't happy because it was Nate who found you and brought Jessica here—he thinks I shouldn't have anything to do with him outside of work. I tried to explain but he wasn't really listening to anything I had to say.' She made a wry face. 'I suppose I'll still be in his bad books when I go round there to help out with Charlie. It'll give him another chance to have a go… But there was one good thing—he's really pleased that you're safe and sound.'

Rob gave a quick smile at that. Sophie guessed he missed living with his father. He went to see him as often as possible but that wasn't the same. 'I can give Dad a hand this morning if you want,' he offered. 'I know you normally have breakfast with him. It'll give me a chance to talk to him and I can take Charlie out for a walk, if you like.'

'Oh, that would be great, thanks. It will give me time to phone the midwife and sort things out before work. I'll let him know you're coming.' She was pleased he wanted to do that. It would do him good to talk to his father.

'Did I hear you say you were going to take Charlie for a walk? How about I come with you?' Jessica came into the kitchen, blonde hair gleaming, her expression showing her delight at being with her family.

'Yeah, why not?' Rob smiled a greeting and they all sat round the table, tucking into toast and perfectly cooked eggs. They talked about things that had been going on in their lives, but most of all it seemed that Rob and Jessica were relieved to be back home in the village where they were born.

'I've set up an appointment for you with the local midwife for tomorrow morning,' Sophie told her sister as she was getting ready to leave for work a short time later. 'She lives in the village, so she knows our family well. She's going to arrange things with the maternity unit at the hospital.'

'Thanks, Sophie.' Jessica patted her abdomen. 'I wish baby would hurry up—it can't be much longer, surely?'

Rob's eyes widened in momentary panic. 'Just don't have him yet, okay? Just leave it till the weekend when Sophie's around…yeah?'

'Of course, bro—whatever you say!' Jessica laughed and ruffled his hair. Smiling, Sophie said goodbye and left for the hospital.

She did the rounds of the Neonatal Unit and then went on to see patients who'd been admitted to the Children's Unit. Josh's condition was less critical now as his head injury healed, and Sophie and Nate had decided it was time to gradually reduce his level of sedation. They had to wait and see what the outcome might be as he slowly recovered consciousness, but Nate had said he wanted to check on him later today when they brought the boy fully out of his induced coma.

She and Nate had both been busy all day and hadn't had time to stop and talk, but she met up with him by the nurses' station late in the afternoon. He was holding out a newspaper.

'Have you seen this in the daily paper?' He looked harassed and on edge, not at all his usual calm self.

'What is it?' She took the paper from him and scanned the article he'd been reading.

Villagers Protest about Homes up for Sale!

Peninsula Holdings are ready to make an offer for the Branscombe estate. Lord Branscombe, once involved in piloting a plane that crashed causing devastating injuries to his former Estate Manager, lost several millions of pounds in an ill-fated business venture overseas and now hopes to recoup his losses.

It's thought that he borrowed money to finance the investment. He suffered a heart attack recently and is now recovering in a convalescent home.

The villagers are seeking urgent talks with his son and heir, Nate Branscombe. Nate was unavailable for comment last night.

She sent him an anxious look. 'Is it true? Are the houses up for sale? Have you made a deal with Peninsula?'

'That's just it… I haven't spoken to the company yet. They finished their surveys last week and prepared a report for their head office. They're supposed to be getting in touch with me some time this week with a preliminary offer, but I've no idea what it will be.' His jaw tightened. 'They'd no right to leak this to the press and stir up trouble all over again.'

'What will you do?'

He pulled a face. 'The parish council has asked me to address an emergency meeting in the village hall later today. They've obviously been spooked by this article. I said I would do it providing there was no press intrusion, but I would have preferred to wait until I'd sorted things out. It all takes time—I have to meet with the accountants, try to set things up. They don't seem to realise that.'

She swallowed hard. 'I think people do understand... but everyone's nervous about the future. My own family's worried. I've just told Rob he can stay with me until we sort out better arrangements for him—he puts on an outward show of being okay but he needs stability. My dad said he can go and live with him once we clear out the spare room—but, even if he goes there, we don't know how long that set-up will be safe. They could both be uprooted before he has a chance to settle.'

'I told you, you don't have any reason to be concerned.' His mouth made a firm line and his green eyes were fiercely determined. 'I'll make sure the changes don't make things bad for you.'

She shook her head. 'I know you mean well, Nate, but once you sell out to Peninsula things could change. I'm sure their lawyers are clever enough to find ways to tear up any agreement. According to one of the men from the company, my dad's house will most likely be scheduled for demolition so they can build on the land. He's been worried about it ever since. Everyone's upset. No one knows how long they will be able to stay in their homes. Some people have lived in their houses since they were children. It's more than bricks and mortar that are at stake—it's the foundation of their lives.'

Nate cupped her shoulders with his hands. 'I do understand that, Sophie, and I'm doing my best to work things out…but there's a lot involved and it's not something I can do overnight.'

'I know.' She frowned. 'Perhaps it will help if you keep people updated with what you're trying to do. As things are, everyone's in the dark and coming up with worst-case scenarios.'

'I suppose you're right. I'll talk to them at this meeting.' His thumbs made soothing warm circles on her shoulders. It felt good and she wanted him to go on holding her, but he let his hands drop to his sides as Tracey appeared at the far end of the room.

She came over to the workstation and handed him a lab report. 'I thought you'd want to see this as soon as it came in,' the nurse said. 'It's the report on Lucy's angiography.'

'Ah, thanks, Tracey. That was quick.' Tracey smiled and walked away, leaving Nate to quickly read the lab's analysis. 'Apparently the treatment went well this morning,' he told Sophie. 'The blood flow to her kidneys has improved dramatically. There was a fibrous thickening causing an obstruction in both arteries, but that's been resolved now.'

Her mouth curved. 'It's all good, isn't it? When I looked in on her a little while ago, her blood pressure readings were getting back to normal. Do we know what caused the thickening in the first place?'

He shook his head. 'These cases are always difficult—there might be a genetic cause, but we can't know for certain. All we can do at the moment is try to put things right.' He glanced at his watch. 'It's getting late—there was an emergency with one of the patients and I missed out on lunch. Do you want to go and grab a coffee with me and maybe a snack?'

Her mouth turned down at the corners. 'I can't, I'm afraid. I said I would go and see Jake for a few minutes in my afternoon break. He's been so busy we haven't had time to get together for a while, but he sent me a text message this afternoon to see how things were going with Rob and Jessica. I think I need to let him know what's happening.'

A muscle flicked in his jaw and she guessed he wasn't happy about her seeing Jake.

She said cautiously, 'He and I are just friends, you know.'

'Hmm. Maybe.' Nate straightened. 'I'll see you later, then. Is there any chance you might come to the meeting at the village hall this evening? I'd like to have you there with me.'

She nodded. 'Yes, of course I'll go with you.'

She turned away to go and meet up with Jake, conscious all the time of Nate's narrowed gaze on her. Then Tracey came back and she heard her telling him about a problem that had cropped up with one of his patients, and he went off to deal with the situation. She guessed he wouldn't be getting the break he wanted.

Sophie took the lift up to the next floor. Jake would still be in his office. He'd told her earlier that he'd been busy all day, talking to suppliers and arranging new contracts.

'Sophie, it's good to see you.' His smile widened as she entered the room and he moved some of his paperwork to one side.

She gave him an answering smile. 'How are things going?'

'Oh, I've been deluged with work. The bosses want a

lot of changes from the old system—more ways to save money and so on.'

'I suppose that's always going to be how things are. They're always trying to get a quart out of a pint pot. I don't envy you trying to make things work. You've put in a lot of overtime on this latest project, haven't you?'

'Yes, I have—it's taken a good deal of effort to put all this together.' He waved a hand over the files that were stacked up on his desk.

'Have you had time to eat? I could go to the cafeteria and bring you back some lunch if you can't get away?'

'Oh, that's okay—I went out to lunch with a couple of colleagues. We tried out the new restaurant by the river.' He glanced at her and said quietly, 'I'm sorry I haven't been there for you these last few days. You've a lot going on just now.'

'It's okay. You have, too.' She gave him a thoughtful look. 'You've been very busy.'

He frowned. 'Yes…yes…I was over in Cornwall again yesterday, talking to Cheryl and Matt about their systems and practices, or I'd have been in touch sooner.'

'Ah, yes, Cheryl…' Her brow creased as she tried to remember. 'I think I met her at one of the hospital's social functions. Nice girl. I seem to remember you liked her quite a lot.'

He looked at her oddly, seemingly nonplussed. Perhaps he'd thought she hadn't noticed. 'I… Well, she…'

She smiled. 'You'll have to let me know how things go with her.'

He shook his head. 'It's a non-starter. She only has eyes for someone else—a bit like you with Nate, I think…I can tell you both care for one another, but you must see that Nate never shows any sign of wanting to settle down. He's a heartbreaker, Sophie, and if he had his mind set on it, I dare say he would make a determined play for you. I suppose he's too involved with this estate business right now, though, and with his father being ill he's preoccupied.'

'That's probably true.' She started to walk towards the door. She didn't know what she thought about Nate, so she didn't want to talk to Jake about it just yet. 'I'll see you later, Jake.'

'I don't want to see you fall any further under his spell, Sophie. He already has you confused—I can tell. We should talk some more.'

'Yes, okay, we can do that. But I have to go now. I need to get back to work.'

'Shall I see you after work?'

'No, not today—I can't manage it. I have to go to a meeting at the village hall—about the estate being taken over. Tomorrow, perhaps.'

'Okay.'

She stopped to pick up a couple of coffees in disposable cups from the cafeteria, along with a pack of sandwiches for Nate. He'd said he hadn't eaten and he might appreciate some food.

Nate's expression was taut when she went back to the Children's Unit, and she wondered if he was still annoyed about the article in the paper and on edge about the meeting that was to take place later today. She approached him cautiously, not wanting to break into his introspection, but he acknowledged her with a brief nod.

'You weren't with Jake for very long,' he said, glancing up from the computer monitor where he was studying a series of CT images.

'No. We're both busy people,' she said. 'He just took a five-minute break.'

Nate seemed relieved. She pushed a coffee cup towards him and handed him the carton of sandwiches. 'I thought you might be hungry as you said you missed lunch.'

His eyes widened and he gave her a beaming smile. 'Bless you, Sophie. You're an angel.' He broke open the flip pack and bit into a chicken-and-mayo sandwich like a starving man. 'Mmm…this is great. Thank you—it was really thoughtful of you to do this.'

'You're welcome.' She turned the conversation back to work. 'You told me earlier that you wanted to look in on Josh before we finish here. Do you want to do that as soon as you've finished eating?'

He nodded. 'It's always a bit fraught, taking children off sedation after a head injury. I remember how it felt for me when I was a child, coming round a few days after my accident. I was intensely irritable and I didn't really understand anything that was going on. The nurses were great, though, incredibly patient.' He swallowed his coffee. 'My mother calmed me just by being there, talking to me and holding my hand. I don't remember what she said but it made me feel a lot better.' His features darkened momentarily as he recalled that time and for an instant his expression was bleak.

She wanted to reach out and hold him, to try to soothe his troubles away and make up for all the bad things that had happened in his life, but the fact that they were in a public place stopped her. 'It must bring back painful memories for you,' she said. He'd loved his mother and she'd been torn from him not too long after that.

'Yes, it does, even now.' He finished off his coffee

and shrugged off his pensive manner. 'Let's go and see how Josh is getting along, shall we?'

'Okay.' She went with him to the side ward where they found Josh being looked after by Hannah. The five-year-old was agitated and restless, pulling at tubes and monitor cables, while his parents were looking on anxiously.

'What's happening to him?' his father asked, looking at Nate. 'Is this a sign that something's wrong?'

'Not at all.' Nate shook his head and drew up a chair so that he could sit down beside the parents. 'It's quite normal for a child to be agitated when he's coming off sedation. Hannah will make sure that he's comfortable and that he can't harm himself in any way. You don't need to worry—it looks alarming but, believe me, it's quite normal.'

He went on gently trying to reassure them. 'We need to check that he's not in any pain or suffering discomfort of any kind. Hannah will stay with him to see to that. We find it's best to keep everything reasonably quiet and dim the lights…but if you talk to Josh and try to encourage him, that might help to calm him down. He'll take a while to process information as his brain recovers, so don't expect a clear response from him just yet. You need to take things slowly.'

The man nodded. 'We will.' He reached out to hold his son's hand and spoke to him softly, and the little boy seemed to quieten at the sound of his father's voice. The child was very pale, his fair hair damp against his forehead.

After checking him over and conferring with Sophie as to his medication, Nate took his leave of the parents and thanked Hannah for doing a good job of looking after the child.

They started to walk back towards the desk but Nate's phone rang before they reached it. He listened carefully to the person at the other end of the line and then said curtly, 'Okay, I'll come over. Give me half an hour.'

He was silent and a bit grim-faced as he cut the call and Sophie said cautiously, 'Are you all right? Is something bothering you?'

He gave an awkward shrug. 'I just heard from the convalescent home that my father has taken a turn for the worse. He has a chest infection, so they have him on oxygen and high-strength antibiotics. I need to go and see him before I go to the meeting—it'll be a bit of a rush but I'll pick you up from your house at around a quarter to seven, if that's all right with you?'

'Yes, that's fine.' She laid a comforting hand on his arm. 'I'm sorry he's not doing so well.'

'Thanks.' He smiled at her and squeezed her hand in response. For a second or two he moved closer and bent his head towards her as though he might drop a kiss on her forehead, but at the last moment he straightened and gently disengaged his arm.

Sophie had to suppress an odd sensation of regret for what might have been. More and more lately, she found herself wanting closer contact with him. Instinct told her she could end up hurt and ultimately abandoned if she let herself get involved with him—his track record with women wasn't good but she couldn't help the way she felt.

She walked with him back to the computer station

and prepared to go home. 'I'll see you later,' she said. 'I hope there's some good news about your father.'

'You too,' he answered. 'Good luck with Rob and Jessica. I imagine they're settling in all right?'

'I'm sure they'll be fine.'

She went home and phoned her father to make sure he was all right before hurrying to get changed for the meeting.

'Do you think Dad's still annoyed with you? How did he sound on the phone?' Rob asked. 'He's been on edge all day. Even Jessica had to try to calm him down. She took him a shepherd's pie a little while ago—it used to be his favourite.'

'It still is.' Sophie nodded. 'He told me to tell her how much he enjoyed it. Yes, he's still disappointed in me. I think he's also a bit apprehensive about this meeting tonight. He said he's going along to have his say. A friend's taking him.' She sighed. 'I wish the press hadn't stirred everything up. Nate says he's working on sorting things out but he needs time and no one's giving him that.'

'Well, good luck, anyway,' Jessica said. 'I'm glad I'm not going to be there to see sparks fly.' She had made dinner for the three of them and they sat round the table and talked for a while, enjoying being together.

Nate called for Sophie as he had promised. Jessica thanked him profusely for the cot and the chair, and Rob thanked him for giving him a lift to Sophie's house.

'I'm glad I was some help.' Nate gave them both a quick smile and then flicked a glance over Sophie, who was wearing a navy pencil-line dress teamed with navy stiletto heeled shoes. His dark brows shot up and he gave a silent whistle. 'Wow!' he said under his breath as they went out to his car. 'You look stunning.'

'Thank you.' She'd aimed to dress simply but stylishly for the occasion and she hadn't expected such a reaction from him. It felt good, though, to know that he thought she looked good. 'How is your father?' she asked.

He grimaced. 'He seems to be comfortable at the moment.'

They drove to the village green, where he parked his car near to the hall where the meeting was due to take place at seven-thirty. People were already going inside, but there were a lot more cars parked than Sophie had expected. The parish council had obviously been busy letting everyone know about the event. They stepped out of the car and Nate looked around, straightening his shoulders as though he was preparing himself for what was to come.

'There you are, Sophie! Your father said you would be here. I've been waiting for ages.' The familiar female voice startled Sophie and she looked around, her mouth opening in shock as she saw her mother standing by a bench seat that was set into the pavement.

'Mum, what are you doing here?'

Her mother looked animated, her eyes bright, her cheeks showing spots of bright colour, and her tawny, naturally curly hair was tousled as though she'd been running her fingers through it. Sophie's heart sank. Those weren't good signs. They were all indicators that her mother had been leaving off her medication.

'I wasn't expecting to see you until next weekend.'

'Well, I came to see you, of course.' She saw Nate standing beside Sophie and glared at him in recognition. 'Please go away. I want to talk to my daughter.'

Sophie looked at him in alarm, but Nate held up his hands, palms flat, and took a couple of steps backwards.

He knew about her mother's condition and wasn't going to argue with her.

Her mother seemed satisfied with that for the moment. She clearly had other things on her mind. She quickly turned her attention back to Sophie and said, 'No one was at the cottage when I got here this afternoon, so I phoned your father.' She rolled her eyes. 'He wasn't any help at all. He told me to go back home. As if I would! I want to see Rob and Jessica—I thought we could all go for a picnic on the green to celebrate us being together.' She was talking fast, full of excitement about her plans.

'Mum—this isn't a good time. We're just about to go into a meeting.'

'Oh, who cares about meetings? I've a basket full of food in the car—I thought we'd spread out a cloth on the grass and enjoy ourselves.'

Sophie sucked in a swift breath. Beside her, she felt Nate stiffen and she couldn't help worrying about what he might be thinking. It was embarrassing when her mother had these manic episodes because to her everything seemed normal and she didn't see that she was doing anything out of the ordinary.

All the times before in the past when her mother had gone off her medication came flooding back, making her stomach churn. Her mother could either go into a deep depression or feel so full of energy that she could take on the world. It was difficult to know how to deal with her sometimes. From experience, Sophie knew that any attempt to turn her mother off her goal would only end in her taking offence. Despite her seeming confidence, her illness meant she was in a highly vulnerable state.

'All right,' Sophie said, trying to talk in a soothing

manner. 'Let's think about this. It's going to be dark by the time we get things sorted—so perhaps this isn't the ideal place for a picnic. How would it be if I take you back to the cottage to see Rob and Jessica? I'm sure they would love to see you and take a look at the food you've brought with you. They could help you set it out and you could have a picnic at the cottage.'

Her mother moved her head from side to side as she thought about that. 'Okay,' she said at last, and Sophie gave a silent sigh of relief.

'Good. Where's your car? Is it close by?'

'Yes, it's over there.' Her mother waved a hand towards a side street.

'Ah, I see it.' Sophie swallowed carefully, conscious all the while of time passing by and of the village hall filling up with people. She was worried about the effect this disruption must be having on Nate but he stayed silent, simply watching her with her mother, his mouth making a flat line. He was clearly disturbed by the turn of events but he wasn't going to interfere and make the situation worse. Sophie had said she would go with him to the meeting and she didn't want to let him down, but she had to take care of her mother. 'Mum, have you brought your tablets with you—are they in your bag?'

'Tablets? I hate taking them…and I don't need them. I feel great!'

'I know you do…but do you have them with you? Can I look at them?'

'Oh, this is wasting precious time.' Even so, her mother searched in her bag and triumphantly produced a bottle of capsules. 'Here, you might as well throw them away.'

Sophie took the plastic bottle and slipped it into her

own bag. While her mother was preoccupied with the contents of her leather purse, she glanced at Nate and said softly, 'I'll drive her to the cottage—Rob and Jessica will look after her. It shouldn't take too long—I'll try to be back for the start of the meeting.'

'You'd better send them a message to let them know you're on your way.'

She nodded. 'I'm sorry about this.' It seemed she was always having to apologise. 'I did tell you my family is always going through problems of one sort or another.'

'Yes, you did, and I remember how it was from when you all lived here before, but it's okay. It can't be helped. I'll follow you in my car and make sure everything's all right.'

She hadn't expected him to do that. 'Are you sure? What about the meeting?'

'With any luck, we should be back in time.'

'Thanks.' She exhaled slowly. She felt better already. She turned back to her mother. 'Come on, Mum,' she said, taking her arm and leading her away. 'It's been disturbing for you lately, hasn't it, with everything that's been going on at home? But it's all working out fine.'

'Yes, it's good now. Rob and Jess are with you. They'll be all right.'

Sophie settled her mother in the car and took a moment to phone Jessica and tell her that they were on their way.

'Don't worry,' Jessica said. 'I'll make sure she takes her tablets. She'll probably sleep for a while afterwards. They often have that effect on her after she's left them off for a while.'

'Thanks.'

Back at the cottage, Jessica and Rob welcomed their

mother and settled her in the recliner armchair. They started to talk to her about things that were on her mind. Over the years, they'd all found this was the best way to deal with her wild mood swings.

Satisfied that she was being well looked after, Sophie went out and slid into the passenger seat of Nate's car.

'Is she okay?'

'I think so. Rob's setting out the food and Jessica has persuaded her to take a tablet.'

'Good.' He started the car and they set off once more for the meeting.

Nate pulled up opposite the village hall. He cut the engine and looked about him, frowning. There were men and women outside the hall, holding cameras aloft, and some had recording devices. These weren't villagers.

'It's the press,' Nate said through his teeth, his mouth making a grim line. 'Who would have told them about the meeting?'

'Isn't that the chairperson from the parish council speaking to one of them?' Sophie murmured. 'He looks quite pleased with himself. I think we can guess who told them.'

'He's gone too far this time.' Nate stepped out of the car and went towards the gathering of people. Sophie followed him.

'There he is.' The crowd surged towards him, cameras flashing, following him as he walked into the hall.

'Are you selling out, Branscombe?' a reporter shouted.

'Are you going after the money like your father?' another called out.

Nate tried to speak to the assembled people but was cut off by another journalist. 'Sins of the father,' the man said. 'What do you say to that, eh? Makes a good headline, don't you think?'

Nate tried to go on with what he wanted to say. People seemed disturbed by what was going on and Sophie caught a glimpse of her father in his wheelchair at the side of the hall, being kept back out of harm's way by his friend. He looked concerned by the turn of events.

'I agreed to come here this evening to talk to all of you and try to put your minds at rest,' Nate began. He didn't get a chance to go on.

'How can you do that? Your father's landed you right in it, hasn't he?' one of the reporters interrupted.

'Yeah, how are you going to sort out his mess?' another one enquired. 'Are you going to make a mint from selling out to Peninsula?'

Nate braced his shoulders. 'Okay, that's enough,' he announced in a brisk tone. 'Either you back off or this meeting is not going ahead.'

'Peninsula Holdings are going to put this place on the map. They'll build hotels and a shopping mall. That'll all be down to you, won't it?' A man with a camera stepped up to Nate and took his picture.

Another held out his recording device. 'What do you say to the people who want to keep their village exactly as it is now?'

Nate's jaw clenched. 'That's it. I'm leaving. If the people who are villagers or tenants on the estate want to talk to me, they can come to the Manor House tomorrow evening at seven. The press are not invited.'

He looked at Sophie. 'Are you coming with me? I'll understand if you don't want to.' He swivelled around and walked swiftly back to the car.

Sophie followed him, eyes wide, anxious about the

disastrous way things had erupted and desperate to talk to him. As she turned to go, she couldn't be sure but she thought she saw Jake among the crowd. Had he gone there to take part in the meeting?

Then, as she hurried away, she caught sight of her father's expression. 'I'm sorry,' she mouthed silently. He was taut with disbelief at the way things had gone. She didn't like to dwell on what he thought of her being with the son of the man who'd caused his disability, but at that moment she felt like a traitor.

She slid into the car beside Nate and he gunned the engine into life. The journalists were blocking the road back to the cottage, so he reversed quickly, turned the car around and headed out along the main highway.

'Where are we going?' she asked.

'To the Manor House.' He shot her a quick glance. 'Is that okay with you?'

'I suppose so.' She frowned. 'I can't help thinking it would have been better if you'd stayed to talk to the villagers.'

'You're probably right, but I wasn't going to take part in a circus. I told the organisers "no press" but they didn't keep to their word.'

'They'll probably be on their way to the Manor right now,' she said quietly. 'You could be heading right into another confrontation.'

'Yes, I expect that's true. I could drive to the Wayfarer's Inn instead—it's out of the way, no one will guess we're there, and we can talk over dinner. What do you think?'

'Sounds good.'

The Wayfarer's Inn was off the beaten track along a country lane and served the residents of another small village further inland. It was set against a backdrop of tall trees and had a garden where people could sit outside at rustic tables lit by old-style lanterns. Sophie and Nate chose to go inside and found a table in a corner made private by a wooden trellis and strategically placed tubs filled with greenery.

Sophie was surprised to find she had an appetite despite the fact that she'd shared a meal with her brother and sister less than three hours ago, but Nate was making up for missing out on a proper meal earlier that day. They ate chilli con carne with pilau rice and sour cream, and finished off with apple-and-raspberry crumble. They talked about his father, who was struggling with lung problems after his heart attack.

It was only later, when Nate's mood had mellowed a little, that Sophie asked him about his plans for the estate.

'What would you have said at the meeting?' she asked him as they drank rich dark coffee. 'Do you think you would have managed to appease them?'

'Some people might have been satisfied, but others possibly not. The thing is, I don't have a lot of options. My father borrowed money to finance his investment abroad and that has to be paid back.'

She frowned. 'I can see why it's been such a worry.'

'Yes.' He made a wry face. 'I've been trying to organise ways to save the estate, but they won't be to everyone's liking. For a start, I would have to terminate short-term leases so that I can sell those properties. That would only apply to newcomers who rent property for the holiday season. We get a few people who come over from France or Spain, wanting a change of scenery. In the winter, the houses are difficult to let unless business people want to stay while they're over here for conferences and so on.'

He refilled his cup from a cafetière and spooned brown sugar crystals into his coffee. 'I'll see if I can start some kind of farming project, and I thought we could make more use of the lake—maybe restock it with fish and organise fishing weekends. I'm sure they would go down well.'

'You'd have to have somewhere for them to stay locally.'

He nodded. 'I could get some log cabins built by the lake…have facilities put in and so on, but it will cost quite a bit initially. I'll put my own money into that but it will be some time before the venture pays for itself.'

'So, all in all, it would have been simpler for you to sell up and have none of this problem?'

'It would. It's taken a while for the accountants to look into everything but I'm fairly sure we have some viable options now. I think I can safely turn down any offer Peninsula makes.'

She smiled. 'That's such a relief. It sounds as though you've tried really hard to find a solution.'

'I have.' He reached for her hand across the table. 'Above all, I'm doing this for you, Sophie. I told you I would do everything I can to make sure you and your father can keep your homes. I'm going down this route because I feel we—my father and I—owe it to your father to help him any way we can to make up for what happened to him, and I'm doing it because I care about you and I want you to be happy.'

'Thank you. I…I don't know what to say. I'm so grateful to you.' She leaned forward in her seat and placed her free hand in his palm. He cupped her hands and bent his head towards her, brushing her lips with his own, sending an instant wave of heat to course through her body.

'You know I want you, Sophie…more than anything. I'd move heaven and earth for you. I want to take you in my arms and kiss you right now and let you know just how much I'm aching for you.'

She kissed him, closing her eyes, oblivious to their surroundings. Her lips were aflame, her blood fizzing with excitement. Hidden by the screen, they were in their own secluded world, and in that moment she wanted him every bit as much as he wanted her.

'We could get a room here,' he said softly, his voice rough around the edges, his hands trembling a little. 'I need you so much. Tell me you feel the same way.'

'I want you,' she said huskily. 'I do…but…I'm not sure it would be the wisest thing… There are so many reasons why this would be all wrong… You and me— we're from different worlds.'

'That doesn't matter. Why should it matter?'

She thought about it. He was offering her a night of bliss, of joy and ecstasy, the fulfilment of all her longings…but that was all he was offering. Could she put her uncertainties about everything that had happened between them and the problems between their families to one side and give in to temptation, take what he was prepared to give, for now?

Her musings were short-lived. A waiter approached and they broke apart, just as her mobile phone started to trill. Still shaken by her need for Nate, she did nothing, but took deep, slow breaths, trying to bring herself back to normal.

The phone kept on ringing. 'They're persistent, whoever they are,' Nate said drily. 'Perhaps you'd better answer it. It might be to do with your sister, or your mother.'

She nodded. The waiter asked if there was anything they needed and Nate asked for the bill. He had himself under control, as if nothing had happened between them. Either that or he was very good at hiding his feelings.

He'd had to remind her about the worries over Jessica and her mother. What had she been thinking? How could she possibly spend the night here with him when her family needed her? She couldn't leave them to their own devices so soon.

She looked down at the screen on her phone. 'It's Jake,' she said flatly. 'I thought I saw him outside the village hall earlier. He's probably worried in case the press caught up with us.'

Nate's head went back a fraction and his gaze narrowed on her. He didn't like the fact that Jake was calling her.

Jake's voice was brisk and matter-of-fact. 'I had to ring you,' he said. 'I tried to get to the Manor House in case you were there, but there are a dozen reporters at the gate. I know you're with Nate—I saw you leave the meeting with him—but I don't feel I had any choice but to get in touch. Your father's very concerned about what happened at the hall tonight. I spoke to him and he's in a bad way, very shaken up. I think he might be suffering a panic attack of some sort.'

'Thanks for letting me know, Jake. I'll go and see him.'

'I told him you would.'

'Yes...okay.'

She cut the call and told Nate what was happening.

'I'll have to go over to Dad's house and try to calm him down. You can stay here, if you want—Jake said the journalists are at the Manor. I'll get a taxi to take me home.'

He shook his head. 'I'll take you, and then I'll go to the Manor House. I'm not going to let a bunch of reporters keep me away.'

She frowned. 'So we could have gone there earlier?'

'I guess so.' He nodded. 'It's just that when you suggested there might be a problem, I thought this place might be more romantic—I suppose I leapt at the chance to spend time with you somewhere you might feel comfortable. I didn't have an ulterior motive, but I wanted you to be able to relax.'

'Hmm…and I did. You're right—this is a lovely inn.' She made a wry smile. 'And I was relaxed enough to be very tempted by your offer of spending the night, until I started to think about everything that's happened. My family has to come first. We've had more than one chance but it's just not meant to be.'

'I won't let you down again, Sophie,' he said.

'I'd like to believe that.' She stood up and he went with her towards the exit door.

'And you know I won't give up trying to win you over, don't you?'

'Mmm… I guessed as much. You always were persistent.'

He studied her as he held open the door to let her through. 'You don't believe I can be good for you, do you?'

She returned his gaze. 'No. There are so many reasons why I should steer clear of you, and an equal number of reasons why I can't—my head and my heart are at war and I've no idea what to do about that.'

He smiled. 'That's easy. Listen to your heart every time…and let me take care of the rest.'

CHAPTER SIX

'YOU WERE THERE with him at the meeting—you were there with Nate Branscombe.' Sophie's father glared at her angrily next morning. 'How could you do that? How could you ally yourself with him when you know how I feel about that family?'

'Nate's okay—he's not done anything wrong. He wasn't the one who hurt us.' Sophie tried to defend Nate but her father wasn't having any of it.

'He's in charge now and if things don't go his way he'll sell us out, plain and simple. He's a Branscombe through and through. And all this time you and he have been getting close again—I can see it in the way you look at him, in the way you talk about him... Don't fool yourself that he cares about you, Sophie. He'll do the same as he's always done with women and drop you as soon as things start getting serious. Didn't you learn anything when he left after my accident? He didn't stay around to help you pick up the pieces, did he?'

'I made it too difficult for him. I was angry and upset and I wouldn't listen. I thought someone—he—should have known his father was having angina attacks. I lashed out at him.'

'You weren't to blame for him leaving. He'd have

gone anyway. I worked for his father, remember? I know how his kind think. They simply move on.'

'Nate's different, Dad. He's a decent man.'

'He's messing with you. James Branscombe always made it clear to me that his son was to marry aristocracy. It was always uppermost in his mind that his son would carry on the line and keep that upper-crust heritage. His family's place in society means everything to James. And his son won't go against him.'

Sophie flinched at the things he was saying. She'd probably known it all along, but having it spelled out for her so graphically made her stomach churn. Her father was upset and angry but she understood he was only trying to look out for her. He wanted to warn her there was no future for her with Nate, but deep down she already knew it, didn't she? Her problem was that she had trouble accepting it.

'I'm not looking to marry him,' she said. 'No one said anything about that.' But if she had the chance to be with Nate for ever, wouldn't she grasp it with both hands? Wasn't she lying to herself if she said anything different? But she couldn't say any of that to her father, could she? He wouldn't understand. 'Try not to upset yourself. You'll only end up having another panic attack like you did last night.' She knelt down beside her father's chair. 'Look, Dad, I'm sorry you feel this way… but I told you how Nate plans to put things right about the estate. He's doing the best he can in difficult circumstances. If you're not convinced, you'll be able to talk to him at the Manor House tonight.'

'Hmmph. We'll see.' He frowned. 'You'll be there, I suppose?'

She nodded. 'I'm going with Rob. He said he wants

to know what's going on. Do you want me to take you, or will your friend be driving you there?'

'I've already made arrangements.'

'Okay.' She stood up. 'If there's nothing else I can do for you, I'd better get back to the cottage. Jessica was having some kind of cramps in her abdomen this morning. They may be nothing, but I need to take her for her check-up at the hospital.'

He nodded. 'Let me know how she goes on. Where's your mother staying? I don't suppose there's room for her at the cottage, is there? Is she any calmer?'

'She seems to be all right now. We're making sure she's taking her tablets and she's booked herself into a room at the village pub. Tom will come over when he gets the chance but it's difficult for him because he has to go to work every day and can't get away easily. Anyway, Mum says she's going to stay there until Jess has the baby. Don't worry. We'll look after her.' She laid a hand on his shoulder and bent to kiss him lightly on the forehead. 'I'll see you later, Dad. Rob will be along in an hour or so to make a start on clearing out the spare room. He's really keen to get things organised.'

She went out by the kitchen. Charlie's tail thumped happily on the floor as she stroked him before leaving the house. She'd spent a fraught half hour with her father and she was almost relieved to be going home.

Jessica was still feeling uncomfortable when Sophie arrived back at the cottage, and she did her best to reassure her. 'We'd perhaps better take your overnight case with us to the hospital,' she said. 'They might want to keep you in.'

Some half an hour later, she took her over to the maternity unit. 'Stay with me when I see the doctor, will you?' Jessica asked. 'And I want you to be there when the baby comes—I don't even know if Ryan will be able to be here for the birth. I need to have you with me.'

'That's all right. Of course I'll stay with you—and once we know that you're in labour, we can get in touch with Ryan. With any luck, he'll be able to fly home at short notice.'

'Thanks, Sophie.'

The obstetrician examined Jessica carefully and looked at the ultrasound scans. 'I think we'll admit you for observation,' she said. 'If things don't start to happen overnight, we'll induce labour in the morning.'

They found a bed for Jessica on the ward and Sophie helped her settle in. 'You can walk about if you want, use the day room and talk to the other mums-to-be,' the midwife told Jessica. 'But make sure you get some rest if you feel you need it. We'll be checking your pulse and blood pressure and listening to the foetal heartbeat and so on at regular intervals.'

'I'm leaving you in good hands,' Sophie told her sister a little later. She glanced at her watch. 'I'm here on borrowed time—I need to go over to the Children's Unit and get to work, but I'll come over to see you later.' She left Jessica making a phone call to Ryan.

The rest of the day passed without anything untoward happening, and after checking on Jessica once more in the late afternoon, Sophie spent some time getting ready for the meeting at the Manor House. She missed Nate and wanted to be with him, but she hadn't seen much of him all day. They'd both been busy with their own lists of patients, and now she was edgy with anticipation at the thought of seeing him again at his home. Last night at the Wayfarer's Inn, he'd kissed her and made it very clear how much he wanted her. How would it have been if she'd spent the night there with him? A frisson of nervous excitement rippled through her at the thought.

A crowd of reporters had gathered outside the gates of the Manor by the time Rob and Sophie arrived, but security staff were on hand to make sure none of them had access to the grounds. They'd been told to expect Sophie and her brother, so they were allowed in without any fuss, and Sophie was able to drive up to the house without restriction.

Nate met her and Rob in the wide hallway and immediately took them to one side. 'Hey, I'm glad you came.' He greeted them cheerfully, but after a moment or two of general chit-chat, Rob excused himself and went to find his father. Nate drew Sophie into a side room.

As soon as they were alone, he put his arms around her and held her close. 'I wish there wasn't such a crowd here tonight,' he said. 'I'd much rather it was just you and me—I'd like to have the time to show you properly just how glad I am to see you.'

'That might not be such a good idea.' She felt warm and safe in his arms, but even so, she looked at him uncertainly, her father's warnings echoing in her head.

'No?' He took no notice of her doubts, folding her to him and sweeping away her qualms with a kiss that was passionate, fervent and full of pent-up desire, as though he'd been holding back and couldn't resist any longer. His kiss left her breathless, clinging to him in startled wonder, definitely wanting more.

'Oh, wow!' she said. 'I wasn't expecting that.' He held her so that her body meshed with his and she smiled up at him, loving his nearness. She was all too conscious of the way his hands were moving slowly over her, shaping her curves, exploring the soft hills and valleys of her body. It made her feel good, made her tingle all over with longing.

'I can't get enough of you,' he said, his voice ragged as he bent his head to nuzzle the silky-smooth column of her throat. He nudged aside the flimsy fabric of her top, exposing her bare shoulder. 'I've been thinking about you all night and all day, waiting until I could get you alone.' He ran the flat of his palm lightly down her spine, moving ever lower until he drew her against him and his strong thighs tangled with hers. 'You're so, so beautiful,' he whispered. 'You tantalise me every time I'm with you.'

She kissed him, a deep-seated need growing in her. She wanted this, was desperate to be with him. And yet, even as she returned his kisses and ran her fingers over his taut biceps, at the back of her mind the doubts were creeping in. Why did it have to be so difficult for her to give in to her heart's desire?

Perhaps it was because she knew, deep down, that she would never be satisfied with a relationship that was going nowhere. She wanted more, much more from Nate, but was he prepared to give it? Her whole life had been torn apart when her parents' marriage broke up, and her own relationships with men had been fraught up to now. Perhaps those experiences had made her afraid. She couldn't face being hurt again and if Nate let her down she would be devastated. More than anything, she needed to experience a love that would last—and she was coming to realise that it was *his* love she wanted above all.

She ran her hand lightly over his ribcage as though she would memorise the feel of him. She wanted him and needed him, but… When she looked up into his eyes, she knew he read the uncertainty in hers. 'I won't let you down,' he said. He kissed her passionately, his hand moving to the small of her back, crushing her soft curves to blend with his.

A clock chimed the hour and he sighed, releasing her slowly. 'We should go,' he murmured reluctantly, resting his head lightly against her temple, and she nodded. 'I didn't want any of this,' he said quietly. 'This business of the Manor and the estate. I simply wanted to be a doctor.'

They broke apart and she spent a moment tidying herself up, straightening her camisole top and smoothing a hand over her jeans. 'Is my hair a mess?' she asked and he gave her an amused smile.

'You look fantastic,' he said. 'You always do. That's part of the problem.' There was a faint note of regret in his voice.

They went into the main hall, where people were beginning to take their places around a long, rectangular solid wood table, and Sophie slid into a seat next to her brother and her father. The walls in here were panelled in oak and the evening light filtered in through leaded panes, casting a warm glow over everything.

Nate welcomed everyone. He'd provided them with tea and coffee and soft drinks or wine, and there was a buffet table at the side of the room behind Sophie, where a selection of finger food had been set out. Sophie guessed that his housekeeper, Charlotte, had been busy organising things. She noticed that as well as a variety of tiny sandwiches, there were mini Yorkshire puddings with rare beef and mustard and horseradish sauce, bruschetta with goat's cheese, basil and tomato, and blinis with smoked salmon. He'd done his best to make sure his guests were treated well.

His efforts certainly helped to put his audience in a better mood and encourage them to listen to what he had to say. He told them of the plans he'd outlined to Sophie, and added that he was hoping to start an organic farming business on the land that up to now had been left to pasture. 'I'll need skilled workers to help me with that,' he said.

There were some dissenting voices. Some people didn't like the fact that he was planning to organise fishing weekends. 'There'll be a lot of strangers roaming around, and they'll start up competitions and so on,' one man said. 'The village won't be the same.'

'It's better than having to sell the houses to Peninsula, though, don't you think?' Nate pointed out the advantages but added, 'The costings aren't all in yet, so I'm making no promises…but this is what I'm aiming for. I'll do my best to hold off any sale.'

When the meeting finished, people stayed to eat some more and talk for a while and ask questions but gradually they started to drift away. Sophie's father spoke to her briefly. He seemed slightly appeased by what he'd heard but said tetchily, 'I'm going home. I can't be in this place without remembering all my dealings with James Branscombe. He was a difficult man to work with. I don't know if his son's going to be different—let's hope he is.'

Rob frowned, watching his father leave. 'He's very bitter still, isn't he? I can't blame him. His whole life changed after the accident. I just don't know why he stayed with Lord Branscombe so long if he felt that way about him.'

'I think the money was probably good, and the work

suited him. It kept a roof over our heads. People put up with a lot to have a secure life.'

'Perhaps he'll feel better when I go to live with him. I'll be able to help him out if he's struggling.'

'That's true.' Sophie nodded. 'Though sometimes it might do him good to struggle a bit.'

Rob frowned. 'How can that be?'

'It might help him to do things for himself as much as possible.'

'But he can't, can he? He's in a wheelchair.'

Nate came to join them. 'I couldn't help overhearing the last bit of your conversation,' he said. 'I think Sophie means that if your father has to try to do some things within his ability, it will help strengthen his muscles. Being able to pull himself up to a standing position, for instance, will help—though he'll need someone to be there with him to make sure he doesn't fall.'

'Oh, I see.' Rob nodded thoughtfully. 'Yes, I can do that.'

Nate studied him. 'How are you doing these days, Rob? Are you feeling any brighter in yourself?'

Rob pulled a face. 'I think I'm better now I'm a bit more settled. I have mood swings and I don't understand why I feel that way. I worry about it sometimes.'

'That's understandable.' Nate was sympathetic. 'Sophie told me you were afraid you might be suffering from bipolar disorder like your mother but, to be honest, seeing you and hearing how you react to things, I think you're going through what every teenage boy goes through. Your hormones are all over the place. It's a difficult time for you.'

'I think Nate's right.' Sophie joined in. She was glad Nate had taken the time to try to reassure her brother.

'You've been better in yourself since you came here and met up with some of your old friends. You said a few of them are studying at the college in town—perhaps you might want to look into signing up for one of the courses that start soon. You've already done a year of Psychology—why not try to finish your studies?'

Rob gave it some thought and then nodded, seemingly invigorated. 'Yeah, I might do that. My mate has to go to an Open Day in a couple of weeks. I could go along with him.'

'That's a great idea.'

Nate glanced at Sophie. 'How's the rest of the family doing?'

'They're fine, thanks.' He already knew about Jessica being admitted to hospital. 'Jess's still having odd abdominal cramps—they're not really contractions as such but she's quite uncomfortable. Her back's aching and she doesn't like being on her own in hospital. And I checked on Mum before we came here and made sure she took her tablets.' She sent him a quick concerned glance. 'Is there any news of your father?'

'He's much the same. He's been readmitted to hospital so he can have intensive treatment. They have him on antibiotics and diuretics to try to reduce the fluid in his tissues, but he seems to be struggling.'

'I'm sorry.'

She and Rob had to go soon after that so that Sophie could drive to the hospital and check on Jessica. She was reluctant to leave Nate—she wanted to stay and talk some more—but her sister was uppermost in her mind just then.

Jessica was thrilled to see her and Rob. They spoke for a short time and Sophie rubbed her back for her, but

Jess was tired and soon dozed off. It looked as though they would go ahead with inducing labour in the morning.

Everything went as planned. A whole day went by after the midwife inserted the pessary that would hopefully start things off. By then the weekend was almost on them and Sophie was glad because it meant she would be able to spend time at the hospital without worrying about having to take time off work.

She went to the village High Street on Saturday morning to buy things that Jessica might need, like baby bottles, nappies and wipes. She found a lovely congratulations card and some of Jessica's favourite chocolates. Lost in thought, she came back out on to the street only to be pulled up short in surprise as she saw Nate coming out of the post office. Her pulse quickened.

'Hi there. It's good to see you.' He smiled and gave her a hug. 'I wasn't sure if I would see anything of you over the next couple of days, with Jessica being in hospital, but here you are. It's my lucky day.' He waved a hand towards the post office. 'I had to send off a registered letter—' He glanced at her packages. 'It looks as though you've been stocking up on essentials in preparation for the baby.'

She nodded. 'Jessica brought a few things with her on the train, but there was a limit to what she could get in her case. As it was, it was a good thing it had wheels on it.' They walked along the street together to where she had parked her car.

'Are you headed for the hospital now?'

'Yes, I—' She broke off, frowning as she noticed a small boy walking with his mother. They were going

towards the pharmacy nearby and the child was coughing quite badly, dragging his feet as though being out
and about was too much for him. He was a thin little
boy around seven years old and he was breathless and
didn't look at all well. His mother looked at him worriedly, supporting him, and as Sophie and Nate looked
on, the little boy's knees started to buckle under him.

Nate reached them and helped to catch the child
before he collapsed completely. 'Can I help you?' he
asked the mother. 'He looks quite poorly.' He held the
child, kneeling down and cradling him in his arms as
his mother nodded anxiously.

'Oh, yes…please can you help?' She knelt down beside him, saying urgently, 'I recognise you—you're Nate
Branscombe, aren't you? Can you do something for him?
You're a doctor, aren't you? I tried to get to see our GP
but the surgery's closed.'

She dragged in a shaky breath. 'My little boy's had
a cough for about a week but the antibiotics the doctor
gave him don't seem to be working. I'm on my own this
weekend. I've been so worried. I'm new to the village
and I have no transport and no one I can leave him with
while I try to sort out what to do. I was going to the
pharmacy to see if anyone could help, but he suddenly
got worse. I knew he was ill but I didn't think it was so
bad—I think I need to call for an ambulance.'

'Yes, that would probably be best,' Nate said. He
glanced up at Sophie but she was already dialling the
number. 'He's feverish and not breathing properly,' Nate
went on. 'He needs oxygen.' He looked at Sophie once
more. 'Do you have your medical kit in your car? I
have mine but I'm parked further down the road.' He
checked the boy over, feeling for a pulse. 'His lips are

a bluish colour already. I'm afraid we may need to intubate him fast.'

'Yes, I'll go and get it.' Finishing the call, she hurriedly opened the boot of her car and hauled out her copious medical bag. Taking off her jacket, she rolled it up into the shape of a pillow and placed it under the boy's head. She placed an SpO2 monitor on his finger and connected it to the portable machine that gave an oxygen read-out.

'What's his name?' Nate asked the mother.

'Shaun.'

'Okay.' He spoke directly to the boy. 'Shaun, I'm going to listen to your chest.' The boy didn't respond but Nate reached for a stethoscope and was quiet for a moment, running the diaphragm over Shaun's ribcage. 'It sounds like pneumonia,' he said after a while. He checked the SpO2 reading. 'His blood oxygen saturation is very low,' he told Sophie. 'The most important thing right now is to get a tube into his windpipe and give him the oxygen he needs.'

Sophie helped him, introducing a cannula into Shaun's hand and giving him a sedative and anaesthetic so that Nate could get easier access to insert the tube into his throat. They worked quickly, taping the tube in place on the boy's cheek. Nate connected the tube to the bag and mask device and then attached this to an oxygen canister. He began to squeeze the bag rhythmically, getting life-saving oxygen into Shaun's lungs.

Sophie explained the procedure to the mother and then said, 'When he gets to the hospital he'll most likely be given an X-ray and possibly a CT scan to take a better look at his lungs. They'll want to do tests to see what's causing the problem and they'll give him a stronger broad spectrum antibiotic in the meantime.'

In the distance, they heard the sound of the ambulance siren. Nate looked up, frowning slightly as he saw that a crowd of onlookers had gathered around them. They were mostly silent, just watching, but Nate was too busy to take much notice. 'I'm going to give him nebulised adrenaline,' he told Sophie. 'Will you take over here while I set it up?'

'Of course.' She squeezed the oxygen bag while he prepared the nebulised solution. It would help to relax the child's airways and allow him to breathe more easily. After a while, when the boy was still unresponsive, he gave him a shot of corticosteroid, aiming to reduce any inflammation that was causing a problem. Sophie went on squeezing the oxygen bag and Nate spoke quietly to the child's mother, trying to reassure her.

The ambulance drew up close by. 'Hi, Doc—hi, Sophie...' The paramedics arrived and listened carefully as Nate outlined the situation.

'We need to have a team waiting for us at the hospital. He should go straight to Paediatric Intensive Care.'

'Okay, we'll let them know.'

They transferred Shaun to the ambulance and connected him to the monitors that would tell them his heart and respiratory rate, along with the level of oxygen in his blood. It was improving but it was still very low because of the infection in his lungs. Shaun's mother sat alongside her son and Nate climbed into the vehicle to make the journey with them.

He glanced at Sophie. 'Thanks for everything you did back there, Sophie. Maybe I'll see you at the hospital later?' He was looking at her packages, abandoned on the pavement.

She nodded. 'Yes, I'll be there most of the day, I expect.' She watched the ambulance pull away and then went to gather up all her equipment.

The small crowd of people were still watching. 'You and the other doctor did all right, there,' one man said. 'Do you think the boy will pull through?'

'Well, we've done everything we can and he'll be in the right place to get the care he needs,' she answered carefully.

'I never thought of Nate Branscombe working as an emergency doctor,' another bystander said. 'I only ever saw him coming and going from the Manor House.' He nodded slowly, deep in thought. 'Just goes to show, you never really know someone.'

Sophie collected her supplies and put them back into her medical bag. She stowed it away in the boot of her car, along with her shopping. A woman who Sophie recognised from around the village picked up one of the bags from the pavement and handed it to her. 'Baby things,' she said with a smile. 'I guessed your sister would be due any time now. I hope things go well for her.'

'Thanks.' Sophie smiled and slid into the driver's seat. She and Nate had spent a worrying half hour or so with the boy and she was almost looking forward to enjoying a more relaxed time in the maternity unit with Jessica.

Perhaps she ought to have known it wasn't to be. Life was never that easy for her, and when she arrived on the ward Jessica was nowhere to be seen.

'Oh, she's been taken to the delivery suite,' a nurse

told her. 'She's not doing too well, poor girl. The contractions have been painful and they've been going on for quite a long time through the night. The doctor's given her an epidural to give her some relief.'

'But she didn't tell me... Why wouldn't she have phoned me?'

'She said if it was going to be a long haul she didn't want to worry you. I was about to call you, though. Things are beginning to speed up quite significantly.'

'I'll go and see her.'

Sophie hurried away to find Jessica. She was lying on the bed looking very pale, with a sheen of sweat on her brow. 'Oh, Jessica, you were supposed to ring me,' Sophie said, going over to her to give her a hug. 'Did you change your mind about wanting me here?'

'No! Never!' Jessica smiled tiredly. 'It's just that it all started to happen in the night and I guessed you'd be asleep. I didn't want to disturb you. And Mum was here earlier. She can be a bit exhausting when she's in full flow. I'm not sure she's taken her tablets.'

'Oh, heavens! Where is she now?'

'She's gone to get a cup of coffee. Do you think you might be able to persuade her to swallow her meds with a bun or something?'

'I will...but shouldn't I be here with you?'

'You will be. They say it will be a while yet.' Jessica smiled, laying a hand on her abdomen as another contraction swept over her. 'I can feel it but since I had the epidural there's no pain. I'll be fine. I think Ryan's on his way to the hospital. He said he was going to catch a flight last night.'

'That's good. All right, I'll go and see if I can find Mum and calm her down—though I suppose you can't really blame her for being excited with a grandson on the way!'

Jessica smiled. 'Yes, maybe.'

Sophie found her mother in the cafeteria, happily sending messages from her phone to all her friends. 'I can't believe it's actually happening,' she said. 'But she's been in labour for ages.'

'It's taking a while, isn't it?' Sophie agreed. 'But a first grandchild is something special…worth waiting for.'

'Oh, I can't wait to hold him!'

'I know. I feel the same way.'

They chatted and she persuaded her mother to eat something and swallow her tablets. Tom phoned a little later and Sophie took the opportunity to slip away while her mother was preoccupied with the call. 'I'll see you in a little while,' she mouthed as she left the cafeteria and her mother smiled.

She went back into the delivery room and saw, to her relief, that Ryan had arrived. He was holding Jessica's hand.

She and Ryan greeted one another and then Sophie went to stand at the other side of the bed. 'I'm so glad you made it in time,' she told him. But, even as she said it, things started to happen all at once. Another major contraction started.

'I can see the baby's head,' the midwife said. 'Try to give a big push.'

The baby's head appeared, but instead of being followed by the appearance of his shoulders, everything seemed to stop. They waited for Jessica's next contraction, but even then the baby's shoulders stayed firmly in place and when the midwife intervened it was no use.

'The shoulder's stuck,' she said, looking worried. The baby's face was turning grey and Sophie was becoming more alarmed with every minute that passed. If the baby stayed in this position for too long, the umbilical cord would be squashed and oxygen wouldn't get through to him.

The midwife had signalled for help and the room filled with people: obstetricians, paediatricians, midwives, an anaesthetist. They all had a specific job to do but seeing them all there, trying to bring this baby into the world, was terrifying. As a doctor, Sophie knew the dangers but this was different—this was her sister at risk, along with her unborn baby.

Two midwives helped Jessica to get into a better knees-up position to facilitate the birth, the doctor made a deeper episiotomy cut and another midwife pressed down hard on Jessica's abdomen. The baby was in distress and Jessica began to haemorrhage. It was horrifying to stand there and see it happen, and for Sophie to know that she had to keep out of the way and let the doctors and nurses do their jobs. This was her sister and her nephew who were in danger and she was frightened for both of them.

In the next minute the baby was born, but he didn't make any sound. He was a bluish colour and floppy, and immediately the paediatrician took him and began to try to resuscitate him. A midwife wrapped him in a blanket to keep him warm and then the doctor suctioned him to clear away the secretions that were blocking his airway. They placed him in an incubator and started to give him oxygen, attaching vital monitor leads to him before wheeling him away to the Neonatal Intensive Care Unit.

Sophie wanted to rush after him and do anything she

could to help, but her sister needed her too. Ryan was white with shock and looked about ready to pass out, while Jessica was clammy with exhaustion and loss of blood. She was still bleeding and the midwives were doing everything they could to stem the flow. Sophie tried to stay calm, urging Ryan to sit down and put his head between his knees for a while to restore his blood pressure, and then she went to hold Jessica's hand once more.

Over the next hour, as the doctors and the nurses did everything they could to bring the bleeding under control, Jessica kept vomiting. All Sophie and Ryan could do was to try to make her comfortable. Sophie spoke to her mother and tried to reassure her—they'd been allowed to take it in turns to be in the delivery room.

'I believe things have calmed down finally,' the doctor said at last. 'She's stable, and the best thing to do now is to let her rest.'

Sophie and her mother left Jessica alone with Ryan from time to time over the next couple of hours, to give them some space. Her mother went to fetch coffees for everyone and Sophie went outside for a breath of fresh air.

Her phone rang. It was Nate, and relief washed over her at the sound of his voice. Everything seemed better when he was close by, even if he was only at the end of a phone line.

'I wondered how things were going,' he asked. 'I've been thinking about all of you.'

'She's had a really tough time and I'm worried about the baby,' she told him. 'I don't know exactly how he's doing, yet, but I think he's out of the woods. Jessica's still retching. They're giving her oxygen through nasal tubes and she's on intravenous fluids, so she's gradually improving.'

'I'm sorry, Sophie. It sounds as though it's been rough on her and the baby. Are you going to stay there through the night?'

'No, Ryan's the only one who can be with her then. The rest of the time they're not allowing more than two visitors at the bedside and Mum's going to be there for a while. Actually, I was almost expecting her to be over-excited despite her medication, but she's been remarkably subdued.'

'She's probably worried, like everyone else. I guess when she takes her medication she's fine.'

'Yes.' She frowned. 'I'm glad you understand, Nate.' Somehow, it was becoming more and more important to her that he accepted her family as they were. 'I was afraid you might be uncomfortable around my family. They can be difficult to handle at times.'

He gave a short laugh. 'I'm hardly likely to feel that way—there are skeletons in most family backgrounds, mine included, and my father isn't exactly a prime example of how to behave.'

'I suppose not.' She wished he could be here with her right now. She yearned for his soothing presence but it wasn't to be. He was probably going to spend time with his father.

Sophie cut the call a little later, after telling him, 'I'll stay with Jessica for another couple of hours and then I'm going to see Dad and Rob and let them know what's happening. After that I'm going home. It's been a traumatic day.'

Before going back to Maternity, Sophie looked in on the Children's Unit and checked up on Shaun to see how he was getting on. He'd been in a bad way when the ambulance brought him to the hospital earlier that morning and she was worried about his condition.

'He's on powerful antibiotics,' Tracey told her. 'He'll stay on the ventilator for some time, but he seems to be responding to the treatment.'

'That's something, anyway,' Sophie said. 'Thanks, Tracey.' She checked on Josh, the five-year-old who had the head injury, but he was doing fine. He was almost well enough to be discharged home.

She went to see her sister one more time. Her mother was keeping her company, concerned for her youngest daughter and holding her hand.

'I feel so dizzy,' Jessica murmured, glancing at Sophie. 'The baby—is he all right? I wish he was here. Have you been to look at him? Ryan's gone to see him.'

'Yes, I looked in on him in the Neonatal Unit,' Sophie told her. 'They're keeping him warm and giving him oxygen. When you're a little stronger and the baby's more up to it, you'll be able to hold him.'

'I wish I didn't feel so tired,' Jessica said. 'I feel so weak—the room's spinning.'

Sophie gently squeezed her hand. 'It's because you haemorrhaged—you're very short on iron, so they're going to give you a transfusion. You should start to feel much better after that.'

Sophie's mother left to go and meet her husband and tell him what had been happening, but Jessica asked Sophie to stay. 'I feel better having you and Ryan with me,' she said.

Jessica had the blood transfusion soon after that, and an hour later Ryan wheeled the baby into the side room where she was recovering. The baby was a much healthier colour now and looked none the worse for his ordeal. He was well wrapped up in a shawl and had a soft wool hat on his head to keep him warm.

Ryan carefully laid the baby on Jessica's chest and she wrapped an arm around the sleeping infant. 'We're going to call him Casey,' she said with a smile, and her husband kissed her tenderly. She was still very weak, but the three of them were together at last and Sophie breathed a sigh of relief, watching them. It looked as though mother and son were out of danger. She took some photos for posterity and then slipped out of the room to give them some privacy.

She went to see her father and tell him about the new addition to the family. Rob was with him, getting the spare room ready while they waited for news, and he and her father were both glad to hear that disaster had been avoided. 'I think the baby is a bit jaundiced,' she told them, 'so the medical team might have to deal with that, as well as making sure that Jessica recovers her strength.'

'Maybe we could go and see her if she's going to be staying in hospital for a few days,' her father said and Sophie nodded.

'Yes, I'll take both of you. Ryan's going to stay with her until they let her come home and then she'll come back to live with me for a while, until he finishes this project he's working on. As soon as that's done, he's going to take paternity leave to be with her and the baby.'

'I'm glad he made it back here in time.' Rob was proud to be an uncle and pored over the photos with his father.

She left them a little later and went home. It was late evening by then and she realised she had missed out on a meal. Her stomach was rumbling and she set about making a quick broccoli, pasta and cheese bake.

The doorbell rang as she set the table and she wondered if Rob had forgotten his key.

'Hi, Sophie.' Nate stood outside her front door, looking wonderful, his dark eyes glittering as he gazed at her in the evening light, his body honed and full of vitality. He was wearing smart casuals, chinos and a dark shirt.

'Come in.' She smiled at him and showed him along the hallway to the kitchen. 'I wasn't expecting you, but you must have smelled the food. There's plenty. Would you like to eat with me?'

'Mmm…smells good. It'll have to be a quick bite, though,' he said regretfully. 'I've been with my father most of the day and I need to go back to the hospital in a while.'

She frowned. 'It's bad, then?'

He nodded. 'I came away for a while so that the nurses could tend to him. I thought I'd check up on you—see how you're bearing up. I guessed you'd be back by now.' He folded her into his arms. 'I've been thinking about you all day, wondering how you were getting on, missing you.'

'I'm fine—we're all doing great after all the worry.'

'I'm glad about that.' He kissed her tenderly, holding her close and making her body surge with heat.

She kissed him, loving the way his hand rested on the swell of her hip, until all at once there was a loud beeping sound that erupted on the airwaves and destroyed the moment.

'Oh…it's the oven timer,' she said in dismay. 'My broccoli bake is ready to serve.'

He laughed. 'We'd better go and see to it, then, before it spoils.'

'Okay.' She pulled herself together and fetched hot plates from the oven and served out the food. 'Sit down. Help yourself to extra cheese and there's hot crusty bread and a green salad to go with it, if you want.'

He sat across the table from her and began to eat. 'Mmm…it's delicious,' he said, and she smiled.

'Rob and Jessica like this—it's one of their favourite meals. They always ask for it when they come to visit.'

He studied her thoughtfully. 'You've always looked after them, haven't you? I suppose with your mother's condition affecting her so badly in those first few years they turned to you?'

'Pretty much, yes. Sometimes Mum would go off for days at a time, so we had to manage as best we could. I felt so guilty when I left to go to Medical School. I came home whenever I could—most weekends and sometimes in the week if my shifts allowed for it. And of course I spent my holidays with them. They were still so young and things were topsy-turvy for them.'

'But now things seem to be turning out all right—Rob is back with your father and planning on going to college, and Jessica is a mother herself.' He speared a forkful of salad and glanced at her. 'That must seem strange to you—it's happened so soon, while she's still so very young. Do you ever think of having a family of your own?'

She nodded. 'One day, yes, I'd like that. I hope it will happen. Seeing Jess's baby has made me feel even more maternal. He's so soft and warm and beautiful.' She drew in a deep, happy breath. 'They let me hold him and it's the best feeling in the world.' He smiled and she said quietly, 'What about you, Nate? Have you thought what it might be like to have your own babies up at the Manor House?'

He was still for a moment, his fork poised in mid-air. Then he let it settle once more on his plate and flicked a glance over her, his gaze searching, intent. 'I've thought about it,' he said at last. 'Sometimes, especially of late, I wonder what it would be like. I'm not sure, though. It's becoming more difficult for me to contemplate as time goes on.'

She studied him cautiously. 'Because you haven't found the right woman or because you don't want to deal with that aristocratic heritage and all that goes along with it?'

'It's neither of those things, really. I suppose, in my heart of hearts, I'm afraid to open up to any woman. It's only happening now because of you, I think. I never understood it before, but of late I've been thinking things through, trying to sort out my feelings. I don't feel I can trust things to work out right. I think the way I am has a lot to do with my mother dying when I was so very young… When you have that wonderful relationship with your mother, you have a right to expect it to last for ever, and as a child I was shocked to the core when it was taken from me.'

'You didn't ever get over it?'

He shrugged. 'You do, of course—not get over it, exactly, but you learn to adjust. There was a void in my life. But then, after a while, my father started to bring girlfriends back to the Manor… He was determined never to marry again—no one could replace my mother in his eyes, I think…but those relationships would last at most two, three years, maybe, and during that time I grew attached to a couple of the girls. They were decent women and I think they meant well—they were each affectionate and sweet towards me and I liked having them around, being able to confide in them…but then the relationship with my father would come to an end and they would disappear back where they came from and I never saw them again. I felt…empty…and lost.'

He shook his head, deep in thought. 'Bringing children into the world is a huge responsibility. They need stability but I don't know what it's like to have a lasting, loving relationship and I'm almost afraid that for me it doesn't exist. The experience has left me feeling that I can't risk putting all my faith in one woman. I tend to think that, somehow or other, I'll always be let down.'

'So it's best not to care too much in the first place?' She gave him a regretful, sympathetic look. 'That's a sad way to go through life but I understand how you feel. I have the same fears sometimes. Maybe we should both try to be braver and learn to take a bit of a risk in our lives.'

He gave her a wistful smile. 'Maybe.' His eyes darkened. 'I'm beginning to realise there's only one woman who could persuade me to take a chance on love…and that's you, Sophie. You mean more to me than I can put into words. I couldn't bear to lose you but I… After what my father put your family through, I'm not sure I deserve you.'

Sophie's eyes widened at the revelation. It wasn't exactly a declaration of love but it was probably as near as he'd ever come to it. 'You mustn't think that way,' she said. Her heart burned with longing. Would he one day be able to tell her what she wanted to hear—that he loved her every bit as much as she loved him?

'I wish—' He might have been about to say more but his phone began to trill and he looked down at the screen and read the text message there. 'It's my father,' he said. 'The doctor thinks I should go to see him. It sounds urgent.'

'I'm sorry.'

He stood up. 'Thanks for the meal, Sophie. I'm glad Jessica and the baby are all right.'

She went with him to the door and opened it to let him into the night. She didn't want him to go but knew that he had no choice. Then, as he walked away from her along the path, she saw to her dismay that Jake was heading towards her. The two men crossed by each other on the path and she saw Nate look at Jake and frown before nodding to him and going on his way. What must he be thinking?

It was more than likely he would be disturbed and concerned, jealous, even, but after what he'd just said to her, would he ever be persuaded that he could trust in her love? Could she ever hope to have a future with him?

'Sophie,' Jake said, coming over to her. 'I hope you don't mind me dropping in like this. I bought a present for Jessica's baby—and some course notes for Rob. He was asking me about working in a hospital and what kind of courses he should follow.'

'That's brilliant, Jake. Thanks.' She gave an inward sigh and braced herself. 'Come in.'

CHAPTER SEVEN

'DO YOU THINK Casey's skin's a better colour now, Sophie?' In her room in the Maternity Unit Jessica held her baby close to her, unwrapping his shawl and lifting his vest to show his chest. 'He was so yellow before with the jaundice but I think the treatment's working, don't you?'

Sophie smiled. 'Oh, yes…he looks much better now.' He was a beautiful baby, with a sweet rosebud mouth and perfect little fingers that curled into fists.

Jessica looked relieved. She wrapped the baby up warmly and held him against her. 'I've been so worried. The last thing you want is for your baby to have to stay in hospital for treatment when he's so tiny. Poor little man—having to have his eyes covered while he's under the special lamp for two or three hours at a time.'

'I would think he only needs a few more hours of phototherapy and then his levels of bilirubin will be back to normal,' Sophie said. 'I know it's been difficult but he's slept through it for the most part, so I don't think it's bothered him too much.'

The midwife had explained the problem of jaundice to Jessica but as a new young mother she was understandably worried. Quite often in newborn babies it was possible that the liver didn't work all that efficiently for the first couple of weeks, so the level of bilirubin could build up in the blood. Usually, it cleared up on its own, but if that didn't happen the baby could be given photo-therapy. The light used in this treatment helped to change the bilirubin to a form that could be more easily broken down by the liver.

'I'm so glad you and Ryan have been able to be here with me,' Jessica said. 'It's made everything so much better. I know you have to work, but it's been good hav-ing you come in several times a day to see us. And Mum will be coming again at the weekend. It's all worked out far better than I expected.'

'Of course it has. And I have everything waiting for you back at home when you're ready to be discharged.'

Her day's work had ended some time ago and Sophie left her sister and the baby a little later, to go back to the cottage once more. If only the rest of her worries could be so easily resolved.

She was anxious for Nate. While she and her family had celebrated a wonderful new addition to the family, his own situation had become tragic. His father's health had steadily deteriorated and a few days ago Nate had broken the bad news to her that his father had passed away.

'He had another heart attack,' he'd said flatly. 'I have a lot of things to deal with, so I probably won't be able to see you for a while. I'm going to take a few days off work to make the funeral arrangements, and I have to get in touch with all my relatives. They're scattered far and wide over the country, so I expect a good many of them will want to come and stay at the Manor for a while.'

'Are you coping all right? Is there anything I can do?' Sophie asked, but he'd been determined to manage by himself. She wanted to be with him but he'd shut himself away to grieve alone. Sophie's only consolation was that Charlotte was with him and would do her best to comfort him and steer him through this difficult time.

Back at the cottage Sophie prepared for the funeral that was being held next day. Nate had said he hoped she would be there. She'd picked out a black suit with a fitted jacket and a pencil-line skirt that she felt would be suitable for the occasion. Teamed with a grey silk blouse and black stiletto heels, she felt the outfit would give her a bit more confidence.

Her father had received a formal invitation too, because he had been for a long time a trusted worker on Lord Branscombe's estate. He showed the beautifully embossed card to Sophie. 'It came with a letter too,' he said. 'I suppose that was thoughtful of Nate Branscombe—that personal touch—knowing how I felt about his father.'

'Will you go to the service?' Sophie had asked.

To her surprise, he nodded. 'Rob said he'll take me. I thought about it long and hard before I made the decision. I've been bitter and resentful for such a long time, feeling that I was treated badly. All along, I blamed James for insisting I went on that flight with him, for not listening to reason when people told him he shouldn't pilot the plane while he was feeling unwell…but the truth is, I should have refused to go with him. It was my own weakness in not standing up to him that led to me being in the position I'm in now. I only have myself to blame.'

'Oh, Dad…' Sophie's voice broke in a sob as she knelt down beside her father's wheelchair. 'You're not to blame for anything,' she protested, laying a hand on his arm. 'I think most people would have accepted his word for it that he felt he was up to it. He was your boss and in the end you went along with what he said because ultimately you trusted him to do the right thing.'

She gently squeezed his arm, wanting to show her support. 'You always did everything you thought was for the best…and you've worked so hard to try to walk again; you've been so stoical this last couple of years. I'm proud of the way you've pushed yourself. And you're getting there… It's taking a while but you *will* walk again. Rob's told me how hard you've been working with him at your physio. You're making progress all the while. Please don't blame yourself for any of this.'

He patted her hand. 'You're a sweet girl. You've always been there for me. I'm sorry I've given you such a hard time these last few weeks over James's son. I suppose I've been harsh in judging Nate. None of this is his fault.'

She looked at him in surprise. 'Are you telling me you've changed your mind about him?'

He shrugged awkwardly. 'Let's say I'm reserving my opinion of him. I heard the talk in the village about how you and he saved that little boy—the one who collapsed and couldn't breathe. I know the child's still in hospital but he's a lot better, isn't he? It made me think about Nate in a different way. And then I heard he got in touch with the mother's family to make sure she had some support. Apparently her cousin has come over here to stay with her. They were good friends before they eventually lost touch with one another, the woman said.'

Sophie's eyes widened. 'I hadn't heard that—Nate didn't say anything to me about it.'

'Ah, well, the boy's mother's been chatting in the post office.' He smiled. 'You know how word gets around.'

She nodded. 'I do.' It made her feel warm inside to know that Nate had done what he could to help the boy's mother.

The weather blessed them on the day of the funeral. Summer was drifting into autumn and the leaves on the trees were turning to red and gold. There was a faint breeze blowing but the sun put in an appearance through puffy white clouds so that the mourners could gather in peace. The service and the rest of the proceedings went without a hitch.

Nate was immaculately dressed, surrounded by a host of relatives Sophie had never met before. He introduced her to them but the names soon became a blur. She smiled politely and made sympathetic comments and hoped that she was being of some help to Nate by being there alongside him.

'I hadn't expected so many people from the village to turn up,' he commented as they ate canapés at the reception afterwards.

'No, nor did I.' She made a slight smile. 'But I think your standing in the village has gone up lately, since you helped young Shaun…and since you outlined your plans to save the estate.'

'Hmm…I only hope I'll be able to live up to what I said back then.' He was frowning and she looked at him curiously.

'Is there a problem?'

'I think there might be but I'm not sure how much of a setback it's going to be. My father's solicitor wants an urgent meeting with me. All I can say is that from the initial conversation I've had with him, the situation doesn't sound promising.'

She sucked in a quick breath. 'Will you let me know if things change?'

'Of course.' He was solemn but his expression became taut all at once, and when she followed the line of his gaze, she saw he was looking directly at Jake. Jake was there as a mutual friend but it seemed Nate didn't want to speak to him just then. 'I'll leave you two alone together,' he said, excusing himself and moving away from her as Jake came towards them. 'I should go and talk to some of my relatives.'

'But Jake will be wanting to speak to you,' she protested. 'He'll want to offer his condolences.'

He shook his head. 'I don't think so. He's looking at you, Sophie. He's been looking at you for the last half hour. Besides, I ought to circulate a bit.'

Jake had been watching her? She was startled Nate had noticed something to which she'd been totally oblivious, but it was clear he wasn't intending to stay around. Nate left her and went to speak to an uncle who had taken up a position by the buffet table.

Sophie exhaled slowly and greeted Jake with a slight nod of her head. 'Hi, Jake. I'm sorry we have to meet again on an occasion like this.'

'Yes, me too.' Jake studied her. 'I hope you know what you're doing with Nate. He let you down before and he'll quite likely do it again.'

'He didn't let me down. I think he went away because he had to come to terms with what his father had done and he couldn't bear to see the pain it caused our family. He tried to talk to me about it but I wasn't ready to listen back then.'

She laid a hand on his arm. 'Thank you for looking

out for me. You've always been a great friend to me,' she said quietly. 'One I'll always treasure.'

'Likewise.'

She smiled. 'Have you heard any more from Cheryl?'

He shook his head. 'A couple of emails. That's all.'

'Hmm. I think you were wrong about her wanting someone else. I happen to know that she's very keen to meet up with you again.' She lifted her brows. 'I heard she was desperately hoping you might want to take her to the annual get-together next month.'

He laughed. 'You're joking with me! How would you hear something like that?'

'The hospital grapevine, you know? She confided in a friend, who told another friend, who spilled the beans to someone who works in Accounts.'

A faint smile curved his mouth. Sophie knew she had set him thinking about a particular course of action but she said no more about it. Instead, she let her glance wander across the room to where Nate was standing. He was looking at her intently, frowning, but when she caught his gaze he turned away and spoke to his companion. He didn't look at all happy, seeing her with Jake. Perhaps he'd misinterpreted their smiles and gestures. No matter what she'd told him to the contrary, he clearly believed she and Jake were an item.

She didn't see Nate again for a few days. When she tried phoning him, he was too busy to say much and she was left feeling dissatisfied and unhappy. She desperately wanted to be with him, to be able to comfort him, but it seemed he simply wanted to be left alone.

He went to London to meet with his father's solicitor and to have further talks with Peninsula. He hadn't told Sophie what the talks were about, except to say that he wanted to clarify things after his father's passing…but when she walked Charlie by the Manor one day and saw valuable paintings being loaded on to a prominent art dealer's van, she guessed something was very wrong. This was a legitimate fine-art dealer from London. Selling the paintings had never been part of Nate's plan to recover the estate.

Whatever the outcome of those appointments in London, Sophie was shocked, along with everyone else in the village, when Peninsula announced just a few days later that they were holding a meeting in the village hall on Saturday afternoon. 'We want to discuss possibilities for the area,' their spokesman said. 'Come along and listen to what we have to say.'

Sophie went to the hall with her father. Nate was nowhere to be seen and it took only a few minutes, less than half an hour, for the spokesman to cause uproar among his audience.

'We've great plans to make changes that will benefit everyone in this area,' the spokesman said. 'If everything goes ahead as we hope, we'll be in a position to make all your lives better, so we're looking for your support.'

A man from the audience stood up. 'What plans are you talking about? Why are you back here telling us how you want to change our village? Has Nate Branscombe sold out to you?'

'He hasn't signed the papers yet but our offer is definitely back on the table,' the spokesman answered. He clicked a computer mouse and brought up on the screen in front of them an enlarged photo of their village, nestled in the valley around the beautiful blue bay. 'There's a prime position for a five-star hotel,' he said, pointing to an area on the cliff top to the east. 'Just think how that will boost the prosperity of the area.' He clicked the mouse again. 'And here's the outline of what the proposed shopping mall will look like. There will be restaurants, a leisure centre, a gymnasium, cinema…'

A woman stood up, angrily voicing her thoughts. 'And along with all that there will be tourists with their cars and takeaway food cartons littering the countryside… broken bottles on the beach… What next—a casino open all hours?'

People stood up, shouting, anxious for their voices to be heard. Some remained seated, Sophie noticed. Not everyone was against change but the majority were adamant that it shouldn't happen, not in their idyllic part of the world.

She left the meeting with her father, taking him back to his home. 'Do you think Nate meant for this to happen?' he asked as she wheeled his chair up the ramp into the house. Charlie woke up from his snooze in the kitchen and came to greet them, tail wagging enthusiastically.

'I don't think so.' She flicked the switch on the kettle. 'But there was some kind of problem—he had to go to see his father's solicitor in London, so I suspect there are financial problems he didn't know about. He hasn't told me anything about it, but I'm guessing it's serious.'

'So you think he'll sell to Peninsula after all?'

'I don't know. I know he doesn't want to.'

Her father was obviously worried as they talked about the possibilities of Peninsula Holdings taking over. 'This place will be the first to go,' he said, looking around the kitchen. 'What are they going to offer me in its place? A ground-floor retirement flat in the suburbs? Their representative seemed to think that would be perfect for me—a place in a warden-assisted block, he said. I could look out on to the street on the front with the shops directly opposite and a communal garden at the back. How would I look after Charlie in a situation like that?'

A look of despair crossed his face. 'I'm used to being in this beautiful place, with trees and shrubs and countryside and the sea not far away, neighbours who pop in to say hello whenever they have five minutes to spare. I can't bear the thought of moving.'

'Perhaps it won't come to that.' She handed him a mug of coffee and slid a plate of his favourite cheese straws towards him. 'I'll go and see Nate—see if he'll talk to me. Maybe together we can come up with some ideas that will help him keep the estate.'

'Bless you, Sophie. I hope there's some way out of the situation.'

The kitchen door opened just then and Jessica came in, wheeling the baby in the pram. Sophie wedged the door open temporarily to allow her into the kitchen and then stopped to coo over the baby. 'Oh, isn't he gorgeous?' He was fast asleep, his little pink hands curled into fists either side of his cheeks. 'He's perfect.'

Jessica smiled. 'He would be if he managed to sleep for more than two hours at a time. I thought if I walked him over here the motion of the pram would rock him to sleep.' She looked down at her baby. 'Oh...I might have known. He's awake again.' She chuckled and carefully lifted him out, wrapping his shawl around him once more. 'I think your grandad wants to see you, young man.'

Her father nodded. 'Oh, definitely. I'll grab my chance to hold him while Rob's spending time down at the beach with his friends. I might not get a look in otherwise.'

'Here you go.' Jessica gently placed Casey in her father's arms. 'Sophie gets to hold him a lot,' she told him with a smile, 'so you get first dibs.'

They sat around the table and talked, taking turns in holding the baby until Charlie began to get restless. He came and laid his head on Sophie's lap, looking at her with big eyes.

Sophie reached for his lead. 'I'll take him out for a walk,' she said. 'Maybe I'll go along the cliff path and up by the Manor. Nate came back from London yesterday, so he might be home. Perhaps I'll get the chance to talk to him.'

'Good idea. Thanks, Sophie.' Her father watched her leave with Charlie. His expression was sad for a moment until he turned back to Jessica and Sophie heard him ask her about Ryan's job and how much longer he would be away.

Sophie loved walking along the cliff top, looking out over the sparkling blue water below. She stood and watched as the waves rolled in to shore, leaving behind bands of white foam and forming rock pools among the shells and pebbles on the sandy beach. Whenever she could, she loved to walk down there, collecting pretty white spiral shells or glossy cowries and periwinkles.

Today, though, she kept to the path and clambered steadily up the hill towards the Manor House. She hoped the gates would be open so that she could simply walk up to the main door, but since the press had taken to bombarding Nate with questions, and generally intruding on his everyday life, he'd taken to using security measures.

She pressed the buzzer and spoke into the intercom.

'It's Sophie,' she said, when Charlotte answered. 'I wondered if I might see Nate.'

'Oh, hello, Sophie.' There was a pause and then she added, 'He says you're to come right in. Is that your dog I can hear alongside you?'

'It is.'

'Ah, he's a lovely dog, is Charlie.' The wrought-iron gates started to swing open and Sophie set out to walk along the long sweeping drive up to the house.

Nate met her halfway. 'Hello, Sophie,' he said. 'It's good to see you.' He hugged her, looking into her eyes with hungry intensity as though he would absorb every part of her. 'I've missed you.'

She clung to him, needing that close, warm contact. 'I missed you too.' She sent him a troubled look. 'I wanted to come and see you before this, but I know you've been busy with family visitors staying over...as well as the business in London. And the press were here a lot, I heard.'

'Yes. Actually, some of them were sympathetic for once, so I spoke to a couple of them briefly. They wanted to concentrate on the fact that I'm a doctor and how it feels to take over the title.'

She smiled. 'There was a beautiful aerial photograph of the Manor House and the estate in one of the national papers.'

'Yes, I saw it. It was a good article too, considering I hadn't given an interview.' He sent her a thoughtful look. 'I was going to come and see you later today—but you've beaten me to it. I expect you're worried about this business with Peninsula?'

'I am. Leastways, my dad's really concerned about what's going to happen.'

'Yes, I guessed as much. I feel bad that you're having to go through all this worry.' He bent down to stroke an eager Charlie and tickle him behind the ears. 'Shall we walk for a while or would you rather go up to the house?'

She smiled. 'I think Charlie would appreciate the walk. I think he was born for the hills and dales—he can go for miles.'

He chuckled. 'Okay. We'll take a stroll by the lake.' He put an arm around her shoulders as they turned on to the perimeter path. It felt good being this close to him, having the warmth of his fingers filter through the fine material of her cashmere top. He pointed out a few changes along the way. 'If you look closely through the trees, you'll see a few log cabins have sprung up here and there. We're still in the process of getting facilities connected—it'll take time, but at least we've made a start.'

She looked at him curiously. 'You're going ahead with your plans, then? I thought everything might have been put on hold when Peninsula started talking about what they wanted to do.'

They were walking through the copse towards the lake, a silver expanse of water bordered by ancient willow trees that dipped their branches gracefully into the water and where spreading oaks mingled with elderberry and blackberry brambles that were luscious with ripening fruit.

'I'll do as much as I can to hold on to the estate, but I'm afraid things are much worse than I realised. Unfortunately, my father hadn't told me the full extent of his liabilities. That's what the solicitor wanted to talk to me about.' He led her to a bench seat set back from the water, close by a landing stage. They sat down and Charlie flopped to the ground at their feet, his tongue hanging out as he panted happily. Sophie looked around. A boat, a small motor launch, was moored by the wooden jetty.

'So the projects you hoped would put things right and cover the debts won't be enough?'

He nodded. 'That's right. My father's financial situation was far worse than he'd said. I think he didn't tell me because he hoped his other investments would come right, but that isn't happening as yet. I'll do what I can to sort out the mess but I'm still working through my options. I've submitted a plan of action to the bank manager and he's going through it with his advisers.'

She reached for his hand and covered his fingers with hers. 'I don't know what to say. I wish there was something I could do to help.'

He smiled. 'It helps just having you by my side, Sophie. I know you're only here because you're worried for your father, but at least I have you for a little while.'

She frowned. 'I don't understand. Why would you say that? I'd be here anyway—don't you know that? I want to be with you.'

'You're seeing Jake, though, aren't you?' A knot formed in his brow. 'There have been rumours. I saw the way you and he acted together on the day of the funeral. He was smiling, relieved almost, after you spoke to him. Up till then I thought I might be in with a chance but after that I realised it could never happen, you and me.'

'Oh, no…I think you misunderstood the situation completely. As to rumours—you know how people get things wrong. They see me having coffee with him in the cafeteria and suddenly it's a full-blown relationship.' She smiled, a small glow starting up inside her. He'd said it—he wanted to be with her. 'There's nothing going on between me and Jake. I told you—we're friends. He was just pleased because I told him someone else is interested in him.'

He drew in a quick stunned breath, his eyes widening.

She said gently, 'I only have feelings for you, Nate. I love you. It's always been you. I just need to hear that you feel the same way towards me.'

He lifted a hand, stroking his thumb lightly across her cheek. 'I wish it were that simple, Sophie.' His eyes darkened, becoming unfathomable like the rippling surface of the lake. 'I love you too, with all my heart, with all my soul, but I can't give in to my feelings for you.'

Anguished, she lifted her hands to his chest, laying her palms flat against the top of his ribcage. 'I don't understand, Nate. I've waited so long to hear you say that you love me. If you feel the same way, why can't we be together?'

He shook his head. 'How can I let it happen when my family has been responsible for so much heartache heaped on your father, on you—perhaps ultimately on everyone who is a part of this estate? My father was responsible for the accident that crippled your father. I can't ever hope to make up for the horror of that.'

'You don't have to...'

'I do.' He straightened. 'I owe you so much but right now I may be about to lose everything I have. Everything I am, my whole existence, my heritage, my family name, is tied up in this place and it's all coming crashing down around me. I can't...I won't...ask you or your family to suffer any more because of my failures. I love you, Sophie, but I can't ask you to be with me, to marry me, until I've restored the family pride and I can offer you the future you deserve.'

She looked at him in shock. 'But I love you, Nate.

Isn't that enough to see us through this? Surely, nothing else matters? We can work this out together, can't we?'

'No, we can't. I'm sorry, Sophie.' He clasped her hands in his. 'When I saw you with Jake, when I didn't see anything of you these last few days, it hit me like a ten-ton truck that I want you more than anything else in the world—I want to be with you, I love you, it's going to be unbearable without you...but I won't put you or your family through any more hardship because of me.'

He kissed her gently, briefly, on the mouth, as though he daren't linger a moment longer for fear of losing himself entirely. Then he stood up. 'I'll walk you back to the gates. Perhaps it's best if we don't see each other for a while.'

Sophie scrambled to her feet and went blindly along beside him. 'You can't do this, Nate. There has to be another way. We can work through this together.'

He didn't answer and that silence made things a hundred times worse. She couldn't feel, couldn't think. She was in shock, her whole body trembling, but she knew there would be no point in trying to speak to him about it any more. He wouldn't talk about it. He had made up his mind and there was nothing she could do to persuade him otherwise.

CHAPTER EIGHT

'YOU'VE JUST COME from the Neonatal Unit again, haven't you?' Hannah smiled as Sophie went over to the coffee machine in the staff lounge. 'I can always tell. Either that or your sister brought the baby in to work to see you.'

'Ah…I can't seem to help myself,' Sophie said, reaching for a mug. 'There's just something about those tiny babies that gets me here, every time.' She pressed the flat of her hand over her heart. 'They're so vulnerable, with tubes for this and that and all the monitoring equipment. I've been doing screening tests today—checking nutrient levels and urea and electrolytes. If there was time, I would spend most of the day in the unit, to be honest.' She smiled. 'But my other patients can be just as adorable. It's so satisfying to see them getting stronger day by day.'

Hannah washed her cup out at the sink. 'I bet you've loved having your sister and her baby staying with you. To look at him you wouldn't think he had such a hard time being born.'

Sophie nodded. 'I've loved every minute of it, and yes, he's doing really well now. He's gaining weight—still not sleeping through the night, of course.'

'Ah—now I know why you've had that peaky look

about you of late.' Hannah grinned and started towards the door. 'I'd better get back to work,' she said.

'Okay.' Sophie concentrated on pouring hot coffee into her mug. Peaky? There was only one reason for her being under par lately and that was because of Nate. Why was he so determined that things couldn't work out between them?

'Hi—how are you doing?'

She gave a small start of surprise as she realised Nate had come into the room as Hannah was leaving. The kitchen area was slightly hidden from the entrance. 'Hi. I didn't see you there,' she said as he came to stand alongside her, reaching for a porcelain mug. 'Shall I pour you a coffee?'

'Thanks.'

'How does it feel to be back at work?'

'It feels okay.' He accepted the mug she slid towards him. 'I wasn't sure how it would be, but it's actually good. The chief called me into his office this morning and for a minute I wondered if something was wrong— I was only here on a temporary contract and I'd had to take time off—but he offered me a permanent post.'

Her eyes widened. 'Will you take it?'

He nodded. 'Yes, I like working here. I like the people and the set-up.'

'I'm glad for you.' She sipped her coffee, looking at him over the rim of her cup. 'I suppose at least being here helps take your mind off all your other problems.'

'True.' He searched in the fridge and found a box of doughnuts. 'I brought these in to share out—would you like one?'

'Thanks.' She helped herself, biting into the cake and carefully licking the sugar off her fingers. Nate watched her, as though fascinated by her actions, until he gave himself a shake and put the box back in the fridge.

'So, what's happening with everyone at home?' he asked. 'I feel as though I've been a bit out of touch these last few days while I've been busy trying to sort out problems with the estate.'

'Oh, we're all doing fine. Rob's started a psychology course at college and my dad's doing really well with his physiotherapy. He's taking a few steps on his own now, with the aid of a walking frame. He says he's going to progress from there to walking with elbow crutches.'

'I thought he would manage it, given time. He's always been a determined man. He just needs to strengthen his muscles now.' He studied her. 'I expect Jessica will be going home soon—how will you feel about that? You've enjoyed being with her and the baby, haven't you? I heard you telling Hannah a bit about him.'

Her mouth turned down at the corners. 'I'll hate it when she leaves but Ryan's coming back next week and they'll want to be together in their own home, of course. I'm taking a few days off work to go there with her to help her settle back in...just until Ryan's home.'

'That sounds like a good idea.' He frowned. 'She doesn't like it there, though, does she? She mentioned something to me about it, and I remember you telling me her house is not up to much and there's no garden, just a small yard out back.'

'That's right. It was all they could afford at the time.' She sighed. 'She says she wants to move back to the village. It was where she was born, after all. Ryan's happy to do that but they have to find the right place, somewhere within their budget.'

'Won't Jessica miss your mother if she does that?'

Sophie nodded. 'I'm sure she will…but it's only about an hour away on the train—a bit longer by car. Up to now we've taken it in turns to make the journey, so we all get to see each other at least once a week. It seems to have worked out reasonably well, so far.'

Nate was deep in thought for a minute or two and she looked at him questioningly. 'Is everything all right?'

'Yes, absolutely. I was just wondering whether they might want to live at the Manor. The place is far too big for me. It takes me all my time to use the main part of the house, and then there are the East and the West Wings that can be more or less turned into self-contained units if necessary. If they had part of the East Wing, for instance, they would have access to a terrace and the garden, and there's a kitchen there that used to be the old scullery. They could stay as long as they wanted, make it their home or use it while they build up their finances to get a place of their own.' He sent her a cautious glance. 'What do you think?'

She gasped, her eyes widening. 'What do I think? Oh, Nate!' She flung her arms around his neck and kissed him soundly on the mouth. 'I think you're wonderful, fantastic, beyond words.'

He looked at her in stunned surprise, laughing uncertainly as his hands went automatically around her waist as though they belonged there. She kissed him again, a longer kiss this time, equally fervent. 'No wonder I love you so much,' she said in a contented whisper. She clung to him, her soft curves crushed against his hard body.

'Sophie…I… We said we wouldn't do this…' He gently tried to push her away but his hands were trembling and the knowledge that he was so affected by her made her blood sizzle with renewed vigour.

'You've got to be kidding,' she said, smiling up at him.

He shook his head, a look of anguish on his face. 'It's too difficult for me if you wrap yourself around me this way,' he said in a distracted, ragged tone. 'I'm only flesh and blood—you're making it way too hard for me to resist you.'

'Good. I'm glad.' She looked at him with sparkling, mischievous eyes. 'It was a silly idea in the first place. Why on earth would you want to keep me away when I can help you get through this awful time? I won't stay away. That's not what love's about, is it? Love is about being there for each other through the hard times. Why should you struggle on your own when I can share your troubles with you? You know what they say—a problem shared is a problem halved?'

'Ah… Sophie…that's not always the case but…' At last he gave in with a small shuddery sigh that seemed to ricochet through his whole body. Joy surged in her at his capitulation, and when he bent his head and rested his forehead against hers, she knew the sweet scent of success. 'I hope you don't come to regret this,' he said huskily. 'Don't say I didn't try to warn you.'

'Yeah, you did…but it didn't work.' She smiled impishly and he kissed her feverishly, with growing passion until she was breathless with longing.

They came up for air just as they heard the door open and someone came into the room. By the time Tracey came over to the coffee machine and saw them there, they had managed to compose themselves once more.

'Oh, hi there,' Tracey said, pausing to look in the fridge. 'Did I hear there were doughnuts to be had?'

'There certainly are—in the white box.' Nate smiled at her. 'They say an army marches on its stomach. I think the same goes for hospital staff—we can't work properly if we're hungry.'

Tracey laughed and bit into the doughnut. 'Mmm… delicious. Just what I needed.' She looked at Nate. 'I saw an article on the Manor House in the paper the other day—the photo that went alongside it was beautiful with the sun glowing on the stonework…and the stable block at the back through the courtyard…and the grounds looked so lush. I can't imagine living in a place like that…I'd never want to come in to work—I'd want to go out and explore it every day. It makes me think how it might have been in Regency times—peaceful and perfect and genteel.'

'There is that, I suppose.' Nate thought about it. 'There are portraits of the ancestors in the West Wing— women in their ballgowns or day dresses, and the men rigged out in their finery. I take it for granted, probably, and I tend not to think about it too much—I'm too busy trying to be a doctor.'

'Yes…I can see you have your priorities sorted.' Tracey smiled and helped herself to coffee while Sophie and Nate excused themselves and prepared to go back to the Children's Unit.

'You didn't send the ancestral portraits to auction, then?' Sophie said quietly as they walked along the corridor. 'I saw some of the paintings being collected one day when I was walking Charlie.'

He shook his head. 'No, only some that I really didn't like. Quite a few were stored in the attic and hadn't seen the light of day for many years. The proceeds will go towards the work on the fishing lodges.'

She glanced at him. 'You know, Tracey may have come up with something when she mentioned the Regency period of the Manor House. You often get film companies or TV production companies wanting to use historic houses as locations. It might be worth thinking of that as an option. I don't know whether it would make much of a difference to your situation.'

To her surprise, he nodded. 'Actually, ever since that picture appeared in the paper I've been receiving requests from companies interested in using the property. I wasn't sure how much of a disruption it would be—but I'm told it would be the ideal location for a TV drama series set in the mid-nineteenth century, and also there's a company looking to make a period adventure film with a grand mansion at its centre. I'm not sure. They won't need to use the whole house, but they're happy that there's plenty of space for the trucks and equipment. They won't be there for too long, I imagine. What do you think?'

Her eyes widened. 'I think it sounds really exciting, and I can't see too many problems as long as you're dealing with companies that have good reputations. I think you need to give it some deep thought. It's your home, after all.' She frowned. 'Perhaps you could persuade them to keep the disruption to a minimum—have them use separate entrances, maybe? And I guess the vehicles might be hidden by the trees and shrubs if they used the West side of the house. What matters is that you feel comfortable with your decision.'

'Thanks, Sophie. I knew you would put it all into perspective for me.' He put his arm around her and briefly hugged her. 'You're right. I need to give it a lot of thought.'

They went their separate ways, attending to their small patients. Sophie's mind was buzzing with questions yet to be answered as she checked lab reports and studied X-ray films and CT scans. What would he decide?

Sophie was away from home for the next few days, so she didn't get the chance to be with him and work through the choices he might make. Instead, she helped Jessica get her house organised and pristine once more after the boiler and central-heating repairs.

'I can hardly believe Nate is being so generous, offering us a place in his home,' Jessica said excitedly. 'I talked to Ryan about it on the phone and he thinks it's a great idea…though, with all the business of the film-company offer and so on, Nate probably has too much on his mind. He might have had second thoughts about it.'

Sophie shook her head. 'No, he called me this morning and said you can move in whenever you want.' She looked at the baby lying in his cradle. He opened his eyes and looked at her, making little gurgling sounds and blowing tiny bubbles from his perfect mouth. Sophie lightly stroked his soft palm and he gripped her fingers tightly in response. She smiled down at him. 'Nate said there's a room that can be turned into a nursery,' she told Jessica. 'You just need to let him know how you want it decorated and he'll get things organised.'

'Oh, I can't wait!'

Ryan came home next day and Sophie left the two of them to spend time together with their baby. She arrived home and a bit later she went over to her father's house, to find him and Rob preparing for another meeting at the Manor. It was Friday evening and Nate had phoned her earlier to make sure she would be able to come along.

'He's invited all the villagers from the estate, plus any

others who are interested in knowing what he plans to do,' her father said. 'Do you know what he has in mind?'

She shook her head. 'I don't. He was sifting through various options, talking with the bank manager and so on, last time I spoke to him about it.' She looked at her father, spruce in a dark grey suit and shiny polished shoes. 'You're looking very smart,' she said. 'It's not a formal do, is it? Nate didn't mention anything like that.' She was a bit concerned that she might not be dressed for the occasion. She was wearing a soft wool dress with a slightly off-the-shoulder neckline and three-quarter sleeves. It was comfortable and classic and she felt good in it.

Her father laughed. 'No, it isn't a formal do...I just wanted to celebrate being able to get out of the wheelchair and stand up for a while. See?' He stood up carefully, taking his time, and Rob came over to him and handed him a couple of elbow crutches.

'One step at a time, Dad,' he said. 'Remember how we practised this...'

Sophie watched as her father slowly walked across the room, straight-backed and proud. 'Oh, Dad,' she cried, going over to him. 'It's wonderful. I'm so happy for you.' She hugged him, and hugged her brother. 'Now look what you've both done,' she said, choked up. 'I'm all tearful and at this rate I'll have to do my make-up all over again!'

They both laughed and a few minutes later they all set off for the Manor House.

Nate greeted them and showed them into the long panelled room where everyone was assembled, helping themselves to refreshments. There was a variety of food, as before, with southern fried chicken, spring rolls and salsa dips, and a range of desserts that included straw-berry bruschetta and dishes of Eton mess.

Nate drew Sophie to him and dropped a kiss on her mouth. 'I'm really glad you're back,' he said, grabbing her hand and leading her over to the side of the room where a bar had been set up. He handed her a glass of wine and murmured, 'I have to go and talk to every-one—help yourself to food and sit down close by me, will you? It's good to have you here. I can't tell you how much I worried while you were away. I thought you might have changed your mind about us, knowing what might lie ahead.'

She looked at him thoughtfully. 'You're still worried I might disappear out of your life?'

He moved his shoulders awkwardly. 'I wanted so much for things to work out for us. I hardly dared hope...'

'You know I'll be here for you, always. The way I feel won't ever change, Nate.'

He exhaled slowly and gently squeezed her fingers. 'I'm glad. Hearing you say it makes me feel so much better.' He braced himself. 'Here goes, then.'

He called for everyone to take a seat, and when they were settled, he said, 'Thank you for coming here today. I know you've all been worried about what might hap-pen to the estate...to your homes. I'm here to tell you what's been decided and how we'll be going forward from now on. None of it involves Peninsula Holdings. I turned their offer down and they won't be coming back.'

A cheer went up and he smiled. 'Yes, I thought you would like that. But I have accepted a couple of other offers that might affect you in a roundabout way. I've agreed to let a TV company use the West Wing of the

Manor House in order to make a period drama series, and I've also signed an agreement to allow a film company to use the house at a later date.'

There were gasps of astonishment from the villagers and a buzz of excited conversation started up. People started asking questions and Nate held his hand up for quiet. 'I know there are things you want to ask,' he said, 'and there will be time for that. Let me just say that the activities of the companies will take a matter of months and there shouldn't be any impact on the village—apart from perhaps a few more customers in the shops or the pub for a while.'

'Will we get a visit from Colin Firth?' one woman called out hopefully.

'Does Daniel Craig do period drama?' another asked with a wistful expression.

Sophie laughed, and Nate smiled. 'I wouldn't know about that,' he said. 'All I want to say, to finish, is that your houses are safe and you need have no worries for the future on that account.'

Everyone started talking at once and Sophie took a moment to quietly say to him, 'Has it really solved all of your problems? Are you out of the woods now?'

He nodded. 'Oh, yes,' he said. 'They're paying me an embarrassing amount of money—a lot of it up front, so I can categorically say the future's looking rosy.'

She laid a hand on his arm, her fingers curling around his sleeve. 'I'm so happy for you. I know how much all this means to you.'

'It means everything to me to know that your father's house is safe and his way of life won't be disrupted any more. He's doing so well, isn't he? And you and I... Now we can have a future together, can't we, Sophie?'

'We always could,' she said. 'You know I don't need a Manor House and all the trappings of an estate to keep me happy. I just want you—the man who saves a little boy's life when he collapses in the street, or feeds a baby in Neonatal—the man who brings my sister to me and gives my brother a lift late at night. You're everything I want, Nate.'

He bent his head to her and kissed her. 'I can't wait for everyone to go,' he said under his breath. 'I want you all to myself.'

She chuckled and went with him to mingle with the crowd and answer questions about the TV production and his plans for the estate.

Her father hugged her as he said goodbye a while later. 'You and Nate are obviously very happy with one another,' he said. 'I'm pleased for you. Does your mother know?'

'I mentioned it to her when I went over to Jessica's house. She seemed to accept it. I think she'll be happy as long as you're happy with it.'

He nodded. 'I'll give her a call.'

He and Rob left to go home, and gradually the rest of the villagers began to take their leave. Nate and Sophie saw them off, and when the last one had gone, Nate gave a soft sigh of relief.

'Come into the drawing room with me,' he said, taking Sophie by the hand and leading her into a room off the wide hallway. 'I have something for you.'

Sophie looked around. She remembered this room from before, with its pale silk wall coverings, cream sofas and luxurious oriental rug. The curtains were drawn now, beautiful brocade drapes that elegantly skirted the floor. Several lamps were lit in here, casting a golden glow over the room, and the wood-burning stove flickered with gentle heat in the inglenook fireplace.

Nate went over to a bureau in the corner of the room. He took a small box from a drawer and turned to her. 'I wanted to give you this,' he said, going over to where she stood in the middle of the room and getting down on one knee in front of her. He carefully opened the box to reveal an exquisite sparkling diamond ring nestled on a bed of silk. Brilliant light was reflected from every perfect facet.

Sophie gasped. 'Oh, Nate...'

'Will you marry me, Sophie?' he asked. 'Will you accept this ring as a token of my love and as my promise that I will always be yours?'

'Oh, Nate...yes.' Her voice broke with emotion. 'I will. I'm overwhelmed.'

He exhaled slowly as though he'd been holding his breath in preparation for her answer. He stood up and placed the box on a table, taking out the ring and turning towards her once more. He reached for her left hand and carefully slid the ring on to her finger. 'It fits perfectly, doesn't it?' he said. 'I asked Jessica your ring size.'

'Ah...that's how you knew. Yes, it does... Wait till I see her—she didn't say a word to me about this! Nate, it's so beautiful.' She looked at him, her eyes shining with happiness.

'It's where it belongs—on your finger. There's a wedding ring made to go with it. Perhaps we could make it a short engagement? I know it's traditional to have a summer wedding, but I was thinking maybe Christmas would be a good time? We could be married in the village church and then come back here for the celebrations. What do you think?'

She lifted her arms to him and wound them lightly around his neck. 'I think that sounds wonderful,' she said.

He wrapped his hands around her waist and drew her to him. 'We could honeymoon in the Caribbean, after the festivities. Do you think you would like that?'

'Anywhere would be lovely,' she murmured, 'as long as I'm with you.'

He smiled and kissed her tenderly, with growing passion. 'I've a feeling that life is going to be sheer bliss from now on,' he said after a while, his voice roughened.

She came up for air briefly. 'Oh, yes, definitely.' She kissed him again and neither of them spoke for a long, long time after that. They were far too busy showing their love for one another.

* * * * *

THE HEAT
BETWEEN US

CHERIS HODGES

This book is dedicated to my readers. Without your support, I'd probably be wondering what to do with all of these stories floating around in my head. Thank you for allowing me to share them with you!

Chapter 1

Michael Jane, also known as MJ, yawned as she leaned back in her office chair while reading over the latest edition of the local newspaper. It wasn't that the story was boring—she just hated Monday mornings, and this one was particularly difficult. Mimi had talked her into a three-mile run, and then a green smoothie for breakfast.

No wonder the caramel beauty was tired and ready for a power nap. MJ looked at her reflection in her compact mirror. Her light brown eyes were sparkling and her auburn curls were actually in perfect form today, despite her run this morning. MJ was often complimented on her full lips, especially when she smiled. It was the one trait she'd got from her mother that she appreciated. Her lips and the beauty mark near her bottom lip.

"Miss Jane," her assistant said. "You have a visitor."

"Who is it?" Michael stifled another yawn. She knew she didn't have any appointments this morning, which was the only reason she'd allowed Mimi to talk her into that crazy run.

"Nicolas Prince."

Michael groaned and tugged at her auburn tresses. "Send him in."

Before the door opened, Michael smoothed the corners of her mouth then sat up straight in her chair.

Nicolas Prince used to be the man of her dreams, the man she'd seen standing at the altar on her wedding day. Now he was simply the client she wished she'd never signed to her marketing company. Nic, who'd always had a healthy dose of confidence, leaned on the strength of their friendship to show up without an appointment. It wasn't a good look.

"Good morning, beautiful," he said as he walked in and took a seat in front of her desk.

"What do you want, Nic?" She sighed and ran her fingers through her hair. MJ played with her bouncy curls when she was annoyed. Nic's unannounced visit was very annoying. Granted, there was a time when seeing Nic would've sent her heart fluttering and made her smile. She'd even gone so far as to fantasize about a future with him. But that was before he'd made it clear that he didn't have the same feelings for her that she had for him, leaving her crushed. Nic had used her to get what he wanted and she vowed that she'd never be used by another man again. Mimi Collins-Daniels, MJ's best friend, had tried to warn her that Nic was a player, but Michael had wanted to see the best in him. She wanted to believe that she could be the one to bring out the love in him, like a princess in a fairy tale. Unfortunately, life wasn't a fairy tale and neither was her one-sided relationship with Nic.

At least she'd learned her lesson. She'd never make the mistake of falling for a player again.

"What's up with the attitude this morning?"

"Why are you here without an appointment? Mondays are busy days for me." She raised her right eyebrow. "You could've at least brought coffee and bagels if you were going to come in here unannounced."

Nic shook his head. "Well, I apologize, but I have an amazing idea and I need your help to make it sizzle."

MJ sighed. "I'm listening."

"Are you?" He rolled his eyes. "Stayed out partying last night?"

Michael gave him a look. "Get on with it. I have another appointment." The sooner he said what he had to say, the quicker she could get him out of her office. "And how I spend my nights aren't your concern. What's your idea?"

"The Great Atlanta Jazz Fest. A two-day citywide event to spotlight the growing scene here and give New Orleans a little competition."

MJ perked up in her seat. "Go on."

"Of course my spot would get the most publicity because I'd be a main sponsor and host all of the after-parties."

Michael gave him an icy glance. "Yeah, I imagine you would expect that. What about the artists?"

"I have a few ideas. A few of the groups I've had at the club would be great headliners. But we need some big names."

"Okay, so how are we going to work this event and get the city on board?"

Nic nodded. Michael turned to her computer and pulled up her internet browser. "We need to make sure we don't have any of the same artists who were in New Orleans headlining here. We want Atlanta's jazz fest to be different, our own thing."

Even if this festival was Nic's idea, MJ knew having her company attached to a successful event like this would put her business at the top when it came to landing multimillion-dollar accounts. She needed this to work, even if it meant working with Nic.

Nic slapped the edge of her desk with excitement. "And this is why I came to you. I knew you could make this work. You're one of the only other people I know who can take an idea and make it as big as it needs to be."

"Me and my staff…"

"No, MJ, I'm only working with you on this. I know your people are sharp, but you're the best."

"Everyone here is capable of making this a stellar—"

He interrupted her. "We have a contract, remember? It says that we—"

"Clearly, I know what it says," she snapped. "Give me a couple of days to get a proposal together. Then we can start firming up plans."

"Miss Jane," her assistant said over the intercom. "Mimi Collins is here for you."

Nic rose to his feet. "My cue to leave. I'll call you to make an appointment so that we can go over this in more detail."

"Please do," she replied as Mimi walked in.

There was no love lost between Michael's best friend and Nic. Ever since they were undergrads at Spelman and Morehouse, Mimi and Nic had butted heads. MJ could never put her finger on why, and at this point she'd chalked it up as one of life's unexplained mysteries.

"Ooh," Mimi said, giving Nic a cool glance. "Am I, hopefully, interrupting something?"

"Hello and goodbye, Mimi. I was just leaving." Nic strode to the door.

"Don't let me stop you." Mimi took the seat that Nic had vacated.

"Guys, this is my office, not the quad," Michael said. "Nic, we'll talk soon."

Mimi made a face and crossed her legs as Nic walked out the door. "Please tell me that was about business."

"It was and you're rude!" MJ broke out into laughter. "I don't get you two."

"Whatever. Are you in as much pain as I am?"

"Not you, Miss Marathon Queen." MJ rolled her eyes. "Let me just go on record and remind you that this morning's run was your idea."

Mimi yawned. "Well, I had a bit of a workout last night with my loving husband, so three miles was a bit much this morning." Mimi stretched her left foot out. "And these heels are murderous. But I had to show up at the Blog-Her conference looking like a million bucks."

"Umm, TMI, Mimi! How's the conference going so

far?" Michael asked, quickly changing the subject. MJ had watched her friend rise to fame and infamy with the power of the keystroke as the creator of the *Mis-Adventures of Mimi* blog. After her public spat with the online dating website *Fast Love*, Mimi had fallen in love with her attorney, Brent Daniels. Michael had hoped their real love story would've made her friend a little less controversial on her blog. It hadn't and that was why the public loved her. Mimi still wrote about relationships and real life issues.

Her last post had been about women not waiting for a man's potential to kick in while dating. The post had gotten over seven million hits.

"I think I might have started something positive," Mimi said with a smirk.

"Why does that statement scare me?"

"Because you're nuts. I met a web designer who wants to make a site that celebrates women. Highlights our trials and tribulations. Falls from grace and comebacks. There are a few sisters looking to create some dating apps that aren't just about your looks and can match couples by the books they've read."

"That does sound positive. I could see myself logging on to an app like that." MJ smiled. "And what else has been going on at the conference?"

Mimi smiled and excitement sparkled in her eyes. "A lot of good ideas in our early sessions. There's even talk of a *No More Mistresses* website that would list all of the married men pretending to be single on dating websites." Mimi kicked off her shoes. "Enough about me. Why was Nic here?"

"Business. He wants to do a citywide jazz fest and

I'd be handling the marketing for it. We're just sketching things out right now. But it sounds like it could be a great idea."

"I hope it's successful for your sake. But Nic can hug and kiss my—"

"Got it, Mimi."

"I forgot to tell you this morning, but Jamal asked about you over dinner."

MJ smiled and Mimi pointed at her. "What?"

"You and Jamal. What's that all about?"

MJ sucked her teeth. "Jamal and I are just friends. He's a foodie, despite the fact that he looks like he eats nothing but protein bars. We were going out Saturday night, but I got a call from a client because of some negative social-media reviews. We had brunch Sunday morning. Then he had to set up security at a venue for a concert or something."

"So, this thing with you and Jamal is still light and fun or…"

"Stop it. Because for the last time, we're just friends." And Michael wondered if they would ever be more than that. If she was honest with herself, she'd admit that she wanted to be more than Jamal's friend, but she also knew his reputation as a ladies' man, so she kept her heart as guarded as possible. The last thing she would be was another name on his list of conquests. And she wasn't about to get her heart smashed again by expecting too much from a man who didn't know what he wanted.

Jamal loved his family, especially his grandmother Ethel. Every Monday, she called him to make sure he was taking care of himself—as if he was a teenager away at boarding school. And every Monday, he looked forward to his early morning conversations with his beloved grandmother.

But at this moment, he needed to get off the phone. A blast from his not-so-distant past had just made eye contact with him.

"Gran, I have to go," he said as he saw a woman walking toward him with a smile on her face. How was it that the one morning he decided to go out for breakfast, he ran into Loony Lu-Lu, also known as Lucy Becker? The wannabe Atlanta socialite couldn't fathom that Jamal rejected her advances and she couldn't take no for an answer. And she always seemed to show up out of nowhere like a ghost of bad dates past. Jamal had gone out with Lucy only once. They'd attended a concert where she spent most of the night on her phone Tweeting and taking selfies for Instagram. It was a boring date, and when she outlined her plans for being on a reality show, Jamal knew he'd never go out with that crazy bird again.

Too bad she hadn't gotten the message.

"Jamal, I do wish you would settle down like Brent. Look at him and Mimi, just as happy as they can be," Ethel said.

"Gran, how do you know that they're happy?"

"Because I read her blog! Anyway, go ahead and do whatever it is you said that you had to do and make sure you get me some fresh crawfish for my Savannah boil this year. I know that stuff you brought last year was frozen."

Jamal chuckled, surprised that his grandmother read Mimi's saucy blog. He remembered how Brent had gotten all out of sorts when his wife had written about their kiss on that infamous blog. "All right, Gran, fresh crawfish and settle down like Brent. I'm going to give you a call tomorrow." He disconnected the call and bit back a groan. If Jamal thought he was going to get away from Lu-Lu, he was wrong.

"Jamal Carver," she exclaimed, "you could've invited me to breakfast and I would've gladly accepted. Now you had to eat alone and where is the fun in that?"

"Hello, Lucy. Being alone is always fun—best company ever." He wiped his mouth with a napkin and dropped it on the table. Rising to his feet, Jamal reached for his wallet and left enough cash to pay for his breakfast and tip his waitress. "Well, I'm off to work. Have a nice day," he said.

"How about we have a nice night, together?"

"I'm good," he said then headed for the door. Jamal silently cursed himself out for ever going out with Loony. He'd known his lips were dangerous, but he'd kissed her anyway. And she'd fallen head over heels. If only he had that effect on Michael Jane's sexy ass.

Sighing, he unlocked his Ford Mustang and slid behind the wheel. MJ had been the star of his dreams since they'd met at his buddy's cookout last year. Despite her masculine name, Michael was all woman, with dangerous curves he wanted to ride like the wind. And those expressive brown eyes. Sometimes, he'd just stare at her to watch the golden flecks in them. MJ's dimples were another reason why he'd always tried to make the caramel beauty smile.

But she had wanted to keep things light. Normally, he'd be all for that, but something about MJ made him look for more. Was his gran right about it being time to settle down?

When he arrived at his security firm in the heart of downtown Atlanta, he focused on the breakdown in coverage at a concert his firm was providing security for where a deadly shooting had happened. He needed answers and someone was going to lose their job today. Jamal prided himself and his company on keeping people safe. His reputation wasn't going to be sullied by people not doing their jobs. And then there was always the possibility of a lawsuit.

Better call Brent after this meeting, he thought. Jamal walked into the conference room and looked around at his staff. Three of the men had been with him for a decade, and two of the guys had come highly recommended from his marine buddy, Walter Ramirez.

"What in the hell happened last night?" Jamal demanded.

"J," Harry Mancini began, "I was in charge last night and I take full responsibility for what happened. Around twelve thirty, the crowd started clearing out and I let two of the guys go home. Then the rest of us had to do security detail for the talent. We had no idea that there had been an argument."

"How did a weapon get on the premises? We were supposed to be checking cars as well! Did you guys not pat folks down?" Jamal asked, disappointed that he was going to have to let Harry go. But he'd dropped the ball big-time.

"We were, but…"

"No buts, Harry. What happened last night was unacceptable and you were in charge. A life was lost. I have no choice but to let you go."

Gasps filled the room, but Jamal wasn't finished. "The rest of you are off duty until further notice. I can't have people on my team who don't follow the rules. We're the First Line of Defense and last night we were worse than rent-a-cops."

Harry rose to his feet and headed for the door. "Jamal, I'm sorry about what happened, but these guys don't deserve this punishment."

"And that's not your choice to make."

Jamal waited for the men to file out of the room before he dropped his head on the table. What he did had to be done but it still wasn't easy to do. Pulling out his cell phone, he called Brent.

"What's up, Jamal?" Brent asked when he answered.

"I'm in trouble," Jamal began. "Or potentially in trouble."

"What's her name?"

"Bruh, this is serious. First Line of Defense was the security company at that concert over the weekend."

"Oh, shit. And people are talking about suing you already?"

"No, but it's only a matter of time. This is America and after the tragedy comes the lawsuit."

"Yeah, but they will probably go after the promoter and the artist first. That's where the money is."

"Still, my guys failed to do their job and I feel responsible."

"Don't say that to anyone else. I know you take your job seriously and you have an impeccable reputation, but you can't save everybody and no one is going to hold you responsible."

"That's what you say until someone files a lawsuit."

"If they do, then you know I got your back. Stop borrowing trouble."

"You're right, but I had one of my top guys running the point on this concert and I had to fire him today."

"Damn, that was harsh."

"So was not following my rules. But whatever. I'm going to go do some paperwork."

"Dude, this is not like you at all. What's the real problem?"

MJ.

"Who said I had a problem?"

"Your actions and your attitude. The last time I saw you act like this was during the… What's her name?"

Jamal groaned. "It's MJ."

"I knew it. I thought you guys were just kicking it and having a good time?"

"And I thought I could handle that," Jamal said. "Any other woman, I would've been good with that, but there is something different about Michael."

"Yeah, she doesn't want you. Forbidden fruit is always the sweetest."

"Says the man who married his former client. I guess you would know."

"I'm going to chalk that up to you not getting any and being jealous. You know nothing happened between Mimi and me before I settled her case. Not that it matters now, because she's my wife and whatever I did worked."

"I know. As a matter of fact, I should send your wife a few dozen roses to get her to help me win MJ over."

Brent broke out into laughter. "You know if you ask Mimi for help, you might end up fodder for her blog."

"Umm, I forgot about that. You know my gran reads her blog. Still, I don't know how and why Michael has gotten under my skin the way she has," Jamal said. "I feel like I'm one step away from being Loony Lu-Lu."

"Is that woman still after you?"

"Sadly. Like they say, it's the ones you don't want who are always chasing after you."

"That's what happens when you have too many ones," Brent said. "I got to go, but I can tell you this— I might be having lunch with my wife and her best friend at the new Sunshine Café in the West End around one thirty."

"You might be getting a six-pack of craft beer to relax with this weekend. I'll see y'all at one thirty," Jamal said.

After hanging up the phone with Brent, Jamal felt a little better about everything.

He glanced at the clock on the wall and realized that he had too much time on his hands to sit there and think about Michael. So, he logged on to his computer and pulled up his rules-of-engagement document for his employees and printed it out. He didn't want any more excuses about not knowing what to do.

Chapter 2

Michael and Mimi were still sitting in her office when Brent called his wife. As she listened to Mimi cooing and laughing into the phone, Michael could only shake her head. But she had to admit, love looked really good on her friend. She couldn't believe she'd ever thought that a narcissist like Nic was capable of making her feel like this. *Get over it.* Turning to her computer, she googled the lineup for the past New Orleans jazz fest and made notes of the artists who had performed there. She wanted to make sure they didn't book the same people for the Atlanta event. Then an idea hit her. What if they used local bands? That would really give the Peach City its own thing. The food would have to be amazing as well. She then started searching some of the restaurants that Jamal had introduced her to that she enjoyed. As she thought about her dinner with him last week, she couldn't help but laugh. They had been sitting on the patio at a new Peachtree Street eatery when a woman walked over to Jamal and threw a glass of water in his face.

She'd gone off on him for not returning her phone calls and proceeded to call him every name in the book. Then Jamal had dried his face with a napkin and stood up and handed her a dollar.

"Maybe this will help you buy a clue as to why I didn't call."

It had been funny to Michael, even as a part of her wondered if this was what it would be like dating a playboy like Jamal.

But they *weren't* dating.

"What are you giggling about?" Mimi asked as she dropped her phone in her purse.

"Nothing as exciting as whatever Brent was saying to you."

"He was reminding me that we shouldn't be late for lunch." The smile on her friend's face told Michael that was not all he'd said. "Come on, MJ. Leave those files and let's get moving. You know how traffic is around here."

"Yeah. But you're driving since you made me run this morning."

"And we're running tomorrow as well, so get ready for it."

Michael groaned as she rose to her feet. "I never thought I'd say this, but I can't wait for you to go back to New Orleans."

"Whatever. You know you miss me when I'm not here. And luckily for you, once my travel series is over, I'll be back in Atlanta full-time. That means we can run every morning."

"No, ma'am."

Mimi rose to her feet and told her friend that she and Brent would see her at the restaurant in about an hour. Before MJ could tell her friend goodbye, her phone rang.

Monday was actually turning into a busy day for her.

Finally, after she wrapped up her calls and reports for her clients about their marketing campaigns, it was time for lunch.

If it hadn't been for the fact that Michael had been clamoring to try the new West End restaurant, Sunshine Café, she wouldn't have agreed to be the third wheel on Brent and Mimi's lunch date. She started to tell her friend not to become that married woman who was always trying to hook up her single friends.

Mimi and Brent were the perfect couple, in her opinion. He was the calm where Mimi was the storm and it worked for them. Her friendship with Jamal was a bit like that. The more time they spent together, the more she found things to really like about him.

The fact that he was a foodie and found the most off-the-beaten-path restaurants in the city always made her smile. She hoped that she could introduce him to a place for a change.

If only he wasn't such a playboy…

Walking into the restaurant, she smiled when she saw Mimi waving for her. "Brent got held up on a case at work," she said when Michael made it to the table. "This place seems really nice."

"I know. I was hoping to tell Jamal about it, since he is always finding cool places for us to eat around the city."

Mimi laughed. "Were you expecting him for lunch? Because here he comes."

Michael turned toward the door and smiled when she saw him walking her way. Their eyes locked and Michael's heart rate increased. *Relax*, she told herself.

Jamal Carver was a beautiful, yet rugged, man. His caramel-brown skin was smooth as silk and that goatee gave him the right mix of tough and sexy. His bedroom eyes gave hints of mystery and sex, and that brilliant smile just made her melt every time. Even if she tried to deny there was an attraction between them that went beyond friendship.

Then he had a body that seemed chiseled from mythological marble and wood, crafted by a sensual deity for pleasure and desire. But since she wasn't the friends-with-benefits type, she kept her wanton thoughts under wraps.

"Hello, ladies," he said when he reached the table, then leaned in and gave Michael a kiss on the cheek.

Mimi smiled. "Jamal, what are you doing here?"

"Thought I'd check this place out and I see that great minds think alike," he said then winked at Michael as he took a seat across from her.

"And here I was hoping to scope it out and bring you someplace new for a change," Michael replied.

"Have you all ordered yet?" Jamal asked.

"No, and I'm going to go," Mimi said as she waved her phone, a peculiar gleam in her eye. "Brent wants me to meet him at the office."

Jamal and Michael shared knowing glances. "Umm, huh," Michael said. "I bet he doesn't need you."

"Anyway. You two enjoy—lunch, that is," Mimi said as she rose to her feet and sauntered away.

"Were we set up or what?" Michael asked.

Jamal shrugged innocently. "I have no idea what you're talking about. You know how I love new restaurants."

"Sure you do," she quipped. "How's your Monday going?"

"It just got a thousand times better," he said with a wink. Michael felt herself blush.

"Glad I could help," she said. "Hopefully this place is as good as it smells."

Jamal reached across the table and took her hand in his. "What are you doing tonight? I have something I want to show you."

"What?"

"Why would I tell you now?" He stroked the back of her hand with his thumb. Shivers of delight attacked her spine as his fingers caressed her. It wasn't as if he hadn't held her hand before, but today felt different. She slipped her hand from underneath his, urging her heart to return to its normal pace.

"Because I hate surprises."

"Too bad. About nine, meet me at my place."

"Jamal, I… Okay."

"Don't get all excited on me," he quipped.

"Oh, stop," she said with a giggle.

A few moments later, a waitress appeared at the table to go over the day's specials. Michael decided to go with the shrimp, chicken and grits, while Jamal was a bit more adventurous and chose a crawfish jambalaya pie.

"Wow," Michael said. "Now, that was a bold choice."

"Have to try it first to see if I don't like it."

She nodded in agreement. "But if you don't, my grits are so off-limits."

"Just selfish. But I'm sure this food is going to be amazing. If not, I have good company."

"Flattery is not going to get you a spoonful of my grits," she joked. Michael liked being with him—laughing was so easy. But she couldn't and didn't want to risk her heart again or get hurt. Jamal was everything that she knew wasn't good for her. A playboy. Would he even want to settle down with one woman? Could he?

"MJ?" Jamal said, breaking into her thoughts.

"Yes?"

"Where did your mind go?"

"Work. A client who came in today wants to do a citywide jazz fest."

"Mmm, that could be a logistics nightmare, depending on how many venues you plan to use."

"Not when I know a dream team that can help." Michael smiled. "First Line of Defense, perhaps."

"I'd be happy to help, but I have to be honest with you. We had an incident over the weekend."

"What happened?"

He told her about the shooting at the concert and

how his team hadn't been able to prevent it. "Ten years in business and nothing like this had ever happened."

"People make mistakes, Jamal."

"But this is bigger than a mistake. Someone died."

"And that's not your fault."

"Wish I felt that way," he said as the waitress made her way to the table with their food.

Jamal was silent until he and MJ took their first bite of food. Then they were singing the praises of the dishes and Jamal wasn't thinking of last night's tragedy. "These are the best grits I've ever had!"

Jamal nodded in agreement. "And the corn bread is tender and sweet. Reminds me of something else."

She rolled her eyes. "And what would that be?"

"You."

"Jamal, you probably say that to all of the girls." Michael wiped her mouth with her napkin.

"Being that you're the first girl I've eaten with here, you're the only one who gets treated to this."

"For now."

"This is officially going to be our spot. It's going to be MJ and Jamal's, not the Sunshine Café. Should I carve our names in the table right now?"

She hid her grin as she shook her head. "You're a mess."

"And? If I was Joe Regular, you wouldn't be here with me, now would you?"

She smiled and nodded. "You're right. And that pie looks delicious."

"It is." Jamal held a fork full of his savory meal out

to her. When Michael closed her lips around the fork, he was jealous. That fork had what he wanted. Michael's lips and tongue. Then Michael moaned. He could make her moan like that. She just needed to give him the chance.

"So good."

Jamal nodded. "Like I said, this is our spot. And for the record, I want points for sharing my food."

She nodded. "Ten points for sharing your food. Only if the dessert is as good as the entrées."

Jamal slowly allowed his eyes to roam over Michael's lithe body. "Where does it all go?"

"What?"

"The food."

"Burns off in the gym. You should join me for one of my morning workouts."

Jamal laughed. "You're not ready. Have you forgotten that I'm a marine?"

"Sounds like you're challenging me and I'm always up for a challenge. You haven't learned from that spades game at Brent's place?"

"Yeah, but you won't have your partner in crime Mimi this time. Name the time and the place."

"Six a.m., Anytime Fitness in midtown."

"Hope you like burpees."

Michael rolled her eyes. "I'm the burpee queen. Hope you like losing."

"Want to know a secret? Brent and I let you ladies win that day because he wanted to get in Mimi's pants."

"That's bull and you know it. Brent was going to get

into her pants win or lose. When you guys want a re-match, we're not hard to find."

Why did she have to say "hard"? Thinking about her in a pair of spandex shorts and a sports bra made him harder than a brick. "I hear you talking, beautiful. But this time we will show no mercy. Brent already has his woman." *And soon enough, I'm going to get mine.*

"And just like Mimi, I don't like to lose." Michael winked at him then waved for the waitress.

"Yes, ma'am?" she asked as she approached the table.

"Do you have a dessert menu?"

"Of course. I'll bring it right over to you."

Michael looked at Jamal with a smile on her lips. "I hope they have chocolate cake."

"With lots of icing." He winked at her, and then his cell phone rang. When he saw Brent's name, he started to ignore it, but he excused himself from the table and took the call.

Michael watched as Jamal walked away, talking on the phone. Part of her wondered if it was one of his women. *This is stupid. If I can't trust him, why am I here?*

The waitress returned to the table and handed her a menu. "Is that your man? Because, girl, you are lucky."

"Oh, we're just friends."

The waitress's mouth dropped open. "Does he know that?"

"Well aware. Question—do you guys have a choco-late cake?"

She nodded excitedly. "And it is very good. Moist, and the icing is homemade."

"I need two big slices."

The waitress nodded and smiled as Jamal walked back toward the table. "He has the hots for you," she whispered to Michael. "You better take advantage of it before I do."

Michael offered her a mock salute. "I'll take that under advisement."

Jamal sat down and placed his hand on top of Michael's. "Sorry about that."

"No worries."

"That was Brent. He had news for me about the shooting this past weekend. So far, it looks as if we have a legal standing if lawsuits start piling up because the promoter should've…"

Michael threw her hand up. "You don't have to explain anything to me. You get phone calls."

Jamal shook his head then polished off the last of his pie. "Did you find anything you liked on the dessert menu?"

"Oh, yeah. I think it's coming our way right now." She nodded toward the waitress.

"That's some good-looking cake," he said as the waitress set the hunking slices on the table.

"Just wait until you taste it." The waitress gave Jamal a wink and Michael felt a twinge of jealousy. Was this woman really flirting with him in front of her face? But then again, she'd just told her that she and Jamal were only friends.

"You wouldn't happen to have any milk, would you?" Michael asked, wanting to send her away.

"Soy, almond or regular?"

"Definitely almond with a side of ice."

The waitress turned to Jamal. "Can I get you some milk as well?"

"No, just some water." When the waitress left, Jamal took a glance at Michael as she took a big bite of her cake slice. "I know you aren't going to eat all of that."

She stuffed it in her mouth and smiled. "Mmm."

Jamal followed her lead and took a big bite of the cake as well. It was good, but when he saw a drop of chocolate on Michael's bottom lip, he didn't care about how the cake tasted because he wanted to taste her.

"What?"

Jamal leaned forward and wiped the chocolate from her lip with his thumb. "Just a drop of chocolate on your face."

Chapter 3

Michael shivered at the feel of Jamal's thumb against her lip. Something about his touch just made her body tingle. She wanted him, but knew it probably wasn't a smart thing to want. Playboys were like leopards—their spots didn't change simply because you wanted them to.

"Th-thanks," she said.

"No problem. Got to keep that pretty face clean. Or you could've used that shot to market this cake."

"They haven't hired me yet, so no free advertising."

"You're hard-core, huh?" He stuck his finger in the chocolate icing and brushed it across her full bottom lip. Just as he was about to lean in and kiss the confection away, Michael beat him to it and licked the chocolate herself.

"Okay, this icing is so good that I would give them a shout-out for free."

"How nice of you," he said. "Don't forget to meet me at nine tonight."

"For a surprise, right?"

Jamal kissed her hand. "Yes. And, no, I'm not telling you what it is. But I do have to run. I have a meeting in the heart of the city and I'm about to be late."

"Have a good meeting and I guess I will see you tonight."

"Come on—you can't act like that."

"Here's the second surprise—if I show up or not. And you should probably save your seduction skills for some-one else." MJ nodded toward the waitress who was clear-ing a table not far from theirs. "She'd like it, I'm sure."

Jamal pulled out his wallet and left enough cash on the table to pay for their meals. "You think I'm trying to seduce you?"

She rolled her eyes. "You're telling me that you're not?"

"Babe, if I was trying to seduce you, you'd be in my arms right now. Just make sure you're not late tonight." He winked at her then headed for the door.

Michael watched him walk away and realized that he was right. She'd see him at nine, and no matter what his surprise was, she was going to enjoy it. Be happy about it and pretend that it didn't make her heart and soul melt.

"I'm in so much trouble," she muttered as the wait-ress walked over with her glass of milk.

* * *

Jamal hopped into his car and drove to the Atlanta Metro Credit Union. He was meeting with the head of security there to revamp their security protocol. As he walked into the building, his mind was on MJ's lips. That woman wore that chocolate like the most delicious lipstick. He'd wanted nothing more than to kiss her and taste that sweetness on her. But she was faster than he'd expected and had licked the chocolate away.

Seeing her tongue pass over that full bottom lip had made his blood pressure rise off the charts. What was it about this woman that made him want her so badly? Maybe it was because she told him no or the fact that she didn't act like the typical Atlanta women he'd dated. She didn't think that three dates meant they were in a relationship or that the fifth date meant an engagement ring was coming next.

MJ was the exact opposite. She didn't take herself, or what they had going on, seriously. At first, he'd enjoyed it. Felt as if he could be himself around her. He could be silly. He could be serious. They could talk politics in one sitting then turn around and debate about who the best comedian of all time was. Jamal had never found that range of conversation with another woman.

And the woman liked football. When he'd scored two tickets to the Atlanta Falcons season opener, he'd taken MJ with him and she'd been an avid fan of the game. Especially the star cornerback. Jamal had been impressed because most women he'd taken to a game knew only the quarterback and maybe a wide receiver or two.

"Defense wins championships, and the way Atlanta looks right now, we're going to the big game!" Michael had said at the end of the game.

"It's just the first game of the season."

"You have no faith."

"I know we have Carolina twice this season and their offense is finally as explosive as their defense," he'd said.

"Please. We're going to eat them up."

Smiling at the memory, Jamal walked up to the receptionist and asked for Craig Franklin.

Michael returned to her office and decided to throw herself into work. She didn't want to think about Jamal, but in the silence of her office, all she could do was think about him. If his finger was any indication, his kiss would be damn near deadly. Shivering, she wondered if anything would happen beyond the heat between them. Would the fire burn out and she end up like the woman who tossed that drink in Jamal's face?

"Nope. I'm not going to let that happen." Logging on to her computer, Michael did immerse herself in her work for about thirty minutes, and then her phone rang. When she saw Mimi's number, she answered because she was going to give her BFF a small piece of her mind.

"You're not slick, Mimi."

"What are you talking about? I had to meet my husband."

"Sure you did. You and Brent aren't slick at all."

"I had no idea that Jamal was going to show up at

lunch. That was all Brent because he said his boy was having a bad day."

"And I'm supposed to be the make-him-feel-better girl?"

"It worked, didn't it? I don't get you two."

"Wait a minute! You were totally against me getting serious with Jamal and called him a rebound."

"And you said you guys weren't serious." Michael could imagine her friend's eyebrow raised to the heavens. "So, what's the problem here?"

"We're friends, Mimi. Just friends. I don't understand why people don't get that. And I'm not looking for another dead-end relationship that is going to end up with me looking like a fool again."

"You like him more than you want to admit. Michael, remember the words of wisdom you used to give me? Time to take your own advice. Stop running and go after what your heart wants."

Michael rolled her eyes. "Because you took my advice, Mimi?"

"Umm, well, had I listened to you about that *Fast Love* post, I would've never had the chance to get close to Brent and fall in love with him. And you wouldn't have met Jamal. Then you'd still be sitting here pining for Nic."

"That's not true."

"What part isn't true? You meeting Jamal or still trying to show Nic that you're in love with him."

"Let's put Nic in the past, where he belongs. I wasted a lot of time trying to make him think we should've been a power couple. I own that. I'm over that."

"Then why are you working with him?"

"Contract."

Mimi sucked her teeth. "So."

"And if this event is as big as I want it to be, this is going to mean more high-profile clients, more big events and the success I've been chasing."

"You're already successful. You run this city," Mimi said.

"From your mouth to God's ear. People know I'm Mimi's friend, but they have no idea what I can really do."

"Whatever. How was the food at the café, though?"

"Amazing, and the dessert was superb. Maybe you and Brent should go there for dinner, since you guys set up that bogus lunch."

"For the record, it didn't start that way, but if you must blame someone, blame Mr. Law and Order. He told Jamal where we were having lunch."

"Oh, there you go. Let me tell you something, Mimi Collins-Daniels. If I read your blog and see any parts of me and Jamal on there, I'm going to hurt you."

"You mean like real names?"

"Don't play with me, Mimi!"

"All right, I'll try."

Michael sighed. "You better do more than try."

"You have my word, unless something really juicy happens. And don't say anything else, because I do write about myself on my blog."

"What does that have to…? Mimi, my brand isn't like yours, and if you…"

"Let me stop playing with you. I won't do it. And you better be ready to run in the morning."

Michael grinned. "About that run. I'm going to work out with Jamal in the morning."

"Ooh. With or without clothes?"

"Stop it. We're going to the gym. And he wants me to come see him tonight."

"You mean he wants to go on a date?"

"It's not a date. It's a…"

"D-A-T-E! Stop living in the land of denial. You two are getting to be annoying."

"Spoken like someone who has been annoying for years."

"And on that note, I'm hanging up."

"I love you, Mimi," Michael said through her laughter. After hanging up, she opened a file on her computer and started planning logistics for the jazz festival. When she typed in *security*, the only company she could think of to handle the job was First Line of Defense. Michael picked up the phone and called Jamal.

Voice mail.

"Jamal, this is MJ. Give me a call when you get a chance. I have a proposal, a business proposal, for you. I wanted to discuss it with you before I see you tonight, if possible. Thanks."

Jamal shook hands with Craig Franklin. "You've been really lucky," Jamal told the bank CEO.

"And I don't want to continue to press my luck. Your security ideas are just what we need to make the bank more secure from inside and outside jobs."

"You also shouldn't give an employee access to the video system. Not saying that you have someone stealing from you, but you have to be proactive instead of reactive."

"Makes sense. I look forward to your report and I'm sure the board will agree to the project."

Jamal nodded. "Let me know when you guys want me to get started and I'll send my tech team in."

The two men walked to the lobby and shook hands again. "Looking forward to working with you," Craig said.

Jamal nodded and told his client goodbye. When his phone vibrated in his pocket, he pulled it out and smiled when he saw a missed call and voice mail from MJ. If she was trying to back out of his surprise evening, he was not going to allow it. Tonight, he'd show her a side of him no other woman had ever seen.

Once he got into the car, Jamal listened to Michael's message. *Business proposal? Interesting*, he thought as he called her back.

"Hey, Jamal. I hope you got my message." Michael's voice was like a sweet song that he wanted to keep on Repeat.

"I did. Do you want to meet tomorrow and talk about it?"

"Aren't we getting together tonight?"

"Just looked at my watch and First Line of Defense is closed."

"Jamal."

"MJ. Listen, you do too much. Tonight, we're going to relax and not say a word about your proposal."

"All right. But you are considering it, right?"

"I'll tell you in the morning. When's a good time for us to get together?"

He could hear the keys on her computer moving at a rapid pace. "I have an opening at nine forty-five."

"That's about the time I have breakfast. Want to see if the Sunshine Café has better eggs than West Egg?"

"No, but I'll meet you at West Egg because those potatoes are just amazing."

"Good. See you later," he said.

"And what are we doing tonight?"

"You'll see when you get there. 'Bye, MJ."

Looking at her phone, Michael couldn't help but smile when she and Jamal hung up. He always made her smile. But that doubtful voice in her head kept telling her that they would never be serious. He was a player. And what made her think that she could be the woman who would change his mind about his lifestyle? The last thing she wanted was to be another one of those women who saw him out on the town and had an emotional breakdown.

That's not my style, she thought as she shut her computer down and prepared to leave the office. It wasn't easy to keep saying and pretending that she didn't want more from him. She just couldn't say it to him. Fear froze her tongue every time she tried. As she walked out of the office toward her car, she decided to head to the gym to burn off some nervous energy.

Would tonight be the night that she and Jamal took the next step in their relationship?

What was this big surprise? She knew that he wasn't going to propose. That thought made her laugh. It wasn't as if they'd known each other long enough for her to start fantasizing about being Mrs. Carver. She put the blame squarely on Mimi's shoulders for making marriage look so good.

As she pulled into the parking lot of the gym, Michael's cell phone rang. She wasn't happy at all when she saw Nic's name flash across the screen. She started to ignore the call, but she knew he wouldn't stop calling because obviously he needed something.

"Yes, Nic."

"Don't sound so excited. I just wanted to see if you had time to meet with me tomorrow. I have some great ideas that I want us to look at for the jazz festival."

"You do realize that it is way after office hours, right?"

"Since when did we start standing on ceremony?" Nic's laughter actually made her blood boil.

"Nic, you're simply a client. We aren't in a space where you can call me in the middle of the night because you have an idea. You made it clear that we're all about business. So, respect me enough not to invade my personal time because you have a freaking idea."

"I'm sorry—am I interrupting you and Mimi talking about whatever it is you two cackle about when you get together?"

"No, you're interrupting me and a very handsome man making a beeline between my thighs. Good night."

She ended the call and tossed the phone in the glove compartment. Michael was ready to punch something really hard now.

It was times like this when Jamal was glad he lived out in the burbs. Tonight he'd have a clear view of the sky and he had a fire pit that he didn't have to worry about getting zoning permission to light. He took his telescope to the edge of the woods that abutted his property and gave him the clearest view of the sky. Not many people knew that Jamal was an astronomy nerd. Since he was a kid, he'd enjoyed looking to the stars for answers. He would've been an astronaut if the *Challenger* incident hadn't scarred him. But still, he enjoyed watching the universe. And though he wouldn't tell his boys, he was a man who wished on stars sometimes. Especially when he was in Iraq. He'd prayed and wished for all of his comrades to make it through the night. He'd prayed and wished that the people he shot in the heat of battle were terrorists and not human shields.

The stars calmed him, made him feel as if he'd have his normal life back. After two years in the Middle East and an injury that left him unfit for combat, Jamal had lost partial sight in his right eye. And though he had surgery to correct the injury and remove the shrapnel from his eye, he hadn't been able to pass the physical requirements of the Marines to rejoin the corps. For about a year, he'd been a recruiter in Alabama. But Jamal missed action. Missed helping people and saving lives.

Deciding not to reenlist, Jamal had moved back to Atlanta and opened First Line of Defense. His grandmother had not been pleased. The matriarch of the Carver family wanted her only grandson, at the time, out of harm's way. She needed him to settle down and carry on the family name. For years, he'd ignored her constant nagging about finding the one. Jamal wasn't interested in a family. His father was MIA and that had had a huge impact on his life. He'd watched his mother cry over this man who'd broken his promises. One thing that Jamal could say about the women he dated was that he never made promises to them. He tried not to play with their emotions and make them believe that he was going to provide them a future.

In all these years he'd taken three women to his family's annual low-country boil in Savannah, but he now knew it had been a mistake to take any of them there. Introducing a woman to his family was unfair to her if he wasn't serious about the relationship, so Jamal had decided that the next woman he took to Savannah would be the one he planned a future with. And for a long time, he'd felt he wouldn't be bringing anyone down there for a while.

But lately, Jamal had caught himself wondering what it would be like to take MJ to Savannah. Would she even want to go with him this year? He figured that she'd say no. But he liked the idea of Gran and the family meeting her. He wouldn't even step in if they started asking uncomfortable questions like *Are you guys serious?*

That was a question he wanted an answer to. Could they be serious? What was holding her back from being his? Glancing at his watch, Jamal saw that he needed to get the shrimp on the grill and grab the graham crackers

Chapter 4

Michael stood under the cool shower spray after her hour-and-a-half workout. She'd hit the heavy bag, run for three miles on the treadmill and flipped a 350-pound tire thirty times. She was sore and tired. She wanted to call Jamal and see if they could reschedule, but she wanted to see him. She was excited about his surprise. Closing her eyes, she imagined him slipping in behind her, his big hands stroking her breasts until her nipples were rock-hard. Leaning her head back underneath the shower spray, she slipped her hand between her thighs, imagining that her fingers were Jamal's tongue. Hearing a throaty moan escape her mouth, Michael snapped back to reality.

Shutting the water off, she grabbed her towel and dried off. *Lord, grant me self-control when I see this man.*

After getting dressed in her favorite purple romper and silver sandals, Michael decided to get a surprise for Jamal as well. She drove to the Sunshine Café and ordered two slices of the sinfully delicious chocolate cake. She waved at her favorite waitress as the latter crossed the full dining room to greet her.

"Cake, huh? Where is Mr. He-Is-Just-My-Friend?"

"I'm taking this cake to him, because friends do stuff like that." Michael smiled.

"Umm, my mama would say that you're working on getting to his heart through his stomach. Good job. But you better learn how to cook, if you don't know how to already."

Michael broke out into laughter. "I'm so not after his heart and I can cook."

"And Shakespeare would say, *the lady doth protest too much.* Girl, if you don't jump on that man, I know a bunch of women in Atlanta who will."

Michael held her tongue because she knew a bunch of women in Atlanta already had. *How am I any different?*

"Well? I hope you have a thong and a cute bra on underneath that outfit." She wiggled her eyebrows.

"Not at all," Michael said. "Just friends."

"Keep in mind that we do cater weddings."

Michael took her slices and shook her head. "You're worse than my friend Mimi. Sounds like something she'd say on her blog."

"As in Mimi Collins? You know her."

"Yep."

"Tell her I'm her biggest fan. I comment on her blog as Cheyenne twelve-eighteen."

"I will let her know and maybe even bring her back for lunch tomorrow." Michael winked at her then headed out the door. Glancing at her watch, she saw that she was going to be late if traffic was bad.

For once, it wasn't. She arrived at Jamal's house right on time. She loved the quietness in his neighborhood. No sounds from the highway, no blaring horns and sirens every five minutes. And his lawn was always amazing. The little girl in her wanted to kick off her shoes and run through the manicured grass.

"Hello, beautiful."

She locked eyes with Jamal, who met her at the door dressed in a pair of cargo shorts and a white tank top. He looked so delicious and youthful as well as sexy. "Hey, you." He enveloped her in his arms and she inhaled sharply. He smelled good, woodsy and clean.

"Ready to be surprised?"

She rolled her eyes. "I guess I have to be."

"You're going to love it," he said. Kissing her on the cheek, he led her into the backyard. Michael was all smiles when she saw the fire pit glowing and the food on the table. But it was the telescope that caught her eye.

"What's this?"

"Some people call it dinner." Jamal's arms went around her waist. "Shrimp, grilled peppers and hush puppies. Because I know you love them."

"Really? I can't lie—they are pretty awesome. And I have dessert. Shoot, I left it in the car."

"We can have it for breakfast."

"Breakfast? You assume I'm spending the night."

"Not assuming, just stating a fact. I plan to keep you up all night."

Michael blinked and her mouth fell open. Images of her body pressed against Jamal's naked one flashed in her head. "I didn't come here to sleep with you, and if…"

"Whoa, little red Corvette, slow down. While I would never kick you out of bed, tonight isn't the night." Jamal pointed to the telescope. "Tonight, I'm going to give you the universe."

"The universe, huh?"

"First, we eat." Jamal led her to the table and pulled the chair out for her like a perfect gentleman. "And you can tell me what you have against surprises."

"What do you know about astronomy?" Michael asked as she dug into her shrimp. "And I don't like surprises because most of the time, it turns out to be something bad."

"That's because you haven't had the right kind of surprises. Stick with me, baby girl, and every day will be a happy surprise."

"I hear you talking. You're going to have to show and prove. I'm curious, though. How did you get into all of this?"

"I'm what you'd call a nerd—a sexy nerd, but a nerd nonetheless. When I was a kid, I'd always escape into the stars."

"Did you ever find anything up there?"

"Sometimes I did. But my big dream was to fly to the moon."

"Yet you joined the Marines and went to war?"

Jamal shrugged as he stabbed at his shrimp. "What can I say? I wanted to serve my country and I don't regret a minute of it. But when they get that space shuttle ready for commercial flights, I'm going to be the first one on it. Play your cards right and I might take you with me."

Michael almost choked on her juicy shrimp. "I'll watch you from down here while you shoot for the moon."

Jamal handed her a glass of wine. "Where's your sense of adventure?"

"Planted right here on the ground."

"Chicken."

Nodding, Michael took a sip of wine then set her glass on the table. "I'll be that. But I don't want to leave the Earth's atmosphere."

Jamal watched MJ eat her shrimp and his loins ached as he imagined her lips wrapped around him like that. Her tongue gliding across his hardness the way she licked the garlic sauce from the jumbo shrimp. He shifted in his seat, growing harder than a brick while watching her eat. He couldn't remember the last time the simple act of a woman eating had aroused him so much.

"This is so good."

"I bet you are."

"What?"

"Thank you."

"Who taught you how to cook?"

"My gran. She doesn't believe any Carver, male or

female, should be unable to feed themselves. So, when she went in the kitchen, she grabbed one of us to be her assistant. Then there was a quiz."

"Your gran seems like she doesn't play."

"She doesn't. You guys would probably get along famously."

"You think so?"

Jamal nodded. "We do a low-country boil at the end of the summer, when the whole clan goes down to Savannah. We all have a part of the meal we're responsible for. I'm the crawfish king."

"Sounds like fun. My family does catering and indoor reunions, once every five years."

Jamal popped a shrimp in his mouth. "You and your family aren't close?"

She shrugged. "We're busy and a small group, so… I guess we're not close. Mimi and I decided to make our own family."

"Y'all are very close."

"That's my crazy sister."

"She's mine, too, but always remember you and I are not related." He poured them both more wine. "Come on—let me take you to the moon." They walked over to the telescope and Jamal pointed to the pillows underneath the stand. "Don't take this the wrong way, but get on your knees."

Michael sucked her teeth. "You know…"

"I'm not the one with the dirty mind, baby. That's you."

She laughed and followed his directions. Then he wrapped his arms around her waist as he knelt behind her. "Now, if you turn your head to the left, you will see Orion."

Michael looked to the left with the telescope. "Wow. Now, is this the same as Orion's Belt?"

"That's the top of the constellation. But look at the whole thing. That's the thing about stars. When you look beyond the surface you see so much more."

She turned around and looked at him. "Why can't people be that easy?"

"People are that easy, if you take a deeper look." He brought his face closer to hers, his lips inches away from hers. The heat of her breath teased him and made him want her with a force so strong that he could barely think. His body was on fire with need for her. He'd never felt this way about a woman before in his life. He didn't know when she'd gotten under his skin like this.

"Jamal..."

Capturing her lips, he devoured her mouth, savoring the softness of her lips and the taste of her tongue. Jamal pulled her closer as if he was trying to melt with her. She didn't fight the heat. Her spicy response made him harder than concrete. But just like the end of a summer rain shower, she pushed him away.

"We can't do this." Her voice was a husky whisper. Could she get any sexier?

"Why not?"

"Because we're friends and this is just going to complicate everything." Rising to her feet, Michael smoothed her hands down her thighs. "I have to go."

"Don't go," he said as he closed the dark space between them. "My intentions were to show you the stars.

I don't want you to do anything that you're not ready for."

"I saw stars all right. Jamal, it's getting late and we have a meeting in the morning. I can't stargaze all night."

He stroked her arm. "That's fine. We're still going to eat the cake for breakfast, just in your office." Winking at her, Jamal walked over to the fire pit and doused the flames. "Next time we'll make the s'mores."

"You had s'mores?"

"Why else would I have a fire going in the summer?"

MJ smiled and stroked his cheek. "Aren't you just full of surprises, Mr. Carver. Next time, lead with the chocolate."

"Oh, so there will be a next time?"

She shook her head. "You're something else, but this was a good surprise and thank you for sharing the stars with me."

I'd share a lot more if you'd let me. Jamal took her hand in his and walked her to the driveway. "Call me and let me know you made it home safely," he said as he opened her car door.

"I will. And thank you again for dinner," MJ said as she closed the door. Watching her drive away, Jamal could only shake his head. He wanted this woman in his arms tonight, even if they kept all of their clothes on.

As Michael drove home, all she could think about was Jamal's kiss. That hot, soul-searing kiss had made her knees weak. Now her body ached with need. She needed Jamal's touch. Needed to feel him between her thighs.

Why did she kiss him? It wasn't their first kiss. She'd kissed him last year when they'd met at his house to talk about his situation with his mother and Brent's father. At that time, Jamal had been an emotional mess because Brent didn't know that his father was also Jamal's little brother's father. According to Jamal, Brent had unresolved anger issues with his father and he wondered how that would play into his relationship with the little boy after Brent Sr.'s death.

But that had been a gentle kiss. A friendly smooch that said, *I support you.* But this kiss... This kiss said, *I want you. I need you.* And boy, did she want him. It just wasn't going to be good for her heart.

He was a playboy. He'd even admitted that he hadn't wanted to settle down. Had something changed? Was he really trying to be with her as more than a friend or had they just gotten caught up in the heat of the moment?

As she pulled into her driveway, Michael sent Jamal a text. I made it home.

She wasn't sure if hearing his voice would make her turn around and live out her shower fantasy with him. Grabbing the cake slices, she exited the car and walked up to her front door. When her phone rang, shattering the silence around her, she nearly dropped her purse and the cake.

"Hello?"

"Your text was nice, but I could've sworn I asked you to call me."

"Jamal, go to bed."

"I will, at some point. Have you walked in the house yet?"

"Unlocking the door now."

"Good. And when you activate your security system, I'll let you go."

"You're all about protection, huh?" Michael keyed in her alarm code. "Done."

"Sleep well, beautiful. See you in the morning."

"Good night." Michael floated to her bedroom on the promise of seeing Jamal in the morning. She didn't even notice the text message she'd missed from Nic.

Jamal didn't sleep well, so when morning came it felt as if it was too soon. His body was so keyed up from wanting MJ that he would have to take a run, and a cold shower would certainly follow. Now he understood Lu-Lu's insanity from one kiss. Well, kind of. Lu-Lu was crazy, while he was just falling hard for the most amazing woman he'd ever met. Pulling himself out of bed, Jamal tugged on his running shorts, grabbed his sneakers and a bottle of water. Even though it was five after six, it was hot in Atlanta already. Jamal started with a slow jog and sped up as he started thinking about what Michael was doing this morning.

Did she sleep alone last night? Did he cross her mind? Was she going to act as if nothing had happened between them when he walked into her office in a few hours? He slowed his gait; he was going to see her in a few hours. Would he be able to handle that?

I got this, he thought as he started running again. Mile one was easy. Mile two, he ran into Lucy.

"Good morning, handsome," she said, seeming to appear from nowhere.

"Morning."

"Isn't this a beautiful green space? I love running here. I wish I'd known that you were working out this morning."

Jamal stopped and gave her a sidelong glance. "Yeah. Lucy, enjoy your run." He tore off as if he was Usain Bolt. Once he'd run for three miles, Jamal was tired. Glancing at his watch, he saw that it was time to head home so that he could get ready to meet MJ.

As he ran home, Jamal glanced over his shoulder to make sure Lucy hadn't followed him. He smiled when he made it home without encountering her again. Now he could focus his attention on MJ. And he hoped that she'd brought the chocolate cake in for them to enjoy over coffee. That cold shower was going to work miracles for him after his morning run.

Michael wanted to call in sick, but since she was the boss, that couldn't happen. Besides, she was the one who'd invited Jamal and his company to work on the biggest account in her company's history.

"What was I thinking?" she muttered as she rose from her bed and headed to the shower. She'd missed two calls from Mimi and she didn't care because she was in no position to run this morning. All night, Michael had dreamed of Jamal taking his kiss deeper and making all of her fantasies come true. But when she woke up holding her pillow and not Jamal, she had to get her act together.

Business. Focus on business.

Michael took the coldest shower that she could stand.

Her mind had conjured up erotic visions of Jamal last night, of his magical tongue touching her most sensitive spots. But in the light of day, she realized that she had to sit across from him and talk real business. She had to listen to him plan how to keep this jazz fest safe.

Get your hormones under control, girl, she thought as she stepped underneath the cold spray. *It was just one amazing kiss. Not as if it was your first amazing kiss.*

But it was. Michael let the cold water wash over her shoulders. She'd never been kissed like that before, and if she was honest, she knew she wanted more. Needed more. Jamal had awakened a passion inside her that she'd never felt before. He was everything she wanted and that scared her because she had a nagging fear that she might not be enough for him.

God, help me, she thought as she shut the water off.

Chapter 5

Michael walked into her office with a smile on her face and the bag containing the cake slices. Not the most nutritious breakfast, but she didn't mind sharing an unhealthy heap of goodness with Jamal.

"Good morning, Ms. Jane. Your nine o'clock is here."

"He's early." Michael looked at her watch and then glanced at the waiting area. "Nic? What are you doing here?"

Nic rose to his feet, smiling as he walked over to her. "I sent you a text last night, but I guess you were busy." He nodded toward the Sunshine Café bag in her hand. "Is that place any good?"

"I don't have time for this, Nic. I have… You know what? Let's kill two birds with one stone. I'm meeting with the head of a security company and you guys will have to meet eventually, so let's do it now."

"Great. What company are you thinking of using?"

"First Line of Defense. Let's go into my office." She expelled a frustrated sigh as they walked down the narrow hallway.

"MJ, I'm sorry about yesterday. I had no right to assume I could monopolize your private time. I miss our brainstorming sessions, you know."

Facing him with her hand on her office door, Michael sighed. "Nic, once upon a time, I thought we were going to be together. So, those brainstorming sessions and telling you all of my dreams and plans when you let me get a word in edgewise really meant something more than business to me. At the end of the day, I wasted a lot of time auditioning to be your woman and I didn't get the part. And since I didn't get the part, I will no longer be playing the role."

"Don't be like that. Bitter doesn't look good on you."

Michael raised her right eyebrow then smiled. "Bitter? Hardly. Babe, I'm better and I prove that every time I look at you and don't punch you in your face." She opened the door and walked in the office.

Nic followed and sat across from her desk. "I have reached out to some local artists and they're super excited about the jazz fest. So, I wanted to bring over some of their music for you to listen to. Then we could come up with a marketing plan to attract their listeners and let people who don't know about them discover them at the jazz fest."

"That's an interesting idea. I was thinking that we

do a jazz sampler CD and put them around different hot spots in the city. And we should expand the number of venues that we use."

"As long as my club gets top billing, I don't mind."

Michael leaned back in her chair. "About that… You can't be so self-serving, Nic. The reason why the New Orleans festivals work so well is that all of the clubs and venues come together to make it successful. There are about fifteen other clubs in the Atlanta area that could bring in more people, more artists, and from a marketing standpoint, this would put you in front of people who don't know about your club."

"That's what I'm talking about. What clubs are you thinking about bringing on board?"

Michael pulled out her tablet and handed it to him. "Here's the list of clubs."

As Nic read over the list, Michael's receptionist announced that Jamal was there to see her.

"Give me just a minute and I'll be out to meet him." Turning to Nic, she asked, "What do you think about the list?"

"There are two clubs here that I don't want to be involved with."

"Don't tell me there is beef in the jazz community."

"Vonnie Love is not someone I trust," he said, pointing to the Love Jazz listing. "He…"

"Used to be your partner. I know. I thought you guys had straightened everything out?"

Nic grimaced. "Not working with Love or Lucy Becker."

Michael rose to her feet and smoothed her pencil skirt. "I'll be right back and we can discuss this later."

Jamal looked around the waiting area and was impressed by MJ's style. Earth tones, abstract art on the walls. This was the kind of setting that made you not hate waiting. Calming, for someone else. Right now, he wanted to see her. They'd get to business, but he had to kiss her again.

And there she was, looking sexier than a woman should look this time of morning. That green skirt hugged those curves like he wanted to and the white ruffled shirt made her look like a present for him to unwrap.

"Good morning, beautiful." Jamal crossed over to her and drew Michael into his arms.

"Hi, Jamal." She took a step back. "Sorry to keep you waiting."

"Not a problem."

"Nic, the guy who's putting the jazz fest together, is here, and since you're going to do security for the festival, I thought you two should meet and talk about your plans."

"Oh, I'm hired like that?"

Michael smiled. "Yes. If you want the job it's yours."

"Is today the day I get everything I want? Because…"

"Down, boy." She pressed her hand against his chest. "We'll see how you hold up after the burpees."

Not willing to wait another second to feel her lips, Jamal leaned in and kissed her deep and slow. His hands roamed her back as she seemed to melt against him. All he wanted to do was lift her in his arms and bury himself inside her sweetness until she sang out in pleasure.

Business. I'm here for a business meeting. Jamal pulled back. "Sorry about that. But…"

"We'd better stop this. Nic is waiting inside." She wiped the lipstick from his lips.

"You still got my cake, right? I skipped breakfast for that."

"The cake is still waiting. Let's go."

Jamal was happy to walk behind Michael if for no other reason than to admire that skirt and silently thank the designer who made it.

Once they walked in the office, Nic and Jamal locked eyes. "Gentlemen," Michael began. "Jamal, meet Nicolas Prince. Nic, meet Jamal Carver, owner of First Line of Defense."

They shook hands then sat down. "First Line of Defense, huh? Were you a football player or something?"

"No, I'm a marine, so I know about defending and protecting real people." Jamal decided that he didn't like this Nic fellow.

"Excuse me."

Michael intervened. "Now, let's talk about what we're going to need to keep this event safe."

Jamal reached into his jacket pocket and pulled out his tablet. "Here's my plan for venue safety. There will be a guard posted at the entrance and at all doors. You're going to be looking at more people than you would normally have at any of these venues. Metal detectors are a good idea as well."

"Metal detectors, Jamal?" Michael questioned. "It's not that kind of crowd."

"I'm with Michael on this. For one, metal detectors

will cost us money. Plus, they turn people off and remind them of why they hate airports."

"Show of hands—how many people in this room run
a security firm?" Jamal raised his hand. "Safety matters, and if you want to ensure safety and keep your insurance costs down, you need metal detectors. Nothing
is going to sink your event like a riot or crowd injury."

Michael nodded. "Good point."

"Well, I still don't like the idea. Why not a pat down?
Metal detectors are going to slow the lines down."

"And keep people alive," Jamal interjected. "You
handle the music and the booze and leave the security
to me." He winked at Michael then moved on to the next
plan for the outdoor part of the security detail, which
included working with the Atlanta Police Department
for crowd control and patrols around the venues.

"This is very impressive," Michael said. "But then
again, I wouldn't expect anything less from you, Jamal."

Nic shot them questioning glances but didn't say anything for a beat. "I've seen you in my club."

"Yes, you have. It's a great place." *But you better
believe you won't see me there again.*

"Thanks. I try to keep it upscale. And it's one of the
best places to meet women, but you already know that."

Jamal clenched his teeth then glanced at Michael.
Her expression was unreadable.

"Guys, can we focus on the jazz festival? Jamal, can
you get me a copy of the security plan? Nic, I think we
need to get you on some local shows and featured in
some entertainment magazines to build a buzz. Once
we get the partnerships with the other jazz clubs nailed

down, we will see if we can get a segment on *Good Day Atlanta*. And you need to play nice with Mimi because I want her to feature this on her blog."

"Oh, Lord."

"She has millions of followers."

"Yeah, Mimi's minions." Nic rolled his eyes. "Isn't she in New Orleans now?"

"New Orleans and Atlanta," Jamal said.

"You follow her blog?" Nic asked incredulously.

"She's married to my best friend." *Clown.*

"Oh, yeah. I forgot Firecracker got married. God bless him."

"Nic!"

He threw his hands up. "Just kidding. Well, it seems as if we're going in the right direction here. Thank you for the meeting, Michael. Let's do this again next week." Nic glanced over at Jamal. "Michael, may I have a word with you in private?"

Jamal shook his head and smirked. "I'll wait for you outside."

"No, wait here," she said. "Nic, I'll walk you outside."

Alone in Michael's office, Jamal walked over to the window and looked out over the city. Nic was acting like a jealous ex. He couldn't help but wonder if he was the reason MJ was skeptical about getting serious with him.

"What did she ever see in that self-righteous prick?"

"Is that the guy who took a trip between your thighs last night?"

"Really? This is what you wanted to talk about?"

Nic placed his hand on her shoulder. "That guy is a player, and if you're trying to…"

Michael snatched away from him. "I'm going to stop you right here. My personal life is none of your concern. I don't need your advice, your opinion or thoughts on what I should do or who I should do it with."

"I know we didn't end up the way you wanted us to, but I was always honest with you."

"Nicolas, whatever we had is officially history. And for the record, Jamal and I are friends, not that it is any of your business."

"I miss you being my friend, Michael."

"We were never friends. And if the way you just behaved in that meeting is how you do friendship, I'm not interested. After this event, we're done, Nic. Business and personal."

He gave her a sidelong glance. "Well, if that's how you want it."

"That's how it's going to be. And if I were you, I'd send Mimi an orchid. She loves those flowers."

"Yeah, I'll take it under advisement."

Michael pressed the elevator button. "Goodbye, Nic." She didn't even wait for the door to close before heading back to her office. Internally, though, she was muddled with emotions. It wasn't as if she didn't know that Jamal was a man about town. But somehow, hearing it come out of Nic's mouth made her feel as if she was being foolish to think that there could be something between them more than sizzling kisses. Did everybody know he was a player? Was he okay with that?

"Jamal and I are just friends," she muttered as she walked back to her office. "Nice view, huh?"

Jamal turned around. "I think this is a better one."

"Ready for that cake?"

He nodded and crossed over to her. "Tell me something. Did you and Nic date?"

"Something like that, but it was a long time ago."

"Left you scarred, though?"

Michael speared him with an icy glance. "Jamal, I don't want to talk about it. We can eat cake or you can leave."

"Ouch."

She arched her eyebrow at him as if she was waiting for his decision. "I'm always going to choose cake," he said then gave her backside a soft smack. "But let me say this—we're not all alike."

"I know that. And I don't think you go to Nic's club trolling for women, either." Michael pulled the cake out of her desk drawer.

"There's something I've always wanted to ask you."

Michael handed Jamal his hunk of cake and a plastic fork. "I might answer."

"How did you end up with the name 'Michael'?"

She broke out laughing as she unwrapped her cake. "You know I must like you because I'm going to tell you the truth."

"The truth?"

"My marketing response to this question is that my parents thought I was going to be a boy and pre-wrote the birth certificate. But the truth is, my mother was a horrible speller. She wanted to name me Michelle. She couldn't spell it and I ended up Michael."

Jamal covered his grin with his hand. And Michael shook her head. "Go on and laugh," she said then took a bite of her cake. "You and Mimi are the only two people who know the truth."

"I'm willing to bet that your name has opened many doors."

"Yeah, well, it was hell getting into Spelman."

"What are your plans for tonight?" Jamal placed his hand on top of hers and peered into her eyes.

"You got another group of stars to show me?"

"No. I want to show you the moon and Venus."

Michael slipped her hand from underneath his and laughed. "You really are a nerd."

"Only you and my gran know this. When I was growing up, my mom had some issues. For most of my childhood, she was in and out of my life. It wasn't until I was ten that she was diagnosed with bipolar disorder. Once she got the right medication, everything was fine. But until she got better, it was Gran who took care of me. She showed me the universe and it started my fascination with the stars."

"How is your mom doing?"

"She and Daveon are doing well. They actually moved down to Savannah. I think Brent Sr.'s death hit Mom harder than she wanted to admit."

"How does Brent feel about all of this?"

"He and Daveon are getting closer and that's the important thing."

Michael nodded in agreement as she munched on her cake. "So, taking me to Venus tonight?"

"Yes. And this is a rare trip, Ms. Jane."

"Is that so?" She placed her fork on the side of her box. "Now, is this going to be after our little gym thing? I'm sorry I missed our scheduled time this morning, but I wasn't feeling it."

What she didn't say was how his kiss had kept her up all night with erotic dreams that made her think about calling him for a booty call.

"You want to lose, huh?" Jamal leaned back in his chair. "You're trying to set me up with this cake, but it is not going to work."

"We'll see, cake man. All of yours is gone and I still have half of mine to eat as I celebrate my victory."

Jamal was about to say something when his cell phone rang. "I have to take this. I'll see you at the gym around six, right?"

"Sounds good." As Michael watched him walk out the door, she wondered if the call he had to take was from another woman. Standing up and looking out the window, Michael decided she wasn't going to drive herself crazy. Jamal was her friend, they were having fun and she couldn't expect him not to see other people.

"I'm worse than Mimi," she muttered.

Chapter 6

"**B**rent, slow down. Did you say my company is named in this lawsuit?" Jamal slammed into his car.

"I got a copy of it about an hour ago. Listen, we can beat this. I just need to know what kind of security plan you had and if the promoter made any changes."

"Nothing on paper, but from what the guys were saying, the shooting happened outside and we weren't hired to protect the parking lot. However, I expected my guys to make sure no guns got on the property. The sheriff's department should've handled that. Shit, I don't need this right now."

"I know. But we need to get in front of this right now and get the promoter to take the heat."

Jamal muttered a string of curse words. "I'm on my

way." He sped to his buddy's office and hoped that the story of this lawsuit wouldn't make the news.

When Jamal arrived at Brent's office, his good mood from talking with Michael had worn off. Part of him could hear Nic telling her that he wouldn't work with First Line of Defense because of this lawsuit.

Brent met Jamal in the lobby. "You look like hell and we haven't even gone over the suit yet."

"I was thinking about the projects that I'm probably going to lose because of this suit, including the jazz fest."

"You and Michael working on that together?"

"Was with her when you called. Met that dude Nic and I can see him talking a lot of shit."

"Let's take this in my office," Brent said then pointed to his assistant. "Can we get some coffee? And hold my calls, unless it's Mimi."

"Yes, sir," she said.

Any other time, Jamal would've made a joke about Brent being whipped. He was definitely going to keep this under his hat for now. Brent sat down and pulled out the paperwork.

"Here's what we're going to do. We're calling the promoter. The Wright family seemed as if they wanted to blame the entire world for their son's death. It's understandable, but ridiculous. Your company, the Fulton County Sheriff's Office and the promoter are named in the lawsuit."

"And how is that going to get me off the hook on this lawsuit?"

"Let me do my thing," he said as he dialed the number. "This is Brent Daniels. I need to speak with Roger Kelly. I'll hold."

Jamal shook his head as Brent scowled at the phone. When Jamal's cell phone chimed in his pocket, he gritted his teeth because it was a Google alert. He didn't even have to look at it to know the lawsuit had gone public. This was going to be a cluster.

"Yes, I received the lawsuit against you and that's why I'm calling. First Line of Defense is my client and you didn't hire them to provide security in the parking lot. I'm looking at that now. Can I represent you? As soon as you get out front and say my current client had nothing to do with the shooting that happened at your event, I'll take it under consideration." Brent hung up the phone and shot his friend an I-told-you-so look. "Crisis controlled."

"Yeah, but the news is already out there." Jamal held his phone out to Brent. "The blogs are talking as well as the local papers."

"Well, I can't do anything about that until the promoter issues a statement."

When Jamal's phone rang, he knew he had to get to his office and try to put part of this fire out. Brent shot him a stern look.

"Jamal, don't talk to the media."

"Hopefully, they aren't camped out outside my office. Leslie is calling. And my receptionist never calls me." Jamal stood up and shook Brent's hand. "Thanks for helping me with this."

"Thank me later when you get the bill."

"Whatever."

* * *

Michael picked up her phone then put it down again. She looked at the news alert for the third time. *He has to be so upset.* Rising to her feet, she paced the length of her office. She felt horrible for Jamal and like a jerk for thinking that he'd run out to talk to another woman. He'd probably gotten a call about the lawsuit and gone to see his lawyer. Walking over to her desk, Michael grabbed her purse. She needed some air. As soon as she got to the parking lot, Michael saw Mimi coming her way.

"What's up, lady? I was coming to see if you and Jamal were huddled together about this lawsuit."

"No. I was just going to take a drive and… Mimi, I'm a jerk."

Mimi raised her eyebrow at her friend. "Now, why would you say that?"

"Jamal was here earlier. He's going to do security for the jazz fest. And Nic was here."

"Oh. My. God! What did old, stupid and thoughtless do?"

Michael dropped her head for a moment. "Got inside my head. He was like, *oh, Jamal, I see you leaving my club with a bunch of women.* Then when I walked him out, he was all *I hope you're not serious about him. He's a player.* So, I'm sitting here feeling like boo-boo the fool and Jamal got a phone call and left suddenly. All I could think was he must be going to meet with some other woman."

"Wait. Why do you care what your friend does and

who he does it with?" Mimi laughed. "Somebody is catching feelings."

"This is why I can't talk to you sometimes," MJ groaned. "I don't know what I was more upset about— Nic calling himself looking out for me or actually falling for Jamal's sexy nerd act last night."

"Sexy nerd? Okay, I need details," Mimi exclaimed.

"Nothing to tell. He cooked dinner and we stargazed." Because she didn't want to hear Mimi go on and on about her hiding her feelings, MJ left out the part about the kiss.

"Are you serious?"

"It was actually endearing," MJ replied.

"I bet it was. And I hope you told Nic where he could stick his unsolicited advice. That asshole."

"You're missing the bigger point, Mimi. That call was about this news alert and his company. How am I going to get serious with him when I have all of these doubts?"

"First, you have to stop driving yourself crazy. Secondly, if you want him, go get him."

"Jamal is happy being single, and I'm…"

"You don't know if he's happy or not because you haven't talked to him about how he feels. You just assume. I told you that you should've been honest with him a long time away."

"And I would take advice from the woman who ran to New Orleans when she realized that she was in love because…?"

"Funny. Real funny, MJ. My point is, learn from my

mistakes. Don't head to another city or state when what you want is staring you right in your face."

But what if he wants something entirely different? Not looking to get my heart broken again, Mimi.

"I know that look, MJ. And your heart wouldn't have been broken in the first place if Nic wasn't a jerk who was more concerned about what you could do for him than how you felt about him. Despite my first impression of Jamal, the one thing he's not is a big jerk."

Michael smiled. "I know."

Mimi furrowed her brows. "Okay. So, you know when a guy opens up to you the way Jamal did, it's not just because he wants to only get into your pants."

"I can't. I'm not ready to get my heart stomped on again."

"And you know this is going to happen because you can see into the future now? Girl, give me those Powerball numbers."

"Shut up." She sighed in exasperation at her friend. "What's wrong with being a little cautious?"

"Nothing, but you're not being cautious. You're being ridiculous. How about you stop acting as if you can read that man's mind? Talk to him, please. Or I'm writing about this on my blog."

"And I will drop you in Lake Lanier."

Mimi grinned and folded her arms across her chest. "Whatever. Let's go find him."

"How about I do it on my own and you go sit on your husband's lap."

"Good idea, and when you find Jamal, tell him how you feel. Because this has moved way beyond a rebound thing and I'm glad. MJ, you deserve to be happy, and from what I see, Jamal makes you happy."

Michael had known for the longest time that Jamal was far from a rebound fling. She hoped that he was the real thing, but how could she be sure when she'd been so wrong about Nic? Granted, she was over Nic, but she couldn't forget the moment she knew she'd made a fool of herself. She'd poured her heart out to Nic, only to hear him tell her that she was a great friend, but he couldn't see himself settling down with her.

Broken and hurt beyond words, Michael had vowed to never allow another man to make her feel so small. Not when she'd worked so hard to be the perfect half to a successful man. She hadn't wanted to be like her mother, always feeling subservient to a man. Michael's father had been a teacher at the local high school and her mother hadn't earned a high school diploma. He'd lorded that over her for years.

Michael knew she would never be with a man who treated her that way. She'd thought that she and Nic were equals and he'd see that together they'd be an unstoppable force. But that night, she understood how her mother had felt all those years. She felt the pain of being treated as if she wasn't good enough.

If she could do it over, she'd be a better daughter to her mom and not always take her father's side.

Now here she was in that same spot—again. Because expecting Jamal Carver to settle down just seemed stupid. Still, she headed to his office and hoped to find him alone so that they could have the conversation that she'd been dreading.

Mimi was right about one thing, though. Jamal did make her happy. Would telling him how she felt change all of that?

Jamal had entered his office from the back entrance and was avoiding all phone calls. He had been trying to take Brent's advice. But all of the reporters outside of his office made him want to say something to clear his name. He'd fired the men who'd dropped the ball on the security inside the event. But it wasn't his fault that the sheriff hadn't provided adequate security outside of the concert.

This lawsuit could bankrupt him or make it difficult for First Line of Defense to gain new clients. "Shit," he muttered as he grabbed a bottle of whiskey from his desk drawer. Jamal started to ignore the ringing of his cell phone, but he saw Michael's picture flash across the screen. Then he answered. "Hey."

"Where are you?"

"At my office."

"I'm on my way over there. Jamal, I think I can help you deal with the media."

"That would be awesome. Come in the back entrance. I'll be waiting for you."

"See you in about twenty minutes." Michael hoped she didn't run into a traffic jam. Her prayers were answered and she arrived at Jamal's office fifteen minutes after they'd hung up. She wasn't surprised to see that a number of media folks were roaming around the parking lot. "News travels way too fast these days." She parked in the back like Jamal had suggested and saw him sitting on the top of his Mustang's trunk.

"Hi."

Jamal hopped off the car and crossed over to MJ. She wrapped her arms around him, thinking that her hug would comfort him. But the heat from his body simply drove her crazy. Inhaling, she filled her soul with his masculine scent. Pulling back, she stroked his cheek. "You okay?"

"As okay as one can be in a media circus." Jamal held her around the waist.

"Maybe I can help you with this."

"No. Our relationship is becoming too business-oriented."

"But, Jamal, this is what I do. And friends help each other in times of need, right?"

Smirking, he shook his head. "Friends, huh? Ever think about what things would be like between us if we were more than friends?"

Michael blinked, wondering if she'd been broadcasting her emotions or if Jamal really wanted to move beyond no-strings. "Do you really think you and I should be focusing on that right now?"

"Today. Tomorrow. Next week. It doesn't matter. Just answer the question."

"Jamal, I—I..." Before Michael could utter another word, flashbulbs went off in their faces. Then the questions.

"Mr. Carver, what are your thoughts on the lawsuit?"

"Were your guards negligent in protecting the parking lot?"

"How did the gun get into the venue?"

Jamal dropped his hands from Michael's waist and turned toward the door of the office, moving to usher her inside. Michael's instincts took over. "Mr. Carver will release a statement in a few days, but right now is not the time to talk about a suit that my client hasn't had a chance to review with his attorney. At this time we offer our condolences to the family."

When the media backed away, she looked up at Jamal, who was giving her a slow handclap as they headed inside.

"I see you're really awesome at what you do. You just came up with that off the top of your head?"

"Yep. It's classic crisis-control verbiage. We're all sorry when someone dies, and while I'm sure you and Brent have looked over the lawsuit, I don't know what you've discussed."

"I might need to take you up on that offer."

Michael raised her right eyebrow. "I can't believe you thought you could do this without me."

"Now I'm forever in your debt. I'll do anything you want to pay it off." Jamal pulled Michael against his chest. She melted in his arms, and as much as she wanted to open her mouth and spill all of her feelings to him, she couldn't. Wouldn't. Didn't. Their lips touched, and in one swift motion, they were locked in a hot kiss. Michael wasn't even sure how it happened—whether she kissed him or not. But when their tongues touched, it didn't matter. She felt as if she was going to pass out as he deepened the kiss; her thighs trembled when he sucked her tongue, making her mouth feel as if it was made of honey. And when he nibbled her bottom lip, her panties were soaked with desire. What kind of magical lips did this man have?

Placing her hand on his chest, Michael pulled away from him, breathless. "Well, that's one way to work off your debt."

"Then I'm going to have to get in trouble more often to create more debt."

"Please don't." She released a deep sigh. "I don't know if I can handle those payments."

"That's just the beginning." Jamal kissed her on the forehead. "So, let's get this statement together."

"I can have it written and ready for you to hand out before you take me to lunch." She winked at him and followed him down the hallway to his office.

When Michael sat at his desk, she seemed as if she belonged there. "Once we're done, we can email the document to Brent to make sure he's all right with everything I say."

"Which is going to be?"

MJ typed without saying a word and then she turned the screen around to Jamal. "Everything I said to those reporters outside."

"Cool. Yeah, send that to Brent because he told me not to talk to the media." When his cell phone rang, Jamal wasn't surprised to see that it was his lawyer. "What's up, Brent?"

"I see you have MJ handling the media. Smart move. The promoter just released a statement about your involvement in the security for the club."

"Saying what?"

"That what happened in the parking lot had nothing to do with First Line of Defense and now this family is trying to sue everyone associated with the concert. We're backing away from this like we have skates on."

"Good. Maybe these reporters are gone now," Jamal said as he walked toward the lobby. He was happy to see the parking lot was empty. "I'm no longer a hot topic."

"That's a good thing. I'm going to let you get back to MJ, because my lunch—I mean, my wife—just walked in."

"Whipped."

"You want to be. Take a page out of my book and go after that woman. I'm about to get mine. Later."

Jamal shook his head when he shoved his phone in his pocket. He never thought that he'd be jealous of a married man. But he wanted that now. Jamal knew from the moment he kissed Michael that he didn't want every woman in Atlanta. He needed MJ to be his one-and-only.

Now, how was he going to convince her of that? Jamal returned to his office, and while he stood in the doorway, he watched Michael sending a text. How could she be so sexy doing something so simple? He wanted to take her crossed legs and wrap them around his waist as he dived deep into her sweet wetness. He wanted to hear her moan his name as she came. Wanted to feel her nails scratch his back as he made her come again and again.

"Jamal?"

"Yes?"

"Did you hear anything I said?"

"Yeah, yeah. Lunch, right?"

MJ stood up and crossed over to him. "No, silly." She tapped his cheek. "I said I can't make lunch because I have another fire to put out. But I'm looking forward to seeing Venus tonight."

He grabbed her hand and kissed it. "I'll see you at the gym first, though."

"We're going to have to reschedule your beatdown. See you tonight." Watching MJ walk out the door made him harder than a man should get watching a fully dressed woman walk away from him. She had a shape like the iconic soft-drink bottle and all he wanted to do was peel those clothes off her and spread her across his desk and make love to her.

"Damn it, I got to make her mine," he muttered as he crossed over to his desk.

Chapter 7

Michael sat at her desk and groaned. Three hours. Three hours of whining and complaining. She was going to drop Cleo Parker as a client as soon as the check cleared. Marketing an author shouldn't be this hard, but if Cleo was going to argue with every reader who didn't like her sci-fi romance novels, she couldn't expect that she was going to make any bestseller list.

When that woman walked out of her office, Michael stood up and did a happy dance. Glancing at her watch, she realized that she wasn't going to make her spin class before going to see Jamal. *Maybe I should just let him work out my thighs. Stop it! This is how it all falls apart, adding sex to the mix. But God knows I want this man.*

Grabbing her purse, she tried to get her hormones

under control before heading to Jamal's. *Cold shower on deck.*

When Michael arrived at her place, she was shocked to see Nic parked on the curb. She parked her car and said a silent prayer before getting out and walking over to Nic.

"What's up?" she asked when he got out of the car.

"I'm sure you've seen the news about your boy's lawsuit."

"And I'm sure you've seen the update about him not being responsible for the shooting. This could've been handled with a phone call—better yet, a text."

"I'm worried about you. I know how women get when they see their friends fall into a happily-ever-after. Don't think that you have to settle for a man like Jamal."

"A man like Jamal?"

"Yes."

"And do you have a better suggestion for my life, since I'm obviously under some kind of undue influence and can't make decisions for myself."

Nic wiped his hand across his face. "That's not what I'm saying, but just because Mimi got married, it doesn't mean that her husband's best friend is the one for you."

"Was I unclear earlier when I told you that my personal life is *not* your concern?"

"Even if you don't consider me your friend, I still care about you, MJ. I want you to be happy, and if I'm not the guy to…"

"Go home, Nic. Go home and don't ever say these words to me ever again. You don't have the right to offer me advice about my love life when you held it hostage for years because you love yourself more than you can ever love me or anyone else." She fought the urge to slap the taste out of his mouth. The mouth that she once craved and dreamed of kissing for the rest of her life. Shaking her head, she realized that after kissing Jamal, she'd learned that she would've shortchanged herself for life if she'd stayed on with Nic.

"When your heart gets broken, don't say I didn't warn you."

Michael walked away because she wasn't sure how long she'd be able to keep her hands to herself.

Jamal decided that tonight, he'd bring MJ inside for dinner. He made lemon pepper chicken and linguine. Then to add some veggies to the mix, he prepared a green salad with spicy vinaigrette dressing on the side. Gran would be proud.

Jamal just hoped that his dessert would be MJ, naked. After they saw Venus, of course, because he didn't want her to know he'd brought her there just to seduce her. But that was his endgame.

However, this wasn't typical playboy Jamal seduction. He wanted to brand her as his tonight. Wanted to make her realize that he was hers for the taking and all she needed to do was open her arms.

Walking into his sunroom, he lit two candles and then opened the blackout blinds so the last rays of the sun could filter into the room. When the moon rose and the stars came out, this was going to be the most amazing backdrop for dinner. Pulling out two big pillows, he set up the table for intimacy. How much longer did he have to wait for her to show up, though? When the doorbell rang, Jamal rushed to the door hoping to see MJ's smiling face on the other side. But when he opened the door and saw Lucy on his doorstep, he wanted to disappear. *I should've never brought her here to wait for Triple A that night,* he thought, remembering the one time he wished he hadn't been such a gentleman.

Jamal swung the door open and leaned against the doorjamb. "What are you doing here?"

"Oh, Jamal, I saw the news about the shooting and the lawsuit. Are you all right?"

"Yeah, I'm good, but I'm a little busy right now."

Lucy stood on her tiptoes in an attempt to look over Jamal's shoulder. "I guess you have someone in here comforting you already, huh? So typical."

"Lu-Lucy, I've had enough of your quasi-stalking. We went out once. One date. I never made any kind of promises to you for you to be acting like this."

"Jamal, I know we have a connection. Just give us a chance." She took a step closer to him.

"Leave or I'm going to call the police."

"One day, you're going to be so sorry about how you treat women. Someone is going to make you pay!" Lucy stomped off the porch and slammed into her car. Jamal could only shake his head as she sped down the road.

Michael wiped the bright red lipstick from her lips and glanced at herself in the mirror. Why did she feel like she was getting ready for the prom? This wasn't her first date with Jamal, but something about tonight felt different.

She reapplied her lipstick and adjusted her strapless sundress. Maybe tonight she would follow Mimi's advice and tell him how she felt. Maybe.

On the ride over to Jamal's, she forced herself not to allow Nic's asinine comments get under her skin. People could change, and who was to say that Jamal hadn't? They'd been hanging out together quite frequently, and other than the incident at the restaurant, there were no signs of him seeing other people.

"You shouldn't have to be a private investigator to date," she muttered as she turned into Jamal's neighborhood. She didn't notice the car parked across the street taking pictures of her as she emerged from the car.

Jamal opened the door before Michael could ring the bell. "Don't you look amazing," he said.

Michael's mouth hung open as she drank in Jamal's physique in black linen pants and a formfitting white T-shirt that hugged his rippling muscles. His ebony brown skin was smooth and reminded her of the finest chocolate. Her mouth watered as she thought about running her tongue across his chest. "As do you." Her voice was husky with yearning. She didn't care about seeing Venus; she wanted to see what was underneath those clothes. Feel his body pressed against hers as they kissed again.

"Come on in. Dinner is waiting in the sunroom."

She followed him inside and was very impressed by the open space of the sunroom. The flickering candles and glowing night sky were breathtaking. "No telescope tonight?"

"Not yet. This room is one of the main reasons I

bought this house. In the winter, I come in here and watch the sky sparkle."

"You're really a nerd."

He kissed her on the cheek then helped her down onto one of the oversize pillows. "I'm only going to take a few more nerd comments."

"What are you going to do, nerd?"

"Take your food away." Jamal reached for her plate and she grabbed his wrist.

"That's just cruel."

He leaned into her, pressing his nose against her. "Do you know how delicious your lips look right now? I'm thinking about cherry pie."

Before she could reply, Jamal captured her lips in a hot kiss—nibbling and sucking on her full bottom lip until she shivered. Pulling back, Jamal smiled at her then licked his lips. "You taste even better than you look."

"Jamal, if you keep kissing me like that, we're not going to make it through dinner."

Lowering his head, he brushed his lips across hers. "Promise?"

"I'm hungry and this food smells so good. Can we eat?"

Jamal bit his bottom lip. "I know what I'd like to eat, but I won't be selfish right now." He took his seat beside her and they dug into their meals. Michael was once again impressed by Jamal's culinary skills.

"If you ever want a third career, I think I see chef in your future." Michael struggled not to slurp her noodles. "Why do we even go out to eat?"

"Because I hate washing dishes. But, if you promise to wear that red lipstick more often, I will cook for you every night."

"Wow, you're easy."

"I'm choosing to take that as a compliment." Jamal rose to his feet. "I forgot the drinks. Sweet tea work for you?"

"Come on, now. Who doesn't want sweet tea?"

As Jamal walked out of the room, Michael gazed out of the windows, amazed by the view of the night sky. Being surrounded by all of the natural beauty, she felt comfortable and ready to open up to Jamal. Tonight was as good a night as any to tell him how she felt about him.

"Here we go." He handed her a glass of tea as she turned around. "Beautiful, isn't it?"

"It is. Makes me wish I could paint. This would be a great painting."

Jamal set his glass down and pulled Michael into his arms. "Look," he said as he pointed to a group of stars. "The Big Dipper. Actually, it's not a constellation, but only the most visible part of Ursa Major, which is the constellation The Big Bear. And don't you dare say it."

"I'm not, because it's just stating the obvious." MJ gave him a quick kiss on the cheek. "Looking at the sky is getting interesting because of you."

Jamal stroked her hair and snuggled closer to her. "MJ." His lips were so close to her ear, she could feel his words. "There are a lot of things that have gotten interesting because of you."

"What are we doing? Jamal, I know you're... I can't pretend we're just friends anymore."

"Good, because I'm tired of doing that myself."

"Can we be honest for a second? I don't want to be hurt and I don't want you to feel like…"

"MJ, I'd never hurt you. And since we're being honest, I've never felt this way about a woman before."

"Jamal."

He stroked her cheek before devouring her lips. His kiss stirred her soul, made her desire drip between her thighs like a summer rain. He slipped his hands underneath her dress and between her thighs. Michael moaned as his thumbs brushed against her wetness. Her panties were soaked and a wet annoyance. She almost wanted to snatch them off, but Jamal made quick work of removing them. As quickly as he tossed them aside, Jamal dived between her thighs and lapped her sweetness. Michael tossed her head back, moaning in delight as his tongue danced around her clit, crying out his name as he stroked her thighs. She grabbed the back of his head, pushing him deeper inside.

When Michael came, it felt like an explosion from her soul. "Oh, Jamal!" Her body went limp and he drew her into his arms.

"You're officially my favorite dessert." He kissed her shoulder. "And that friend question is answered. We're no longer just friends. MJ, tonight I'm making every inch of you mine." He slowly slid her dress below her breasts and unsnapped her bra. "You're so beautiful." Slowly, he licked and sucked her rock-hard nipples while sliding her dress all the way down. Every touch, every lick ignited a fire inside her. Jamal made her body move to his will.

Moving down to her navel, Jamal used his tongue to explore Michael's curves and silky skin.

"Need to get a condom," he moaned. "Because I have to be inside you."

Michael nodded, unable to speak because she wanted him so badly.

Jamal practically ran into the bathroom. He grabbed a condom and stripped out of his pants and T-shirt. To-night he felt like he was going to be making love for the first time. He paused. He would be making love to MJ. This wasn't a hookup, a fling or something that wouldn't mean anything in the morning. He was going to make love to the woman he was falling in love with. The one woman he was never going to let out of his heart.

Walking into the sunroom, he looked at MJ lying on the pillows. The word *goddess* came to mind. "MJ," he said as he crossed over to her. "I know I keep saying it, but you are beautiful."

She propped herself up on her elbows and her eyes roamed his nearly naked body. "And you don't look half-bad yourself. Come here."

"Yes, baby?"

MJ reached for the waistband of his boxer briefs. Tugging them down, she reached for his hardness and Jamal shook with anticipation when he felt the heat of her breath against his tip. Stroke. Lick. Suck. Jamal's knees quaked. Her tongue was magical and the softness of her lips nearly took him to the brink.

"Michael, Michael, Michael!" He stroked her hair as

she licked him like he was a melting ice-cream cone. "Need to be inside you, baby."

She pulled back from him, ending his sensuous torture. "I need you inside me, now."

Jamal ripped the condom package open and slid the sheath in place. As he joined her on the pillows, he thought about seeing her belly filled with his child while she wore his wedding ring. The image made him go still for a beat. Never in his life had he ever thought about family and marriage with a naked woman lying in wait.

He wrapped her legs around his waist and drove into her wetness. They ground against each other, dancing an erotic tango. She felt like heaven. Felt better than anything he'd ever experienced as she matched him thrust for thrust.

Any fantasy he'd ever had about MJ didn't match up to the reality and he couldn't be happier. "Yes, yes," she cried as they rocked back and forth. She tightened her thighs around him and Jamal exploded.

"Damn, baby, damn!"

MJ licked the side of his neck as she reached her climax. "Oh, Jamal."

He wrapped his arms around her and decided that he never wanted to let her go. "I may never let you leave."

"I may not want to." Moments later, they were both asleep and sated.

About an hour later, the sound of smashing glass woke the couple. Jamal leaped to his feet and pulled on his boxer briefs. "What in the hell?"

"What's going on?"

Jamal dashed down the hall to find out while Michael covered herself with her dress. When he got to the front door, he saw one of his planters had fallen and broken the side window. *This is weird*, he thought then brushed it off as a stray animal roaming his property.

"Everything all right?" Michael called out.

"Yeah. Probably a deer looking to eat my plants. I'm going to the garage to get some plywood." Opening the door, Jamal looked around to see if Bambi or his cousins were still running through the yard. When he didn't see anything, he crossed over to the garage and grabbed some wood to patch the window for the night.

He didn't notice a car at the end of the street and the driver watching his every move.

Chapter 8

Michael looked up at the ink-black sky and smiled. It was nice to know she wasn't in a one-sided romance. Jamal made her feel as if they were going to have a great future and she could open her heart to him without getting hurt.

"Hey," Jamal said when he walked into the sunroom. "You good?"

"Yeah. What time is it?"

He looked at his watch. "Two thirty. Let's go upstairs and sleep in the bed."

She shook her head. "I like it down here. It's still beautiful." Michael pointed to the sky. "Can't wait to see what it looks like when the sun rises."

Jamal eased down on the pillows with Michael and

pulled her into his arms. "It won't compare to you at all."

She leaned against his chest, and they looked up at the stars until they drifted back to sleep.

MJ woke up with a start, wondering if last night had been another dream. But her naked body let her know she hadn't been dreaming at all. Making love to Jamal had been better than a dream. He was as tender as he was passionate. A lover who gave as well as he received.

Turning to her side, she wondered where he was. The scent of coffee gave her an indication. Stretching her arms above her head, she drank in the beauty of the golden sunlight pouring in through wide windows. The warmth of the sun reflected MJ's mood, and the cheerful scene was made even better when Jamal walked in the room holding two mugs of coffee.

"Good morning, beautiful." He held out one of the cups to her after she sat up.

MJ inhaled the aroma of the coffee and smiled. "Umm, Dancing Goat blend. Mimi strikes again."

"I knew about Dancing Goat before she used it to seduce my boy."

Michael laughed. "It worked."

Leaning in and kissing her on the shoulder, Jamal grinned. "Is it working now?"

"We'll see. What are you going to do about that window?"

"I'm going to call someone out to replace it later. You hungry?"

"Starving."

"Let's cook something," he said as he set his coffee cup on the table.

"All right." Michael pulled her dress on and followed a shirtless Jamal into the kitchen. "Breakfast is my favorite meal."

"Then maybe I should sit back and watch."

"Well, you've cooked dinner for me, so I will be happy to cook you my famous cheese omelets."

"And I have to have garlic toast to go along with it."

She thrust her hip into his. "I like the way you think." Michael was impressed by Jamal's gourmet kitchen, stainless-steel appliances, copper pots hanging over the stove and a spice rack on the back of the stove.

"I see you, Bobby Flay."

"I told you my gran said you need to know how to cook. Let me see what you're working with."

"Point me to the eggs and cheese." Michael grabbed a frying pan and placed it on the stove. Jamal showed her where all the ingredients were for what she needed then sat back and watched her cook.

When she finished the omelets and baked the toast, Jamal was impressed by the beauty's skills in the kitchen. "I think we're never going to have to eat out again." Jamal accepted the plate Michael set in front of him.

"Don't get used to this. We still have to go to the Sunshine Café because I can't bake."

"Me either."

Jamal dug into his food and it was delicious. "This is good. We should just open a restaurant. You handle breakfast and I'll do dinner."

"What about lunch?"

"That's when we do each other." Jamal winked at her as she walked over to the other side of the bar with her plate.

"You are so bad."

"And I'm really good at it."

"As much as I'd love to hear and feel more about your bad behavior, I have some meetings about the jazz fest in a couple of hours."

Jamal's jaw tightened. "With Nic?"

"You don't like him much, huh?"

Jamal stuffed a piece of toast in his mouth. "What's the deal with you two?"

"There is no deal. He's a client."

Jamal raised his eyebrow at her. "Really?"

Michael tilted her head at him. "I know you're not playing the jealous-of-your-past card. Are you really serious right now?"

"Wait—you're turning my question into an argument?"

"No, but the implication of…"

"Let me stop you right there. I have nothing to do with any of my exes, but you and Nic are always around each other. I just want to make sure I'm not going to be blindsided."

"I don't roll like that, Jamal. If I had a smidgen of feelings for another man, I wouldn't have been with you last night, or even hanging out with you these past few months. But don't be that guy. Don't be the guy who acts like no other man was interested in a woman until he looked at her."

"Ouch."

"Jamal, I'm not going to bite my tongue because you gave me an orgasm."

He clasped his hands together. "How did we go from having a wonderful breakfast to having our first argument?"

"This isn't an argument. I was just setting you straight."

"Excuse me. Come here. We have to make up now." Jamal opened his arms to her. Michael laughed as she fell into his embrace.

"Maybe I overreacted. Fatal flaw of mine."

"And you probably keep things bottled up, too, don't you?"

She nodded. Jamal lifted her chin. "We're going to have to work on that."

"And just for the record, Nic and I don't have anything between us, and since I had to be honest with myself about him months ago, we never did have anything between us."

"We're not going to bring him up again unless it's in your office and we're talking about the jazz fest."

Michael backed out of his arms. "Shoot. I have to call the city about permits today. I'm glad you reminded me."

"Back to the real world."

"Yeah. But why don't you come by my place for dinner tonight? We can have cake for breakfast."

Jamal playfully swatted her backside. "Sounds like a plan."

After cleaning up the kitchen, Jamal and Michael went their separate ways. Jamal still couldn't help but wonder if there was more behind Michael's outburst about Nic. It had been a simple question. But he couldn't deny that he had a past and there were several women in Atlanta who could make a scene if they saw him and MJ out in public. He couldn't judge her for having a past, but it didn't stop him from being jealous as hell.

Michael walked into her office and sighed. She'd made a plum fool of herself at Jamal's over breakfast. He'd had a legitimate question, but she felt some kind of way when she was reminded about her one-sided relationship with Nic. She'd spent so much time hoping to prove that she was good enough for Nic and all she'd gotten in return was the ultimate kiss-off. She'd been hurt by it, but she was now over it. She just didn't understand why she'd gotten so upset this morning.

Was everything going to be different between them now? Would he want to have sex with her every time they saw each other now? Would they continue to explore restaurants and keep their friendship together, or would this be that friends-with-benefits thing that she was trying to avoid?

Picking up her desk phone, she called Mimi. Voice mail. Michael took that as a sign that she needed to figure this out on her own. Diving into work, she got most of the groundwork set for the jazz fest, securing permits for the venues and setting up meetings with the other clubs that would be participating in the festival.

Then she called Nic to see if he'd made any headway with the jazz mixer that they were going to use to promote the festival. As she listened to the phone ring,

Michael couldn't wait until this thing was over and she didn't have to deal with Nic anymore.

"Morning, Michael. You must have been reading my mind."

"Nic, I need to know when you're going to get that jazz compilation together and how long it will take to get it reproduced."

"All business, huh?"

"I'm not about to go back and forth with you today. I have a lot to do."

"Let's get together for lunch," he said. "I have some things to show you and it's a little early for me."

Michael sighed then looked at her calendar on her phone. "I can meet you at one thirty."

"Great. Why don't we go to that new café you like so much?"

"No. We can meet at Houston's on Lenox Road because I'll be coming from a meeting in that area."

"All right. Michael, is everything okay with you?"

"Everything is great. Thanks for asking."

"Why am I getting so much attitude from you?"

"Nic, you're not getting attitude. You're just not getting what you want."

"If things were that bad between us, why…? You know what? I'll see you at one thirty."

Michael was tempted to slam the phone down, but she hung up normally. Why had she wasted so much time with Nic when she'd known nothing good would come from it? Mimi had tried to warn her; hell, Nic had told her on several occasions that he wasn't trying to commit. But she'd stayed around hoping he would change his mind. Now she was shaken about this thing with Jamal.

What if Jamal changed his mind? What if he decided that he didn't want a commitment? And what about the other women? Could he be satisfied with one woman when he'd spent so many years dating many? If Michael was honest, it had been her fear that started the argument this morning. She needed to get over that. But how?

Rising from her seat, Michael looked out the window and decided that she was going to have to have faith in what she and Jamal had. She pulled her phone out of her pocket and sent him a text.

You just crossed my mind and I wanted to say hi.

Jamal smiled when he read MJ's text. Any other woman who would've sent a text like that would go on the do-not-call list. But Michael wasn't just any woman.

Thinking of you, too. Window is fixed. Going to email you the final security plan.

Okay. What do you have a taste for tonight?

Other than you? Surprise me.

Ha. Don't be nasty—right now. I'm still at work.

But you're the boss. I can come and have you for lunch later.

Damn, I have a meeting. Guess we'll have to wait for dinner.

Counting down the hours.

Jamal stuffed his phone in his pocket then hopped in his car. When he glanced in the rearview mirror, he saw Lucy's car.

"She's taking crazy to a whole new level," he muttered as he turned down a side road to see if she would follow. She did.

Then his phone rang.

"Yeah."

"I'm not stalking you. I just want to talk to you about last night."

"Lucy, we don't need to talk at all. You should just stop calling me, showing up at my place and following me."

"Jamal, I really care about you, and if…"

"Lucy. Lose. My. Number." Jamal hung up the phone and glanced in his rearview mirror to see if she was still following him. He started wondering if Lucy had been the deer who'd broken his window last night.

Michael glanced at her watch. She hated it when people were late without a call or email. Lucy Becker was pissing her off. Maybe Nic had been right about not wanting to work with her. If she didn't show up in the next five minutes, Michael was going to cut her from the list.

"Ms. Jane, Lucy Becker is here."

"Great. Send her in." *Late ass.*

Lucy walked into Michael's office looking like a glamorous jazz singer, rather than a club owner. She was supermodel-tall with a creamy caramel complexion and coal-black eyes. Michael was tempted to ask her if she could scat.

"Michael Jane, you are definitely not what I expected." Lucy extended her hand to her.

"I get that a lot. Lucy, thank you for coming in today."

"This jazz festival sounds like a great opportunity. What do you need me to do?"

Be on time. Michael smiled. "I want the jazz scene in Atlanta to come together and make this festival explode. You own one of the biggest clubs in the city. We wouldn't be able to put this on without you."

"That's true." Lucy smiled arrogantly. "What kind of groups are you booking to perform?"

"I'm leaving that to the experts like yourself and Nicolas Prince. Nic is actually in charge of getting the major acts together."

"No wonder you called me. That jackass doesn't know talent."

Michael stifled her laughter. Lucy, despite her lateness, might be all right. The women talked and laughed for about an hour before Lucy agreed to help with the jazz fest and start building a buzz about it at her club.

"Just one thing," she said as she grabbed her purse. "I want to make sure Nic knows he is not the only club owner sponsoring this. I hope that my place will benefit from some of this marketing and that I'm included in some of the after-hours events as well."

"Of course," Michael said.

Lucy smiled. "Great."

Once she was alone in her office, Michael wondered if all club owners were egomaniacs like Lucy and Nic. She'd find out when she met with the owner of Brown Sound Entertainment.

Dontae Brown was a pleasure to meet with, even if he was a bit of a flirt. He had been happy to throw his support behind the jazz fest and was even willing to help Nic host all the after-parties that he wanted. He'd kept asking Michael to join him for dinner, which she respectfully declined five times.

"You're the prettiest Michael I've ever met. At least take a selfie with me for Instagram."

"I can do that." She smiled as he held up his phone and snapped the picture. Then he kissed her on the cheek and took another photo.

"Team too much," she admonished.

"You kept telling me no. I had to steal a kiss."

"See you, Brown." Michael headed out the door. All she could do was hope her meeting with Nic would be quick and painless.

Jamal walked into Brent's office and caught him kissing his wife as if they were the only people in the world.

"Y'all keep this up, I'm going to be a godfather soon."

The couple broke their kiss then turned around and glared at Jamal. "Ever heard of knocking?" Brent asked.

"I did. I guess Mimi had her tongue in your ear and you didn't hear me."

"Shut up," Mimi said then threw a pen at Jamal. "Brent, I will see you in two days. Me, you and hot beignets."

"Keep talking like that and you'll see me on the plane with you." Brent kissed her one more time and Jamal turned away. Mimi and Brent made him smile and see that this was everything he wanted. He could see him and Michael having a relationship similar to this one, but there was no way he could let MJ live in another city even if she did commute back and forth. He needed her within arm's reach. Needed her lips against his in the morning, in the middle of the night, hell, right now.

"Hello," Brent said as he snapped his fingers in his friend's face. "What's wrong with you?"

Jamal smiled then waved goodbye to Mimi. When he and Brent were alone, Jamal sat down and smiled.

"I want that."

"You better define what *that* is, because if you're talking about my wife I'm going to have to punch you in your face."

"No, fool. I'm talking about what you and Mimi have. I think Michael and I can have that. I'm falling in love with her."

"Really? When did that happen?"

"Probably from the day I met her, but I know she feels the same way now, so I'm ready to settle down and be a one-woman man."

Brett looked out the window. "Has hell frozen over?

Are you serious? I mean, I hope you're right because if you hurt that woman I'm never gonna hear the end of it."

"Last night I realized that you don't need every woman in the world to be satisfied. You just need the right one, and MJ is the right one."

"Oh, shit, hell has frozen over."

Jamal shook his head. "I come to pour my heart out to you and you got jokes. I love this woman, or at least, I'm falling in love with her."

"What makes Michael different? I mean, how do you know that this is going to last? You need to know that before you get bored or get upset because Michael is Mimi's best friend. I can't get caught in the middle of one of your relationship mishaps."

"Have you ever heard me say this about a woman before? I'm always honest, and I'm going to be honest with Michael. I want her in my life for the long haul. I just got to make her believe that because I feel like, even though we have a connection, she's holding back."

"Maybe she has the same questions I have. Jamal, you've made it pretty clear that you don't want a serious relationship. Atlanta is your playground, right?"

"Used to be. I'm not playing a game with Michael."

"You better not be."

Jamal glared at his friend. "What? I can't change?"

"Just make sure this is real change and not you charming your way into Michael's pants."

Folding his arms across his chest, Jamal was starting to get angry. Though he could understand Brent's line of thinking. "Trust me when I say this—Michael is more than a woman I want to sleep with. We've stargazed."

Brent eyed his friend incredulously. "If you told her your astronaut story, then I might believe you."

"Told her the story, showed her Orion and explained the Big Dipper to her."

"Yep. Hell has frozen over. You're in love."

"I need your help. Find out from Mimi what the real deal is with MJ and Nic. When we met earlier this week, dude was acting like a jealous ex, and he was telling her that I come to his place to pick up women."

"Well, you do."

Jamal shot Brent an icy look. "Used to. I'm not trying to be her rebound if there is still something between them." He told Brent about the disagreement he and MJ had this morning.

Brent laughed at the end of the story. "I'm surprised she didn't punch you in the face. You, of all people, should never question a woman about her past. If she did that to you, which she has the right to do, you would be pissed off."

"There isn't a woman in this city that I'm working with and we've had a past anything."

"Oh, so you're jealous?"

"Don't be silly. I'm Jamal Carver. I don't do jealousy."

Brent laughed. "You're doing a good job of it right now. Your eyes are turning green like the Hulk."

"Shut up."

"Come on. I'll let you buy me lunch and listen to how you're not jealous." The two men headed for the

Chapter 9

What is this? Keep Michael Waiting Day? she thought as she sat in Houston's waiting for Nic.

When the waiter came over to refresh her glass of water, Michael looked up at the entrance and saw Nic kissing some young woman.

She smiled, thinking, *Good for him. Maybe now he can mind his business and stay out of my life.*

Then he shooed the woman away and made his way over to the table where Michael was sitting. "Hi. Sorry I'm late. Was a little busy."

"No problem, but a call or text would've been nice," Michael said. "I do have other things to do, but I have made a lot of headway with the jazz fest. We should be good for October, maybe November."

"November's the holiday season. People aren't going

to want to spend money on tickets when they have to buy Christmas gifts and turkey dinners to bake."

MJ shook her head. "Your timeline is a little ridiculous if we're going to market this right and make this a successful event. If you just want to put together some random jazz groups and call it a festival, why are you working me so hard?"

Nic leaned back in his seat and smiled. "I hope you're not giving me attitude because of what you just saw."

"Unlike you, Nic, I couldn't care less about what you do with your personal life. But what I do care about is you showing up twenty minutes late for a one-thirty meeting when I've been running around all day talking to all of these club owners so that we can get the jazz fest going. You may have been getting busy, but you weren't working on what's important."

"Excuse me. I appreciate all the work you're doing, and despite what you think, I have been working. The promotional compilation will be ready tomorrow. And I sent you an email with some different art ideas."

"Great." Michael reached into her purse and handed Nic a proposal that she'd drawn up after her meeting with Lucy and Brown.

"You have been busy." He flipped through the pages. "Lucy really wants to be a part of this? Not surprised that she wants some events at her place. She is a lunatic."

"Well, she thinks you're a jackass." Michael picked up her glass of water and took a sip. Nic rolled his eyes and continued reading.

"Why do you want to move the date to October? All

of this stuff can be done and we can have it on Labor Day, like I want."

"And having a new Labor Day event means we're going to have a lot of competition. Established events that people go to every year. Had we had more time, we could've put together the event for August and branded it as end of summer. But we'll have to do it next year. It's October or nothing if you want this event to go well. We just need to make sure all of the groups you've lined up are able to perform."

"As long as I get the contracts signed, we're good."

"Well, as long as you deliver the artists, then I think we can produce the best fall jazz festival that will blow the city away."

"I just have one concern," Nic said. "What about security? You can't still want to use First Line of Defense after the lawsuit and everything."

Michael gritted her teeth. "Yes, I'm still using First Line of Defense because they're good at what they do. If you paid attention to the news, you'd see that they had nothing to do with what happened in the parking lot."

"And this has nothing to do with the fact that you're sleeping with the head of the security firm?"

"Assuming things again. Check their record. They have handled security for some of the biggest events in the city. We'd be stupid not to use them."

"I'm not crazy about using a security firm that's caught up in bad publicity. And I still don't like the metal detectors. We're going for a more mature crowd. Detectors are going to offend a lot of the people."

MJ shifted in her seat. "Do you want to be liable if

there is an incident because we didn't have metal detectors? Also, insurance will be a lot cheaper if we have more security measures in place."

From the look on Nic's face, she knew she had him. "All right. I guess the metal detectors will be what we do. I still don't like them."

"At this point, it's not about what you like. It's about what's best for the safety of the people who will be attending the event. So are we done here?"

"You got a point, even if you're trying to have a lunch meeting without lunch."

"I wasn't late—you were. But if I'm honest, I'm hungry, too."

Smiling, Nic patted the back of her hand and picked up a menu. "Since you've worked so hard, I'll even spring for lunch."

"As if you had a choice."

Brent knew something was wrong the moment he saw Jamal's fist clench. Then he followed his friend's gaze and saw Michael and Nic sitting at a table. Jamal turned to Brent. "Let's go someplace else."

"No. Now you got me wanting cabbage and a Biltmore. You really think that's more than a business lunch?"

"The hell does it look like to you? Is he holding her hand and she's letting him? What part of a business lunch is that?" Jamal narrowed his eyes at them.

"Look, she just snatched her hand away and doesn't even know you're stalking her." Brent chuckled. "I'm actually glad Mimi isn't here to see this. I wouldn't be able to stop her from writing about this and I wouldn't try."

"I'm going to speak to them."

"Do not make a scene. You still have to work with that man, and MJ doesn't strike me as a woman who likes drama played out in public."

"He looks like he wants to put her on a plate."

"Stop projecting and staring at them. If this is you in love, I'm scared."

"Shut up."

"If you're going to go over there, be an adult."

"Don't judge me." Jamal crossed over to MJ and Nic. "Hello, guys."

MJ smiled as if she was happy to see him, but Jamal noticed Nic's scowl.

"What are you doing here?" she asked as she rose to her feet and kissed him on the cheek.

"Mimi went back to New Orleans today and Brent is depressed."

Nic snorted. "I find that hard to believe. That man is probably celebrating."

MJ speared him with an icy look and Jamal had the common sense to hold back his caustic comment. "This was the work study restaurant back in the day."

"Yes. Because the spinach dip is to die for," MJ said.

Nic cleared his throat. "Maybe we should order one."

"Good idea. You guys enjoy. MJ, I'll see you later." Jamal walked away without saying another word to Nic. If that wasn't being adult, he didn't know what was.

Brent shook his head as Jamal returned to the front door, where they'd been waiting for a table. "No yell-ing and no glasses thrown. Looks like you're not as scary as I thought."

"Want to know what he said about your wife?"

"That mother…"

"No, no, you have to be an adult." Jamal shook his head. "I don't know what she ever saw in him."

"Does it matter? She's with you."

"Yeah. Let's get this cabbage and get out of here before I forget that she's mine."

Michael tried to focus on whatever Nic was saying, but her eyes kept wandering over to where Brent and Jamal were sitting. Jamal seemed to know it, too, because when their eyes met he'd lick the tortilla chip, reminding her what his tongue could do.

"Hello? Are you listening to me?"

Michael focused on Nic's face. "No."

"My God, you really are sleeping with him."

"Didn't you spend part of your afternoon doing that with the young lady you brought here earlier? And for the last time, my personal life is none of your business."

"You have your finger on the nuclear bomb, but if that's what…"

"Shut up."

Nic shook his head. "I'm done."

"Thank you."

After they ordered, Nic received a phone call and excused himself from the table. "Hey," Michael said. "Lunch is on you, remember."

He opened his wallet and handed her two twenties

then dashed out the door. Michael was alone for only a few seconds.

"Excuse me, pretty lady? Is this seat taken?"

"It will be if you sit down, Jamal."

"Where did Mr. Personality go?" he asked as he sank into the chair across from her.

Michael shrugged. "Got a phone call and ran out of here. Did you dump Brent?"

"I wish. He's coming over here after he gets the last bit of spinach dip out of that bowl."

"So, do I have time to lean over for a kiss?"

Jamal nodded and gave her the kiss they'd both wanted since they saw each other moments ago.

"My God, people trying to eat. Get a room."

"Don't be a hater because your wife is gone." Jamal licked his lips and winked at Michael.

"My wife will be back in two days. Don't make me be that annoying friend that hangs out with you the whole time she's gone."

Michael laughed. "You can't do that, Brent. I'm sorry we have plans."

Brent smiled at the happy couple. "I'm sure you do. So how is the jazz-festival planning for you guys? All work and no play or a lot of play and a little bit of work?"

"It's coming along. At least we have a great security plan in place. I met with some clubs on this today, and corralling them all together is going to be interesting." She stroked her forehead. "But I think we can make it work."

"Who did you meet with?" Jamal asked.

Michael took a sip of water. "Dontae Brown and Lucy Becker."

Jamal nearly choked on his water. "Lucy Becker? She's nuts."

"And obviously doesn't own a watch. She was so late for our meeting, and that is my number one pet peeve. Why do you say she's nuts?"

Brent stifled a laugh. Michael looked from Brent to Jamal.

"Is anyone going to let me in on the joke?"

Jamal nodded. "We went out once."

"Really?"

"You'd think I'd broken off our engagement when I told her that I wasn't going to see her anymore."

Michael took a gulp of water. Lucy was beautiful, she seemed smart and she couldn't hold Jamal's attention?

"Don't give me that look," he said.

"What look would that be?"

"The 'I can't believe you've dated half of the women in Atlanta' look?" Brent quipped. Jamal turned to his friend and glared at him.

"Not. Helping."

Michael set her glass down and threw her hands up. "I was just drinking water. Besides, we all have a past."

"And she's probably going to try and angle to turn this into a reality show. That seems to be the new thing for mildly successful women in Atlanta."

"Tell me about it," Brent snorted.

"Don't tell me Mimi is…"

Brent shook his head. "No. She is happy being be-hind the computer screen with her blog. But I dated a woman who thought we should've allowed our relationship to play out on a *Real Housewives of Atlanta* type of show."

Jamal laughed. "Denisha Tate, God bless her gold-digging soul. I heard she has landed a show."

"Seriously?"

"*Looking for Love in Hot-lanta.* They contacted FLD about doing security for the show last week."

Michael scoffed. "That show is going to be a hot mess. I can't believe people want to air their dirty laundry for the world to see. That stuff never goes away. I hope Mimi doesn't write about it."

"Me, too," Brent said.

"Oh, does Mimi not know about Denisha?" Jamal asked. "I know…"

"Shut up, Jamal. There's no need for Mimi to know about a failed relationship of mine." He held up his left hand. "We already put rings on it."

Michael began to wonder if she wanted to know more about Jamal's failed relationship with Lucy. Did it matter? They were together and working on their future. Was his past really that important? She mentally shrugged it off. They were going to look forward, not backward.

Once the waiter brought their food over, including another spinach dip, the trio fell into a casual conversation.

"This was fun," Brent said as he glanced at his watch. "But I have to get back to work."

"And you need to pay for your food." Jamal extended his hand to his friend. Brent shook his head.

"Lunch is still on you even if I didn't have to listen to you lament over your...problems."

Michael raised her eyebrow. "Problems?"

"Pay him no mind. I'll get you, Brent. Wait until Mimi comes home."

"You two are horrible." Michael laughed then wiped her mouth. "I have to go as well. Need to get some reports together for this jazz fest and check on a couple of my other clients. I'll be glad when the show is over."

"Me, too," Jamal muttered. Brent waved goodbye to the couple and headed out the door. Jamal stood up and wrapped his arms around Michael's waist.

"This was a pleasant surprise and I'm glad we had this lunch meeting. But you're not off the hook for dinner. I'm thinking a sushi buffet all over your body."

Michael kissed him on the cheek. "Why are you so nasty?"

"Because you like it. See you tonight."

As MJ walked out of the restaurant, Jamal's mind filled with questions about Lucy. Was she angling to work with MJ because she knew they were involved? *She can't know that, but I know when she finds out she's probably going to go off the deep end.*

Calling her was out of the question, and how did he warn MJ without seeming like the playboy she thought he was? The only person he could really talk to was the woman who'd told him to settle down a long time ago. His gran.

"Jamal, what did I do to get an unexpected call from

you? You better not be calling about not finding fresh crawfish."

"I'm starting to feel like you've branded me because you ate that one bad crawfish in the bunch."

"Boy, you know that mess was frozen. Anyway, how are you doing today, grandson?"

"I have to tell you something."

"Please don't tell me you've gotten someone pregnant and you're going to have to marry her because you're not going to let her take your son away from you."

Jamal blinked rapidly. "Are you sure you weren't a writer in a past life? I said I have something to tell you and you've given me a crazy baby mama that I have to marry to keep my kid and you're just assuming it's going to be a boy?"

"What do you have to tell me?"

Jamal laughed. "I think I've met the one."

"Lord, these are the end of days. Jamal, you're really going to get married?"

"Slow down, Gran. We're not there, yet. But Michael is…"

"Did you say 'Michael'? Baby, I didn't know you were gay. I love you just the same and I want you to know we will welcome Michael into the family and celebrate your union because love is love."

"Gran, Michael is a woman. I'm not gay and when you meet her she can explain her name to you. Listen, how do I get MJ to take me seriously and realize that I'm not the cad that people seem to think I am?"

"Jamal, I've always told you that you can't play with women like they are interchangeable Barbie dolls."

"I don't do that." Jamal could imagine his grandmother scoffing at him. "Okay, maybe I did that in the past. But according to you, that's a family trait."

"And I had to break your grandfather from that. You know how? I made him miss me. I left him and he had to learn that I wasn't the kind of woman you could find every day. You better treat her that way now."

"What about the woman I want to leave me alone?"

"Call the police and keep her away from your new woman. Jamal, actions speak louder than words."

"You're right. I love you, Gran."

"I know you do. And you're sure Michael is a girl?"

"One hundred percent."

"All right. Can't wait to meet her."

Jamal couldn't help but laugh when he hung up with his grandmother. Still, he worried that Lucy might cause a serious problem in his budding relationship with MJ.

Chapter 10

Michael was ready to call it a day, but she had one client who needed to be talked through how to use Instagram to market her new line of coffee-infused cupcakes. A fifteen-minute conversation turned into a two-hour workshop. By the time she got off the phone with the baker, Michael knew she needed to hire a social-media guru to handle these things in the future.

"It costs to be the boss." She shut down her computer and placed her phone system on night answer because she wasn't taking another phone call today. Glancing at her watch, she realized that whatever she had planned for dinner wasn't going to work now. She hoped Jamal would enjoy takeout from the Sunshine Café. When she made it outside, she noticed that Lucy was coming her way. *Not now*, she thought as she plastered a smile on her face.

"Michael, I'm glad I caught you." Lucy stood in front of her like an imposing linebacker from the Falcons. "I have a great idea on how we can get more eyes on the festival."

"Awesome. But can it wait until tomorrow? I have dinner plans that I'm running late for."

"Oh, well, I guess. But it will only take a second."

Michael glanced at her watch and sighed. "What is it?"

"One of my dearest friends produces some docuseries for a popular network, and I was telling her about my involvement with this event. She wants to follow me around and film the preparations."

Michael laughed inwardly. Brent and Jamal had been right. "We're talking a reality show?"

"That's what some people call them, but it's really a look into my life, and Nic is on board with it."

"Of course he is."

"But you're the marketing genius and I wanted to get your input. From what I understand, some of the best and brightest of Atlanta is going to be a part of the festival. The world should see what we're about, you know."

"Why don't you send me some details about the show and I'll see if it is a fit for what we're doing. Then we need to make sure everyone involved is all right with being filmed and get waivers."

"Great. I know this has the potential to be golden. Are you available for a breakfast meeting?"

"I'll have to check my schedule and let you know. Lucy, I really have to go."

"Okay. 'Bye, Michael."

Getting into her car, Michael shook her head. She couldn't wait for this festival to be over. How many more months did they have to go?

After ordering dinner and grabbing a bottle of wine, Michael was finally ready to head home. She hated that she didn't have the view of the sky that Jamal had over at his place. But she had a different view she was ready to show him. She reached her place with just enough time to plate their dinners and change into something that would make Jamal see all kinds of stars.

Jamal paid for the two dozen roses and tipped the florist for unlocking the door for him when he arrived. "Next time, I'll come earlier."

"Please do. But thank you." She counted the money and was very impressed with the tip. Jamal headed to his car and sped down the midtown streets. He couldn't wait to see MJ, kiss her and wrap his arms around her.

He was going to listen to Gran and let MJ know she was the only woman he wanted and needed. Jamal just hoped that Lucy wouldn't be a problem. When he was alone, her quasi-stalking hadn't been a problem. Now he didn't want MJ to be in harm's way. He glanced in his rearview mirror to see if Lucy was lurking in the shadows. So far, so good.

Arriving at MJ's, Jamal wasn't thinking about Lucy anymore. He was yearning to see Michael and feel her arms around him. She opened the door before he rang the bell, and when he took a look at her, he nearly dropped the roses in his hand.

Michael stood there in a V-neck red lace teddy that accented her creamy skin and hugged her amazing curves. "Damn."

"I have to apologize. I got off late and didn't have time to cook." She ushered him into the house. "We have takeout from Sunshine Café."

Jamal nodded but couldn't take his eyes off her hips and those legs as she glided across the floor. "MJ."

When she turned around with a smile on her cherry-red lips, Jamal forgot what he was going to say. She touched his hand and took the roses.

"These are for me, right?"

"Yes. And I couldn't care less about dinner, whether you put these roses in water or anything other than those shoes on my shoulders." When she dropped the roses on the counter, Jamal grabbed her and kissed her slow and deep. MJ wrapped one leg around his waist and he felt her heat. And when she thrust her hips into him, Jamal was harder than a ton of bricks. Walking toward the sofa, he laid her on the soft cushions and spread her legs apart. She put those shoes on his shoulders as he pulled the crotch of her teddy to the side and licked her sweet nectar. So wet. So good. She arched her hips up to his lips, allowing him to go deeper inside her. Jamal devoured her, finding her throbbing bud and sucking it until she screamed his name.

He needed to feel her wetness around his hardness. Pulling back from his goddess, Jamal stripped out of his clothes. "You're so beautiful when you're satisfied."

"Then you're the best-kept beauty secret in the world."

"Let's take this to your bedroom. Show me the way." Jamal lifted her into his arms and MJ pointed to the top of the stairs.

"To the left."

Jamal headed into the room she pointed to and laid her on the bed. She looked so alluring on the lavender bedspread. He placed the palm of his hand in the center of her chest. MJ's skin felt like silk. He stroked her hard nipples with his fingertips and she moaned. Jamal leaned in and licked her nipples. "Yes," MJ exclaimed. "Yes."

He slipped his hand between her thighs and stroked her wetness until she hummed. "Jamal. Need. You."

He needed her even more, but he didn't have protection right then. As if she could read his mind, MJ reached underneath her pillow and handed him a condom. "I was a Girl Scout." She winked at him as he tore the package open.

Jamal slid the condom in place then dived into her wetness. "Michael!" They ground against each other at a hurried pace. She tightened her thighs against him and Jamal nearly climaxed. But he pressed on, pushing deeper and deeper inside her until she came down like a summer rain. And when her wetness dripped on him, Jamal exploded like a cherry bomb.

Collapsing in each other's arms, the duo closed their eyes and released a sigh of release.

"Amazing," Michael said.

Jamal kissed her cheek. "Yes, you were."

"Sorry about dinner."

"What are you apologizing for? This was the best dinner I could've had. You worked a lot this week."

"I know, and when I was leaving, Lucy showed up pitching her reality-show idea."

Jamal went still. Did Lucy know about him and MJ? "Was that all she wanted?"

"Doesn't matter. I know what I want. More of you." MJ brushed her lips against his neck. "Think we can have round two, then dinner?"

"Sounds like a great plan."

After making love again for another hour, MJ and Jamal headed downstairs to eat their cold dinner. Jamal was glad MJ had covered her amazing body with a white cotton dress so that he could focus on his dinner.

"Jambalaya pie." She set the plate in front of him and all Jamal wanted was for her to be on that plate. It didn't matter what MJ wore—he wanted her. He wrapped his arms around her waist.

"How about another helping of that Michael Jane pie?" He licked his lips and squeezed her ample bottom.

"You are too much. We do have to work tomorrow."

"That's like fourteen hours away from now." He winked at her and pulled her closer to his chest. "You're beautiful."

"You keep telling me that. I guess I should start believing you."

"Yes, you should. MJ, I want you to know that you're one of the best parts of my life. I've never felt this way about anyone before."

She touched her forehead against his. "You don't have to tell me what you think I want to hear."

"I don't say anything I don't mean." Jamal captured her lips in a hot kiss. She melted in his arms and Jamal knew Michael was the one woman he couldn't live without.

Michael pulled back from Jamal and smiled. "I'm so hungry. And I need my energy if you want some more of this pie."

"Please, eat."

A comfortable silence enveloped them as they ate, and Michael couldn't help but stare at him and wonder if this was really going to work. She couldn't crave him this much, put her heart out there and hope that he didn't hurt her. Of course, this man wasn't Nic. He was with her because of her and not what she could do for him.

"What's that look about?"

"What look?" Michael smiled. "Can't I enjoy eye candy?"

"I feel like a piece of meat," he quipped.

"I could bite you. Jamal, this is fun. I like being with you."

He inched closer to her. "So do I. MJ, I want you to know this—you're the only woman who means anything to me. I've never known anyone like you. When I wake up in the morning, you're the first thing on my mind. I look forward to hearing your voice, seeing your face and feeling your lips against mine."

MJ's heart swelled and she struggled not to let the tears welling up in her eyes fall. Jamal cupped her cheek.

"Are you sure you're ready for just one woman in your life?" Her voice was low. He brushed his lips across hers. "As long as that one woman is you, then yes."

Chapter 11

Michael woke up in Jamal's arms. She wished she could stay there all day but she had work to do. When he tightened his arms around her waist, she decided work could wait and snuggled closer to him.

"Morning." The heat from his breath sent tingles down her spine.

"Morning." She turned to face him.

"How are you this beautiful in the morning? Where's the drool?"

She elbowed him in his stomach. "I don't drool, thank you very much."

"That hurt, woman!"

"Want me to kiss it and make it better?"

"Yes. But if you do that, we're not getting out of this bed today." Jamal glanced at the clock on her nightstand. "And I have a meeting this morning with the producers of that show."

"You're going to do security for them?"

"Depends on the type of show it is. I have some guys who would be excited about pulling fighting women apart. Don't all of those shows have some sort of cat-fighting?"

She shrugged. "I try not to watch those shows. They make women look like man-hungry idiots."

Jamal laughed. "Guessing you have no desire to star in one."

"Not at all. All publicity isn't good publicity—I don't care what people say. If you want to build a brand and develop a name for yourself, the best way to do it is hard work. Do you think Oprah would do a reality show?"

"Hell no. But she's Oprah."

"That's right, and hard work made her Oprah."

"That's what you want? To be like Oprah?"

Michael sighed. "No, I just want to have a legacy that I can be proud of. My family was poor, but proud. That's the reason my mother never fixed my name on my birth certificate."

"Wow."

"It's opened some doors for me. Your friend even thought I was a man."

Jamal raised his eyebrow. "My friend?"

"Lucy."

He scoffed. "She isn't my friend. More like an annoyance."

"Are you sure that's all she is?"

Jamal nodded. "And how about this—you're naked in

my arms. Why are we talking about another woman?" Before she could answer, Jamal captured her lips in a hot, wet kiss. Michael pressed her body against his, feeling his hardness grow against her thighs. She opened her legs, inviting him to her wetness. Just as he was about to enter her, both of their cell phones began ringing.

"Ignore it," he moaned. "Work can wait."

Her silent agreement was when she thrust her hips into his. Protection was the last thing on his mind as Jamal reveled in her wetness. He thrust deeper and deeper inside her. Michael's moans were like a symphony of bliss. The skin-to-skin connection was just delicious. Reckless. So damned good. Jamal tried to hold back his explosive climax, tried to keep himself from giving in to pleasure. But Michael felt so good and he couldn't hold off any longer. She dug her nails into his shoulder as the ripples of her orgasm attacked her body.

"Whoa," she said when she caught her breath. "That's a good way to start the morning."

"Best part of waking up." Jamal winked at her. "Going forward, we're going to have to be more careful."

Michael nodded. "I'm on the pill but nothing is one hundred percent."

"And in case you're wondering, I get tested often for work and I don't have any STIs."

"Good—me either. Still, we're too old to be this irresponsible."

Jamal glanced at Michael's belly, watching a bead of sweat roll down it. What if his careless action made them parents? Normally, he'd be filled with fear and loathing, but he wouldn't mind raising a child with MJ. Watching her belly grow with his little boy and going to get her weird snacks. He even smiled at the image of him in a pair of green scrubs holding her hand as she gave birth to Jamal Jr. Or maybe they would name him Michael as well.

"What's going through that head?" She stroked his cheek.

"Nothing. Just enjoying the view."

"We'd better get out of this bed and go be adults. Run our businesses and whatnot." Michael propped herself up on her elbows and kissed Jamal's collarbone. Neither of them made an effort to move. It took another thirty minutes for them to break their embrace and get ready for work.

Leaving Michael's bed was probably the hardest thing that Jamal had to do. If she'd wanted to play hooky, he would've sent someone else to meet with the producers of the show. But MJ had to be responsible. He loved that about her. Loved a lot of things about her. He was super close to falling in love with her. That scared him a little bit and excited him as well. *Get it together and get some work done.* Jamal picked up his phone to check his missed calls and text messages. When he saw Lucy's number, he wanted to toss his phone out the window.

Miss you so much. Can we talk and see if we can work things out?

The next message from Lucy was angrier. So, you're just going to ignore me? I guess you have some whore in your bed tonight! I'll forgive you, but you have to talk to me.

Jamal deleted the messages and blocked Lucy's number. Hopefully, he wouldn't have to deal with her while MJ helped plan this jazz fest. He was glad that he'd taken his gran's advice and shown MJ that she was the only woman he needed and wanted. Jamal was confident that they would have a great future together.

Then he called the producer back and told him that he was running late for the meeting but he'd be there.

"No worries. We're actually meeting with cast right now and it ran over. I'm glad you're not sitting in the lobby waiting."

"Awesome." Jamal slowed down a bit as he drove. Since things weren't on schedule, he didn't have to rush. Any other day, he'd be pissed because he would've been sitting out there in the lobby waiting with an attitude.

Michael floated into the office and didn't care that she was the one late for the meeting with Nic. She would've called, but she hadn't felt the need to do so. Nic had kept her waiting so many times and turnabout was fair play.

"Well, it's about time." Nic rose to his feet when he saw Michael crossing the lobby.

"Traffic."

"I called you this morning."

"Talking and driving is very dangerous. Come on—let's get started." Michael walked toward her office, giving a nod and a smile to her receptionist. Once she and Nic entered her office, Michael took her seat and smiled at him.

"What can I help you with this morning?"

Nic rolled his eyes and handed Michael a CD. "You made it seem as if getting this mix done was a priority."

"This is great." She inserted the disc in her computer and turned the speakers on. The sweet sounds of jazz filled the room and Michael swayed in her seat. She knew this was a CD she'd play the next time she and Jamal got together.

"She likes it." Nic extended his hand to Michael as an upbeat song came on.

"I don't think so."

"Come on. This is the hit from the compilation and your reaction is proof of that. Let's dance."

Michael gave in to the beat and danced with Nic. Once upon a time, Nic and Michael were the king and queen of salsa. As they danced, neither of them noticed Lucy standing in the doorway snapping pictures on her cell phone until the song ended.

"Well, you two are very cozy." Lucy walked in and sat down across from Michael's desk. Nic shook his head and Michael walked over to the computer to turn the music off.

"This is the mix that we're going to use to promote the jazz festival," Michael said. "It sounds great."

"I see. I had no idea I was walking into a dance party. I would've worn different shoes."

"Anyway," Nic said. "I have about five thousand copies printed. They're being delivered to all of the participating clubs. And we have permits for all of the outdoor locations that we want to hold performances at. Ladies, we are good to go." He placed a folder on Michael's desk.

"Almost," Michael interjected as she took a seat. "We need to get the security details for each location. So, I'm going to talk to Jamal about sending folks out to get a..."

"Jamal Carver?" Lucy asked.

"Yes. First Line of Defense is handling security for the event."

"They are a good group. Jamal is pretty awesome."

Nic sucked his teeth. "Why don't y'all start a fan club for the guy?"

"Jealous, Nic?" Lucy quipped. "I'm sure you're the president of your own fan club."

"And you're the queen of yours."

Michael hid her smile. She hadn't seen anyone get under Nic's skin like this except Mimi. Maybe Lucy wasn't as bad as Jamal said she was. Maybe.

"Are we done here?" Michael rose from her seat. "I want to get these locations to Jamal so that we can start getting the security plan in place."

"Oh, I can do that," Lucy said with a smile. She held her hand out for the file Nic had given Michael.

"I got this."

Lucy's face hardened for a minute, leading Michael to believe that Jamal may have been right about her. At any rate, she wanted everyone out of her office.

"This has been great, but I have another meeting in about ten minutes."

"With Jamal?" Lucy asked. Nic shot her a questioning look as Michael shook her head.

"I do have other clients. So, we're done, right?"

Lucy cleared her throat and stood up. "Yes, we are. When can I expect to have these CDs in my club?"

"They're being delivered now," Nic said. "Mikey, thanks for the dance." As he headed out the door, Michael wanted to throw something at him. But she was happy to see him and Lucy leave. She picked up her phone and sent Jamal a text.

Hope your meeting went better than mine.

Jamal shook hands with the reality-show producer, who said, "I look forward to our partnership."

"Me, too," Jamal said. "I'm going to have my crew come over tomorrow and introduce themselves to you and the ladies."

"Sounds good. Too bad you won't be around. You could get some scene time and send hearts racing."

"I'm good with that." Jamal pulled his phone out of his pocket and smiled at MJ's message. "Have a good day."

Meeting was great. Sorry you didn't have the same experience. Want me to kiss it and make it better?

You bet. Lunch?

You're on the menu?

That can be arranged.

See you at one?

Cool.

Glancing at his watch, Jamal saw that he had time to go to his office and get his crew together to head to the production office. He missed Harry, because he would've put him in charge of this assignment.

Had he acted in haste when he fired him? When he arrived at his office, he called Harry. Voice mail. He wondered if his old friend and colleague was salty about the firing. "Hey, Harry, this is Jamal. Give me a call when you get this. We need to talk."

After hanging up the phone, he called his staff in to tell them about the new assignment. Jamal had no problem finding guys who wanted to work on the reality-show set. Because he knew men could be distracted by some of Atlanta's sexiest women, he decided to put Diana Jones in charge of the group.

"Really?" she asked.

"Yes. You're ready. We're going to get started next week and it runs for eight weeks. Each one of you will have to sign an agreement saying that you won't talk about the show or reveal the winner." Jamal pointed at his team. "You guys are going to have to go to the studio and get your credentials and sign those contracts."

"Guess this means we're back!" Marcel Carpenter exclaimed.

"Yes. We've been cleared in the lawsuit. We're also

under contract to work a jazz festival later this year. So, it looks as if we are back."

Everyone cheered and Jamal held his hands up. "Since we have these big contracts coming up, we have to be on point."

The crew nodded in agreement. "That's all," Jamal said. "Thank you guys for all of your hard work."

As the meeting ended, Jamal couldn't help but smile. He loved his crew and was sure that they were going to rock out both events. As he glanced at his watch, his smile got even bigger. It was time to go see Michael.

Michael wanted to bang her head against her desk after her meeting with the most computer-illiterate business owner in Atlanta. This man had no idea about social media and marketing his restaurant on it. Trying to explain Twitter and Facebook to the sixty-year-old felt like pulling teeth. But after two hours, she'd finally gotten him to get it. By the time he left, Michael had set up his social-media accounts and he had a couple of hundred followers already.

She was glad that she could hand this account off to one of her social-media mavens. Just as she was about to head to the bathroom to freshen her makeup, the receptionist buzzed her.

"Mr. Carver is here to see you."

Michael looked at her watch. He was early. "Send him in."

Jamal strode into the office, crossing over to Michael and pulling her into his arms. He didn't say hello, just captured her mouth in a hot kiss. She melted in his arms and returned his kiss with fervor. Their tongues danced a sensual tango and she was tempted to push everything off her desk and make love to him right there. Jamal tore his mouth away from hers and smiled.

"Better?"

"Much."

Jamal stroked her cheek. "Sorry your meeting sucked."

Michael groaned. "Lucy and Nic are two hardheaded people. Then I had a meeting with a new client who didn't even know what Facebook was. It's been an afternoon. Thank goodness for the amazing morning I had with you." She winked at him. "So, what's for lunch?"

"If I'm not mistaken, it's you—right?"

"And that's a good thing for you, but I'm hungry." She thrust her hip into him.

"Then if you want something to eat, you better not do that again. Want to order in? I have some questions for you about the security plan for the jazz fest."

"I need to get away from this desk." *Because if we stay in here, we might just end up on top of it.*

"All right. Let's get out of here."

Michael grabbed her purse and Jamal took her hand in his. "Ready to ride fast?"

"Why don't you hand me the keys and let me show you how fast works." Michael held out her hand. "One of the first things I ever wanted from you was to drive the fastback Mustang."

"Using me for my car. I feel so cheap." Jamal placed the key in her hand. "Be gentle with her."

Michael shook her head. "What is it about you men and your cars?"

"The control, the power and the beauty. It's like a woman."

"You should stop while you're behind."

"Yes, ma'am."

When they arrived at the car, Michael smiled. "Well, she is beautiful."

"Wait until you feel her power."

She slid in the driver's seat and cranked the car as Jamal got into the passenger side. The roar of the engine gave her a thrill. "How many tickets have you gotten in this car?"

"I'm going to plead the Fifth. But let's just say I don't drive through Paulding County anymore."

MJ pressed her foot on the gas pedal and tore out of the parking lot. "Yes!"

Jamal gripped his seat belt as if he was about to be tossed out of the car. "Guess you're going to get banned from Fulton County."

She slowed down a bit. "That's not going to happen. Where do you want to eat?"

"There's this barbecue joint in East Point that will give you a chance to open Sally up on the highway."

"You named your car Sally?"

Jamal grinned. "She has her own theme song."

"And let me guess—you have it on your smartphone."

Jamal leaned over and turned the radio on. The sounds of Wilson Pickett filled the car. Jamal and Michael began singing to the legend's voice. When they passed a Georgia State Patrol car, Michael slowed down.

"I see why you're banned in Paulding County. This car is awesome."

"The driver is much better." He placed his hand on her thigh.

"I always wanted a Mustang, but I figured it would be too hard to put a car seat and a diaper bag in."

"Really? But you don't have kids."

Michael sighed and tightened her grip on the steering wheel. "Let's just say when I planned my life, I thought I'd have a couple of kids by now."

Jamal glanced out the window and didn't say a word. Michael noted his silence and sighed. "You know how it goes. We make plans and God laughs."

"Who did you imagine as the father of these paper babies?"

"Doesn't matter because my life has taken a different direction and I'm pretty happy with it."

"That's a good thing."

"A great thing." She smiled. "So, where am I going?"

"Next exit."

She nodded and took the exit. Jamal directed her to the small restaurant at the end of a one-lane road.

"How did you find this place?"

"On a drive one day about six months ago. They have the best coleslaw in the metro area."

"How do you eat all of this food and not gain a pound?" She gave him a slow once-over as she parked the car.

"Gym time. And you have been avoiding that challenge. It ends today."

She rolled her eyes. "Fine. But you're going to lose."

"Talk is cheap. So, what do I get when I win?"

Michael broke out into laughter. "Since you're not going to win, the question is, what do I get?"

"Anything you want."

"This car for a week?"

"Anything but that."

"No fair!"

"What about I cook dinner for you for a month?"

She shook her head. "I just want to drive Sally for a week."

"Fine. And when I win, you become my personal chef for a week."

Michael extended her hand to him. "You're on."

They got out of the car and headed inside. The restaurant was rustic and small. The tables were wooden like old school picnic benches. Jamal pointed to a round table in the back. "Let's sit there."

"No hostess?"

He smirked and shook his head. "Come on, woman. You know better." They walked over to the table, and seconds later, a tall woman in a stained apron walked over to them.

"Jamal! Where have you been?"

"Working." He stood and hugged the older woman. "But I have been missing this place."

"I know you have. Bet you haven't had a pulled-pork sandwich—a good one, anyway—in months."

"You're right about that." Jamal turned to Michael. "This is my girlfriend, MJ."

"Well. This is nice. Come on, girl. Give me a hug!"

Michael stood up and hugged the woman. "It's about time he brought a lady friend around here."

MJ smiled. "He says this place is amazing."

"Telling the truth and nothing but the truth. Please tell me you're not one of those vegan women."

"I'm not. Hanging with this guy would make it hard to be one of those."

"Good. I have an idea for what y'all need to eat. A sampler platter."

Jamal gave her a thumbs-up. "Sounds good! Extra coleslaw."

The woman shook her head and walked into the kitchen. After Jamal and MJ settled in their seats, she looked at him and smiled. "You seem at home here."

"Miss Lizzy reminds me of my auntie from Savannah. Good food, advice whether you want it or not and more food."

MJ placed her hand on top of his. He brought her hand to his lips and kissed it. "What's wrong?" he asked.

"Nothing. Just wishing my family had been as close as yours seems to be. But don't let that ruin this meal."

"If you ever want to talk about it, know that I'm here." He stroked her cheek and smiled.

"Thanks. This isn't something that I've talked about much. It just seemed like most of the people I hung out with didn't have strong family ties, and hearing about your family just makes me wonder if we could've and should've been closer."

"Every family is different. If Gran hadn't pulled us together when my mother was going through her stuff, there's no telling how I would've turned out."

Before their conversation could continue, Miss Lizzy walked out with a platter overflowing with food. Short ribs, pulled pork, coleslaw, potato salad, barbecue chicken and hush puppies.

"Give me a second and I'll be right back with a big pitcher of sweet tea. Or as some people around here call it, sweet table wine."

"Miss Lizzy, you have outdone yourself."

"Ooh, I forgot the mac and cheese." She slapped her hands against her thighs. "I'll bring that with the tea."

"Do you think we're going to eat all of this?"

Jamal nodded and took a rib from the platter. "Yes."

MJ grabbed a chicken wing and took a bite. She moaned in delight. "This is good."

"Told you." He held out a hush puppy to her. "This is better than mine, but don't go broadcasting that."

MJ bit into the hush puppy. "Your secret is safe with me. But this is delicious."

Miss Lizzy returned with the mac and cheese and tea. "Enjoy, guys."

About two hours later, MJ and Jamal sat at the table filled with empty plates, stuffed and satisfied.

"Whoo!" Jamal wiped his mouth. "That was amazing."

"I don't think I can eat another bite."

Miss Lizzy returned to the table with two small bowls of banana pudding. "Now, you can't leave without this."

Jamal smiled. "She's right. This banana pudding is the business."

"And I packed it to go, because y'all ate like you haven't had a meal in two weeks."

"You put your foot in this food, Miss Lizzy," Jamal said and Michael nodded in agreement.

"Well, thank you." Miss Lizzy turned to Michael. "You don't have to wait for this guy to bring you back here."

"I won't. This is a great spot. I can't wait to bring Mimi out here."

Jamal paid the bill and they headed to the car. He held his hand out for his keys, but MJ rolled her eyes and got into the driver's seat.

"But I thought this was part of the bet? How is it that you get to drive right now?"

"Because I drove here, it's only right that I drive back to my office."

"Woman logic. I understand."

"That's not sexist at all." Michael started the car. They rode in a comfortable silence, and then Michael put the mix CD in.

"This is dope." Jamal swayed to the music. "Who's the artist?"

"It's a mix of the artists who will be performing at the jazz fest. The CDs will be available at the clubs participating in the event."

"So many people will hear this and buy tickets. I almost want to get four right now."

"We're going to have to switch back to business mode when we get back to the office because we have the sites for the shows in place and I want you to go out there and outline what we need to do to keep people safe."

"I was wondering when you guys were going to get around to that."

MJ smiled. "Well, we finally got our act together."

Chapter 12

Michael was in awe as Jamal drew and wrote on the maps of each venue. Not that she'd had any doubts about his skill, but he obviously knew what he was doing. She was happy that she'd chosen his group to protect the jazz festival. Michael knew this could be a career-making event for her business. Despite all of the nonsense that had gone on in the planning of the festival, its success would make her one of the best marketing companies in Atlanta. Hell, the country.

"That smile is making me hot."

Michael focused on Jamal. "Can I tell you how much I appreciate you?"

"I'd rather you show me." He wiggled his eyebrows at her. "I know this event is important to you and I'm here to make sure there are no incidents that could mar it for you. So, anything I can do to make this successful, I'm all for it."

Michael crossed over to him and wrapped her arms around him. "You don't know what that means to me."

He brushed his lips against hers. "To your empire." Jamal captured her lips in a hot kiss that shook her soul. He was the kind of man she should've always wanted to have in her life. Someone who supported her dreams, looked out for what she was trying to establish for herself and not just what she could do for him. This was what love should feel like. This was the man she could build a future with. Right?

Jamal pulled back from her and smiled. "Don't think that amazing kiss changes the fact that I'm taking you down in the gym tonight."

"I almost want to let you win, but the fighter in me won't let me do that. Six thirty, right?"

"You got it." Jamal gave her a quick kiss on the lips. "So, if I'm going to be on time, I'd better go and take a look at these locations to see if I can implement these security plans."

"All right," she said. "See you tonight and I'm going to kick your ass at the gym."

"So you say." Jamal grinned then headed out the door.

Michael watched him leave and couldn't take her eyes off his tight bottom. She wondered if he wore gray sweatpants in the gym or tight shorts that hugged his muscles like a second skin. Either way, she couldn't wait to see it in a few hours. "'Bye, Jamal."

He turned around and smiled at her. "Don't be late for your beatdown."

* * *

Jamal headed for his car humming one of the jazz songs from the CD as he walked. When he felt a hand on his shoulder, he expected it to be Michael. But turning around, he saw that it was Lucy. *Shit.*

"Jamal, what's going on?"

"Why are you still stalking me?"

Lucy scoffed. "Okay, I'm not stalking you. I'm working with Michael on the jazz festival and we have a meeting. It's just a chance meeting."

"Sure it is. Lucy, what's your game?"

"Are you and Michael seeing each other?"

"How is that any business of yours?"

"Then I guess that is a yes. Wow. It makes sense why Nic said we should create a fan club for you. And I thought he was just jealous because he had competition. You know they have something hot."

"Had."

Lucy pulled out her phone and showed him a picture of MJ and Nic wrapped in each other's arms. Jamal kept his face neutral, but inside he was boiling with anger. Was she still seeing this guy? The asshole whom she claimed she was over? And of all people to see them together, it had to be Lucy?

"Nice," Jamal said.

"So, you're all right with this?"

"Goodbye, Lucy." He strode off from her and headed for his car.

"Jamal, you were all that I needed. All."

Ignoring her, he got into his car and zoomed out of

the parking lot. The aching thud in his chest must have been what it felt like to be heartbroken.

Michael ended her day with a smile on her face. She couldn't wait to see Jamal at the gym. Changing into her workout clothes, she sent him a text.

It's about to go down.

She headed downstairs to her car and drove to the gym, not paying attention to the fact that she hadn't gotten a response from him. When she arrived at the gym, Michael looked around the parking lot for Jamal's Mustang. When she didn't see it, she figured that she'd take advantage of her head start and warm up. After running on the treadmill for half an hour, she began to worry. Had Jamal been in an accident? She slowed her gait. Had something happened at work? Did she miss a text from him? She stopped the machine and pulled her phone from the back pocket of her yoga pants and dialed Jamal.

Voice mail.

Okay. What in hell is going on? Michael called him again. Still voice mail. She dashed out of the gym and sped to his house. As she drove, her mind was racing with the worst-case scenario. Had he been hurt? Did he need her?

Tears welled up in her eyes as she dialed his number again, fearing the worst.

Voice mail.

Jamal had ignored every call from MJ as he sat at the bar downing shot after shot of Fireball Whisky. How could she do this to him, then turn around and smile in his face? This was a game that he'd never played. Now he'd been played. Jamal tapped the bar for another shot. Part of him wanted to head over to Nic's jazz spot and punch him in the face. Then he'd send MJ a picture of her lover. But that would make him look like the jerk. The jerk in this situation was Michael.

His phone rang again. He looked at Michael's smiling face and wanted to toss the phone across the room. But still, he didn't answer. The bartender set another glass of whiskey in front of him. Jamal downed it and turned his back to the bar. When he saw Lucy coming his way, he wished he'd been able to move faster so that he could get away from her.

"Jamal, I thought that was your car outside. How are you doing?" she said as she took a seat beside him.

"What do you want?" He felt the need for another drink.

"Rude."

"I want to be alone."

"And get drunk? What's going on with you?"

Jamal glared at her but kept silent. That didn't keep Lucy from running off at the mouth, though.

"Jamal, I told you that we would be so good together. There is no one in Atlanta that understands you the way I do."

"Please. Stop."

She inched closer to him. "Just give us a chance."

"No. Lucy, let it go. We had one date. It wasn't a good one. You built this fantasy in your head about us being in a relationship, having a relationship or developing a relationship. It's not going to happen. It was never going to happen. So, stop following me around, thinking that I'm going to settle for you."

"At least I would've been faithful. I wouldn't be entertaining another man in my office under the guise of working together. You're going to get what you deserve. The heartbreaker's heart gets broken. Karma actually works." Lucy rose to her feet and stormed out of the bar.

Jamal gritted his teeth. Was he being foolish because he was taking a picture that Loony Lu-Lu showed him as the truth?

Still, he'd had doubts about the real deal with Nic and MJ anyway. The way she'd talked about wanting a family and hoped to have one by now. He had no doubt that she was talking about Nic. Maybe working on this festival was reviving her feelings for him.

Dropping money on the bar, he headed out to his car. When he saw the slashed front tires and cracked windshield, he didn't have to wonder who did it.

"Damn it!" He called AAA to tow the car away, and then he dialed Brent.

"What's up, man? You and Michael came up for air?"

"I need a favor. Can you come pick me up?"

"What's going on?" Brent's voice took on a serious timbre.

Jamal told him about the picture that Lucy had shown him of MJ and Nic embracing in her office and how he'd come to the bar to drown his sorrow in whiskey. Then he recounted how Lucy had shown up and pleaded for the two of them to be together.

"She has gone off the deep end." Brent sighed. "How long has she been stalking you?"

"Who knows? Then I come out to my car and the windshield is smashed and two tires are slashed. The worst thing about all of this is that she's the one who caught MJ with the guy she said she wanted nothing to do with. MJ had said she and Nic were over."

"Ask yourself this—how do you know that picture wasn't photoshopped or that it was a moment that didn't mean anything? Have you talked to Michael?"

"No."

"That's mature."

"Are you coming to get me or do I need to call Uber?"

"On my way. But do me a favor. Fix your attitude before I get there."

Jamal hung up the phone and walked back into the bar. He needed another drink.

Michael was frantic with worry. She paced back and forth in Jamal's driveway. Had he gotten in an accident because of his need for speed in that car? Instead of calling him again, she called Mimi.

"Girl, what's going on?"

"I think something has happened to Jamal. We were supposed to meet two hours ago. He's not answering the phone and he's not at home. Oh, my God, Mimi, I'm so scared."

"Okay, okay, calm down. I'm going to call Brent on three-way and see if he's heard from him."

"Yes, yes, please do that." Michael's hands shook as she waited for Mimi to come back on the line.

"Mimi, calm down. I'm going to pick Jamal up right now." Michael sighed when she heard Brent say that.

"Where is he?" Michael asked.

"Mimi, you got me on three-way?"

"Brent, she was worried."

"Hello!" Michael interjected. "Where is Jamal?"

"He's sitting at a bar. I'm going to pick him up and take him home."

Michael rubbed her forehead. "A bar? He's at a damned bar? I thought he was in a ditch dead and he's drinking at a bar."

"Michael," Brent said. "Calm down. You two need to talk. Why don't you wait for him at his place?"

"Obviously his phone is working because he called you. Do you know how many calls and texts I sent this man? He can talk to the stars, because I'm out."

"Michael, give him a chance to explain himself," Mimi said. "You…"

Michael hung up the phone and hopped in her car. Speeding out of the driveway, she drove to the gym because she needed to punch something, preferably Jamal's face.

Heading for the heavy bag, she picked up a pair of gloves and started punching. An hour later, she was covered in sweat, sore and pissed. If Jamal had been in the bar all of this time, why didn't he answer the phone? Why didn't he respond to her text messages? Snatching her gloves off, she stalked over to the drink machine and bought a liter of water. She downed it in three gulps, but the cold water didn't calm the burning anger inside her. This was the reason she hadn't wanted to open up to Jamal, share her feelings with him and fall in love with him. But she did, and once again, her heart had been smashed in thousands of pieces. Never again.

Michael headed for the shower and drowned her tears in the cold water. She was tired. Tired of believing that she would've been happy with Jamal. Right now, she didn't even care what his excuse was for not showing up or taking her calls. She just wanted to finish working on this jazz festival and get out of his life.

When she made it home, Michael turned off her phone and climbed into bed. Sleep would be her best friend tonight.

Brent pulled into Jamal's driveway and glanced at his friend. "You good over there?"

"Yeah. So, you talked to MJ?"

Brent nodded. "She called Mimi because she was worried about you. Then she got upset. You two need to talk and work this thing out. At the end of the day, you still have to work with her on the jazz fest."

"I have other people who can handle that."

Brent shook his head. "I know you care about this woman, so you need to stop acting like a spoiled ass-hole."

"And if you'd seen a picture of Mimi hugged up with her ex, you would've been all right with that? If I'm not mistaken, you were willing to leave her because of a blog post."

"This has nothing to do with me. My issue with

Mimi dealt more with the legal ramifications of people thinking that I was sleeping with my client. You know, the same thing my father did that landed him in prison."

Jamal ran his hand across his face. "So, I'm out here acting like a fool?"

"You said it."

Jamal reached into his pocket and dialed MJ's number. It went straight to voice mail. "I guess she's playing my game now."

"Can you blame her? She called you for hours and you ignored her."

"Well…"

"And you should've given her a chance to explain. Keep in mind you've dated half of the women in Atlanta. She's watched broads throw drinks in your face and yet gave you the benefit of the doubt. You see one picture and flip out. A picture from a woman who you know would do anything to ruin your life."

"Okay, okay, I messed up. I got to give her a chance to explain, but that was her office. Who knows what happened before Lucy showed up."

Brent slapped his hand on his forehead as he put the car in Park. "For the last time, I'm telling you that you've lost your mind. Maybe you wanted this to happen because you're too afraid to fall in love."

Jamal leaned back in his seat, not wanting to admit that his friend was right. But he was. He wanted to give MJ everything and that picture of her and Nic just made his soul ache.

"I'm going inside. Thanks for bringing me home."

"Truth hurts, huh?"

Jamal, feeling dejected and low, sighed and climbed out of the car. "Thanks again, bruh." Closing the door, Jamal headed for his backyard and eased into a lawn chair. He looked up at the stars and remembered the sweet times he'd shared with MJ. She didn't laugh at his hobby and she seemed to be interested in learning about the constellations and everything. Then there were those sweet kisses and her body in his arms.

What have I done? Jamal pulled out his phone and called MJ again. When he got voice mail this time, too, he figured he'd have to wait until the morning to get an explanation and apologize.

Leaning back in the chair, he closed his eyes and drifted off to sleep. Maybe it was the whiskey that took him into a deep slumber. But when Lucy crept into his backyard and lay down beside him on the chair, he didn't feel a thing.

Chapter 13

The next morning, Michael woke up to the sound of banging. Yawning, she climbed out of bed and padded to the front door. Looking out the window, she was surprised to see Mimi standing there with coffee cups in her hands.

"What are you doing here?" Michael opened the door and smiled.

"I figured my friend needed some Dancing Goat." Mimi handed her a coffee cup and gave her a hug. "Can't believe you were still in bed."

Michael rolled her eyes as she took a sip of the coffee. "You're lucky I answered the door." The women headed to the kitchen and Michael washed her hands. "Hungry?"

"Depends on what you're about to cook."

"Cheese omelets."

"Starving."

Michael started whipping up the ingredients for the omelets. "How long have you been here?"

"Flew in last night. So, have you talked to Jamal?"

Michael shook her head as she whisked the eggs. "Nope. Have no plans to."

Mimi tilted her head to the side. "You two are ridiculous. Brent said when he dropped him off last night he called you and got voice mail."

"Actually, I turned my phone off. He was in a bar. He ignored me all night while I was about to lose my mind thinking this man was dead."

Mimi reached for an apple from the fruit bowl in the center of the breakfast bar. "I know you're pissed and you have every right to be. But shouldn't you let him explain? You guys do have to work together for the next few months."

Michael slammed a frying pan on the stove. "Why do I keep doing this, Mimi?"

"You haven't done anything."

"Yes, I have. I keep mixing business with pleasure and ending up alone and sad."

"How do you know that this can't be worked out? We're not talking about Nic."

Michael flipped one omelet then the other. "Doesn't matter. I'm done with Jamal and the whole male species."

Mimi bit into the apple. "That's harsh and stupid."

"You want this omelet or no?"

Nodding, Mimi took another bite of the apple. "You're going to have to be nicer to me."

"Why?"

Mimi smiled. "Because your goddaughter isn't going to like it when we fight."

Michael whirled around and looked at her friend with a huge smile on her face. "You're pregnant?"

"Yes!" Mimi crossed over to Michael and gave her a tight hug. "I'm probably going to write about the Mis-Adventures of Motherhood now."

"I can't wait to read that and I hope God does give you a daughter." Michael squeezed Mimi's cheek. "You deserve it."

"I'm taking that as a compliment, though I know you're trying to be funny."

After the omelets were ready, Michael and Mimi headed into the dining room. "So, is she going to be a Georgia peach or a New Orleans saint?"

"Of course my husband wants us to spend the next three years in Atlanta, where we have established our lives and don't have to go out house hunting and the like. Besides, I want to be around my bestie while the little one is growing in here." Mimi placed her hand on her still-flat belly. "And these omelets are going to be a part of life."

"Oh, so now I'm your cook?"

"No. But this is what best friends do for their pregnant and scared friends, right?"

"Why are you scared?" Michael placed her hand on top of Mimi's. "You have an amazing husband who loves you more than anything in the world. He's going to be there for you every step of the way. Then you have me, who will be there for you when you drive him crazy."

Mimi sighed. "And that's why I'm going to move back to Atlanta full-time."

"Really? I know New Orleans was your dream."

"Being Mrs. Daniels is a much better dream. Besides, after the first termite swarm, I was kind of over New Orleans."

Michael laughed. "Welcome home, Mimi Collins."

"Where are we going?" Jamal asked as he snapped his seat belt in place.

"Breakfast. I have some big news for you." Brent started his car.

"Hopefully it doesn't come with a side of fireworks. My head is killing me."

"Overdid it last night, huh?"

Jamal sighed. "Ended up sleeping outside like a dope."

"Have you called Michael?"

"Nope. I know she doesn't want to talk to me, so I'm not wasting my time today."

Brent shook his head. "You need to talk to her, because she needs to explain that picture and the two of you are going to be spending a lot of time together."

"Not really."

"Yes, you are. Who do you think is going to be my son's godmother?"

"Son? You actually knocked Mimi up. Congrats, bruh! So, we're having a little raging Cajun?"

"Nah. Mimi has decided she wants to be around familiar things as she prepares for the little one to come into the world."

"Smart." Jamal glanced around and noticed where they were going. "I know you're not taking me to MJ's house."

"Yes, I am." Brent pulled into MJ's driveway. "And look at this. Mimi's here."

"You guys set me up. I'm really starting to question our friendship."

"Play nice." Brent placed the car in Park then opened the door. Jamal walked slowly behind him as Brent rang the doorbell.

"Hey, baby." Mimi swung the door open then flung herself into Brent's arms. Looking over his shoulder, she saw Jamal standing there with a sheepish look on his face. "How's the phone, Jamal?"

"Hello, Mimi. You look beautiful."

"Mimi," Michael called out. "Who's at the door?"

Jamal brushed past Mimi and Brent. "It's me, MJ."

She glared at him, her eyes blazing with anger. "What are you doing here?"

"Can we talk?"

"Nope. When I wanted to talk to you, when I thought you were lying in a ditch dead and your head bashed open, I wanted to talk to you. When I called you more times than a sane woman should call a man, I wanted to talk to you. Now I couldn't care less."

Jamal stroked his chin. "I should've handled things better yesterday. But…"

"But what? You decided that being with one woman

was just too much for you to handle, so you went off and did what you do? What was so bloody important that you couldn't answer your damned phone?"

Jamal closed the space between them. "I saw you and Nic. Wrapped in each other's arms in your office."

Michael gasped. "What?"

"Lucy showed me the picture of you two, and you know what? I was mad. I was pissed because you said he meant nothing to you."

"He doesn't mean anything to me. And what you saw was nothing. You should've given me a chance to explain. Acted like an adult."

"You're right. I made a mistake and I'm sorry. But what was going on in your office?"

MJ shook her head. "You don't trust me. You took the word of a woman whom you have called crazy on several occasions, and didn't bother to ask me what really happened. Do you know how many times I've had to suck it up when one of your exes or a one-night stand of yours shot us the side-eye or threw a drink in your face? Yet you had this myth in your head about Nic and me. I don't give a damn about Nic. And if you must know what was going on, we were dancing to the mix CD. His hands weren't all over my body and it meant nothing."

"I know I was wrong, but…"

"But what? Your ego was bruised and you thought it would be a good idea to try and hurt me? Good job— you win. Now, get out of my house."

"Yeah, I'm not doing that," he said then pulled her

into his arms. "Michael, I'm sorry and I'm not going anywhere until you tell me that you forgive me."

"I'm going to need a little time for that." He could feel her anger wavering and he was going to take full advantage of it. Leaning in, Jamal captured her mouth in a slow kiss. She pressed her hand against his chest as if she was trying to push him away. But in a swift moment, she melted in his arms. When they broke the kiss, they stared into each other's eyes.

Jamal ran his index finger down the side of her cheek. "I'm sorry. And if you still need time, I'll give you that."

"I think I've had enough time. Can we make a promise right now?"

"What's that?"

"That we won't spend another night like last night?"

"That's a promise." Jamal kissed her forehead. "And we need to have an extended makeup session." He glanced over her shoulder and looked over at Mimi and Brent. "Without an audience."

"Guess that is our cue to leave," Brent said.

"Nope," Mimi countered. "I still have omelet on my plate."

MJ shook her head. "Why don't I just cook everybody some breakfast?"

Jamal wrapped his arm around her waist. "I'll help."

"Don't be in there getting nasty on the stove top!"

"Shut up, Mimi." Michael tossed a tangerine at her friend.

Alone in the kitchen, MJ and Jamal made quick work

of whisking the eggs and making two perfect omelets. "Please tell me you have Dancing Goat."

She shook her head. "But Mimi was kind enough to bring me some this morning. Pity you didn't pick up the phone last night."

"How long am I going to wear that?"

She shrugged as she plated the omelets. "Until I get tired of rubbing your nose in it. I mean, you robbed me of my victory at the gym last night."

"I did, but I got a clear morning. We can go ahead and end this right now."

"Let's eat and then we can go get it on."

Walking into the dining room, MJ set the plates on the table and Jamal gave her bottom a squeeze before taking his seat.

Mimi polished off the last of her omelet and smiled. "Babe, looks like our work here is done."

"Ambush reunion. That would be a great reality show."

Jamal shook his head. "Y'all are two of the corniest people I know. MJ, we're going to have to help baby boy Daniels grow up cool."

"You mean little Mimi? She's going to have a girl."

Brent and Mimi exchanged glances. "Maybe we'll have twins." Mimi stuck her fork in Brent's plate and took a piece of his eggs.

"You sure are eating like we are."

She threw her hand up at him. "This is just the beginning."

Jamal glanced over at MJ, remembering their careless night. He couldn't believe that he wanted this. He wanted her sneaking food off his plate, asking for a foot rub and carrying his child. And he'd been stupid enough to almost let it slip away because of Lucy and that picture.

"You don't want your omelet?" Mimi asked Jamal.

"Stay out of my plate. I'm not your husband. I don't have to share." He took a big bite of the omelet.

After breakfast, Mimi and Brent headed home and Jamal cleaned the kitchen while MJ got dressed for the gym. "Hey, MJ. I need to swing by my house and grab my gym bag. Since my ride left, do you mind taking me?"

She bounded down the stairs. "Sure. We can even go to the gym in your neighborhood. That way you can clean out your car and get it ready for me."

He placed his hands on her shoulders. "About my car. Sally is in the hospital."

"Really? What happened?"

"Someone must have been jealous of her beauty. Windshield smashed and a couple of tires slashed."

MJ raised her eyebrow but didn't say anything.

"What?" he asked.

"That sounds like a scorned woman type of thing."

Jamal knew she was right, but he was not ready to get into that conversation right now. He figured that Lucy had damaged his car, but he knew the dive bar probably didn't have security cameras that would show her in the act. "I'm going to write it off as a minivan driver who was just really mad about the current state of his or her vehicle."

"Whatever. Or you did it yourself because you're about to get your butt kicked by a girl." She flexed her muscles and then bounced out the door. Jamal stayed a few steps back so that he could get a full view of her amazing ass.

Michael glanced over at Jamal as she drove. Could they make it? Were they going to be able to put distrust of old relationships behind them and move forward together? Lord knew she'd tried. And Jamal hadn't given her a reason not to believe him.

"What's up?" he asked.

"Just thinking. You know, this wasn't supposed to happen."

He nodded. "Mimi told me to leave you alone."

"Thank you for not listening."

"I knew I had you when you tasted my hush puppies."

"And at some point in this forgiveness thing, you need to whip up a batch for me."

Jamal winked. "Gladly. As a matter of fact, we can have some for lunch. That is if you're still talking to me after you lose this burpee challenge."

Michael rolled her eyes as she pulled into Jamal's driveway. "Whatever."

They headed inside and Jamal dashed into his bedroom, while Michael looked around the living room. Then she crossed over to the sunroom and smiled. The night they'd spent there had been beautiful and so romantic. She almost wanted to pretend that he won the gym challenge and just make love to him on oversize pillows while the sun beat down on them.

"Hey, babe, ready?"

She turned around and smiled at him. "Let's go."

Jamal pulled her into his arms and brushed his lips across hers. "Don't try to use those lips and eyes to get out of this beatdown."

She raised her right eyebrow. "I'm tired of hearing about this. Let's go."

They hopped in the car and drove to the gym. Once they arrived, Jamal pointed to a clear space in the corner with yoga mats. "All right, time to put up or shut up."

When Jamal dropped down and did his first burpee, Michael thought she might be in trouble. Then she fell in line, began to mimic his moves. They met each other stroke for stroke, squat for squat. They'd been going at it for about an hour before either of them noticed that they'd drawn a crowd.

"I need one of them to train me," one of the people watching them said.

She peeked at Jamal. "Anytime you want to quit."

He puffed. "I can do this all day." Jamal did another perfect burpee and Michael followed suit. Their sweat wet the floor, leaving pools. Jamal slipped and Michael leaped to her feet.

"I won!" She jumped up and down.

"Nah, nah. You didn't win. I slipped."

"Don't want to hear it. I won." Michael turned to the crowd. "Did I win? Or did I win?"

A few women in the crowd nodded and cheered while some of the men said Jamal was robbed because of the sweat on the floor. "The women have spoken. I won." Michael kissed him on the cheek.

"Best two out of three."

"No." Michael wiped her forehead. "I'm tired."

They headed for the showers and Michael's legs felt like overcooked noodles. She couldn't have been happier for Jamal's slip. He seemed as if he could go all day. And Michael knew he had plenty of stamina. Stepping out of the shower and wrapping up in a white towel, she was surprised to see Jamal walk in with a towel wrapped around his waist.

"What are you doing in here?"

"I came to kiss the victor. And find out if you hurt as much as I do."

"More, probably."

"Can we go to my place and take a nap like we're in kindergarten?"

Michael nodded happily. "But I expect a juice cup and apple slices when we wake up." She wrapped her arms around him and smiled. The words *I love you* hovered on the tip of her tongue, but fear silenced her.

"I'd better get out of here before some screaming woman comes in."

"Well, this woman can't wait for you to make her scream tonight."

Jamal squeezed her bottom. "Meet you out front."

Chapter 14

Over the next month and a half, Jamal and Michael were basically joined at the hip. They spent their mornings working on the security plans for the upcoming jazz festival and their nights making love. What Michael loved most about being with him was how he made her laugh and how he was such a tender lover.

The more time they spent together, the more she wanted to tell him how much she loved him. But something always stopped her. Whether it was a ringing cell phone or a client showing up out of the blue. Then there were the quiet moments when they were alone and doubt set in.

Just like right now. His lips brushed against her neck and Michael's eyes fluttered open. "Did I wake you?"

"Yes, but you knew you would." Michael looked up

at the stars. Tonight she'd talked Jamal into sleeping in the sunroom.

"I want to show you something. Come outside with me."

"At this time of night?"

He nodded. "Trust me. This is a rare sight."

"Okay. But don't we need clothes?"

"Nope. But if it makes you feel better, we can wrap up in these sheets." They headed outside, looking like college frat boys in togas. Jamal walked her over to the telescope. "I got an alert earlier today that Cancer would be visible tonight."

"Cancer?"

He nodded. "It's a rare constellation to see and I want to share it with a rare beauty." Jamal gave her a quick peck on the cheek.

"You have me looking at the stars so differently these days." She stroked his cheek. "So, Cancer. Point me in the right direction."

Jamal brought the telescope in the right direction. "Look to your left."

Though he'd been showing her all of these different constellations, most of the time Michael just saw stars and smiled. But this was his thing and she was trying to grasp it and failing.

"What am I supposed to be seeing? Crabs?"

Jamal shook his head. "Let's go inside. I think you are one of millions of people who can't see Cancer in the sky. That's fine. Those of us who can know beauty when we see it."

"On this one, I'll have to take your word for it." She

faced him and gave him a hot, wet kiss. Michael moaned as their tongues danced. Jamal's hands reached underneath the sheet and fondled her breasts. She arched closer into his body, giving him carte blanche to touch her everywhere. She wanted and needed to feel his heat. Even though they were outside in the darkness, she knew this was a little dangerous. Pulling back, she smiled at him. "We should take this inside," she said.

Jamal nodded. "Good idea, because I want you so bad." Scooping her into his arms, Jamal turned to the door and almost sprinted inside. They didn't make it to the sunroom as he pressed her against the door once he closed it, and pulled her sheet off. He dropped to his knees and spread her legs apart. Jamal licked and sucked her wetness, seeking her throbbing bud as she screamed his name and gripped his neck.

Michael's knees went weak as the waves of her orgasm washed over her body. "Jamal, Jamal," she moaned.

"Come for me, baby." And to make sure she did, Jamal used his tongue and his finger to keep her wet. Then Michael exploded. She melted against his shoulders. "You taste so good."

"I don't think I can walk right now."

"You know I will carry you." He scooped her up in his arms and carried her to the sunroom. They cuddled together, her head resting on his chest while Jamal cupped her bottom.

"Look. There is the Big Dipper again." Michael pointed up at the sky.

"Good job. I'll make you an astronomy nerd yet." Jamal kissed her cheek.

"I wouldn't go that far." She rolled over on top of him and he was instantly hard.

"How far would you go?"

She spread her thighs and guided him to her wetness. "I'm willing to go this far." Their bodies joined together in pleasure. Michael ground against him as Jamal gripped her hips. They danced a slow grind with their moans filling the air. Michael fell against his chest as he squeezed her bottom, sending waves of pleasure throughout her body.

"Yes, yes, ride me, baby." His voice was a guttural groan as he reached his climax. Then Michael reached her own explosion.

Falling against each other, they drifted off to sleep. But before Michael closed her eyes, she brought her lips to Jamal's ear. "I love you."

Jamal woke up early just to look down at Michael's sleeping face. He didn't know if he had been dreaming last night or if she'd actually whispered those words in his ear. Running his finger down her cheek, Jamal knew he loved this woman completely and unconditionally. As much as he wanted to hold her all morning, he had a meeting with his guys about the reality show and he needed to put the final touches on the security plans for the jazz festival before filing it with the police and sheriff's office. Kissing her on the forehead, Jamal whispered, "Wake up, sleepyhead."

Her eyes fluttered open. "Umm, good morning."

"How are you feeling?"

"Amazing." She stroked his cheek and smiled. "But

I guess we have to get ready for work and do all of that adult stuff, huh?"

Jamal nodded. "But not before we eat and have coffee. I didn't buy eight pounds of Dancing Goat grounds for nothing."

"Eight pounds?"

"Well, I don't want to run out, especially since you don't seem to share your coffee."

She nudged him in the side. "Whatever. You get the coffee going and I'll make some omelets."

"Sounds good." They didn't move.

"Remember the last time we did this, we didn't get up for hours. We had clients waiting and…" Jamal captured her lips, kissing her slow and deep.

When their lips parted, she smiled at him. "Let's get that coffee."

After breakfast, Michael was ready to kiss Jamal goodbye when the doorbell rang. Groaning, he dropped his arms from her waist. "Who is this? It's way too early for visitors."

"I'll clean up the kitchen for you," she said as he walked to the door.

Jamal looked out the window, and when he saw Lucy, he wished he had ignored the doorbell. She rang the bell again. He opened the door and stepped out on the porch.

"What do you want, Lucy?"

"Good morning to you. I wanted to bring you some muffins and talk."

"Not interested in your muffins. But I would like your insurance information."

"Excuse me?"

"I know you smashed my car a couple of weeks ago."

"Please." She toyed with her hair and grinned. "I wouldn't smash a car and mess up my manicure. I guess your girl is in there. I noticed a strange car parked in your driveway."

Jamal grabbed Lucy's arm and pointed her to her car. "This has to stop. I'm tired of you showing up on my doorstep, following me and being extremely creepy. This has to stop. So far I've been trying not to involve the police, but I will. Now, get out of here!"

"You care about her, don't you?"

"Get off my property, Lucy!"

She glared at him and hopped in her car. As she sped out of his driveway, all Jamal could think about was how he was going to explain this episode to MJ. Walking into the house, he sighed and headed to the kitchen.

"What was that all about?"

"Nothing important."

She raised her eyebrow and handed him a cup of coffee. "I think we made too much java."

"Nothing like an extra cup of coffee."

MJ looked at her watch. "I'd better get out of here." She kissed him on the cheek. "I'll see you at lunch."

"You sure will."

As Michael left Jamal's, she couldn't help but think he was hiding something. But she hadn't wanted to question him. That would make him think she didn't trust him.

She didn't want him to think that she doubted him, but she couldn't deny her instincts. He was outside for a minute, longer than it should've taken to tell a sales-person to bug off. What if it was one of his...? *Stop it. You can't claim to love this man and not trust him.*

Michael sighed and drove away. She was going to have to believe in him. He hadn't given her a reason not to trust that he'd been true.

I can hear Mimi now, she thought as she got onto Georgia 400. *I'm simply overreacting.*

When she arrived home, Michael was shocked to see Lucy in her driveway. Glancing at her watch, all she could think was this woman was nuts.

"Michael, hi. Sorry to show up unannounced."

Michael closed her car door. "So, why did you?"

"Can we talk? Girlfriend to girlfriend? Mind if I come in?"

"Actually, I do. If you want to talk to me about business, you can make an appointment and meet me in my office. But showing up at my house is not how I do business."

Lucy folded her arms across her chest. "If that's how you want it. Can we meet for lunch today?"

"When I get to my office, I'll check my calendar and have my assistant call you. Goodbye, Lucy."

Stalking off to her car, Lucy muttered something about "the truth" and Michael shook her head as she walked in the front door. Then a thought hit her like a lightning bolt. *How does that crazy woman know where I live?*

Michael closed her door and made sure it was locked before she went upstairs and got dressed for work. Then she went downstairs and made a green energy smoothie, even though she'd had breakfast with Jamal. She had a feeling that she was going to need a lot of energy for the day, especially if she was going to have to deal with Lucy this afternoon. Part of her wondered what Jamal had ever seen in the other woman apart from her pretty face. Then again, he did say that they'd gone out only once.

That must have been a hell of a date.

Jamal walked into his office and told his assistant to hold his calls for a half hour. He was tired of Lucy and now he could actually call it stalking. Sighing, he kept the lights off in his office, and when his cell phone rang, he almost yelled at his assistant, until he realized it wasn't his office phone.

"Yeah?"

"Jamal, this is Harry. I know I was supposed to get back with you a few weeks ago, but things have been a little hectic for me."

"It's good to hear from you, man."

"You might not say that after what I have to tell you."

"You're not coming back to First Line of Defense?"

"Nope. I'm going to retire and head down to Florida. However, you better be careful and watch your back."

"What do you mean?"

"Jamal, you got a crazy lady on your hands and trust me about that. I passed by your place a few nights ago and I saw she was staking out your place as if she was Atlanta Police."

"Really?"

"Yeah, and I'm sorry that I haven't gotten around to telling you sooner. Lucy acts as if she is classy and has a lot going for herself, but I've heard some stories."

"I don't think I want to know. But hey, man, thanks for calling and I appreciate the warning."

"No problem. Now, if you need anything, give me a call and I got you."

"Thanks, man!" After hanging up the phone, Jamal realized that his break was over. Turning the lights on in his office, he was ready to get to work and push Lucy out of his mind. But he was definitely going to get a security camera set up around his house.

After going through some requests for security, Jamal looked down at his watch and saw that it was about time to meet with MJ. He'd found a flaw in their security plan that they needed to get taken care of before the event. Jamal threw a dart at the calendar on his wall. Two more weeks of this and then he wouldn't have to deal with these crazy club owners anymore.

The threat of Hurricane Dylan forced the Carver low-country boil to be postponed and Gran decided to make it this year's Thanksgiving celebration. Jamal had been happy because he hadn't had a chance to get fresh crawfish with all of the craziness going on.

He couldn't help but think about what Harry had said. Was Lucy dangerous or just a spoiled brat trying to get her way? He shook those thoughts away and headed for his car. Right now, he was going to focus on getting security tight for the jazz festival. He didn't want anything to mar the event. The right people were

watching and he wanted MJ to get all the credit she deserved for putting on a great show.

Michael smiled when noon rolled in and Lucy hadn't
shown up in her office. She buzzed her assistant.

"Yes, Miss Jane?"

"If Lucy Becker shows up, please let her know that
I'm in a meeting."

"Yes, ma'am. Mr. Carver just walked in. Are you
available?"

Michael smiled. "Of course."

"I'll send him in."

She smoothed her skirt and wiped her mouth before
he walked in.

Jamal smiled as he crossed the threshold. "Hello,
beautiful. Sorry to stop by unannounced."

Michael crossed over to him and gave him a tight
hug. "Stop by anytime. What's going on?"

He pointed to her desk. "Let's have a seat. I was
going over the security plan and I saw a few soft spots."
Jamal rolled out the blueprints of all of the outdoor venues where concerts were scheduled and pointed out the
flaws.

"How do we fix that?"

"Easy fix is a gate. Best plan, I think, is a gate and
two more people back there. This is where local law
enforcement will come in handy. I have all hands on
deck and I don't have another man or woman that I can
put back there."

Michael nodded. "If you think having additional officers will keep everyone safe, then that's what we will have to do."

"MJ, I want you to win. Because when this goes well, the city of Atlanta is going to know the marketing genius you are and they are going to beat a path to your front door."

"From your mouth to God's ear."

Jamal walked over to Michael's seat and stood in front of her. With a big smile on his face, he leaned into her—their foreheads pressed against each other's—and brushed his lips against hers. "I see big things in your future. And a big kiss."

"Let me have it."

Jamal captured her lips, nibbling her bottom lip, sucking her tongue and making her moan. She wrapped her arms around his neck, pulling him closer. Jamal's body felt so good. His kiss heated her like a desert afternoon. As his hand slipped between her thighs, Michael knew she wasn't going to get any work done until she had a chance to feel him deep inside her.

"MJ. I've always wondered how comfortable your desk is." Jamal swiped the papers on her desk onto the floor. "Shall we find out?"

"Yes." Her voice was a husky whisper as Jamal lifted her from her seat and laid her on the desk. Hiking her skirt up, he dropped to his knees and pulled her panties down. Spreading her thighs apart, he buried his face between them, lapping and sucking her sweetness. Michael gripped his head as she moaned in pleasure. She pressed her body deeper into his kiss.

"Yes, yes! That feels so good."

Jamal continued pleasuring her, slipping his hands underneath her shirt and tweaking her diamond-hard nipples. Michael's body burned with need as his tongue made circles around her clitoris. Her desire wet his face as she exploded. "Jamal!"

Pulling back from her, he smiled at the sated look on her face. "Oh, we're not done. That was just part one of the desktop fantasy." Winking at her, Jamal dropped his pants to his ankles. She reached down and stroked his hardness. Then she pushed him back in her desk chair. "Was this a part of the fantasy as well?" Michael eased down his body and took the length of him into her mouth. Suck. Lick. Suck.

Jamal groaned as her tongue grazed the tip of his throbbing penis. She felt his shiver as she licked him like the sweet chocolate he was.

"Ooh, ride me, baby. I need to be inside you now."

She mounted him, guiding him inside and reveling in the way he felt as he filled her with desire and pleasure. Grinding and sliding in the chair, Michael and Jamal bumped and ground against each other until they both exploded. She leaned against his chest, trying to catch her breath.

"Did it end like that?"

Jamal shook his head. "But this is one time when I'm happy to say reality outweighed my fantasy." He kissed her gently on the cheek. "We need some food to regain all the energy we just expended, since we still have work to do."

"But we're the bosses, right? Why don't we take the rest of the day off and have lunch in bed?"

Chapter 15

Jamal almost beat MJ to her house. He was so looking forward to spending the rest of the day wrapped in her arms. But when he and MJ arrived at her place, he was shocked to see Lucy there.

"My God," he muttered as he parked his car and got out. The look on MJ's face said she was just as appalled as he was.

Lucy clasped her hands together. "I'm glad both of you are here."

"What are you doing at my house—again?" MJ shook her head in disgust. "We've already had this conversation."

"I know, and I was going to come by your office, but that seemed so indelicate. This is a private matter that I thought we should talk about in private. It's just an added bonus that he's here."

Jamal stood between the two women. "Lucy, you have to stop this."

"Jamal, you're the cause of this!"

He furrowed his brows at her. "What are you talking about?"

"Tell her about the other night."

MJ looked from Lucy to Jamal. "What is she talking about?"

Lucy folded her arms across her chest and tilted her head to the side. "Jamal, you need to come clean. You need to tell her the truth."

Jamal squeezed his forehead. "You're not making any sense."

Lucy pulled her phone from her purse. "This! When are you going to stop acting as if we're not together when we spent the night just a few days ago." She flashed the picture of her draped across Jamal's sleeping body. MJ snatched the phone from her hand and studied the photo.

"This is your backyard, Jamal."

"This didn't happen."

MJ slapped him. "Don't stand here and lie to me. This. Is. Your. Backyard. Your special place that you don't share with anyone."

"I'm sorry you had to find out this way," Lucy interjected. "But Jamal plays these games, toys with women and always comes out looking like a rose."

"How about both of you get the hell off my property!"

"MJ, you can't…"

She threw her hand up in his face. "Don't you say a word to me, you lying bastard."

"MJ, please! You can't..."

"Control what I'm going to do if you don't get out of my face!"

As MJ turned on her heels and slammed inside her house, Jamal crossed over to Lucy and glared at her. "What in the hell kind of game are you playing? You know damn well that nothing has ever happened between us."

"Well, a picture is worth a thousand words, and she believed every one of them. I told you that one day you'd pay for playing with all of these women as if they were pawns on a chessboard. Here is your reckoning." Lucy smiled coldly at him. If Jamal had been a lesser man, he would've stuffed her in his trunk and dropped her off in Lake Lanier. Instead, he bounded toward MJ's door. He wasn't going to leave until she heard him out.

Michael ignored the doorbell for five minutes, because she'd been crying her eyes out and Jamal didn't deserve her tears.

After five more minutes, she was tired of hearing the damn ringing. Why hadn't he left when she told him to? How could he explain that woman lying in his arms in what was supposed to be their special place? He'd been the one who said he didn't take women back there. He'd made her feel special when he showed her the stars and his softer side. Jamal had been so sweet, tender and loving. He'd made her believe that the playboy Jamal Carver had died and he was all hers.

Liar! She'd made a fool of herself again and she was tired of being a fool for love. And she loved him. She loved Jamal more than she had been willing to admit. And once again, she'd found herself on the wrong side of heartbreak.

Another ring. Was he insane? One thing was for sure: Jamal wasn't going to leave and Michael couldn't stand that damned doorbell anymore. She crossed over to the door and snatched it open.

"What part of 'get the hell off my property' don't you understand?"

"MJ, I'm not leaving until you hear me out."

She pushed him against his chest. "What can you say? She was in your backyard, on that precious patio that you never took a woman to until me, right?" She pushed him again. "I don't know why I fell for your lies when I knew you were a snake."

"Really?"

She narrowed her eyes at him, but Michael knew she was being harsh. "I knew you weren't a one-woman man, but I trusted you and you broke that and my heart."

"You can't take her word over mine without giving me a chance to…"

"I'm not taking anyone's word. I saw the picture. She was in our space, in your arms! What's supposed to be the takeaway from that? Jamal, please just go!" Michael felt her eyes burning with unshed tears and she was not going to give him the satisfaction of seeing her cry.

"I'm going to go for now, but I'm not going to give up on us and you're going to see that I was never unfaithful to you. And for the record, we've been down this road with Lucy before. Is it just different now because you keep expecting me to hurt you?"

"Again. She was in our space. A woman who went on one date with a man isn't going to do all of this! Don't expect me to continue to buy the bullshit."

Michael walked over to the door and opened it. She didn't say a word as Jamal walked out. But when he left, she crumpled to the floor and sobbed.

Jamal left MJ's and drove around the city like a lost tourist. He tried to wrap his mind around how Lucy had gotten that picture. Yes, she was in his backyard and he was sleeping, but... The night came back to him a rush of memories that he'd written off as a dream. A few months ago, when he'd gone to sleep in his backyard after getting a little too tipsy at the bar, he'd felt something against him on the lounge chair. But between him being tired and drunk, he hadn't been able to open his eyes to see what was going on.

The next morning, he'd awakened to the chirping of birds and his sprinkler system spraying him in the face. But other than an extraordinary headache and wet pants, he didn't remember anything else. And he certainly didn't remember being with Lucy that night. How was he going to convince MJ of that?

Jamal wanted to turn around and go back to MJ's place and make her understand that he hadn't hurt her and he wasn't the guy she thought he was. Still, Lucy needed to be put in her place. He knew if he went to the police, he'd get laughed out of the station house. She may have been responsible for vandalizing his car, but there was no proof. She'd taken a picture at his house, but she hadn't broken any laws because he didn't have a No Trespassing sign on his property. He felt as if this woman was holding him prisoner. Jamal pulled out his cell phone and called Brent. Maybe his friend had some idea as to how he could help him.

Mimi shook her head as she shoveled a forkful of chocolate cake in her mouth. "I really thought he'd changed his ways. I was rooting for you guys and even started looking at maternity bridesmaid dresses." She let out a groan and then looked at Michael, who seemed to be on the verge of tears again. "I'm sorry."

"Not as sorry as I am. And that crazy bi... She came to my house, Mimi, twice!"

"She better be grateful that we aren't the M&M of ten years ago. She would be in a world of trouble."

"He isn't even worth dumping five pounds of sugar in her gas tank for." Michael swiped a piece of Mimi's cake. Popping it in her mouth, she tried to tell herself that if she stayed mad that she would hurt less.

Mimi licked her fork. "He is worth it and that's why you're hurting. I thought he'd changed, the way he'd call Brent and... Oops. I'm supposed to be minding my business."

"He'd call Brent and what?"

"Nothing."

Michael snatched Mimi's cake away. "MJ! You can't do this to your godchild."

"He'd call Brent and what?"

"From what I overheard, Jamal was falling hard and

fast for you. That's why something about this seems fishy."

"Mimi, there was a picture. She was all laid up on him in his backyard. Our spot." Michael handed Mimi her plate back then rose to her feet. She was glad her friend had kept her old place in Atlanta. Today, she needed a hiding spot, though Jamal could easily find her since Brent and Mimi did live across the hall in the condo complex. And as much as she wanted to pull up stakes and get out of town, she still had the jazz festival to promote. Looking out of the massive windows, Michael sighed. She had only a day, at the most, to avoid Jamal.

Damn.

"Mimi, are you in here?" Brent asked, causing Michael to turn around. Clearly, she didn't have a day to avoid Jamal because there he was with Brent.

"I'm leaving." Michael walked over to the sofa where Mimi sat, to grab her purse.

"Hear me out before you leave." Jamal stood in front of her, blocking her exit.

"What? What could you possibly have to say?"

"Can we talk alone?"

She shook her head. "I'm not going anywhere with you and I'm really not interested in what you have to say."

"So, I'm just supposed to let go because you said so?"

She turned her back to him and made the mistake of looking at Mimi and Brent. They'd been sitting on the sofa, Brent's arms around Mimi's shoulders and Mimi's head against his chest. For a brief second, she saw her and Jamal in that pose, remembered how happy she'd been in his arms as they looked at the stars. Was she willing to throw that away without giving him a chance to explain?

Was she willing to trust her heart not to get broken again?

"MJ? I just want the same chance I gave you."

She turned around and looked at him. "We have to work together for these next couple of weeks. But I don't have to move beyond that with you."

"You don't have to do anything you don't want to do, but you and I know that we're not over."

She ran her hand across her face, hating that he could see right through her. "If nothing happened between you two, then why did you invite her over?"

Jamal took her face in his hands. "You've seen yourself—she shows up where she wants to show up. I thought about when that picture might have been taken. Remember the night I acted like an ass and thought you'd kissed Nic?"

She nodded.

"I slept outside because I'd had too much to drink that night. Even in the picture you could see I was out cold. MJ, you have to believe in me, believe in us. You're the only woman I want in my life, in my arms and in my bed."

Everything he said made sense and she wanted to trust that he was right. Just as she was about to reply, her cell phone went off. Nic.

She wasn't surprised that he was calling, being that the jazz festival was so close. "Yes, Nic?"

"Is there a reason you're not in your office? Come on, MJ. We got to make sure everything is…"

"Nic, you're not my only client, and I sent you an email about all of the questions you had and a copy of the new security plan. What more do you need?"

"Well, I had a few questions and some suggestions about the after-parties at my club. And there's been a push for more of the mix CDs and I forgot where we've already distributed them. Can I be honest?"

"That would be a first," she quipped as she held her finger up to Jamal.

"I'm scared. This is big and I couldn't have done it without you."

"All right, Nic. I'll meet with you in the morning."

"Thanks."

Smiling, she hung up and focused on Jamal. The look on his face told her he had a lot of questions and Michael wasn't inclined to explain herself at all. "I'm going home."

"MJ." He touched her arm. "Don't give up on us."

She didn't reply as she walked out the door.

Jamal took about two seconds to think before he rushed out the door after MJ left. "MJ! I'm not giving up and I'm not going to let you turn what we've been building into a business relationship. Nothing happened with me and Lucy."

She turned around and faced him. "Why can't you just give me time?"

"Because what I feel can't wait. Damn it, I've waited my whole life to find one woman I could love, and now that I've found you, I'm not going to let anyone or anything come between us."

"This isn't just about you! I'm in this, too, and I'm

not trying to get my heart broken! You're going to break my heart. Maybe you're not going to do it on purpose. Maybe this thing with Lucy is some crazy accident, but what about the next time and the next woman? I knew who you were when I started seeing you."

"You made me better, MJ. You made me see that you're all I want or need." He took her face in his hands. "Don't do this."

Tears filled her eyes and Jamal's heart broke. The last thing he'd wanted was to ever make her cry. He didn't want to hurt MJ and he'd felt as if he'd done just that.

"What am I supposed to do?"

"Trust me, MJ. Trust me. Love me and let me love you." He captured her lips in a slow kiss. Jamal felt her melt against his body, felt as if her resistance was floating away. Pulling back from her, Jamal pressed his forehead against hers. "MJ."

"Jamal, please."

"I know you love me."

"What?"

"Say it."

"No."

"Say it."

"I love you."

"Then you owe it to us to keep going and I won't take no for an answer."

She stroked his cheek. "I'm not going to say no again."

Chapter 16

With the jazz festival less than twenty-four hours away, Michael was amazingly calm. The shows had sold out and the weather was expected to be perfect. She hoped that everything would go off without a hitch.

Nic burst into her office, breaking into her thoughts. "We have a problem."

"Hello to you, too." She shook her head.

"I don't have time for niceties when one of our head-liners just dropped out!" Nic plopped down in the chair in front of Michael's desk.

"Who was it?"

"The Pink Brass Band. Lucy called me and told me five minutes ago. She said you two can't work together anymore as well. What's going on with that?"

Michael typed the band's name into her computer

and looked for their manager's number. The Pink Brass Band was one of the hottest groups in the nation and a huge part of the marketing of the jazz festival. She didn't understand why their management hadn't called her.

She snatched up the receiver on her phone and pounded the number into the keypad.

"Clayton Matthews," a voice answered.

"Clayton, this is Michael Jane. I just got a disturbing message about the Pink Brass Band."

"You were on my list to call this morning because I wanted to know why you guys decided at the last minute to pull my girls. Lucy called about two hours ago and I was shocked."

Michael narrowed her eyes. This woman was playing a serious game that wasn't going to end well. "Clayton, I'm so sorry for this mix-up. Please tell me you all haven't booked anything else."

"We didn't have time. My next booking was going to be at the courthouse to sue you guys for breach of contract. We gave up some big shows to do this festival."

"You don't have to do that. We still need your girls. I'll upgrade your housing for this mix-up."

"Thanks, MJ. I should've known not to listen to that rambling crazy lady."

After hanging up the phone, she held up her finger to Nic and started calling all of the other acts to see if Lucy had tried this trick with them as well.

MJ knew that the success of this festival could make her career, just as it being an epic fail could ruin everything she'd worked so hard for.

About thirty minutes later, she'd confirmed that no one else had received a call from Lucy. The entire time she'd been on the phone, Nic looked as if he was about to lose his lunch. If this hadn't been so important, she would've gotten glee from the torturous look on Nic's face. But this wasn't a game. Finally, MJ could put Nic's mind at ease. "Crisis averted, but why is Lucy trying to ruin this event?"

"I told you she was off in the head. But you insisted on working with her." Nic shook his head.

Michael closed her eyes and squeezed the bridge of her nose. "Listen, we don't have to talk about shoulda, woulda, coulda. We have to make sure this festival goes off without a hitch. We've planned for months and we should have the greatest weekend ever in the jazz community."

"And then what's next for us?" Nic smiled.

"Nothing."

"You have to admit that we made a great team."

She laughed and shook her head. "Nic, we didn't make a great team. You were very difficult to work with and I wish I'd recognized this years ago. But this was a great idea." What she didn't tell him was how she'd already seen a bump in clients because of the branding of the jazz fest and her handling of the marketing.

She also didn't tell him about the drama with Lucy and Jamal. "Do you need anything else?" Michael rose to her feet and glanced at her watch. She was meeting Jamal for lunch and she needed to get going.

"I think we're done. You've done an amazing job and I'm glad we got a chance to work together on this."

She smiled. "It was interesting." She extended her hand to him and Nic laughed.

"This where we are now?"

Michael nodded. Nic pursed his lips. "Girl, give me a hug!" Nic enveloped Michael in his arms and gave her a tight, brotherly hug. "I know that we're not the friends we used to be, but you will always have a place in my heart."

"That's sweet. Nic, I wish you the best."

They headed out the door together and Michael felt as if the book was closed on her and Nic forever, business and personal.

Jamal shut down his computer. He was in need of a kiss from MJ because this jazz fest was getting on his nerves. Between the calls from the police and sheriff's departments about his security plans and watching his back to see if Lucy was lurking around, he was tired.

When his phone rang, he was tempted not to answer, but since it was Gran, he picked up.

"My queen."

"Don't 'my queen' me. I haven't heard from you in a couple of weeks."

"Sorry, Gran, I've been busy, and I know that's no excuse. But I still love you."

"I can't tell. Anyway, you have my crawfish ordered?"

Jamal hated to lie to his gran, but he hadn't ordered the crawfish. "I have."

"You've never been a good liar. If you bring frozen crawfish this year, I'm writing you out of my will."

"No frozen crawfish, not that I've ever brought you frozen crawfish anyway. Gran, I'm bringing someone with me."

"Really? Now, is she the special one you've been asking me questions about?"

"Yes, and MJ is the one."

"You better be sure, because the last thing that you should do is make that woman love you when you have no intentions to make a lasting future with her."

"I don't have a future without MJ."

He could feel the smile on Gran's face through the phone line. "Look who's grown up. I can't wait to meet this woman."

"You will and you're going to love her. I have to go, but I'm glad you called and you know that I love you more than the stars."

"Make sure you show me that love with fresh crawfish!"

After hanging up, Jamal heard the door open. MJ walked in with a huge smile on her face.

"Hey." She kicked her heels off.

"Hey, you." He crossed over to her and pulled her into his arms. "One more day."

"I know."

She sighed as they broke their embrace. Jamal took her face in his hands. "What's wrong?"

"Lucy Becker."

Jamal groaned. "Don't say her name. She might pop up like a ghost. What did she do?"

"Tried to cancel one of our headliners at the last minute. Nic came into my office this morning in a tizzy."

"Really? Did you get it handled?"

"Of course. I'm going to be so happy when this is over."

"Ready to head out for lunch?"

"Why don't we order in?" She smiled. "You're the only person I want to be around right now."

Jamal smiled then licked his lips. "I like the sound of that." He walked over to his computer and pulled up an online menu for his favorite Thai restaurant. Since he and MJ had Thai food at least once a week, he already knew what to order. "The food will be here in about thirty minutes." Jamal rose to his feet and turned the lights off. Then he sat down and motioned for MJ to sit on his lap.

"Thank you for believing in us."

"Thank you for giving me a reason to believe. Jamal, I love you."

"Love you more. You changed my life and I couldn't be happier."

She stroked his cheek. "Jamal."

In a quick swoop, he captured her full lips in a hot kiss. She melted against his chest as the kiss deepened. Jamal was thankful for that skirt she was wearing. His hands had free access to her thighs and that sweet spot between them.

MJ moaned as his thumbs brushed across her throbbing bud, making her body burn with desire. Just as he was about to slip her panties off, there was a knock at the door.

"Damn, just when I was ready to eat."

MJ eased off his lap and Jamal went to get their food.

* * *

While Jamal paid for their lunch, Michael received a Google alert on her phone. When she saw it was about Mimi's blog on the jazz fest, she couldn't wait to read it.

Atlanta is about to host the biggest music festival for jazz lovers. It's going to be chock-full of food, fun and great music. I had a chance to talk to the members of my new favorite band, Pink Brass Band. They're an all-female jazz band from Atlanta. All of their instruments are pink and they sound great! The creator of the band, Nadine Oakley, said she wanted to show the world that women could play real music and didn't have to trade on their bodies to be successful.

Now, make no mistake, these women are beautiful, but you won't see them dancing around the stage in leotards showing off their boobs and booty.

"We are much more than our looks. We write our music, we play our music and we look good doing it fully dressed."

They got the idea to be a brass band after a trip to New Orleans when they were college students. Seeing the music at the clubs and on the street made them want to bring part of that back to Atlanta.

"But we had to put our spin on it. When we painted our instruments pink, we gained a lot of attention. Then people listened to us and they were hooked."

They started headlining regional festivals, and three years ago, they signed a deal with one of the biggest jazz labels in the country. Then pink became the color of success. The group was nominated for a Grammy and have two platinum records under their belt.

Even with their critical success, there are people in the A who haven't heard the Pink Brass Band play. That all changes tomorrow when they take the main stage at the inaugural Atlanta Jazz Festival. Things get started at noon.

Log on to www.atlantajazzfest.org for a list of performance times and all of the food trucks that will be on the scene, including the amazing Sunshine Café's mobile restaurant.

"Good job, Mimi," she said as she set her phone on Jamal's desk.

Jamal crossed over to MJ. "Food. What are you smiling about?"

"Mimi's blog."

"Do I even want to know?"

"It's about the jazz fest." MJ playfully punched him on the shoulder. "That food smells delicious. Let's eat."

Licking his lips, Jamal smiled. "I know what I was trying to eat."

"So nasty." She smiled as Jamal pulled the food out of the bags.

They sat down and enjoyed pad Thai orange chicken and rice. After they finished eating, Jamal and MJ nestled on the love seat in the corner of his office and drifted off to sleep. And she didn't have to dream, because it had come true already.

Chapter 17

The morning of the jazz fest, the nerves finally hit Michael. She was praying that everything would go off without a hitch. Her duties were technically done, but she was connected to the event, and if anything went wrong she would be linked to it.

Sighing, she called Mimi again. Yes, it was early, yes, her best friend was pregnant, but today she needed a run.

"Hello?"

"Mimi, it's about time you answered."

"MJ, if you're not dying, I'm going to kill you."

"Can we go for a quick run and talk?"

Mimi exhaled into the phone. "Sure. The doctor said I should stay active and I haven't taken a run in two days. Can you do me a favor, though?"

"What?"

"Two chocolate doughnuts from Krispy Kreme. I've been craving one for two weeks and Brent won't get one for me."

"Why not? Because if your husband isn't on board with feeding you junk food, there is probably a good reason."

"He's mean and he claims that I should watch my sugar intake."

"I agree. So, I'll get you half a doughnut—only because I woke you up this morning."

"You're mean, too. I'll see you in fifteen minutes."

After hanging up with Mimi, Michael headed out to her balcony to get some fresh air. Smiling, she thought about Jamal and how he'd spent the night talking to her on the phone. It felt like being back in high school again.

She didn't notice that she was being watched from across the street.

Jamal and his security staff walked around the main stage area, making sure everything was set up properly for crowd control. It was early, but he wanted to make sure there were no glitches. Jamal was taking securing the jazz festival extra personal because he knew how important this was to MJ. She'd worked too hard for anything that he could prevent to go wrong.

"Have we gotten the reports from the metal detectors? They're online, right?"

"Yes, sir," Brad Stoops, the field commander, said. "We're waiting on the contractor to come in and put the fence up in the back of the park and then we're done."

"Great. I'm going to check the second location and then I need you guys to meet me at the office so that I can issue the vests."

"Got it."

As Jamal headed to his car, he pulled out his cell phone and called MJ.

"You're up early," she said when she answered.

"So are you. How are you feeling this morning?"

"Nervous, scared, excited."

"Well, I have some great news for you—security is tight."

She laughed and Jamal felt the warmness of her smile through the phone line. "I knew it would be. That's why I wanted First Line of Defense."

"And I thought it was just because you wanted me."

"I was going to have you anyway."

"Is that so?"

"Please, don't act like you would've said no."

Jamal laughed. "You're right. What are you doing right now?"

"Standing on the balcony, watching the sunrise and waiting for Mimi so that we can go on a run."

"I talked to Mimi yesterday. Is she trying to get you to get her chocolate doughnuts?"

"Yes. What's up with that?"

"Brent said the doctor told her she has to cut down on her caffeine intake. No chocolate and no coffee."

"She's not going to make it. Poor Mimi."

"Well, as her best friend and the future godmother of my godson, you need to make sure you keep her de-caffeinated."

"Will do." Jamal heard MJ's doorbell ring.

"I'd better go. I think Mimi is here."

"MJ, I love you. See you later."

"Love you, too."

After hanging up with his woman, Jamal was all smiles. He couldn't help thinking about Brent and Mimi, though. He wanted the life they were having, preparing to welcome a baby into the world. MJ in a white dress flashed before his eyes, and though he needed to check on security measures at the other venues, he wanted to go and look at engagement rings. Today was going to be the day that he asked MJ to marry him.

As soon as Michael opened the door, Mimi asked, "Where's my doughnut?"

Michael shook her head. "Not doing it. Jamal told me what the doctor said about chocolate and coffee. I have to protect my future goddaughter."

Mimi rolled her eyes. "Fine."

"But I do have something for you. A blueberry smoothie."

Mimi folded her arms across her chest. Michael laughed.

"If you close your eyes you can pretend that it's a chocolate milk shake." They headed into the kitchen.

"When I announce my pregnancy on the blog, I'm so telling this story."

"When are you going to do that? I've been waiting to see how your readers are going to react to the news. I'm still trying to wrap my mind around it myself." Michael dropped the blueberries and ice in the blender. "Almond milk or soy milk?"

"No dairy?"

"Nope."

"Soy. And Brent isn't exactly excited about our private life going public again. That's why I've been holding back. I get where he's coming from, but over the years, I feel like my blog has become more than just a place for me to rant. I share my joy and pain with my readers and this is the best thing that has ever happened to me and I want to share it with the world."

"This opens a whole new avenue for you and your blog. The Mis-Adventures of Motherhood."

Mimi reached out and hugged her friend. "You are a marketing genius. I'm so scared, MJ. I don't know if I'm ready to be a mom."

"Girl, you're going to be awesome. You have so much love to give and a great support system."

Tears welled up in Mimi's eyes. "I'm glad you're here for me. There are some things men don't get and I need you to listen."

"You know I got you. And we're going to drink these smoothies until you give birth."

Mimi looked at the purple juice in the blender. "Yeah, no."

Michael poured the smoothies in two glasses. "Drink."

They drank the smoothies and then headed out for their run. Instead of their normal three miles, they ran one mile in silence. Michael's mind was on the jazz festival and she silently prayed that nothing would go wrong over the next two days.

"Can we stop now?" Mimi asked.

"Yes! I was wondering if you were going to be super pregnant woman."

"So did I, but I see that I can't do it all." Mimi took a deep breath. "I think this is going to be my first blog post."

"I can't wait to read it and you better tell the whole truth."

Once they were back at Michael's, Mimi and her best friend settled down on the sofa and love seat then went to sleep.

The ringing of MJ's cell phone woke them up. "Hello?"

"Where are you, MJ?"

"Oh, Jamal, Mimi and I went to sleep. Give me about twenty minutes and I'll be at the park." Michael rose to her feet, and then she woke Mimi up.

"Everything is actually looking good around here. The food trucks are getting set up and it smells amazing."

"Have people started coming out yet?"

"There are a few hundred people here so far."

"Okay. Let me and Mimi get ready and we're on our way."

Mimi stretched her arms above her head. "I guess that nap was way too good."

Michael nodded. "I meant to get to the park around nine thirty, but sometimes you have to listen to your body."

Mimi picked up her keys and told MJ she'd see her at the park.

"Meet me by the main stage. Jamal said it's getting pretty crowded out there."

"Cool. I know Brent said that he'd come out after court this afternoon. I want to hit up the food trucks without his watchful eye on me."

"Umm, huh. You're still staying away from chocolate," Michael called out as she walked out the door.

MJ hopped in the shower and got dressed then sped to the park. Jamal met her at the entrance of the park and walked her through the metal detectors. "You look amazing," he said as he drank in her image in her white sundress and strappy sandals.

She spun around. "You like? Got to love Atlanta weather. It's October and still seventy degrees. I couldn't have ordered a better day from Mother Nature herself."

He nodded and took her into his arms. "I don't just like it—I love it. White looks good on you."

MJ looked around the park, happy to see the crowds growing. "This is really nice."

"You worked hard on this event. You should be proud." Jamal kissed her on the forehead.

"Thank you. I'm glad the work is over."

Jamal nodded as he watched people entering the park.

"I'm glad we ended up using the metal detectors," MJ said. "I feel a lot more comfortable with this given the state of the world."

Jamal nodded. "I can't believe we actually had an

argument about it. But that's neither here nor there. We get to have fun now."

Locking hands, Jamal and MJ headed toward the food truck staging area to check out the grub.

In the distance, Lucy watched the couple, her face showing how angry she was seeing them together. "What does she have that I don't?" she muttered as she followed them with her eyes. "I told him he was going to pay for playing with people's hearts and it's time for him to do just that."

As the music started, Jamal watched MJ's hips sway while she took a bite of a funnel cake corn dog. Those lips. His lips. He loved everything about this woman and he couldn't wait to ask her to be his wife. He hadn't gotten the ring he wanted for her, but the emerald-and-diamond ring in his pocket was the pre-engagement ring he was going to give her when he asked her to marry him later today. He wanted to take his fiancée to Savannah, not his girlfriend.

"What? Do I have powdered sugar on my face?" She locked eyes with him.

"No. I was just thinking that you should share." He laughed. MJ held her corn dog out to him and Jamal took a big bite. Huge mistake.

"My God, that is too sweet."

"That's what makes it great. However, I don't think I'd add this to my daily food choices. Like a wise man once told me, you have to try it to make sure you don't like it."

Jamal pointed to a pizza food truck. "I'm going to keep it safe and simple."

"Chicken."

They walked over to the food truck. After Jamal ordered his slice, MJ turned to him with a smile on her face.

"How many security guards do you have working today?"

"Between the two locations, I have about a hundred guards and then I have a crew that works the after-parties. Speaking of, are we going to hit up any of them?"

MJ shook her head furiously. "I don't want to be out when the sun goes down because I'm so over this."

Jamal kissed her cheek. "I'm so glad to hear you say that. Because tonight, I want to wrap you up in my arms and watch the stars."

"In the sunroom?"

"Yes. And we can make love all night long."

MJ moaned slightly. "Can we leave now?"

"That would be so irresponsible." He winked at her. "But I'm very tempted." Looking at MJ again in that white dress, he couldn't help but think about watching her walk down the aisle into his arms. Though the band on the stage was playing an up-tempo rendition of Stevie Wonder's "Ribbon in the Sky," all Jamal heard was the "Wedding March."

"Jamal? Are you okay?"

"Yeah, yeah, just thinking about your naked body and how irresponsible I want to be right now."

She pinched him on the shoulder. "Stop it."

Taking his pizza slice, Jamal and MJ moved toward the stage to listen to the music for a while.

"I love the sound of this band," MJ said, still moving to the beat. "I think they were on the CD compilation."

"They do sound great." Jamal tossed his pizza crust in a nearby trash can. "Let's dance." Taking her in his arms, Jamal spun Michael around as the band played. The people around them smiled as they watched their moves. Jamal dipped MJ twice and she broke into a salsa move that drew cheers from the crowd.

Once the song ended, Jamal and MJ drew as much applause as the band. "I need water," MJ said. "That was fun."

"It was." As they turned to head for one of the drink stations, they ran into Lucy.

"Well, isn't this cozy." She folded her arms across her chest.

"Lucy, please don't make a scene," Jamal said.

"A scene? I'm here for retribution!" Lucy reached into her purse and Jamal leaped into action. He tackled Lucy and a .22 caliber pistol spilled from her purse. MJ kicked it away as Jamal reached for his zip tie to secure Lucy's hands.

"You can't do this to me! You've played with hearts and you broke mine! I hate you!"

Jamal pressed the button on the radio on his shoulder to call for backup. Lucy looked up at MJ. "You're not special. He's going to toss you aside like trash soon enough."

"One date." Jamal gritted his teeth. "We went on one date and it didn't work out. Get over it, Lucy."

MJ backed away from them and released a sigh. She had no idea that Lucy was that insane. "How did she get a gun in here?" MJ watched as two Atlanta PD officers hauled Lucy off.

"I don't know, but I'm about to find out." Jamal took long strides to the entrance. He grabbed the guy manning the metal detectors. "How in hell did someone get in here with a gun?"

"Everyone has been going through the metal detectors. I don't know what happened."

The guard watched as Lucy was carted out. "Is she the one?"

"Yes."

"Jamal, she told me that she was one of the organizers and she didn't have to go through the security."

Releasing a low growl, Jamal thought about firing the man on the spot, but he could understand how Lucy had fooled him. "Everybody goes through the metal detectors, no excuses. I don't care if it's the mayor, the president or the Pope."

Jamal headed back to where MJ was standing. He could see she was shaken up. "Come on, babe. I'm getting you out of here." He wrapped his arms around her shoulders and headed for the back exit.

MJ shook her head. "I'm still in shock right now."

Getting into his car, they headed for his place.

On the ride over to Jamal's house, Michael called Mimi and told her what happened at the park.

"My goodness. Brent and I are going to meet you guys at Jamal's."

They all pulled up at Jamal's place at the same time.

Brent hopped out of the car and gave MJ a tight hug. "That had to be some scary stuff. Are you all right?"

"I'm fine, thanks to this guy." She nodded to Jamal.

Mimi rushed over to Jamal and gave him a hug as well. "I knew you were a good dude underneath all that playboy exterior."

"I would do anything for the woman I love, including taking a bullet for her."

MJ crossed over to Jamal and kissed him slow and deep. "You don't know how thankful I am that you love me that much."

The group headed inside and settled in the sunroom. "I can't believe Lucy was that crazy." Brent shook his head.

"Are you sure it was just one date?" Mimi asked.

"So, I kissed her." Jamal shrugged his shoulders.

MJ raised her eyebrow. "One kiss and one date led this woman to stalk you and try to shoot us or you?"

Jamal held his hands up. "I don't know."

"I don't mean to make light of this situation, but can we get some food in here?" Mimi asked. They all broke into laughter.

"Let's feed Mimi." Jamal rose to his feet and headed to the kitchen. MJ followed him. Alone in the kitchen, Jamal pulled MJ into his arms.

"I was so scared out there." Jamal kissed her on the forehead. "If anything ever happens to you, I don't know what I'd do."

"You could've gotten hurt, too."

"And I would've gotten over that, but not losing you." Jamal smiled. "This is *not* the plan I had for the day."

"Yeah, we didn't even get to the Sunshine Café truck."

Jamal crossed over to his refrigerator and pulled out some cheese and cold cuts. He grabbed a beer for Brent and bottles of water for him, Mimi and MJ. "MJ, the food truck wasn't what I was thinking about." Facing her, he smiled. "I wanted today to be special. Wanted to celebrate your success with the event. Well, I'm sorry it was ruined."

"Jamal, we're still here and alive. Nothing was ruined." She grabbed the drinks as Jamal placed the cheese and cold cuts on a plate.

"Y'all better not be in there doing anything nasty around the food!" Mimi called out.

Shaking her head, MJ headed for the sunroom.

Chapter 18

The rest of the festival went off without any more incidents. Jamal made sure his staff followed all of the rules about security. MJ, however, didn't return to the festival, but she kept her eye on the reports about it.

By all accounts, everyone was having a good time. As she sat in her office, Michael was proud of what she'd done. Now she was preparing proposals for other clients. She was in high demand and she couldn't be happier. Since her staff had worked so hard on the jazz fest, she'd given them two days off.

"Knock, knock," Jamal said as he walked into MJ's office. "Where is everybody?"

"At the festival or at home. I gave everybody time off. I'm just getting new clients lined up."

"So we're all alone, huh?" Jamal closed the door and locked it.

"What are you doing?" Michael smiled, knowing what was coming next. Jamal crossed over to her.

"First, I'm going to take off all of your clothes." He was glad she was wearing a sundress. He slid the straps down her shoulders, exposing her smooth brown skin. The dress fluttered to the floor. MJ stood there in black lace underwear making him smile.

"So, what's next?"

Jamal responded by stripping down to his boxer briefs. Michael marveled at the sight of his chiseled body. Strong thighs, six-pack abs and muscular arms that always made her feel safe when she was wrapped up in them.

The evidence of his arousal made her mouth water. She reached for the waistband of his underwear and tugged them down. She stroked his hardness and Jamal groaned in delight. Dropping down to her knees, MJ took him into her mouth, licking and sucking him until he called out her name.

Just when he felt as if he was going to explode, MJ pulled back and Jamal lifted her up and dropped her on her desk. "Let me take those panties off." Jamal didn't slide them off; he just ripped the lace off then spread her thighs apart. He buried his face between her thighs, sucking and lapping her wetness until her thighs quaked. "Yes, Jamal! Yes!"

He deepened his kiss, sucking on her throbbing bud, and Michael exploded. She pushed him back in her chair then mounted him. Slowly, she ground against him. Jamal plunged deeper and deeper inside her.

"That's it, baby. Ride me."

MJ threw her head back while Jamal sucked her breasts, sending waves of pleasure up and down her spine. Her moans floated through the air as she reached her climax and collapsed against his chest. Their bodies were covered in sweat and their hearts shared the same beat.

"That was amazing," she whispered.

"You always are. God, I love you, woman."

Michael closed her eyes and let the warmth of his love wash over her. "We should get out of town."

"Great minds think alike. I was wondering if you wanted to go to Savannah with me next week. It's time for the Carver low-country boil."

"I'd love to go."

"We can make a vacation of it, stay for a week, hang out on Tybee Island and stay away from crowds."

MJ nodded. "That sounds heavenly."

"But tonight, we're going to find Hercules in the sky."

"Such a sexy nerd. I can't wait."

Epilogue

Savannah, Georgia.

MJ hadn't expected so many people at the Carver family low-country boil, even if it was Thanksgiving. She thought it would just be family members, not half the town. It was like a smaller version of the jazz festival. She stood back and drank in the crowd and the pots of seafood. Everyone was either cooking or serving plates to the older people who were seated at the wooden picnic tables. MJ had been in charge of the rice—serving it, anyway. Jamal's gran, Miss Ethel, had said she'd let MJ cook something next year.

"You have to earn a cooking slot here because we will let you know if your food is not up to par. You're the first one of Jamal's women to actually ask to help out." The older woman had smiled at MJ. "I like you a whole lot."

"Penny for your thoughts." Jamal wrapped his arms around MJ's waist.

"Was thinking about your grandmother and what I'm going to cook next year."

"You better mean it because she doesn't forget anything." MJ whirled around and faced Jamal. He was cute in his red apron and chef's hat.

"Are all of these people your relatives?"

Shaking his head, Jamal explained what the lowcountry boil was all about. It had started out as the Carver family reunion, but then they had ended up with so much food left over that they had to throw it out or give it away. So, Ethel decided to invite the whole neighborhood. Those who could bring something would, but everybody ate.

"Your grandmother is an amazing woman."

Jamal nodded then rubbed his nose against MJ's. "I figured something out."

"What's that?"

"You're a lot like Gran. Smart, successful, won't take no for an answer and very independent."

"Okay, sounds good to me."

"And here's something else that I realize. MJ, I can't live my life without you." He dropped his hands from her hips and got down on one knee. All eyes turned to the couple and a few oohs and awws rose from the crowd.

"Michael Jane, make me the happiest man in the world and say you will marry me."

She brought her hand to her mouth as Jamal pulled a black velvet box from his pocket. "Oh, my God. I don't know what to say."

"'Yes' would be good."

"Yes, yes, of course I will marry you!"

Jamal lifted her into his arms and spun her around. The crowd broke out into applause as he kissed MJ long and deep. He knew that he'd found the only woman he'd ever need and he couldn't have been happier.

Written with permission...

When she said yes, a player died. When she said yes, he became the protector of one heart: hers.

A couple of years ago, my best friend was ready to give up on love. She'd let the wrong guy worm his way into her heart—despite my warnings. So when she finally let him go, I gave her some advice that a lot of you didn't like too much. I told her to rebound, have fun and not to take dating too seriously. Of course, at the time, I was taking dating too seriously. I have to say that I'm glad she didn't take my advice. She looked past his playboy exterior and saw his heart. And he was able to make her believe in love again. They danced around their feelings as if they were in a ballroom for a while, but when things got real, she said yes.

He took her home and introduced her to all of the important people in his family. And when he got down on one knee to propose, she said yes. So, you know what this means. This is the first Mis-Adventures Couple! Though I'd like to take credit for this wonderful

union, *I'm not going to do that. I'm just going to wish
them the best!*

   XOXO-Mimi.

* * * * *

MILLS & BOON
MEDICAL
Pulse-Racing Passion

Set your pulse racing with dedicated, delectable doctors in the high-pressure world of medicine, where emotions run high and passion, comfort and love are the best medicine.

LET'S TALK
Romance

For exclusive extracts, competitions
and special offers, find us online:

MILLS & BOON

THE HEART OF ROMANCE

A ROMANCE FOR EVERY READER

ODERN
Prepare to be swept off your feet by sophisticated, sexy and seductive heroes, in some of the world's most glamourous and romantic locations, where power and passion collide.

STORICAL
Escape with historical heroes from time gone by. Whether your passion is for wicked Regency Rakes, muscled Vikings or rugged Highlanders, awaken the romance of the past.

EDICAL
Set your pulse racing with dedicated, delectable doctors in the high-pressure world of medicine, where emotions run high and passion, comfort and love are the best medicine.

ue Love
Celebrate true love with tender stories of heartfelt romance, from the rush of falling in love to the joy a new baby can bring, and a focus on the emotional heart of a relationship.

Desire
Indulge in secrets and scandal, intense drama and plenty of sizzling hot action with powerful and passionate heroes who have it all: wealth, status, good looks…everything but the right woman.

EROES
Experience all the excitement of a gripping thriller, with an intense romance at its heart. Resourceful, true-to-life women and strong, fearless men face danger and desire - a killer combination!

To see which titles are coming soon, please visit

millsandboon.co.uk/nextmonth